# Loving Lee

Happy Pride

♡ Cozy

# Loving Lee

## Confession: Book One

**COZY DUBOIS**

Copyright © 2024 by Cozy DuBois

All rights reserved.

No part of this publication may be reproduced, distributed, or transmitted in any form or by any means, including photocopying, recording, or other electronic or mechanical methods, without the prior written permission of the publisher, except as permitted by U.S. copyright law. For permission requests, contact Heartwood Forest Publishing LLC.

The story, all names, characters, and incidents portrayed in this production are fictitious. No identification with actual persons (living or deceased), places, buildings, and products is intended or should be inferred.

Book Cover by Marta Susic.

Interior Formatting by Cozy DuBois.

No generative Artificial Intelligence was used in the process of developing, writing, or designing this publication.

Ebook ISBN: 978-1-964386-04-1

Paperback ISBN: 978-1-964386-00-3

First edition 2024

To the queer bars that feel like home.
And to the city of Dubuque, for erasing you from existence.
You're Bellamy now.

# Author's Note

WELCOME AND THANK YOU for picking up *Loving Lee!* Unless we're related, in which case: Thanks for the support. but please put down the book!

Like many people, I took up writing as a hobby during lockdown and—missing my bar friends and the community with whom I could be myself—set out to write a compilation of short stories centered around the interesting people who make gay bars their second home. As a result, this book is set in 2019, and the series continues through 2021 in an alternate timeline without real-world current events, even if real-world issues still impact the story.

The story changed from the original vision, even if the setting didn't. Friendships grew, feelings deepened, and character arcs took precedence over the brief connections between strangers. It became a novel, and then a series, and eventually outgrew the romance genre I originally set out to write in.

*Loving Lee* is not a romance novel that fits the standard formula, with two characters who meet and fall in love and live happily ever after. The *Confession* series is the story of Lee and his family—Tara, Blanche, and Sunny—and their coming-of-age journey where they grow together and fall in love along the way. Their Happily Ever Afters happen, of course—this is still technically a romance, after all, I'm not about to undermine the whole genre—but romance is not the biggest plot. Queer love is more than just who we love romantically—our relationships don't necessarily follow heteronormative milestones, our family ties are not always bonded through blood or law, our friendships are powerful influences in our lives, and our relationship with ourselves can be complicated yet illuminating. Trauma isn't cured through the power of ~~dick~~ love, and people don't remain in stasis while their bestie gets their heart broken. Character arcs don't wait for someone else's happy ending before they begin and they don't end with an "I love you." Their journeys continue together as their family changes and grows, even after they've found their happily ever after.

This series is an ode to the queer community I love and the people in it. LGBTQ people of color are the heart and soul of what it means to be queer in America and have always driven our community forward. Even though I am not a person of color, my goal as a writer is to put more books with happy endings for queer people out into the world. To tell queer stories, it would be a disservice to minimize queer Black experiences as merely a tokenized sassy-gay-friend side character or the flat love interest of a white person. Queer Black people, like Lee and Antonio, are the main characters and always will be.

That's not to say that this book is intended to be an authentic representation of what it is to be Black and gay in America—though the amazing sensitivity readers I worked with helped shape this into something that (hopefully) isn't horribly offensive and out of touch. I will never be the person who can write that story, so I encourage everyone to read #ownvoices books by queer Black authors. Some of my favorites are Kacen Callender, Claire Kann, Rebecca Weatherspoon, Julian Winters, Morgan Rogers, R.M. Virtues, Mia McKenzie, Kosoko Jackson, Chencia Higgins, and many more.

# Content Advisory

I'd like to preface this by affirming that this series centers queer joy. That said, the characters in these books haven't had the easiest lives and deal with the lingering impacts of past trauma. Proceed with caution if the below may be uncomfortable. If you see anything that may be a dealbreaker for you, I have a more detailed explanation (with some spoilers) on my website http://cozydubois.com/.

- Substance use, including frequent alcohol and marijuana use; One POV character in recovery from addiction.

- Sexual content between people of all genders to varying intensity; Brief non-graphic flashback to past assault during non-consensual kiss; Unintentionally coercive relationship.

- Difficulties managing mental health, including depictions of panic attacks, dissociation, flashbacks, and substance use to cope with emotions.

- The main characters come in a wide range of body types and appearances. This book takes a body-neutral approach, however some characters have biases and insecurities.

- References to past traumatic events occur off-page but may be heavy for some readers.

# Thursday, April Twenty-Fifth

# Chapter One

## Lee

"Buttercup, please don't hate me." Lee's fist hovered near Tara's open bedroom door; he'd meant to knock first. *Damn, starting off strong.* He dropped his hand back to his side uselessly.

Tara's attention snapped away from her laptop, her green eyes narrowing in suspicion. Curled up in the last patch of afternoon sun at the end of her twin bed, she took her earbuds out, looking at him expectantly.

As he hovered in the doorframe, Lee struggled to find an explanation that wouldn't piss her off. He wiped the sweat beading on his palms on his jeans and put on his best apologetic wince as he worked up the courage to spit it out.

"What'd you do?" Tara finally demanded. The warning in her tone only made him sweatier; he should have been used to it after ten years of disappointing her. Her anxiety about what he might say was always worse than her anger at the truth. But the fact that she was already on defense *before* Lee could tell her he'd ruined her birthday was not a good start.

He pushed his glasses up his nose. "Chas put me on the schedule. For Saturday."

"Lee! You were supposed to take off work!"

Lee barely ducked the pillow that flew at his head. "I did! I promise!" Retrieving it from the floor, he pulled one of her red curls from it and let it flutter to the floor. The hallway would get vacuumed way sooner than Tara's room.

He hated making anyone mad, let alone Tara. Tara Sanderson had been his best friend, his platonic soulmate, the light of his life ever since they'd met nearly a decade ago at the naive age of fifteen. She deserved everything good in the world, not flaky excuses. But she'd forgive him. If he could count on anyone to put up with him, it was Tara.

"Chas has a new queen starting Saturday. Apparently, she's high maintenance, and you know Freddy can barely handle the usual set list without me." Lee squeezed into the room, shuffling sideways between the bed and the closet door to bring the pillow back. "You know I'd much rather celebrate with you, but they need me."

Entering Tara's cramped room, the smallest in the apartment they stayed at with their friend Blanche, was usually more work than it was worth. His larger frame—tall, heavy-set, painfully noticeable—barely fit between the bed and the closet door. Lee's wasn't much better, but at least he had a full-size mattress and *didn't* feel like a claustrophobic giant. Not that he was ungrateful. Any room was an improvement from most of the places they'd stayed. Even if Tara's room would be better suited as a closet.

Tara leaned forward expectantly. He smacked her with the pillow before he tucked it behind her. The grin that broke across her face was gone when Tara leaned back into it and crossed her arms.

He folded himself next to her, the shady-ass twin bed creaking under his weight. "I'm sorry, Buttercup, but you know I can't say no to anyone, especially not Chas. What can I do to make it better? I can get you a VIP table for the show!"

Her sour expression pained him. He'd planned the perfect night—just Tara, Lee, Blanche, and Sunny. Tara's three friends were the only company she'd want on her birthday; that he'd convinced her to go out in public this year was a miracle.

Tara never saw the point of birthday parties, but every year Lee begged her to let him plan one, just like he did for Sunny and himself (Blanche always had other plans). This year, Tara had finally given in; her birthday was on a Saturday and she hadn't immediately hated Lee's suggestion of an arcade. No small feat, as he'd expected she'd veto everything he came up with.

For Tara, not hating something was practically enthusiastic.

He put on his best pleading pout and took her hands, his deep brown skin framing her freckles. She would never admit it, but affection always won her over. Affection, the little things he did to show he cared, and snacks were the keys to Tara's heart.

Tara's eyebrow arched, but she squeezed his hands in return. "Maybe we'll go to the arcade without you."

Lee couldn't hide his skeptical look. "Really? Sunny will kick your ass at every game, and Blanche can't even play Pacman."

Tara would have no fun losing to Sunny all night, and Blanche would just people-watch. Besides, Lee wanted to be there for Tara's first ever birthday party, even if he had to watch from the control room. If Tara came to the show, Lee could make sure she had fun and danced a little. Not that Tara could dance. A newborn giraffe on a trampoline would have better moves than her.

"Maybe."

"So, you're gonna take the bus, then? I can't drive your ass around if I'm at work." Tara's patience wouldn't survive the spotty bus service between Eastside and South Bellamy, where the arcade was. And there was no way Lee would let her drive his admittedly shitty Sonata. He couldn't afford a new transmission, let alone fix whatever Tara would do to it.

Lee pointed a warning finger before she could respond. "And don't you dare say you'll just stay home—you've never had a real birthday party, and I refuse to let you go another year without one." All those years persuading Tara to celebrate herself, and here he was, flaking on the plans he'd made.

"Ugh! Fine." Tara threw her head back. "I guess walking home is better than the damn bus. Probably a better chance of getting laid at Confession, too."

"*Or*... Ask someone on a date instead of hooking up with a stranger again?"

Tara shot him a skeptical look. "Oh, like *you* do?"

"Hey! I want to date more." Lee pushed his glasses up as they threatened to slide down his nose. Taking a breath to erase the bitter edge to his voice, he added quietly, "Just no one wants to date me."

"You're really convincing me, here," Tara deadpanned. "But seriously, any man would be lucky to have you. You're a goddamn catch and don't you forget it!"

Lee smiled despite himself; Tara always did her best to inflate his ego. If anyone had ever wanted him to stick around *after* they'd hooked up, he might have believed her. "Are we okay?"

Despite Tara's protests, she still wanted to spend her birthday with him. He would never *say* he mattered more to her than anyone else in her life (he wasn't *that* conceited), but he did. She mattered more to him, too. Blanche often described them as codependent, which Sunny would follow up with a joke that *codependent* was an understatement. And they weren't wrong.

"Of course, we're okay." Tara kept her scowl, but her thumbs gently traced his knuckles. "How's this? Get me a VIP table *and* pay for my drinks, and we'll be more than okay."

"Buttercup, I'll do whatever it takes to make it up to you." Lee stood and pressed a kiss into her mop of short red curls. They both knew she hadn't been that upset to begin with; he just hated disappointing her. "Do I look okay? Or should I change?"

"Oh god, this again. You look fine!" Tara huffed in exasperation. "Where are you going?"

"Work." If Tara said he looked fine, he didn't look good enough. A new coworker meant he should make an effort. Like his dad used to preach, seven seconds was all he got to make a good first impression. Raising someone's estimation after they'd formed a bad opinion was difficult. Or in his parents' case, impossible. One moment was all it took to lose their approval forever.

Pulling his hoodie off, Lee distracted himself from *that* train of thought by focusing on the music buzzing from Tara's headphones, still laying on the bed. The R&B melody was familiar, but with Tara's cheap headphones, he couldn't tell what song.

"Why? It's Thursday," Tara said as Lee opened her closet. The closet in his room was tiny, and Tara barely used hers. Her assortment of joggers, leggings, tank tops, and hoodies were carefully folded into a storage bin. Lee's sweaters, button-downs, and vintage crewnecks hung from the bar instead.

"Chas wants me to come in for a meeting with the new queen to plan the set list for Saturday." He buttoned up a blue collared shirt, pulling a maroon crewneck over it. "At least she warned me this time. Half the time, Chas gives me the updated setlist that night. She did say this one is kind of needy, though. Wish me luck, I guess."

"You won't need it. Everyone loves you, and you're great at your job." Tara rolled her eyes as he wordlessly asked for her approval of his outfit. "You look good."

Lee turned around, still skeptical; Tara rarely wore anything besides athleisure. "Okay, but would *I* think I look good?"

"This is what mirrors are for, dude." She eyed him thoughtfully anyway. "Tuck your undershirt into your jeans. And your left sleeve is lumpy. There. Hot as usual."

"Thank you." Picking up a pair of socks she'd tossed on the floor, Lee deposited them in the worn-out mesh hamper wedged behind the door as he shuffled back out of her room. He looked back at her with a grin.

"I'm not a slob, Lee!" Tara tried to cover her laugh with a huff.

"I didn't say a word, Buttercup." Lee didn't have time to tease her properly; he had to go to Confession to meet this new queen.

---

TWENTY MINUTES AND A brisk walk across the Mississippi later, Lee stepped through the employee entrance of his home away from home since he was nineteen. Confession—in all her gay bar glory—was housed in an old warehouse on the Iowa side of Bellamy, sandwiched between Downtown and the river. Originally a pump organ factory, the building had been converted into a skeezy hotel in the '80s. The empty building left behind during the recession had become the first of many urban renewal projects in Downtown Bellamy over the last decade. Since then, Confession had evolved into the nightclub, restaurant, and coworking offices she was today. Because really, a former pump organ factory just begged to be a gay bar.

The owners had kept the industrial charm, and the building's history had inspired the name and church theme. Chains and pulleys draped in plants, neon signs, and erotic art decorated the exposed brick and beams of the space illuminated by stained glass windows. Religious irreverence shone throughout: intricate wood-carved panels—salvaged from actual confessionals—decorated every bathroom door, and religious icons in intimate positions hung on the walls. Chas, the genderfluid owner and devout Catholic, teetered on the edge of camp and heresy.

Despite the late notice Chas had given him for the meeting, he'd arrived fifteen minutes early. As usual. *"Early is on time, and on time is late."* His father's constant lessons had never quite escaped him, despite Lee's best efforts to forget.

Exhaling the memory with a quick breath, Lee forced himself to dawdle on his way upstairs, briefly indulging in small talk with the coworkers and regulars who flagged him down. Chas wouldn't care if he was late, but merely considering being the last one upstairs made him burn with shame.

Confession's ground floor housed the bar and restaurant, which became a dance floor on weekend nights. The second floor was a spacious venue for drag shows, burlesque performances, and private events. Lee spent most of his time there, hooking up mics, hefting speakers around, and running sound in the control room during shows.

He'd stumbled into the audio tech gig after Blanche had introduced him to Chas five years ago. Lee had worked under the table in the beginning, until he was legally of age to be in Confession at all. Technically, he was supposed to get an Associate's Degree in Audio Production before he'd turned twenty-one and they'd hired him officially. That hadn't happened, but Chas hadn't mentioned it again. Lee didn't see the point. He had taught himself what he needed to know, and he was good at it. An expensive piece of paper wasn't magically going to make him better at his job.

Being there on a Thursday felt out-of-pattern. Normally, weeknights were for Dildo Bingo, Dick Tac Toe, or some other game. Sometimes, they'd play shows or movies. But unless Blanche sexiled him and Tara—in which case, they'd hang out in the coworking space on the third floor—Chas only needed him on weeknights for private events. She'd never called him in to review the set list for a new performer before.

Lee groaned when he saw the control room door closed. He knocked loudly, hesitating with his hand on the handle. Quicker than he expected, a "Yer good!" sounded from the other side.

Averting his eyes to be safe, he kicked the doorstop down as he went in. But he needn't have worried. The picture of innocence, Chastity Gomez—better known as Chas Titty, co-owner and headlining drag king—had stolen Lee's usual chair, his boots propped up on Freddy's lap. Freddy, the light designer, gave Lee his usual quick nod in greeting, which Lee returned.

"I'm not late, am I? You're strangely put together considering the door was closed." Not that it was unusual for Chas and Freddy to be alone together in the control room, but neither of them was fixing their hair or readjusting their clothes.

"Ha! No, we were just havin' a chat. We're not *that* unprofessional." Chas's laugh boomed as he winked. "Thanks for comin' in on yer off day. Carlita should be here soon to go over her set list and mic setup. Don't be surprised if she's late, though."

Even offstage, Chas blurred the lines between his onstage persona and real self. Today looked to be at about 90% Chas Titty, 10% Chas Gomez, a sign that today was a he/him day. His cowboy boots with their generous heel brought his height up to a full five foot nothing. Chas liked to joke that he reached five-four on account of his Stetson. Only his face was out of costume, looking more masculine bare of stage makeup and sans mustache.

"Mic—is she going to emcee?" Lee asked. Most performers weren't mic'd, preferring the freedom of lip-syncing to roam around the audience for tips. Chas and whoever else emceed for the night shared one between them.

Chas rubbed his stomach. His generous chest and belly were hidden behind a leather vest, giving the illusion of a beer gut. "She'll start emceein' again soon, but not this weekend. She sings instead of lip-syncin', so she'll need a mic stand."

"She'd prefer a headset over a mic stand!" a melodic voice interrupted from behind.

Lee turned, chest tightening as he met a pair of hazel eyes beaming up at him. As the newcomer slipped past him into the small room, his eyes raked over Lee, smile growing wider with every step. A wiry shoulder brushed Lee's chest and a hand grazed his waist, leaving Lee burning from the contact.

Glasses sliding slowly down his nose, Lee helplessly turned with him, unable to look away. Neither did the other man; he walked backward into the control room with a grin.

"Antonio! Welcome back!" Chas hopped out of his chair.

The man, presumably the new queen, finally turned to greet Chas. Lee wiped his nose and pushed his glasses up when the other guy's back was turned, bringing him into focus. Taller than Chas—but who wasn't—he was willowy, with loose, sandy brown coils tousled over his forehead, a shade darker than his golden-brown skin. His slender figure was well-muscled, especially through his leggings as he bent over to hug Chas.

Trying to remember how to breathe, Lee dragged his eyes away once he realized he was staring hard at this guy's ass. But Freddy's mustache was already twitching. Lee snapped his mouth closed once he noticed it was hanging open.

Of course, Freddy saw that, too.

Freddy didn't talk much, but as the only person who worked closely with Lee, he saw everything. Including Lee's not-infrequent one-sided attraction for the many interesting and confident men who came through Confession.

Luckily—or perhaps unluckily—no one but Freddy seemed to notice. The rare occurrence a coworker had pursued him, they'd either quit soon after, or Lee would pine after them for months after they'd ended things, until his heart finally got the message.

"Tonio, you remember Freddy, of course." Chas gestured toward the paunchy man sitting next to him. Lee always teased Freddy for being middle-aged, but it was more in personality than years. Freddy's black hair didn't have a single gray in it, but his dad uniform of blue checkered shirts and worn-out white sneakers aged him anyway.

Freddy waved two fingers in greeting, like a grizzled semi-driver instead of a mid-thirties white guy born and raised in Eastside.

"How could I forget Freddy? You always make me look my best, don't you, darling?" Antonio cooed. "So much more than a light designer. More of an artist." With a flare of his long fingers, he grazed Freddy's chest, lingering over the buttons.

Freddy blinked a deadpan look in return.

"Hands to yourself, Tonio. I forgot how damn flirty you are." Chas made a face and clapped Lee on the shoulder, the sound drawing Antonio's attention. "And Lee, this is Antonio Flores, better known as Carlita Asada, our prodigal headliner finally back home. Lee Jones here is the best audio tech we've ever had. He started a couple of months after you left."

Lee smiled awkwardly at the compliment, extending his hand. "Pleasure to meet you."

"Trust me, the pleasure's *all* mine." The brown skin surrounding Antonio's hazel eyes broke into smile lines as Antonio beamed up at Lee. "You're the sound guy, huh? Fantastic! You need to make me sound as good as Freddy makes me look."

A strong hand grasped Lee's, who fought to keep his smile passive. Any spark he felt was just in his head, his imagination running wild from an attractive man smiling his way. Nothing new there. "I'm sure you'll make my job as easy as you do for Freddy."

Antonio's smile widened as they shook hands longer than was necessary. Lee let himself pretend he wasn't alone in feeling like the world had shifted under him. His chest tightened breathlessly at the idea of this vision of a man wanting him back.

*Get it together, Lee. A hot guy smiles at you and you're already imagining things.*

"Keep talking like that *and* get me a headset, you'll be a lot more than the sound guy." Antonio didn't let go of Lee's hand.

The warm fingers gripping his own felt like the only thing keeping Lee alive. Those hazel eyes had become a window, allowing Heaven's light into his soul.

*Calm the fuck down.*

Lee would get him a headset if he had to work the next two days straight.

# Chapter Two

## Lee

After an hour drunk off Antonio's smile, Lee barely remembered his promise to Tara, heading to the front desk instead of slipping out the back. His head swam with featherlight touches to his knee and wrist—and a lingering squeeze of his shoulder Lee had not-so-subtly leaned into—as they'd discussed Antonio's tracks. Antonio had looked him up and down with a smirk of approval any time Lee had said anything. His intoxicating laughter made it hard to pay attention to Chas as he'd rearranged the setlist.

Chas hadn't said anything about their blatant flirting, but Freddy had raised an eyebrow a few times. Lee hoped he hadn't acted too foolish. While obviously charming, Antonio was an equal opportunity flirt, teasing Freddy and propositioning Chas as much as he had showered Lee with compliments. Chas and Freddy, normally highly suspicious of anyone encroaching on their "territory," didn't seem to think much of it.

Not like Lee had. His initial attraction to Antonio was already growing into a crush, but Lee refused to hope. Chas's comments earlier about "high maintenance" and "needy" weren't the only warnings; Antonio gave off strong fuckboy vibes—the diamond studs in his ears and effortlessly-styled curls should be red flags.

But his eyes, though! And that smile?

Lee may have been a sucker for a compliment—especially from someone as attractive and charming and funny and attentive as Antonio—but flirting didn't mean Antonio was into him too. *He's just friendly. Unless he hits you up on Grindr, keep it professional.*

He considered himself attractive, but Lee had heard enough comments along the lines of "you're cute...for a Black dude" and "I usually don't go for chubby guys" to be pessimistic about his dating prospects. Sex, sure. He wasn't hard up for hookups when he wanted one. Grindr existed for a reason. Everyone needed to blow off steam sometimes. Dating, on the other hand, was impossible.

When Lee was younger and less jaded, he'd tried harder to find something serious. He'd caught feelings more than a few times. His longest situationship to date was when he'd hooked up with the same guy once a week for a good six months. It seemed like they were on the same page—they had an emotional connection beyond sex worth exploring. Lee had worked up the courage to ask what they were, and that was the last he'd heard from that guy.

He'd learned that lesson the hard way more than once.

These days, Lee took the approach that if someone liked him, they'd let him know. No point in trying to convince the people with "no Blacks," "no fats," or "masc4masc" in their profile to give him a chance. Even if he wasn't particularly feminine, constantly performing masculinity to hold someone's interest was exhausting; he'd done enough of *that* as a kid, when he was still desperate for his dad's approval.

This left him with mostly creeps in his messages, but sometimes a decent person would reach out. Then, the vicious cycle of Lee catching feelings too soon would begin again, never going anywhere. No one wanted him for more than casual hookups. Lee tried not to take it personally. That was just how shit was. Hookup culture reigned supreme everywhere; Bellamy was no exception.

Antonio wouldn't be either.

"You're not supposed to be here on a Thursday," Jackie, the front-of-house manager, greeted Lee with a confused look as he leaned on her podium. She rifled through the schedules on a clipboard, pulling out the pen holding her bun together to scribble a note. Her long braid unwound and fell over her shoulder.

"Hi, nice to see you too," Lee teased. "Chas wanted to go over the setlist changes."

"Oh, for Carlita? I'm so excited Tonio is back! I missed that weirdo," Jackie gushed. "Did you work with him before?"

"No, I started after he left. Hey, can I reserve—"

"Jackie, you still talking shit about me after all these years?" A now familiar voice piped up from behind.

Lee had to bite his lip to keep from grinning.

Jackie squealed—a sound Lee had *never* heard from her before—and greeted Antonio with a hug. "Tonio, you bitch! I had to find out you were moving back from your Insta? What happened to New York?"

Antonio's smile faltered, but he recovered with a dramatic toss of his hand. "I had to work too hard to barely make rent. So I moved home, and my sister got me a job at some middle school."

"You're a teacher?" Lee was surprised to hear his own voice ask the question. He really wanted to ask, "Are you single?" but caught himself. Antonio hadn't made any indication he was into Lee. Other than the touching, the glances, and the smiles that made his heart beat faster.

Antonio flashed another wide smile his way. Lee's heart fluttered predictably in response. "I will be soon. I'm teaching choir this fall, but in a few weeks, I'm doing a music program for the poor suckers in summer school."

Lee couldn't help but smile back. "I wish they had a music class when I had to do summer school back in the day." He'd never been the best student, even before he'd dropped out in ninth grade. He wasn't stupid; he simply didn't connect with most subjects. Which was basically everything but music.

"Aw, you were a poor sucker?" Antonio winked.

*I walked right into that one.* The wink affected him more than it should have, but he managed a flirty response before the moment passed. "Never been called a *poor* sucker before."

Antonio's eyes flicked to his mouth. A tongue peeked out from behind Antonio's grin to wet his lower lip.

"Lee, didn't you need something?" Jackie interrupted. "A room perhaps?"

Embarrassment flooded Lee. He hadn't realized how close they'd gotten—or more accurately, how close he'd edged to Antonio. His knee was pressed against Antonio's thigh, Antonio's hand lightly tracing his forearm as they leaned on the podium. *Keep it professional.* He shot a sheepish smile at Jackie but didn't back away. Antonio didn't either. "Oh yeah, can I reserve a VIP table for Tara's birthday on Saturday? Oh, and I'll get the tab."

Jackie jotted Tara's name down on her clipboard and coiled her hair back into a bun, securing it with her pen. "Before I forget, here are your invites for the employee appreciation party a week from Sunday. We're closing early after the brunch show, so no excuses."

"What if I already have plans?" Antonio took the fliers and handed one to Lee, letting his fingers linger on Lee's wrist.

Lee did nothing to shake off his touch, tucking the invite into his pocket with his other hand. Chas had already given him the flier for the annual employee party weeks ago to give to Blanche, but *Antonio* had given him this one. *Why are you like this?*

"Cancel 'em. It's mandatory, Antonio. You know Chas will take it personally if you don't come. He loves these things." Jackie crossed her arms, her uncharacteristic squeal from earlier replaced by her usual no-nonsense attitude. "And you're emceeing next weekend, so your ass better not flake."

"Some appreciation," Antonio muttered. He stuffed the invite into his back pocket and leaned on the podium, pressing his shoulder against Lee's arm. "So, Lee, does your friend want a birthday shout-out on Saturday? I do a very dramatic rendition of the birthday song."

Lee laughed. "Only if you have a death wish. Tara hates attention. She'd throw hands before you started singing." On impulse, Lee brushed his thumb along Antonio's sharp jawline. "I wouldn't want anything to happen to this face, after all."

*Too far, Lee.* He turned and left before Antonio could react, not wanting to witness the discomfort on Antonio's face.

―――・―――

# Antonio

Antonio fanned himself as he clung to Jackie's podium, staring at Lee's broad shoulders disappearing through the front entrance. "Jackie, *please* tell me Chas's policy on workplace fraternization hasn't changed."

"Are you seriously fanning yourself? Wow, you're still so dramatic!" Jackie laughed. "No change, though. Chas would be the biggest hypocrite if he did."

"Oh, thank God. I think I just swooned. Is he always like that?"

"Lee?"

"Who else would I possibly be talking about?" Antonio swiped Jackie's clipboard and fanned himself harder, trying to cool the flames in his chest. The hot-ass beefcake with glasses and a soft baritone was giving him the best heartburn. A choir of angels, complete with harps and bells, sang "Love at First Sight" by Kylie Minogue in his head.

*Stop being a dramatic bitch.* This rush searing through his veins was probably just nerves. Or indigestion.

*But I've never had angels in my head before.* Antonio chewed his lip. *Honestly, even if these aren't real feelings, Lee could be funner than anything else I got going on. I've been so responsible since moving home. I deserve some fun.*

His stomach twisted, disappointed that the visceral soul-wrenching jolt when he'd first locked eyes with Lee in the control room could be mere lust. He'd felt nothing but lust his whole adult life, and it had never felt like *that* before.

Jackie shrugged. "Lee's always sweet but not *that* flirty. I'm jealous—he's never looked at me like *that*."

Antonio forced himself to look away from Confession's doors, where it was increasingly obvious Lee was not about to return and drag him to the Confessionals. He shot a grin at his old friend. "Jealous, Jackie? You're saying I finally have a chance with you?"

Jackie grabbed her clipboard back. "Nope, still ace. I'm just jealous because that was cute as shit. You looked ready to bust the entire time."

"Ugh, *he's* cute as shit!" Antonio sighed as he draped himself over the podium, sagging in relief that he hadn't been deluding himself. Maybe the longing pounding through his veins *was* real—*Please, let it be real*—but even if the exhilarating rush was simply his new baseline attraction, at least he could potentially do something about it. "Is he single? Or open? Do I have any chance?"

Jackie shrugged. "He's never mentioned it one way or the other. He's cool, but he doesn't talk about himself a lot. Chas and Freddy know him best."

"That is supremely unhelpful, Jackie." He'd have to ask the girls backstage. They'd catch him up on everything he'd missed, and more importantly, how available Lee might be. He doubted Lee would confide in their boss about his sex life. "Is Venus still here?"

"Unfortunately," Jackie scoffed. "But yeah, if anyone knows, it'd be her."

"Tonio." Chas appeared at the podium. "Are you already distractin' Jackie? You haven't changed at all."

A pang of doubt struck Antonio's sternum, dousing the fire in his heart. A sobering reminder that he couldn't afford to get sidetracked by fun, as charming and hot as the fun might be. After the way he'd left Bellamy—how he'd ghosted everyone at Confession—Chas was sticking his neck out for Antonio by letting him come back. He had to do things right this time.

Jackie came to his rescue. "Oh, don't blame him, Chas. I was just teasing him for the big ol' hearts in his eyes for Lee."

"Now, Tonio—"

"Chas, I know *you're* not about to warn me off of getting involved with a coworker." Antonio made a face.

Chas waved his hand. "Psh—no, I know better than to warn *you* off anybody. Y'all are adults. But unless yer stickin' around for once, the right thing to do is leave him be. Lee is practically family, and he's been through enough shit in his life without you breakin' his heart."

"What if he breaks *my* heart?" Antonio pressed his hand to his chest. He shouldn't have been offended that Chas thought so poorly of him; his track record with workplace flings wasn't great. But Chas couldn't have known how perfect Lee's hand felt in his. How his stomach twisted anytime Lee smiled. How he wanted to live the rest of his life staring into Lee's warm brown eyes.

And that was terrifying. He had no idea what to do with...feelings.

For the first time in his life, Antonio's gut screamed that he'd met someone special. All of the emotions he'd never imagined were real when other people described them—emotions he'd never expected to experience—had parted the clouds and illuminated his soul. The stories about sparks flying, a gut feeling of rightness, and "when you know, you know" always sounded like exaggerations.

Until now.

*Don't get ahead of yourself. You can't trust gut feelings. This could be gas. Or nerves about performing again. Or this damn appreciation party.*

Chas shot him a skeptical look. "Since when does Antonio Flores get his heart broken?"

Other than a resigned sigh, Antonio had no response. Chas was right—it wouldn't be the first time he'd imagined romantic feelings and accidentally strung someone along. Impulse control was the right move, as much as he hated it. He was still getting used to his new normal.

*But I owe it to myself to find out if this is real. That's why I came home, isn't it? To rebuild myself into someone better. I'm a new person, even if no one believes me yet.*

# Saturday, April Twenty-Seventh

# Chapter Three

## Sunny

From Sunny's vantage point at the VIP table at Confession, the abstract painting of a giant dong on the brick wall had transformed Tara's short red curls into pubes. Sunny snapped a photo when Tara's head was turned. Only Lee ever watched her Stories, but he'd find it hilarious.

"Please tell me that's not my birthday present." Tara stared at a wilted plant Blanche had set on the stainless steel table.

Sunny blinked. She hadn't even seen Blanche approach. Strange. Normally she couldn't keep her eyes off of them.

Blanche covered the plant's nonexistent ears in mock horror, their long bleached blond hair pooling over their shoulder as they curled protectively around the plant. "Don't listen to her, sweetie. She doesn't deserve you anyway."

Sunny wondered where they'd found this one. Their last "rescued" plant had been retrieved from a dumpster. The dried-up palm had never recovered, but nothing could dissuade Blanche from taking in another charity case. At least this one still had some green in its leaves.

Blanche sat next to Tara and stroked the crispy leaves lovingly with one finger. They leaned back to slouch in the chair. "I found this sweet little rattlesnake plant next to a dumpster behind that new condo by our place. I think it'll make a full recovery."

"Which new condo?" Sunny muttered sarcastically to herself. Just last week, concrete barriers had appeared, blocking off the surface lot across from Blanche's apartment for yet another new overpriced building.

Eastside was being invaded by "luxury" condos, spreading like a disease from the river. The Iowa side of Bellamy had been "renewed" over the past decade, drawing tech companies to the low taxes and cheap real estate. As a result, housing was scarce across the entire Bellamy metro. Developers were taking advantage of Eastside because of it. The single-family homes on the Iowa side and in the Wisconsin suburbs were protected by strict zoning laws, still lingering from when redlining was legal. The mom-and-pop businesses and rowhouses squeezed in between the abandoned warehouses, rail lines, and freeways on the Illinois side of the Mississippi weren't protected by shit. *ABnother way Eastside gets screwed over by historical systematic racism.*

The Eastside Sunny had grown up in had been the "bad" part of town. Now condos went up weekly, touting amenities like "Instagrammable Views" and "Rooftop Event Space." There weren't any fewer gunshots at night or needles on the sidewalks. The only differences now were the white women jogging by and "young professionals" complaining about the "blight" that had existed for decades, as if they weren't part of the problem. Eastside needed grocery stores, doctor's offices, and better schools, not art galleries or luxury housing—

"So I get to celebrate my birthday with a dead plant. Great," Tara said.

Sunny snapped back to the conversation, closing the mental tab about gentrification. It was Tara's day; she could zone out at home.

"It's not dead, just neglected. And a plant is more fun than playing pinball with a bunch of ten-year-olds," Blanche shot back.

Blanche always knew exactly how far to push Tara's buttons. Sunny tried to emulate their innocuous shit-talking, but she usually pissed Tara off. Still, snark and arguments were Tara's love language, so Sunny kept trying. They had a mutual understanding that catty banter and biting sarcasm meant they loved each other.

Tara glowered at her roommate. "Well, thank Lee for ruining his own plans then."

It was all bluster. A grumbly bitch Tara may be, but she loved Lee and Blanche fiercely. For years, Sunny had been *so* nice to make up for the Cookie Incident, but nothing had ever worked. She'd finally earned Tara's trust with a right hook to a creep who wouldn't leave them alone. Tara didn't care about nice; she just needed people to have her back.

Sunny would much rather have gone to the arcade than Confession. But she wouldn't pass up an easy opportunity to tease Tara, so she raised her vodka cran. "To Lee, for saving Tara's birthday!"

Blanche laughed with Sunny, clinking their scotch against her glass.

Tara added her glass to theirs with a grin. "To Lee, for the drinks!"

The lights dimmed and the first bars of "Achy Breaky Heart" got the audience cheering. Blanche whooped loudly when Chas line danced onto the stage. The bronze skin on their stunning cheekbones was unfairly flawless in the low light, even with no makeup. Having the confidence to leave the house without the armor of contouring was goals.

Sunny stirred her drink absentmindedly as Blanche walked to the stage to tip Chas. Long blonde hair hung down their back, emphasizing the flare of their hips. They always claimed they were a natural blond, but Sunny frequently helped bleach the black roots of their hair. It was a little gratifying to know they had one insecurity, even if they stayed blonde mostly because clients paid more.

Blanche Van Horne had been her friend, mentor, and secret crush since Lee had introduced them five years ago. They'd connected her with people, resources, and possibilities she'd never dreamed existed. Sunny lived on the Internet, but Blanche was an encyclopedia of real-world experience and word-of-mouth connections. A social chameleon, they stood out when they wanted to and blended in when they didn't—a necessary skill of their profession as a street worker-turned-dominatrix. Enviably, they were always exactly who they wanted to be. Even in their questionable thrifted denim outfit, they were effortlessly femme and confident.

On the opposite end of the spectrum, Sunny put her foot in her mouth anytime she opened it. Being as serenely confident as Blanche seemed like an unattainable dream.

While her body was closer to the shape she desperately wanted thanks to the miracle of hormones, Sunny still felt like an imposter half the time. It wasn't until she got her breast implants last year that she'd become confident enough to wear a dress in public. Not that Sunny got to dress full femme often anyway; khakis and boring sweatshirts were the unofficial uniform of her software engineer job. Living with her mother, who had a propensity to deadname her when they argued, wasn't exactly validating either. Birdie wasn't unsupportive, per se (she had many trans and gay friends back in Chiang Mai) but she projected her own issues onto Sunny.

Nights out were the only time Sunny could be herself and live out her unfulfilled teenage dreams of wearing cute dresses with fishnets and chokers. Tonight, she could be her true self and pretend she was effortlessly feminine and confid—

"Are you gonna stare at Blanche's ass all night?"

Sunny's cheeks burned. "I'm not *staring*. I just...zoned out in that direction."

"Sure." Tara sipped her whiskey coke, eyebrow raised skeptically.

Fortunately, after five years of bickering, Sunny knew *exactly* how to get Tara's attention off of her not-so-subtle staring at Blanche's ass. "So Tara-Bear, what was your favorite part of being twenty-three?"

Tara shifted, tracing the rim of her glass with a finger. "Don't make it a big deal."

"Of course your birthday is a big deal!" Sunny pulled Tara under her arm. "Tell me what you're looking forward to about being twenty-four!"

"Oh god, stop! We didn't do this shit on *your* birthday. Why are you doing it to me?" Tara wiggled out of Sunny's grasp, pushing her away with a hand to Sunny's throat.

"Doing what?" Blanche asked as they returned to the table.

"She's asking about my feelings and shit." Tara scowled, holding Sunny's neck at arm's length.

Sunny pulled away with a grin and rubbed her throat. "And telling you I love you. And how much you mean to me! And how cute you are in that romper—you should wear real clothes more often."

"Bitch, stop pretending to be nice!"

"Fuck you, I am nice!"

Blanche's face erupted into a wicked smile. "Oh, babes, it's your birthday! Let us love you!" Their arms opened up to help Sunny trap Tara in a group hug.

"You're both doing way too much right now. I'm getting another drink." Tara ducked and scurried away as applause erupted for the end of Chas's number.

# Tara

Annoyed, Tara made herself a spot at the bar as the next song started, muttering a quick non-apology for nudging aside a broad-shouldered man watching the show. She worked her way between him and an older lesbian couple with their hands in each other's pockets. *Just cringe enough to be cute.* That sappy love was not in the cards for her. It looked sweet on them, though.

Tara pulled the hem of her romper down while ordering another whiskey coke from Jackie behind the bar. She'd drained her first drink before the ice could further water down the bite of the whiskey.

Lee surprised her with a hug from behind as she set her empty glass on the bar. She knew it was him without looking: His hands squeezed her shoulders before wrapping around her waist, his linebacker frame pressed against her back, and his familiar scent of rosemary and shea butter told her she was safe. They were attuned to each other in a way she doubted she'd ever experience with another person. After ten years together, particularly during the lower points where they'd slept under overpasses or in Walter's camp, Lee was a familiar presence. No matter what else was happening, she could always sense when he was nearby.

Lee stopped Jackie before she poured rail whiskey into Tara's glass. "Don't give her that cheap shit! My bestie deserves Black Label on her birthday! With a splash of Coke so I still can use the employee discount, though!"

Jackie made an exasperated face but put the bottle down to search for the scotch. "You know that's not how the employee discount works, right?"

"Yeah, but it's her birthday!" Lee squeezed her tighter.

"I'm already doing it, aren't I?" Jackie waved him off. "I gotta run downstairs because apparently, no one checked the damn top-shelf inventory up here."

"What's with all the sappy shit today?" Tara complained, but there was no bite to it. She could handle Lee's affection, even if Sunny's made her want to run away. She leaned back into the hug, resting her head on his shoulder.

Lee kissed the top of her head. "I'm sorry I ruined your birthday, Buttercup. I had the perfect night planned and everything."

"I'm sure you'll plan another party for me next year." Tara smiled up at him. She hadn't been that upset about the arcade, but Lee always over-apologized for everything.

"Damn right! A better one!" He left a loud wet kiss on her forehead and ran back to the control room as the number ended.

Tara turned toward the stage, wiping her forehead. She appreciated drag performances, but she always found herself more entertained by the audience. Sunny and Blanche cheered as Venus DeVille did one last backflip and disappeared backstage.

Sunny's charming smile made her appear deceptively sweet. With her red dress and her long black hair in twin plaits, she shone in all her wannabe-goth-girl glory that only came out on the weekends. She was usually a nerdy space cadet. As much as they harassed each other, Sunny Boonmee had proven herself to be a true friend. Eventually. She had the attention span of a gnat and could never read the room, but she was genuine and loyal.

Her friends looked like complete opposites; Blanche covered in denim that someone's grandma had bedazzled, and Sunny dressed like she'd robbed a Hot Topic. In many ways, they were—Sunny was ditzy and argumentative, while Blanche was observant and unflappable. But both fiercely loved their friends. Tara tried her best to live up to their example. Blanche, Lee, and Sunny were the closest thing to a real family she'd ever had.

Tara adjusted her olive green romper, tugging the hem down where it rode up again. Wearing something this tight and structured—instead of her usual joggers and hoodie—made her skin crawl. But since it was her birthday, she'd let Lee convince her to dress up. Even if she wasn't fond of the seam digging into her ass, her ass did look amazing. The view in the mirror was worth the discomfort. Sometimes. For special occasions.

Jackie handed her the drink after topping the generous pour of Black Label with a splash of Coke—an "employee mixed drink" under Chas's loose rules.

Calling a "thank you" to Jackie, Tara dropped a couple of dollars on the bar for her and leaned back against it. Staying put sounded more appealing than heading back to the table. She needed a moment after the overwhelming love Sunny and Blanche had thrown at her. Even Lee, her security blanket, had left her more vulnerable than was comfortable. *This is why I like to stay home. But if it makes Lee happy...*

She breathed deeply, not bothering to shut her eyes. Staying aware was safer. When Blanche first taught her how to do this meditation shit, she'd have to go somewhere quiet and safe to concentrate on her breathing. But quiet, safe places were rare.

*Inhale, 2, 3, 4, 5. I see the drag king, my friends, and that goddamn plant.*

*Exhale, 4, 3, 2, 1. I feel the bar behind me and the arm of the dude sitting next to me.*

The deep breaths irritated her nose. She snorted back a cough and took a sip of her drink to clear her throat.

*Inhale, 2, 3, 4, 5. I taste my drink. This is straight fucking Black Label, Jesus Christ!* The smooth burn of the scotch overpowered the sweet bubbles from the splash of Coke.

*Exhale, 4, 3, 2, 1. I smell scotch, obviously. Vanilla from somewhere. Lavender from my laundry detergent. Well, Lee's laundry detergent because he does my laundry.*

Going out for a few hours on her birthday was the least she could do to make Lee happy compared to everything he did for her. The whirlwind of discomfort settled down with every breath reminding her that her friends' affection was safe. She smiled into her drink; the last thing she needed tonight was a panic attack.

"So is Buttercup your real name, or is there something else I should call you?"

Tara's train of thought derailed at the deep voice in her ear. The broad-shouldered man smiled at her. She scanned him—a habit refined by advice from Blanche and life experience—checking for signs he might be a threat behind his attractive exterior.

He was classically handsome—strong jaw, Roman nose, and thick brows—but with a softness to his features. His deep-set eyes seemed honest, if insecure. He searched her face for a reaction as she blatantly checked him out. She wondered what color his eyes were outside of Confession's dim blue and pink lighting.

He wore a dark sweater and jeans. No wedding band or tan line on his finger, but his watch looked expensive. Likely single and middle-class, if not richer. Long dark hair spilled over one shoulder, the thick curls cascading down his wide chest into loose ringlets. Tara itched to tangle her fingers in his curls and see if his chest felt as solid as it looked.

*Maybe he'd join me in the Confessionals?* He wasn't straight—*not with that hair*—but his hungry look was clearly not platonic. He reminded her of a puppy sitting impatiently for his treat, tail thumping in excitement. That won her over. No signs of trouble.

*Yet.*

"Call me anything you want. Just not Buttercup." Tara smiled back. The anxiety behind his pretty eyes melted and his smile grew into an earnest grin. *Oh fuck me, he has dimples too?*

---

## Blanche

"We've lost Tara." Sunny slid into Tara's spot, scooting closer to Blanche. "Her newest victim is a guy for once."

Blanche turned from the drag king's performance, finding Tara at the bar flirting with a tall, handsome fellow. Tara may not know how to have healthy relationships, but she sure didn't let that stop her from enjoying casual sex with strangers. It probably felt therapeutic to have someone's attention, even if it didn't heal anything. Tara would actually have to let someone in for *that* to happen.

They nursed their scotch. Tara had pulled an unusually masc person, but she had always cared more about convenience in her hookups than demographics. And since Tara never went anywhere besides Confession, not many men hit on her. Straight men usually circled the bachelorette parties like sharks instead of picking up a grouchy masc woman.

Sunny sighed, gazing with admiration at Tara. "I wish I had her confidence. How does she meet people so easily?"

Blanche laughed. "Babygirl, Tara has many good qualities, but confidence is not one of them. Stubborn, yes. Sensual, yes. Self-preservation, in spades. But that's not confidence."

"Okay, if she's not confident, then what does she have that I don't? I wanna bang hot strangers in the bathroom."

Blanche smiled wryly and closed the distance between them. "Is that what you want? A quick fuck in the bathroom?" they teased, intentionally breathing their words down Sunny's neck.

Sunny shivered, her pupils widening. Blanche loved teasing Sunny like this, despite their better judgment. She was so cute, so suggestible. It was hard to resist, even though Blanche shouldn't encourage her; Sunny's crush wasn't exactly subtle.

"Uh... Yes?" Sunny squeaked out.

*Too far, Blanche. You know better.* As flattering as her crush was, Sunny was their dear friend and they preferred to keep it that way. Indulging in any personal relationship beyond friendship only gave Blanche more to lose. Sunny respected that boundary, so Blanche ignored the obvious other than occasionally teasing her.

With a sigh, they backed out of Sunny's personal space, leaning away to create more distance between them. "Babygirl, what Tara has is trust in her instincts, emotional walls thick enough to survive the apocalypse, and extreme thirst for a pair of thick thighs and pretty eyes. That works for her. You and Tara are not the same."

They wondered how much to say. Sunny liked to get advice, even though she didn't always take it. They searched Sunny's dark eyes in the dim light, reflecting the stage lights like stars. "But, you were right about what you need—confidence. How confident are you in your own skin? How confident are you in demanding what you want from a partner?"

"I'm not. At all." Sunny's gaze fell to her drink, her face crestfallen. "I can barely rub one out when I'm alone, let alone fool around with strangers. I'm hopeless."

Blanche had a sixth sense for predicting where conversations would go. A skill they'd refined over two decades of sex work, from anticipating if a situation would sour. They didn't like it, but the outcome of this one was practically inevitable. "You're not hopeless. You just need more experience to get comfortable with yourself. With or without a partner to help you explore and communicate your boundaries."

Despite Blanche's misgivings, Sunny did need somewhere safe to get to know herself. A tall order for a young trans woman who still shared a bedroom with her little sister.

It wouldn't be the first time Blanche had performed that service. It'd been more frequent when they were young. Blanche and Daisy would claim a bench by the burial mounds, up on the bluff. Everyone in Bellamy who wanted a helping hand (or other body part) knew to find it there. Since specializing as a dominatrix a decade ago, that particular service was less frequent, but Blanche's vanilla clientele still found them by word of mouth.

Sunny sat quietly for a while, watching the show. Until, as expected...

"Blanche? Can I ask a favor from you? Professionally, not a personal favor." Sunny placed her hand on their arm, drawing Blanche's attention. Her dark eyes pleaded with them. "Could I..." She paused, a roaming spotlight briefly illuminating her wide-eyed expression. "Will you be that safe space for me?"

Blanche exhaled their disappointment with a sweet smile. Sunny reminded them so much of Daisy. And they could never turn away someone in need, especially one as dear as Sunny. Playing even the smallest part in helping Sunny find her confidence was worth any number of awkward conversations afterward, no matter the risk to their fragile, hard-won peace.

Not that Sunny would go through with it. Even in the unlikely event that she brought it up again, Lee would see the disaster coming and talk sense into her before it got that far. Blanche religiously honored client privacy, but Sunny would not keep this to herself. She'd go to her best friend for advice, and Lee would tell her to find someone else for help, and Sunny would listen.

But just in case, Blanche had to remind Sunny this had to stay strictly business. *Because if anyone would read too much into it, it'd be Sunny.* They kept their smile on as a mask to hide their hesitation; Sunny would only take it personally. "Only if you promise not to catch feelings for me."

# Chapter Four

## Tara

As Tara leaned in to flirt with Mr. Dimples, his hand slid around her hips. "You won't give me your name?"

Tara shook her head and leaned into him, her chest pressing against his. "You don't need to know it."

"All right, Beautiful, I'll call you pet names until I find one that fits then," Mr. Dimples teased as his fingertips tentatively traced her bare thigh.

Tara smirked as she sipped her drink, basking in the glow of his attention. Sex was the one vice she allowed herself to indulge in whenever the opportunity struck. It wasn't the sex itself, nice as it was. Being wanted by someone—anyone—was intoxicating. The short-term, emotionless desire made leaving the house worth the effort. And this man looked at her like he worshiped her, his blatant want scratching an itch in her soul.

But the man pulled away, his attention drawn to the stage as Chas announced the next performer, whoever the new queen was. Carlita something-or-other. His hand started to drop from her leg.

Tara leaned in close to his ear. "What's your favorite cuss word?"

To her delight, the man's dimples deepened. His hand on her inner thigh burned her skin, edging closer to the hem of her romper as he leaned in. Tara's defenses rose as their faces drew closer. But she stood her ground, relieved when his mouth went to her ear, not her lips. His breath tickled, smelling lightly of whiskey as his deep voice replied, "Easy question. Fuck. Fun to say and even more fun to do."

*Wow, good thing he's hot. That's corny as hell.* Tara could work with it. He didn't need to talk much for what she wanted. Tara's lips grazed his ear as she spoke. "Good choice. Fuck. That's what you can call me when you're railing me in the bathroom."

A faint whine escaped into her ear. He cleared his throat before his voice rumbled again, lips teasing the shell of her ear as she had done to him. "You can call me God then, Angel."

Tara's breath caught. *Who knew corny ass lines did it for me?* She grinned and downed her drink, grabbing his sweater to pull him toward the bathroom.

He hesitated, looking at the new queen onstage with a wince. She made a spot-on Beyonce, but Tara was mildly offended Mr. Dimples would consider watching the show instead of a guaranteed pull.

He dragged his eyes over her again before muttering to himself, "He'll understand." His dimples reappeared. "Let's go, Sweetheart." His hands found her hips as she led him through the crowd to the bathroom.

Tara's favorite part about Confession was the bathrooms, better known as the Confessionals. The stalls were actual rooms—fully enclosed with tiled walls and hand-carved wood panels mounted onto steel doors. Unusual for a nightclub (but perfect for the anonymous sex she enjoyed), they were clean, private, smelled decent, and locked securely.

By design, the Confessionals could accommodate anything anyone might need. Each bathroom was ADA accessible, with its own sink, sharps container, first aid kit, dispensers with condoms, dental dams, lube, tampons, pads, and temporary tattoos (for some reason) packed into each small room. And despite Confession being solidly a 21+ establishment, even a baby changing station hung on the wall. For folks who could stand to pee and didn't need a full bathroom, they had a room of urinals.

Tara dragged the broad-shouldered man into her favorite stall at the far end, locking the door behind her. *Jesus Christ, he's tall.* Tara hadn't noticed when he was sitting down, but he towered over her even more than Lee did.

"Any boundaries, Turtledove?" He crowded her against the door, mouth on her neck.

"Such a gentleman," Tara cooed. Normally, they never asked. "No kissing on the mouth or grabbing my hands or wrists. No health issues, and tell me now if you do so we can work around it. Use a condom. Everything else is fair game."

He smiled against her neck. "Sounds good to me, Sugar. I'm not into degradation, but I'm open to everything else. No health concerns from my end." He wedged a massive thigh between her legs. "Are you familiar with the traffic light system? Green for keep going, yellow for slow down, and red for stop?"

"I doubt we need safewords for a quickie in the bathroom, but I'd love it if you prove me wrong," Tara teased as she squirmed up his muscular frame, the wood carving mounted to the door digging into her back. She was fairly tall at five-foot-nine, but this man was a fucking redwood tree. "Can I touch your hair?" Her fingers had been itching to find out if his loose ringlets were as soft as they looked.

His sharp exhale hissed in her ear as she wrapped both legs around his hips, his hands moving to her ass to support her. "You can touch me anywhere you want, Corazón."

"You didn't say green."

His laugh puffed against her skin. "Green. Pull it if you want."

Tara didn't hesitate. Both hands sank into his thick hair, yanking his head back. His responding groan resonated under her tongue dragging up his neck. *Wow, vocal and he cares about consent? Be still my heart.* Most men she'd been with acted like making sounds was a sign of weakness instead of the wordless praise she craved.

In addition to the faint smell of whiskey from earlier, she caught a hint of vanilla and something woodsy as his pulse fluttered under her lips. *Oak?* She didn't know what exactly oak smelled like, but it *felt* right.

"No bra, Lovely?" he whispered huskily in her ear, tweaking a nipple through the stiff denim of her romper.

Tara arched into his hand as his mouth trailed down her neck, "Spoilers, but no panties either."

Her hands combed his scalp where she had pulled his hair, fingers tangling in his curls. A honeyed "fuck" dripped from his mouth. *God, the voice of this man.* An intoxicating thrill ran through her every time his deep moans echoed in the small bathroom. Tara briefly considered telling him her name just to hear him say it.

His fingers made quick work of the buttons on her romper, giving him access to her pink nipples, already tightened into peaks. He took one in his mouth, pulling her up higher against him. Tara's sharp gasp echoed as he worked her tit with his teeth and tongue. Need burned through her body in waves, hampered only by the stiff seam riding up her ass again.

"Can I get naked? This wedgie is killing me." Untangling herself from him, she stepped out of her romper, finally free of irritation.

His gaze admired her body, taking in her skinny form, all her hard edges, and the abstract tattoos decorating her hips and thighs. Tara didn't let him look too long. She didn't want him to take in how underweight she was, or the old scars hidden under the tattoos. They always gave the most pitying looks when they noticed. She stepped closer, cupping her hand over his erection.

"Oh, fuck," he exhaled, staring down at her. In the softer light of the bathroom, his deep-set eyes were the dark satin brown of coffee. Tara wanted to dive into them. He seemed just as lost, slack-jawed and breathless as she massaged his impressive erection through his jeans.

Tara wanted to taste him, discover how far she could take him in her mouth. An odd fluttery sigh escaped at the thought of choking on his dick. *Okay, embarrassing.*

He bit his lip, his pretty eyes hungry. She allowed herself to drown in his worshiping gaze a little longer. "You're going to ruin me, aren't you, Motek?" A flurry of unidentifiable emotions crossed his handsome face. His mouth opened and closed as if searching for the words to say before quietly commanding, "Hands on the railing." He gestured toward the ADA bar.

*So much for blowing him.* Tara complied, surprised but not displeased at the transformation from eager to authoritative. Normally, she liked to drive, but she'd give him a chance.

His hands gripped her hips, grinding his erection against her ass as he curled around her. His lips brushed the shell of her ear as his deep voice murmured, "I won't touch your hands, but keep them there until I say so. There will be consequences, Darling. Enjoyable ones, but consequences. Color?"

"Green. I'm touched you remembered." Though she kept her tone sarcastic, warmth flickered in her chest. She usually had to remind most people of her rules when they broke them at least once. Letting someone take charge who remembered her boundaries might be fun. Hopefully, he'd keep impressing her. She didn't bend over like this for just anyone.

"Baby, I won't forget any of this," he whispered huskily before his hand burned between her shoulder blades to bend her over further, leaving her cunt exposed to the cool air.

To her surprise, she didn't hear the zip of his jeans or the crinkle of condom foil. Instead, his hands dragged along her ass and thighs, fingers tracing the tattoos across her hips.

Without preamble, his tongue ran a hot stripe along her slit. Her squeak of surprise morphed into a whine of pleasure. He devoured her, tongue delving deep into her. Large hands gripped her ass as she ground back against that goddamn mouth. The filthiest slurping sounds echoed in the small room.

His tongue slid down to her clit and a thick finger filled her, pressing all of her favorite spots without her telling him what to do. He added a second finger, rotating his hand down deeper, harder. Tension spiked through her. A coil of pleasure tightened as he sucked her clit.

"How am I this close already?" she panted, her words becoming nonsense, but she'd say whatever she needed to encourage the magic he was performing on her body. *Men like him don't eat pussy like this.*

If this was what bottoming could be like, maybe she'd let people top her more often. Normally she got herself off while nose-deep between someone's thighs. On a lucky day, they'd return the favor.

He hummed in response. The deep rumble against her clit sent her over the edge. She gasped out a final "Oh god!" that turned into a loud cry as her back arched. His firm grip on her thigh and her death grip on the rail kept her from collapsing to the floor.

Light kisses pressed against her thighs as she shuddered through the lingering aftershocks.

Mr. Brown Eyes straightened up behind her, still kneeling, alternately biting and kissing her ass cheeks. "Color?"

"So fucking green!"

He let out a laugh, exhaling against her ass. "Good."

His fingers curled inside of her. Tara was on the verge telling him to just fuck her already, but he interrupted her begging with a tongue to her asshole.

Tara's brain shorted out. Hands gripping the metal bar, she lost herself in the sensations. A strong arm wrapped around her hips was all that kept her upright. A hot wet tongue worked against her sphincter. Thick fingers pumped inside her cunt. A deft thumb brushed her oversensitive clit.

She was vaguely aware of the vulgar sounds coming from her, but she no longer cared how loud she was. Anyone waiting for a bathroom must have figured out what was happening in this one by now.

Time lost all meaning as he worked her into another orgasm, her brain exploding into a galaxy as expletives and nonsense fell from her lips. She had no idea if it'd been minutes or hours or seconds or what her name was by the time she came down from her high.

"Color?"

Tara couldn't answer, control of her breath slow to return as she regained sensation in her body.

"Duckling, tell me your color," he warned, removing his hands.

"I can't remember my name, let alone colors," she managed to gasp.

He chuckled, standing up. "I'll take that as yellow, Bunny. Let me know when you're ready for me or if you want to stop."

Tara stretched her arms over her head, catching her breath. *Stop? How dare he suggest it?* Turning to face him, she touched his chest, admiring the hard muscles underneath his soft sweater. He waited patiently for her instead of undressing or pulling out a condom.

Her heart fluttered. She must look a mess, but she was beyond caring about how sweat must have ruined the mascara Sunny had made her wear or the flush spreading across her chest. Mr. Redwood Tree was still looking at her like he wanted her desperately and that was all that mattered.

"Oh yeah, green." She tugged on his sweater, eager to see his body.

He looked down at her, mock disappointment on his face. "Did I say you could take your hands off the rail, Naughty?" His hands gripped her hips, and gently pushed her to the handrail.

"Oh no, consequences!" Tara grinned and fought against him halfheartedly. She was surprised to find this was…fun? It was unusual for her to be this comfortable with someone she'd just met. She preferred to be the dominant one; it was safer that way. But even as he steered her to the rail, she was still in control.

"Enjoyable ones." Mr. Brown Eyes pinned her against the wall, leaving her arms free like she'd told him, but her tits and neck were crushed against the cold tile. His broad chest, still clad in his sweater, pressed warmly against her back, his lips hot behind her ear. He paused to give her a chance to change her color.

"Still green." Tara lowered her hands to the rail below her. "I'll listen. For now."

He stepped back, replacing his torso with a firm hand to keep her pressed against the wall. Anticipation crawled up her spine, hoping he'd either fuck her or—

*Smack.* Her ass stung where he slapped it. Her breath caught in her throat.

*Smack.* A backhand to her other cheek made a cry fly from her mouth.

"Oh, fuck yes!" She wanted to bottle him to relive this every night as she fell asleep. Tara hadn't even fucked him yet, but he was going to star in a lot of her fantasies from now on. *Maybe I should ask his name so I know what to call my vibrator.*

"That's one for each hand that left the railing. Don't do it again." His voice dripped into her ear, raw as honey, viscous and thick.

"Can I have a reminder of the consequences?"

He laughed and slapped her ass twice more. "Cheri, I could do that all night, but I want to be inside you. Color?"

"Dude, green!" Tara leaned into the wall, eyes squeezing shut in anticipation, hands gripping the railing. "You don't need to ask so much. I'll tell you if it changes."

"Understood."

She waited, pressing against the cool tile to stay grounded from delirium. If all bar hookups made her feel this good, she'd have to make a rule against it.

The sounds of a zipper and a crinkle of foil echoed in the room. His knuckles grazed her skin as he rolled the condom on. Cool and wet, the lube made her shiver when his erection fell heavy against her back.

"Put your legs on mine, Dear. I've got you, but it might give you some leverage if you want it." As he spoke, he lifted her lower half effortlessly off the ground and gripped an ankle in one massive hand to fold her leg beneath her. She tucked her other leg under to match.

"This is a new position for me," she admitted, kicking her shoes off. Kneeling on his massive thighs midair, her upper half pinned to the wall, was an impressive testament to his creativity and strength.

"That makes two of us." His breath tingled her neck. "Working with the circumstances."

He pushed into her slowly, groaning with her. He felt bigger than most, stretching her cunt delightfully, but she hadn't looked for herself to verify. Tara wondered if his cock looked as gorgeous as it felt inside her.

"Circumstances?" Her voice was breathy even to her own ears. The leverage of his thighs helped her roll her hips back against him, encouraging him to move.

He set an agonizingly slow pace, rolling into her with each phrase as he answered her in a strained voice. "Public bathroom. Height difference. Your boundaries. Mine."

*This man is going to ruin me.* His consideration flooded her with warmth. Impatient and needing to take back some control, she rocked faster, desperate for him to go deeper.

"Oh fuck, you're amazing." He met her eagerness with a bite to her neck, groaning into her ear. "If I give you another, can I come?"

She panted, trying to form words. "Dude, you don't need my permission. I already came twice. If you want to come, come." She bore down as she rolled her hips against him to emphasize her point.

"How are you so perfect?" He was the one babbling now. Tara bit her lip, proud she could make him moan and pant the same way he had done to her. "You feel so good, Kitten."

The praise made her giddy. That weird fluttering sigh tickled her throat again; she stifled a cough with a heavy swallow.

He rocked into her harder, one hand moving to her clit. White-hot pleasure simmered through her body as he fucked her from behind, his forearm wrapped around her hips.

Her oversensitive body couldn't take any more. Tara erupted into another orgasm, a cry tearing from her throat as her muscles convulsed around him. He swore a chain of increasingly loud curses into her neck.

Fucking her through the orgasm shattering through her, he followed her into bliss a few moments later with a muffled shout as his teeth dug into her shoulder. He exhaled soft moans, breath trembling against her skin as his cock flexed inside her.

They gently detangled from each other as they caught their breath, equally dazed.

Tara collapsed onto the toilet to pee, but also because she didn't trust herself to walk. Her legs trembled as she reached for her shoes to put them back on.

"You know, most people wouldn't eat ass at a bar," she tried to joke, distracting herself from the post-orgasm emotions creeping up.

"Your ass looked edible." He shrugged, turning away to dispose of the condom before she could peek. "And you didn't seem to mind."

Tara pouted, disappointed she'd missed her opportunity to see his dick. Or any part of his body. She'd barely touched his sweater. "Not complaining. Just impressed."

He washed his face and hands before working the snarls from his hair. Thick fingers parted the brown-black ringlets, undoing her handiwork.

"Sorry for messing up your hair."

"Kitten, never apologize for anything that we just did." He smiled over his shoulder, plaiting his hair into a messy braid to hide the tangles.

A grin crossed her face involuntarily at the sight of his dimples. "Kitten, huh? That's the nickname you settled on? Kinky. Should I call you Daddy?"

He snorted. "Under *no* circumstance do I ever want to be called Daddy."

Tara flushed the toilet and stood between him and the sink to wash up. His frame was tall and broad enough to encompass her in the mirror. Something about the two of them together…

"Did you know you purr, Kitten?"

Tara blushed. "I might be getting a cold."

"For both our sakes, I hope not," he teased. "I don't know how you made that sound, but I want to hear it again." His hands ran down her sides to rest on her hips. Coffee-brown eyes met her green ones in the mirror as he pressed a kiss to her neck.

Her heart stopped as her breath caught. Time slowed to a halt. Tara wanted to stare at him in the mirror forever and never forget how his arms surrounded her, how his chest pressed warmly against her back, how safe she felt with him.

No.

She shouldn't feel safe with him.

Her pulse roared to life, injecting dread through her veins. Her breath stuck in her throat, unable to reach her lungs or clear the fog curling into the dark corners of her mind.

*Breathe, Tara.* She had to get somewhere truly safe. Alarm bells rang in her head, out of sync with the racing of her heart. Her rapid shallow breaths echoed as if all other sounds had been sucked out of the room, her ears ringing with the shrill panic reverberating in her mind.

"Too bad we're strangers." The sound of her own voice brought her back to her body. Taking a deep breath, Tara stepped out of his arms, shaking out her romper. The post-nut clarity sank in. He was a good fuck but not worth breaking her rules.

"We don't have to stay strangers." His gaze followed her. "I'm down for round two at my place if you are. Or can I give you my number? I'd love to see you again."

Tara froze, fighting the tightening of her chest. "As good as this was, it was a one-time thing. I don't make the mistake of repeats."

His face clouded over. "A mistake. Is that what this was?"

"No, but— Look, it's nothing personal, dude. Just forget about me and get on with your night." She finished buttoning her romper and crossed her arms to hide their shaking.

He glowered at her. "Kitten, I don't think I'll ever forget you."

Tara forced an air of nonchalance into her words, "Well, that sounds like a You problem. See you never, asshole."

His words struck her in the back as she stepped out of the bathroom. "Fucking bitch!"

*So much for "Kitten."* It was for the best though. The fantasy of a quick bar fuck—even an amazing bar fuck—would always be better than the reality of a real person in her life.

Tara pushed past the people waiting in line, ignoring the whistles and applause. She bolted like she always did, shoving down the guilt for pushing him away before giving him a chance, for ditching her friends when they wanted to celebrate her. She packed it away into the hidden corner of her brain where she kept the rest of the feelings she'd rather live without.

Glancing up at the control room where her closest safe space would be, she decided to leave instead. Lee was working and had better things to do than attempt to keep her from spiraling. Already, the familiar sense of dread rose, but she could muffle her inevitable panic attack for the twenty minutes it would take to walk home. Her body and her friends knew the routine by now. Tara could break down as soon as Blanche's front door was securely locked behind her.

*Just breathe.*

# Chapter Five

## Lee

Lee wrapped an extension cord around his forearm, cleaning up equipment in the wings. His head bobbed with the music playing, even though Confession was closed for the night. The bar was practically empty; only a handful of employees and a few regulars were still lingering.

He regretted that Tara's birthday was cut short, but her social battery rarely lasted past intermission. He knew Tara well enough to guess a hookup had gone left, but Blanche would take care of her. Sunny and Blanche had left soon after Tara had dipped; Blanche had texted him that Tara was home safe and drowning her feelings in pizza. His Buttercup would be fine.

Tidying up could probably wait until after the brunch show tomorrow, but leaving before everyone else was done with their closing tasks felt wrong. *"A good leader should be the first to arrive and the last to leave."*

"There you are! I've been looking for you!" Antonio's lilting voice called from behind Lee, thankfully drowning out the memory of one of his dad's many lectures.

Antonio's face was washed clear of Carlita's makeup—though his eyes were somehow more stunning, smudged dark with eyeliner—and his curls were pressed flat from where his wig cap had been. A silk floral robe revealing just as much golden-brown skin as it concealed had replaced the blue sequin dress and padding he'd worn onstage. It fluttered around his thighs as Antonio strode toward him, his stilettos echoing through the wings.

"You were looking for...me?" *Duh. He just said that.* Lee's heart raced as he considered all the improbable possibilities why.

Antonio held out the headset and mic pack. "Where do you want me to put this?"

*Oh, right. Keep it professional.* "I set up a charger in the control room." Lee took it, *not* keeping it professional as he let his touch linger. "You were great tonight."

Carlita was incredibly acrobatic, especially considering she sang live. "Love on Top" was a hard-ass song and she'd sung it flawlessly. All while keeping the audience engaged and not missing a single step of her complicated choreography.

Even more impressive was her rendition of "Poker Face" while doing backflips on beat and in heels. Small wonder Carlita needed a headset. From what Chas had told Lee during intermission, she'd been good before, but Carlita was on another level after five years in New York. She had quickly become a crowd favorite tonight.

Lee's favorite, too. He couldn't look away when Carlita performed. Even in full drag, Antonio was stupid attractive. Maybe it was his confidence, his talent, or the witty banter with the audience that drew Lee's attention. Or maybe Lee was just half in love with him already.

*You gotta chill. Stop doing this to yourself.*

"I was great, wasn't I?" A blush crossed Antonio's cheeks. "Thanks to you, honestly! I know for a fact that Chas didn't have this headset lying around."

Lee rubbed a hand over his short hair. "Yeah, no, Chas likes to hold a mic when he's on stage, but we upgraded the sound system a while ago. It was no big deal to go buy one."

A wicked smile crossed Antonio's lips. "Well, as much as I love a *mic* in my hand, it wouldn't have been the same. You can take a little credit for my flawless performance." He stepped closer. "Can I thank you somehow?"

Lee swallowed, not daring to hope. "What, uh, what did you have in mind?"

"A date, if that's okay?" Panic crossed Antonio's face at Lee's unblinking stare. "Oh, God, I hope I didn't misread this."

Lee nodded quickly, recovering with a nervous smile. "No! Yes! I mean, yeah, it's okay. Date sounds good." *Real smooth, there.* "I wasn't sure if I was reading too much into it either. You're way too hot to be single." *Goddammit! Stop talking!*

Antonio's laughter was the sweetest music. "God, you're cute. I am *very* single. Just haven't met anyone who makes me happier than I make myself. Yet."

"And you think *I* have a chance?" Lee looked around. "Is there someone behind me you're talking to instead?"

Antonio burst into musical laughter. Lee's heart leapt along with the cadence. "Oh, she's got jokes too. I'm so screwed!"

Unable to fight a dopey grin, Lee fought the urge to pinch himself. He was usually one-night stand material at best, especially for someone as charismatic as Antonio. The entranced smile on Antonio's face sent shivers down his spine.

"Oh." Lee realized belatedly that Antonio was waiting for him to say something instead of just grinning like a fool. "Should we get drinks after the brunch show tomorrow?"

Antonio shook his head, a wince dimming his smile. "My family is coming to the show, and they'll stick around. How does coffee on Monday sound? Unless you have another job, of course. I have a few weeks before my nine-to-five starts, but I totally get if you have somewhere to be."

"No, yeah. Coffee sounds great. Here, I'll text you." Dropping the forgotten extension cord with a heavy thump on the wood floors, Lee unlocked his phone and handed it to him.

Antonio texted himself a heart emoji, stepping closer as he handed the phone back to Lee. "Now I have yours too. So no ghosting me, 'kay?"

Lee couldn't imagine a universe where *he* would ghost someone like Antonio. "Never. I have to make you happier than you make yourself, remember?" He edged closer as he tucked his phone into his pocket, Antonio's exhale tickling his neck.

Antonio's tongue darted out to wet his lips. "Is this real?"

Lee barely heard him above the blood rushing in his ears. Even his inner flirt couldn't come up with a response. Instead, he gently pressed his lips against Antonio's, quickly pulling away as he second-guessed that maybe he'd overstepped. Mortification burned through him.

Grabbing his shirt, Antonio pulled him back with a desperate crash. His hesitation and embarrassment evaporating, Lee drank him in, lips slipping against the smile he'd been thinking about for two days as want pulsed through his body.

Antonio's fist gripped Lee's collar as he backed Lee against the wall. Hitting the brick knocked the breath out of him, but he couldn't bear to tear his mouth from Antonio's, no matter how light-headed he was.

Lee didn't know how long they'd kissed, or exactly when he'd wrapped his fingers through Antonio's curls. The brick wall bit into his knuckles as he cradled the back of Antonio's head. He lost track of whatever he'd been doing when he turned to press Antonio against the wall, sliding his hand under the silky robe to grip Antonio's thigh wrapped around his hip. Long fingers grasped his neck and shoulders to pull Lee closer, sending shivers down his spine. The scrape of stubble against his jaw and the nibble against his bottom lip chased every thought away. Kissing Antonio was the only thing that mattered. Their bodies pressing against each other was his only concern.

"Leland, you whore. Stop sucking face and hurry up! We're bored!"

Lee froze as Whatshisname's voice pierced through the ecstasy. *This bitch.* He'd forgotten about his other...friends, for lack of a better word. He pulled away a fraction of an inch from Antonio's kiss, but that was already too far. His forehead fell gently onto Antonio's as they panted. "Sorry. I forgot. I'm driving some friends to a party."

Lee DD'ed every Saturday for a few of the regulars after close. He'd banked on Tara being done socializing long before then, so he hadn't bothered to risk the drama he'd catch for canceling. Whatshisname and his crew weren't exactly close friends of his, but they let him tag along if he drove. Lee went more for the community than the company; there weren't many places in Bellamy where he'd find himself surrounded mostly by queer men of color.

Tara, Blanche, and Sunny were his family, but they would never be the community he craved. He wanted to be a part of a crowd like he was as a kid, at church cookouts and family reunions. Somewhere he fit in, where he wouldn't stand out for being too gay or too big or too Black or too...himself. Not that he wanted to go to church or see his parents again—*God, no*—but he missed the vibe. These parties were the closest he could get.

"Oh." Disappointment flashed through Antonio's eyes.

"Do y—Do you want to come?" Lee asked.

Antonio shook his head, a rueful smile on his face. "I would only make bad decisions if I went. And I want you to be a good decision."

Lee swallowed his disappointment. "We're still on for Monday, though, right?"

Antonio nodded, that easy smile coming back to his face.

Lee kissed him again, needing Antonio to understand he wasn't rejecting him, that Lee wanted to see where this went. This gorgeous man with the heart-melting kiss silenced the inner reasonable voice telling him to calm down. Lee always caught feelings easily, but he'd never caught them from one kiss before.

*This one's gonna hurt like a bitch when it's over.*

"Leland!" Whatshisname's shrill yell echoed through the wings.

Maybe it was better Antonio couldn't come. They were always desperate for new dick to pass around. Lee always stayed out of *that* drama, and he selfishly wanted to keep Antonio to himself. Antonio inevitably leaving with someone better than him would feel real shitty.

Lee regretfully pulled away. It took all his willpower to gather the equipment lying around instead of tossing it all on the ground and kissing Antonio again. Arms full of cables and Antonio's headset, he hurried away with a "See you tomorrow" thrown over his shoulder. If he looked back at Antonio, he'd never leave.

LEE BARELY NOTICED THE vibration in his pocket over the pop music playing on the Bluetooth speaker. *Ooh, maybe Antonio texted me?* He reached for his phone, all the while scolding himself for being delusional.

*Oh. Sweet.* Someone had bought one of his house tracks, so he was twenty bucks richer. Not as nice as a text from Antonio, but still good. He grinned and tapped his fingers on his beer bottle to the beat of the music. Someone out there liked his music enough to pay for it. Maybe this one would be his break.

"Did you get a dick pic? Let's see!" The guy standing next to him grabbed his phone. "Oh, boring. Just your music shit."

Lee snatched his phone back, trying to hide his irritation. He didn't know this guy well enough for him to take his phone without asking. But he tried to take it in stride. "I'd rather get money from my 'music shit' than a dick pic. It's not like any of your broke asses will ever cough up gas money."

The handful of people standing around laughed. He didn't know whose apartment this was; Lee just drove where he was told. This week they were over Eastside. Guys were dancing and laughing in the living room all around them. Others made out on the couch. Clusters were talking shit, smoking, and drinking. Laughter rang out from the bathroom.

Lee never remembered any of their names. He'd hooked up with some of them, so he knew the more memorable dating app usernames. At the party tonight, he'd already awkwardly avoided UncutHungTop *(all lies)*, JustAHole *(accurate, he just laid there)*, and DLTopPBW *(the "top" was very misleading and "DL"? In that shirt? Doubtful)*.

He'd long forgotten the names of the friends he came to these parties with—if he'd ever known them at all. Lee called everyone by some nickname in his head and avoided saying anyone's name out loud. The group he drove included BJSlut *(a very accurate username)*, Amen *(Not a username, more of a catchphrase)*, and Whatshisname, their self-proclaimed leader.

Phone Snatcher rolled his eyes. "Explains why you're single."

"Like you aren't?" Whatshisname shot out. Lee really should learn his name, but it'd been three years since they'd met—too late to ask. "Still, Leland, you gotta stop wasting time on that music shit. If you were any good, you wouldn't be worried about gas for that death trap you drive."

"Amen to that!" agreed Amen. He always agreed with whatever Whatshisname said.

Lee had never hooked up with either of them. Probably for the best. Amen was in love with Whatshisname, but Lee wouldn't even if he wasn't. Whatshisname had tried. But even if Lee *had* been into him, he needed friends far more than he wanted hookups, and Whatshisname ghosted every one of his flings. And since he was Lee's invite to these parties, Lee always found a reason to avoid going home with him so he wouldn't be left behind next week.

"That death trap got you here, didn't it?" Lee's skin prickled with annoyance. "Why hate on me for making a few bucks?"

"Chill, Leland." Whatshisname side-eyed him. "I'm just talking shit. You take everything so damn serious."

"Amen!" contributed Amen.

Lee fell silent, mentally retreating from the conversation to focus on the music playing, tracking the chord progression to figure out the sample. Whatshisname wasn't wrong. If Lee was any good, he'd sell more than a couple of tracks a week. Getting rich wasn't his priority; Lee made music because he enjoyed it. Still, it'd be nice to be a little more successful, considering how much work he put into it.

Lee's downfall was that he wasn't musically inclined. He couldn't sing or play an instrument, but he could figure out what layers would make a beat better, why some songs felt nostalgic when they were sampled and others tacky. Someone else with talent would have to turn his house tracks into a real song.

"Sounds like you need to get laid." Phone Snatcher elbowed him. "Why don't you message one of the people who hit you up on Grindr?"

*Ten bucks says he's one of them.* Phone Snatcher had been hanging strangely close to Lee tonight. Lee usually wasn't the focus of the conversation like this. He preferred to blend into the background.

To be fair, Lee would normally have checked Grindr by now. But, normally, Lee wouldn't have a date lined up with anyone. He swallowed, remembering how Antonio's hazel eyes had fluttered half-closed as they kissed. Not many guys were interested in him, and for *Antonio* to ask *him* out?

*Calm down. It's one date. There won't be a second.*

"Leland's mooning over his new girlfriend. He was sucking face with that new queen earlier." Whatshisname made a show of looking at his nails.

"Ugh, Carlita. I was hoping she'd stay in New York." Phone Snatcher rolled his eyes. "Honestly, I don't know why Chas puts up with her. More drama than she's worth."

Lee took a sip of his beer to hide his skepticism. Antonio didn't seem dramatic, just genuine and talented and funny. Perhaps a little talkative and flirty, but that was cool with— *Wait, is this Venus?*

Other than Chas, Lee wasn't close with any of the performers, but he should probably recognize his coworker of five years. Not that he knew Venus DeVille's real name, either. Trying not to stare, Lee imagined the guy next to him with a wig and makeup; Phone Snatcher was definitely Venus. Lee's skin itched at the realization that some of his coworkers might have seen him outside of work and he'd never known—

"She was asking about you backstage tonight." Venus put his hand on Lee's arm, which did nothing to quell his mortification that his reputation at work might be compromised. Not that he'd ever acted particularly crass at these parties, but still. He wanted his coworkers to like him, and he wasn't exactly virtuous. And Venus was a notorious gossip.

"I told her not to bother, more for your sake than hers. Carlita has a reputation. She acts all obsessed at first, but then she gets bored and ghosts. Awkward as hell for the rest of us when she breaks another heart." Venus pressed against him with a wink. "But I had no idea you chased queens. I woulda talked to you years ago if I'd known."

Pushing up his glasses, Lee bit back the grin at the thought that Antonio had asked about him; better not to let Venus think the smile was for anyone but Antonio. As much as he appreciated the warning, he was not expecting Antonio to stay interested. Being asked on a date was already more than he'd hoped for. It'd be a nice change of pace for someone to act obsessed with him, even if only for a few days.

Whatshisname laughed with a sneer. "Sis, if he's into twunks like you and Carlita, you need to be more worried about getting crushed to death under Leland's fat ass."

"Who are you calling a twunk, Fivehead?" Venus snapped as Lee huffed out a "Really?" Annoyance bristled through him. *Don't take it personally. It's just shit-talking.*

"Please, the only thing fat about Lee is between his legs." BJSlut winked at him. Being objectified for his dick size was not much better than a fat joke, but Lee appreciated that BJSlut stood up for him anytime Whatshisname turned nasty.

"Can we keep me out of this?" Having been chubby his whole life, Lee had grown to like his body. If only everyone who didn't could keep their opinions to themselves...

"Calm your tits, Leland." Whatshisname scoffed, fiddling with his hair in a hopeless attempt to hide his receding hairline. "Who knows, maybe someone *actually* worth your time can make you forget all about Carlita."

Whatshisname and Venus glared at each other.

"Amen!"

*Oh, God.* Lee finished his beer, walking away to grab a second drink and find a different group to talk to. *Ten bucks says this ends with them asking for a threesome.*

Whatever power struggle happening between Venus and Whatshisname had nothing to do with him; he didn't want to be the prize in their battle of egos. At least Antonio liked *him*, if only for a few days.

Monday morning could not come soon enough.

# Chapter Six

## Blanche

Blanche exhaled carefully, trying to make smoke rings. It didn't work. The smoke billowed into a cloud, obscuring the crack in the ceiling above them. Maybe if they sat up instead of laying sideways across the armchair, they could do it. But Blanche had never been very good at smoke rings. Daisy had always been better at shit like that.

"Babes, you're stressed." They passed the joint to Tara. She sat cross-legged on the couch, wrapped in a throw blanket. "Here. Get fucked up with me."

Snaking an arm out of the blanket to take the joint, Tara fiddled with it as she changed the song on her phone. Tara listened to surprisingly romantic music for someone who refused to admit she felt emotions. She called it "alternative R&B." Lee would tease her and say it wasn't "alternative" just because she'd slept on someone until they got popular.

Daisy would have called it "baby-making music." It wasn't bad. Just not Blanche's thing. Daisy had introduced the impressionable young Blanche to grunge when they'd met back in 1998. They hadn't listened to anything else since.

"I'm fine, Blanche." Tara took a hit anyway. She coughed before passing it back and grabbed another slice of the pizza Blanche had picked up on the way home. The box sat open on the coffee table, next to the half-empty bottle of Jack that Blanche had swiped from Confession. Jackie had raised an eyebrow, but they both knew Chas would give

Blanche the whole bar in a heartbeat. A privilege Blanche was careful not to abuse.

Whiskey, weed, and pizza. Everything Tara had truly wanted on her birthday, despite Lee's best efforts to get her to be less of a recluse.

"Girl, you were having a full-on meltdown when I got home." Blanche raised a skeptical eyebrow. "Wanna talk about it?"

Tara shook her head. "Nope. Nothing to talk about," she muttered around her pizza.

"So Mr. Tall, Dark, and Handsome from earlier had nothing to do with you crying under a blanket when I walked in the door?" Blanche asked gently. "If I need to beat his ass, I'd rather know now. He might still be there."

Tara let out a sharp exhale. It was the closest she'd come to a laugh for a while. She always needed time to bounce back from a panic attack. "I would have beaten his ass myself if I needed to. No, he was nice. *Real* nice. I feel kinda bad I ran out on him, but it's whatever. I don't give a shit."

"'Real nice'? Dick was that good, huh?" Blanche teased.

Tara smiled when she exhaled. "Honestly? Fucking rockstar at eating pussy. I came so hard I forgot my own name." This time, Tara actually did laugh. A little sardonic, but still a laugh. "Who knew coming that hard could trigger a panic attack?"

*She is so full of shit.* Blanche saw right through her, even if Tara refused to admit she'd felt an emotion and gotten scared. "You gonna see him again?"

Tara shot them a dirty look, refilling both of their whiskeys. "Do I ever?"

She didn't. Tara hit 'em and quit 'em. Her hookups went from strangers to lovers to ghosted within an hour. In Blanche's professional opinion as a sex worker—basically the next best thing to a therapist—Tara was a little fucked up. Not her own fault. She handled her trauma the best she could. She didn't handle it *well*, but she managed. All of them did.

"I think you should if you run into him again." Blanche took the whiskey from Tara. "If you give anyone a chance, at least let it be someone who knows what they're doing."

"You want to talk about all the things we 'should' be doing? When's the last time you had a date or slept with someone who wasn't a client?"

Blanche's smoke ring fell apart as soon as they exhaled it. "No comment."

"And the last time you saw your therapist?"

"No comment."

"Exactly. I'll break my rules when you start prioritizing yourself."

All three of them had been significantly more messed up when they'd first moved in together than they were now. So, to set a good example, Blanche had told Tara and Lee they were talking to a professional to process their grief.

Their "therapist" was a client. Though he actually *was* a therapist. He wasn't a *good* therapist, but he had a license and a degree from some small Christian college. One of the "ex-gays" who practiced conversion therapy, so the people who hated their kids could pretend they were good parents.

They did weekly house calls for him, which added to the illusion that Blanche was in therapy. He never wanted to get off, instead requesting Blanche put him in a chastity device and a TENS unit to recreate the only therapy that had repressed his "homosexual tendencies": shock therapy with a side of humiliation. He'd lay on his chaise in his home office and tell them about his patients. They'd sit in his chair and shock him every time he said anything remotely empathetic or progressive.

It'd been pretty fucked up, even in Blanche's two decades of sex work. Beyond the blatant HIPAA violations, Blanche firmly believed kink shouldn't cause trauma. Not that kink had to *heal* anything, but a good domme shouldn't make someone's issues *worse*. And Blanche had enabled this man to spout disgusting ideology at these poor queer kids, how they were destined for Hell unless they lived a godly life.

All of the same things the Family had told Blanche when they were a kid.

Their anger for the ethical position this man had put them in made it that much more satisfying to shock the ever-living fuck out of him. And what was more fitting than a trans femme sex worker taking the money that homophobic Christian parents gave him?

Overall, the therapist has been an educational client. Blanche had listened to hours of this man theorizing about human nature in his attempts to justify self-hatred. They researched ahead of their sessions to understand the nuances enough to prove him wrong, leading to lively debates and thoughtful conversations.

And Blanche *had* gotten some healing from it, learning the tools to process their own issues. He'd give Blanche tips on how to psychoanalyze him and what questions to ask that they, in turn, asked themself and Daisy. And later, Tara, and Lee. If it weren't for the fact that he was naked except for the electrodes and the device around his junk, Blanche might have felt like a real therapist.

He'd killed himself a couple years ago. Blanche sent flowers to his funeral. After all, he'd sent flowers after Daisy's death.

Blanche took another hit, avoiding thoughts of Daisy. They might be high enough to risk bad memories, but they needed to be present for a post-panic attack Tara. When she had disappeared during Carlita's act, Blanche knew they'd soon end up at home, pretending everything was fine.

*Carlita. I hope Chas knows what she's doing.*

Carlita had improved in her years away—tighter vocals, better outfits, actually dancing instead of stumbling around the stage drunk—but Blanche would have to check in with Freddy to make sure Chas wasn't stressing herself out by adding that wild card to her plate.

"You good, babes?" Blanche broke the silence. Tara didn't need conversation, just company. Someone to keep her grounded.

"Yeah." Tara swirled her whiskey and took a slow sip. "This is a nice end to the night."

"Sitting quietly and getting trashed at home?"

Tara's still-sardonic laugh was practically a giggle. "Literally the dream birthday. I don't understand why Lee enjoys going out. If I wasn't trying to get laid, I'd stay home every day."

"All the more reason to give Mr. Tall, Dark, and Handsome a chance. Imagine how much better your birthday would be with him waiting in your bed."

Tara shook her head and reached out for the joint. "I have rules for a reason."

"Sometimes, breaking the rules is worth the payoff, babes."

"And sometimes, you can tell people no and put yourself first." Tara mocked their singsong tone before putting the joint to her lips.

Blanche laughed. "I do that enough with my clients."

Many of the therapist's theories had stuck with Blanche over the years. They'd armchair psychoanalyze their friends, wondering why they were so fucked up. Most of it came down to attachment issues and trauma. It stuck with them all in different ways. Sunny, for example, was surprisingly well-adjusted, all things considered. Her issue was she only accepted the reality she wanted. Anything that contradicted her paradigm may as well not exist.

Lee's strict childhood, followed by a tumultuous adolescence, had left him stagnant and anxious. He was sweet, funny, and easygoing. But the second Lee had to make a decision, he froze. If someone—besides Tara—showed a hint of annoyance, he fled. He'd shut down until Tara, Sunny, or Blanche told him what to do and reassured him they weren't going anywhere. Lee felt so pressured to be considerate, he'd never take the time to figure out what he wanted.

Tara, on the other hand, was id-driven. She protected herself from her poor impulse control by withdrawing from the world. If something might feel good, she'd do it without a second thought. And when anything unexpected happened, she'd get scared and run. Which is why she didn't have anyone in her life but Blanche, Lee, and Sunny. The idea of letting people in terrified her.

*Thank god she never got into drugs.* Blanche took the joint back from Tara. Tara was impulsive, not stupid. She needed non-addictive coping mechanisms, like meditation exercises. Meditation had been Blanche's attempt to get Tara to acknowledge her hard feelings for once in her goddamn life. To process them so she wouldn't be caught by a surprise emotion and trigger a panic attack. Or at least see the patterns to make herself a little more functional.

It was helping. Slowly, but surely. After all, Tara had laughed mere minutes ago.

"Remember when we met?" Blanche murmured.

"No." Tara sighed. "That whole night is blurry, and I'd rather keep it that way. My first clear memory is when you handed me tacos. You were my guardian angel, delivering nourishment to cut through the dissociative fog."

They laughed. "Bitch, you get so poetic when you're stoned."

Blanche had met Tara mid-panic attack and made it their mission on the spot to help her. It'd been heart-wrenching to hear her sobs echoing in an alley when Blanche's own grief still burned raw. To see their own helplessness reflected in Lee's face as he held her, trying to reassure her that she was safe when he didn't feel safe himself. As if the universe (or Daisy in whatever afterlife existed) had dropped two traumatized teenagers into their life and said, "Blanchy, babe, get your fucking shit together for them."

But instead of healing alongside them, Blanche helped Tara and Lee to *avoid* their own shit. They'd secured their apartment from a pharmaceutical executive; a home for Tara and Lee was worth binding themself to a piece-of-shit patron. They'd found Lee a job, navigated the red tape around Tara's lack of identification so she could attend community college, and helped Sunny—who'd followed Lee home one day—find doctors and better hormones.

All the while throwing themself into work with problematic clients, who used Blanche to absolve themselves of guilt. Work helped them forget that there was more to surviving than loneliness and anger. Work allowed them to forget their own shit for a while.

"A while" had become five years.

As exhausting as clinging to grief could be, Blanche still wasn't ready to move on. Even if Lee and Tara could land on their feet without them. Even if Sunny had more support and resources. Even if Chas and Freddy were successful and happy and thriving without any help from Blanche. Their anger remained as hot and bitter as when their grief was still fresh. With work, they could channel the dark parts of themself away from their real life so that their loved ones could get the caring, gentle, supportive Blanche they wanted to be.

"Fuck. You're right. I'm high as shit." Tara's sigh was less heavy this time.

Blanche relaxed at the sound of her voice, the tension easing from their shoulders and back. Tara's presence helped keep them grounded as much as Blanche's did for her. They turned in the chair to face Tara, the glow from the construction lights outside casting a halo around her. "You know, you've grown so much in five years. Maybe outgrown some of your rules. You can expand that teeny tiny comfort zone."

"Do you do this to Lee and Sunny too? Or am I the only one you don't enable?"

"Please, I enable all my ducklings equally." Blanche's lips curved into a smile as they brought the joint to their lips.

# Antonio

"You know what happened last time, Tonio," Richard said ominously when he finally answered the phone without a hello.

With his phone pressed hot against his ear, Antonio swallowed his sigh of relief. For as cold as his friend's tone was, Richard's raspy contralto distracted Antonio from the void of the blank TV in his studio apartment. From the darkness creeping in the windows because he still hadn't hung up any curtains. From the bare walls closing in on him as he sat on the couch alone.

For such a small space, Antonio still found himself lost in his new apartment. But at least now he had an anchor. A surly, snobby anchor.

"'Hi, Tonio. How are you? It's so unlike you to call me—is everything okay? Do I need to bring over the ropes again?'" Antonio teased, not bothering to keep the sarcasm out of his voice. Richard wouldn't care. "I'm great, Dicky, thanks for asking! And yeah, I could use support right now, but please don't tie me to the chair again. Freaky ass! I still can't believe *you* have shibari ropes."

"Gabe is probably awake. He's better at this sort of thing than I am."

Antonio snorted. "Duh, Dicky. I called him first. But he sounded upset, so I pretended I was calling to give him shit for not showing up tonight."

"Don't call me Dicky. Especially if you want something from me. Like emotional support." The sneer in Richard's voice was audible even through the tinny speaker.

Antonio laughed. "You say that like it's a disease, Richard."

"The argument could be made."

Antonio sighed. "Look, I appreciate you answering your phone for once, but I need to talk something out. Gabe isn't in a good place to listen, and I don't want to worry my family. As one of my two and a half remaining friends, you're my last resort from overthinking myself into self-sabotage. Or worse, calling Phin. I just need you to tell me if I'm being foolish."

"You're always foolish."

"*After* I talk this out, asshat." Antonio settled into the couch and threw his feet over the arm. "So, you know how tonight was Carlita's first performance since moving back home? Which, not that I expected you and Gabe to show up, but it would have been *nice* if you had."

"I told you I had a prior engagement."

"So...reading at home by yourself?"

Richard paused. "Don't let my personal life distract you."

Antonio scoffed. He'd known his anti-social friends wouldn't show up, but that didn't ease the hurt when neither had even texted him to check in. Luckily, he had no shame in asking for their support when he needed it. "Anyway, I kind of met someone? He's the audio tech at Confession, and he's so sweet and charming and—"

"You did *not* call me to gush about your new fling."

Antonio scowled. "You're *such* a dick."

"You knew this when you called me."

"Ugh, this is the necessary backstory. Just listen!"

Richard was not the friend Antonio went to for emotional support for a reason. But Gabe had sounded so broken when Antonio had called to give him shit, he couldn't add to his plate. Even if Gabe insisted he was fine, concern for his best friend had overtaken any irritation.

And Antonio did talk a lot. Especially compared to the ever-terse Richard, who spoke as if each word cost a fortune. He should try to be concise for the man's tiny social battery. "So, I really like this guy. And not like when I say I like someone to convince myself it's true. I am genuinely into him. I think. He's got this gorgeous voice and he's so hot and—"

"Point, Tonio."

"Okay, okay." Antonio tried his best to explain without getting sidetracked by more fun facts about Lee. "We kissed after the show, and it was so amazing that I had to untuck—"

"Tonio, I'm about to hang up on you."

"Ugh, you never appreciate a good yarn! Like, I think he could be special, right? But then he *left* to go to a party with this other guy who seems...hmm...*catty*. And he invited me along, but I didn't think I should go. That'd be a bad decision, wouldn't it?" Antonio paused, chewing on his lip. That moment with Lee had made him feel more alive than he'd felt in months. And that was a dangerous feeling. Maybe it was merely what lust felt like now, but nothing that felt this good had ever been good for him.

"Parties are always bad."

"Richard, seriously."

"Antonio, tell me what you want from me."

"I want some validation that I did the right thing. That I'm *doing* the right thing." Antonio was already in over his head. New Antonio wanted to stay in Chas's good graces. So instead of climbing Lee like a tree, Antonio had asked him out on a date. Mostly to see if his feelings would still be as strong in the light of day.

But then Lee had kissed him, and the chorus of angels in his head burst out into Beyonce's "Rocket." His plan to take it slow had been replaced with visions of Lee on his knees—sucking him off, smiling up at Antonio as he shampooed Lee's hair, swallowing nervously as he held out a ring.

But then Lee had left to hang out with some other guy at a place where Antonio should not go, and reality had come crashing down. Because Lee was a real person who interacted with other real people and had a normal, functioning, social life. He was not a heaven-sent angel to rescue Antonio from his demons. These visions of their future were wishful thinking.

"To summarize: you like a guy at work—"

"I like like him. This feels like more than a regular like."

"Are we in middle school?" Richard huffed. "Okay, you 'like like' a guy at work who made out with you after the show. He had plans to go to a party and invited you along, but he was going with someone who gave you a bad feeling, so you turned him down. Sounds suspiciously intelligent of you so far. Tell me how he reacted."

Antonio racked his brain to remember anything about the rest of the conversation. All he could think of were Lee's lips pressing against his once more, soothing Antonio's self-doubt and fear. "Disappointed but understanding. I told him I would make bad decisions there, and I wanted him to be a good decision."

Richard's voice hummed through the phone. "That's cute."

Antonio grinned. It was a rare day when Richard complimented anyone, especcially him. "On one hand, my demons are telling me I should have gone with him. But on the other hand, New Antonio thinks he'll be bad for me. But on the third hand, I think—keyword think—that everything is *okay*? Because he asked, I said no, and he didn't pressure me. I didn't say *why* going would be bad, but I think he read between the lines."

"You should tell him sooner than later. People believe what they want to believe until you tell them otherwise."

"You're right, Dicky. I'm trying to be a better me, and that includes being up-front with people." Antonio groaned. "Gross."

He couldn't let his wishful thinking fuck up his life again. His impulse control had always been his downfall; he refused to let it ruin this thing with Lee. He had to play it cool. Take it slow.

Especially if Lee was friends with walking red flags. Especially if Lee went to the kind of house parties Antonio used to attend. Especially since Chas had lectured him about not hurting Lee.

Antonio swallowed the anxiety tightening his throat. He closed his eyes, trying to recapture how serene and alive and whole his brain had become when Lee had kissed him. His therapist would probably be disappointed in him for jumping feet first into a whole mess of emotions that he didn't understand, but Lee felt...right. After that heavenly kiss, he was determined to see this unusual emotional connection through.

"I'm surprised I helped." Richard would never admit it, but a smile brightened his voice.

A snort escaped Antonio. "Honestly, same. Maybe I should call you more often."

"Don't you dare."

# Monday, April Twenty-Ninth

# Chapter Seven

## Lee

*You're ridiculous.* Fifteen minutes early for a date was far too early. Lee shoved his icy hands further into his pockets. He'd forgotten it was still cold enough in the morning to warrant a jacket. A quick glance up at the sign hanging from the brick building confirmed he was at the right place.

*Do I wait inside?* It could get awkward to wait for so long without ordering. This could be somewhere where they'd cough and point to a "no loitering" sign if he didn't order right away. And he wanted to pay for Antonio, so he couldn't order before he got there.

This was why he needed to stop being early to shit.

Not that he expected anything different from himself. The whole situation with Antonio had been incessantly replaying in his mind. Saturday night, he'd been lost in thought, nursing a beer while everyone had talked around him. He'd chalked his sullen mood up to a headache when BJSlut asked if he was good. An excuse that had come in handy when Whatshisname had invited him up as Lee dropped him and Venus off at Whathisname's place later.

He owed himself twenty bucks.

Even expecting that Antonio would tire of him like everyone else did, his disappointment had grown bitter the longer he'd overthought Venus's warning. He'd already let his feelings get caught up in Antonio's charm. It was hard not to read too much into anyone pursuing him, let alone someone who seemed so earnest and genuine.

Part of him wanted to just get it over with. To have the date and feel special and be what Antonio wanted, so he could get over the hurt when Antonio ignored him afterward. Another part of him wanted to bask in Antonio's attention while it lasted.

Already, the signs of fading interest were there. Antonio had left as soon as the brunch show on Sunday had ended, so they didn't get a chance to talk again. Lee told his hurt feelings that Antonio couldn't exactly flirt with Lee when his family was there.

They'd barely texted, aside from Antonio sending him the address of some new coffee shop downtown that Lee hadn't heard of. Lee's "Can't wait!" text was met with a "me either!!!! :-)" from Antonio, but that'd been the extent of their conversation. Maybe Antonio was playing it cool, but most guys would have sent a few risky texts or pictures by now.

Lee had changed his outfit five times that morning, settling on a cornflower blue sweater and dark-wash jeans. He'd only made up his mind because Tara had threatened to pour her coffee on him if he asked her to "rate another damn outfit!" Hopefully, she wasn't lying when she'd said Lee looked good. He had planned to ask her opinion on at least four more options; he was left instead with a lot of time and no distractions from his anxiety. So he'd just left. Without a jacket.

Even taking the time to walk to the damn coffee shop, Lee was still stupid early. As slow as he'd tried to keep his pace, he had crossed the Mississippi in a heartbeat. Partially because the wind blowing downriver was bitterly cold, but mostly because the idea of Antonio getting there before him, of making *Antonio* wait for *him*? *"Never give anyone the opportunity to think you're less than perfect."* Annoyingly, his dad was right in this case. He'd regret giving Antonio any reason to dislike him.

But still, fifteen minutes? For a date? Too much, even for him.

Despite how warm and inviting the coffee shop looked, Lee walked down the block to sit on a bus bench. Pulling out his phone to kill time, he found a video reviewing an audio production app. Paying attention to the video was more challenging than he wanted to admit. His mind kept drifting back to hazel eyes instead, smudged in eyeliner as they'd flickered half-closed. Because he was pathetic.

*You know better than this. You're gonna have a quick date, hook up, and then pine after him for months.* The same thing had happened with the bouncer a year ago, the gogo dancer the year before that, and one of the line cooks when he was twenty.

Less than two minutes into the video, which he was not paying attention to at all, someone clearing their throat startled him.

"Hi." Antonio stood a few feet away, a shy smile on his face. He wore a maroon bomber jacket to keep the spring chill at bay. Pearl earrings matched the necklace Antonio fiddled with.

Yanking out his earbuds, Lee lumbered to his feet. "Hey." He waved once before dropping his arm back down to his side, subtly wiping the sweat from his palms as he shoved the headphones back into his pocket. *Cooler than a motherfucker, Lee.*

Antonio's smile widened. "You're early too, huh? Hope I didn't interrupt you." Without heels, he stood shorter than Lee realized, shorter than Tara or Sunny. Five foot seven at most.

"Yeah, no, just killing time. I have a bad habit of being early," Lee admitted, pushing up his glasses.

"So, you usually come too quick?" Antonio teased with a smirk.

Lee snorted. "I walked right into that."

"You really did. Coming too soon isn't normally a problem for me." Antonio winked before turning away, his cheeks darkening. "No joke, I'm always late to everything, but I was excited to see you!"

"Same." Lee's heart fluttered, silently willing Antonio to look at him like that again. "You want to...?" He gestured to the brick building that held the cafe.

Antonio grinned. "Yeah, let's..." He mimicked Lee's vague gesture as he walked past him toward the entrance.

The recent investment in the Riverfront District had transformed abandoned brick and limestone warehouses and surface lots into art museums, parks, and restaurants. Confession had been one of the earliest renovations; this coffee shop must have been a more recent project. This side of the river was way better than it used to be. Downtown had been empty and depressing when he was a kid.

Lee just wished the "urban renewal" had stayed on the Iowa side. He'd had to find a new barber three times in the past year because their buildings kept getting sold to developers. Tara had offered to line him up whenever she touched up her undercut, but he'd rather get wolfy than let her anywhere close to his hair. Though now as he held the door open for Antonio, he wished he had texted his newest barber. Being overdue for a lineup was not a good impression for the first date he'd been on in months.

Antonio insisted on paying for his herbal tea and Lee's cold press. After a brief power struggle full of intense eye contact and a raised eyebrow from Antonio, Lee reluctantly let him. He silently vowed to buy lunch if this date went that long. *Big "if," but don't start this off by being argumentative.*

They settled into a couple of club chairs in the cozy loft area of the shop, enclosed by bookshelves. As Antonio shifted around in his chair to find a comfortable position, Lee sipped his coffee, unsure of what to say. Their kiss Saturday night was a distant memory come Monday morning.

"So, you wanna tell me about your trauma first or should I start?" Antonio joked, breaking the silence, awkwardly curling up into the chair.

Lee barked out a laugh. "Great first date conversation."

"We're queer Black men. How else will we know if we're compatible unless our issues line up?" Antonio grinned as he tucked one leg underneath him. "Or we could do the coming out stories instead of trauma? Start off easy."

"Aren't those the same story?"

"Not for me. Mine is funny. See? We're already getting to know each other!" Antonio leaned back in this chair. "Seriously, jokes aside, I want to know everything. Tell me about Lee outside of being Confession's best audio tech ever."

Lee opened his mouth but found himself at a loss; most guys didn't bother asking about him. "Uh...I live with my friends Tara and Blanche. Blanche finessed a three-bedroom from their sugar daddy so their 'kids' could stay with them. They never mentioned their 'kids' were homeless teenagers they'd known for all of a week, so Tara and I make ourselves scarce when he's there. It's been like five years at this point, so he probably doesn't care, but we don't want to ruin a good thing—"

"Oh, shit." With a flush of mortification burning up his neck, Lee realized he had shared more than planned. He rushed to explain, in case Antonio might think he'd been homeless due to some personal flaw or choice. "Uh... My parents kicked me out when they found out I was gay when I was fifteen."

Taking a steadying breath, Lee focused on the chord progressions of the folk song playing in the background, ignoring his dad's voice insisting that being gay was both the greatest personal flaw *and* a choice. He forced a smile as he pushed his glasses up, his nose prickling with sweat. "Told you the trauma and coming out story were the same. Sorry. I usually don't share that with most people."

Antonio tilted his head, a soft smile on his face as his eyes searched Lee's face. "No need to apologize! I asked for everything. I take it you and your friends have been through a lot together?"

Lee nodded. *Just answer the question—he doesn't need the whole story.* But Lee couldn't stop himself. Normally guarded about his past, everything strained to burst out of him with Antonio's encouraging smile. "Yeah, I'm lucky. Tara and I met at a shelter, and then my aunt let us stay with her, but she died when we were eighteen."

Trying and failing to keep his knee from bouncing, Lee decided to change course. That story would open the door to a lot of questions that he wasn't sure how to evade. Memories of Auntie Alitrice always made his stomach twist. "We met Blanche a few months later."

Lee sipped his coffee to keep himself from saying more. The night he and Tara had met Blanche was another can of worms to avoid, though the actual memories of the riot at the encampment weren't the issue. Even after five years, Lee still could not fathom why Blanche had asked him and Tara to stay with them, but he was grateful. Without Tara, Aunt Alitrice, and Blanche, Lee wouldn't have made it to adulthood. "I have another friend, Sunny. We've been friends since middle school and she hangs out with us all the time."

There. Sunny was a safe topic. Mostly. As long as Antonio didn't want any stories from before they'd reconnected at age nineteen.

Talking about the memories he'd locked away long ago threatened to drag him down into too-vulnerable emotions. Lee fell into the breath pattern that Blanche had taught Tara to get ahead of her panic attacks. He'd learned along with her, but only enough to keep his memories under control. He sat back, tapping the melody on the arm of the chair, hoping Antonio wouldn't ask any follow-up questions.

Because frankly, Antonio was probably not that interested in his feelings; not many people were. *"Always keep your smile on, even when it hurts."* That was his mom's voice, hushed and stern. *"No one likes a crybaby."* Lee put on the placid half smile she'd taught him to wear, waiting for Antonio's reaction.

"Wait, so your parents kicked you out *and* your aunt died? Don't take this the wrong way, but most people would not call you lucky," Antonio teased, eyes crinkling as his smile widened.

With a rush of relief, Lee couldn't help but return Antonio's smile. Usually, people gave him pitying looks or asked invasive questions. Antonio listened and accepted what Lee had said as if his past was normal.

"Yeah, but they don't have friends like mine." His life hadn't exactly been charmed, but Lee was eternally grateful for Tara, Blanche, and Sunny. They took care of him; he returned the favor however he could. "They're my family now."

"Which friend had their birthday the other day?" Antonio blew on his tea, lips pursed over the brim of his mug to cool it.

Lee stared at the curve of Antonio's cupid's bow, struggling to focus on enjoying the date, instead of fantasizing about what might happen afterward. "Uh...Tara. We were supposed to go to an arcade, but I got put on the schedule, so we moved the party to Confession."

Antonio ducked his head with a grimace. "Sorry, that must have been my fault. Freddy is shit at running sound, even without my needy ass and my headset."

"Right? There's no way he's that bad by accident."

"Still does the bare minimum but manages to keep his job. Guess dicking down the boss on the regular has its perks." Antonio's laugh brought a grin to Lee's face.

"So, why'd you move to New York? And why'd you move back *here*?" More at ease now that the conversation had moved away from him, Lee gestured toward the window as he leaned into the arm of his chair. "Like, there are worse cities, but Bellamy is still cold most of the year with nothing to do."

Antonio took a thoughtful sip before answering. "I don't want to, like, rub it in after what you just shared, but I have a big family who spends way too much time together. Being away from them was the worst. They drive me nuts, but they're my everything."

Lee's heart lurched at the love shining on his face, wishing more than anything he could relate. He'd worried about his little sister before they secretly reconnected on social media a few years ago. But his parents? Never. "They were very enthusiastic about your performance yesterday." Two large tables packed with people had screamed and cheered for Antonio.

"They're always like that, but they're extra happy I'm home." Antonio chuckled softly. "I hustled so hard and barely got paid. Maybe being without my family would be worth it if I could make it big, but after five years, I wanted to come home." He sighed. "Even New York didn't want a drag queen singing house."

"Sorry, you sing house?" At Antonio's nod, Lee fanned himself with a grin. "Oh, damn! I need a moment to get my hard-on under control."

Antonio choked on his tea. "Oh, come on, I'm serious," he sputtered out, coughing through his laughter.

"So am I. Popping a semi over here," Lee teased as he passed Antonio a napkin. "Seriously, I make house beats as a side thing. I love that nineties shit when house got hella gay. Like Moi Renee and Franklin Fuentes. A drag take on house sounds dope. I need your SoundCloud."

"I'll text you the link so you can jerk off to it later, Miss Honey." Antonio grinned, wiping the tea from his hand. "As long as you show me yours. Maybe I can use your tracks for one of my songs."

Lee smiled back. Antonio kept surprising him. With Carlita's polished pop performances from the weekend, Lee never expected to talk house with him. Hopefully, Antonio would still be friendly at work after he got bored with Lee; it'd be nice to have someone to talk music with. None of his friends really understood. Tara, Blanche, and Sunny were more supportive than his other friends, but even they glazed over when he started raving about the nuances of deep house versus Chicago. "I always figured New York would be the best place for a drag take on house."

Antonio's smile fell and he glanced away. "Well...another reason I moved back was to get sober. Addiction can really fuck up a career. I didn't exactly make the healthiest choices before I left, but being in New York made it exponentially worse. I tried to get sober and stay there, but I relapsed every time." His hazel eyes studied Lee's face as if for reassurance. "So, I moved back and went to rehab properly this time. Now, no more pills, no more weed, no more alcohol. Not even caffeine these days."

Addiction was common everywhere in Bellamy; Lee knew how hard it was to kick. His and Tara's neighbors at Walter's camp had enough horror stories that neither dared try anything harder than grass. He resisted the urge to put his hand on Antonio's leg, reminding himself they were in public. Instead, Lee gave him an encouraging smile, hoping he came across as understanding like Antonio had. "I'm so impressed. You want to *teach*? Without *caffeine*? What's your secret?"

"I'm high on life, baby!" Antonio exclaimed with a relieved grin. "Kidding! I'm not *that* corny! Honestly, I'm still figuring it out." He leaned closer with a wince. "Like, I'm a little fucked up, which is not something you're supposed to say on a first date. But I should tell you now so you can make an informed decision about me. Like, I was always out there, but my brain is still getting used to sobriety, so I'm somehow even weirder than I was."

Lee couldn't stop himself from touching Antonio's knee. "You don't seem fucked up."

Antonio smiled ruefully and put his own hand on Lee's. "Okay, but, like, I *am*, though. You'll hear me singing nonsense, and you might need to tell me things eight hundred times. I barely remember anything that happened in New York, and I still can't remember shit."

The vacant look on Antonio's face made Lee turn his palm up to squeeze his hand.

His smile widening, Antonio waved his other hand as if shooing away a fly. "Music is the best way I can remember anything. It's wild, but at least I have that, you know? Who knows why the Benzos spared my musical memory when the rest of my brain is fucked? I *have* to sing when I perform now. I can't remember lyrics or choreo if I'm lip-syncing."

Tracing his thumb over Antonio's fingers, Lee waited while Antonio's eyebrows furrowed and soothed. Small wonder he'd moved back home if he was struggling in New York; sobriety was an uphill battle. Maybe a fresh start with the support of his family was what Antonio needed. And maybe Antonio was no longer the same person Venus had warned him about.

Lee forced that train of thought away. Typical of him to be thinking of himself when Antonio was going through it right in front of him.

Eventually, Antonio's lips curved into a smile again. "It's getting better now that I'm home. I get plenty of sleep, eat my veggies, and go to the gym. Go on dates with cute audio techs."

Lee's heart thudded in his chest. "Meet a lot of those, do you?"

"No, just one in particular. He's pretty great." Antonio winked.

LEE COULD NOT GET enough of Antonio, and the draw seemed mutual. Antonio was probably only being polite, but Lee let himself hope that Antonio wanted to spend time with him. After hours of easy conversation at the coffee shop that Lee was reluctant to end, Antonio surprised Lee by inviting him to find lunch at the food trucks nearby.

Despite Antonio's protests, Lee insisted on paying.

A long lunch of soba noodles became a walk along the riverfront. Their hands grazed but didn't touch as their slow stroll brought them to the modern art museum, where they took increasingly ridiculous pictures in the sculpture garden. Lee had found himself reaching for Antonio's hand while they were both doubled over in laughter more than once, but pulled back when his dad's voice reminded Lee about appropriate behavior in public.

Their walk brought them to a quiet corner of the sculpture garden, where tall box hedges enclosed a series of rebar and stone sculptures. Lee put an arm around Antonio's shoulders as they walked, feeling more confident in the secluded area.

"I like spending time with you," Lee hesitantly admitted, cheeks sore from laughing and smiling so much. The rational part of his brain told him Antonio probably just had free time, but after six hours together, he was starting to believe that maybe Antonio liked his company, too. "This might be the funnest date I've ever had."

Antonio grinned, leaning into Lee's side and stealing his breath. "I feel like I'm pushing my luck. Like I should get out of your hair before you get sick of me. Or before you realize you're on a date with someone in recovery and bounce. I would if I were you." He turned those hazel eyes up at Lee. "But something about you makes it hard to go home."

Lee shook his head. "*Me*, get sick of *you*? You realize I'm a dork with no game?"

"You had game the other night when you kissed me."

"Yeah, I don't know where that came from."

Antonio laughed. He twined his fingers through the hand Lee rested on his shoulder, sending a thrill up Lee's arm. "And yet, I still want to hang out with you. Want to watch a movie at my place? Maybe get a pizza? Or is my luck about to run out?"

Lee ran his thumb across Antonio's, enjoying the warm skin against his. He leaned in conspiratorially. "I'm pretty sure you're about to get lucky," he whispered loudly.

"Wow, you really are a dork!" Antonio's sonorous laugh brought a grin to Lee's face. He pulled Lee behind him as he headed back to where they'd met that morning. "Come on, I'll drive. Just don't say shit about my old ass car."

"Can't be worse than mine." Fighting the hope in his heart, Lee followed behind him, reluctantly dropping hands when they reached the edge of the garden that protected them from view.

Even if Antonio wanted him—maybe even *liked* him—that didn't mean he should read into it. This would be the nice end of a nice date.

But Lee couldn't help but hope that there'd be a second.

# Chapter Eight

## Lee

"So, what are we watching?" Lee sank into the sofa in Antonio's small studio apartment back over Eastside. The older building was not too far from Blanche's, just farther away from the river. Sparsely furnished and decorated, it still felt cluttered. Open boxes lined the wall as if there was no room to unpack anything that Antonio didn't need.

Lee bit into his pizza. Antonio was lactose intolerant and mostly vegan, so they'd gotten a cheeseless veggie pizza. Lee judged him a little—*a lot*—but the pizza turned out okay after Antonio doctored it up with seasonings and vegan parmesan.

After tacking a sheet over the window to block the late afternoon sun, Antonio settled next to him, cuddling under Lee's arm. Sparks tingled under his skin where their bodies pressed together. "Something campy, scary, or a musical?" Antonio gripped Lee's thigh as he stretched for the remote.

"Right, the only three genres." Lee teased. "Can we do one that won't make me cry?"

"Are you secretly a big softie?"

"Yeah, no! Not unless a dog dies in the movie." Lee faked a sniffle. For some reason, sad dog movies brought out the weak ass in him.

"So not *I am Legend*. Got it." Antonio scrolled through the recommendations.

"Don't even joke! Sam was the best part of that movie, and I don't even like dogs."

"You don't like dogs?! Aw, babe, your first red flag! I'm so relieved you're not perfect." Antonio laughed. "How about *Clueless*? No dead dogs, and if you haven't seen it before, we *will* watch it because it's a classic."

"No, yeah, *Clueless* is great." Inside, Lee reeled from the casual endearment. *He probably didn't mean anything by it. Blanche calls everyone by pet names, too.*

Soon enough, they'd polished off the pizza, but Lee couldn't pay attention to the movie. His hand drifted from Antonio's shoulder to his waist, pulling him closer. He struggled to breathe as his heartbeat pounded in his chest.

There was no point in pretending he was at Antonio's apartment for any other reason. And Lee wanted him, to be sure. But his sappy romantic hopes had struggled against his baser instincts, desperate as always to prove that sex wasn't the only thing worthwhile about him. He'd toned down the flirting all day, hoping their date could go on one hour more. Luckily, Antonio hadn't seemed impatient.

Antonio's fingers traced his own, and Lee opened his hand to tangle their fingers together. He risked a glance at where Antonio's head rested on his shoulder, only to meet Antonio's hazel eyes in the dim light, face upturned in Lee's direction with a smile.

Lee didn't hesitate to press his lips to Antonio's. Just like Saturday, nothing came close to the bliss of Antonio's kiss. He tentatively licked the seam of Antonio's lips, which parted with a soft exhale.

Running a hand through Antonio's curls, Lee pulled him closer to get a better angle. There was a good chance he might die if Antonio pulled away. He wasn't sure if he'd been alive before this moment.

*It's just sex, Lee. Don't do this to yourself.*

Without breaking their kiss, Antonio climbed into his lap with a soft moan as Lee wrapped an arm around his hips to grind his erection against him. Lee dragged his mouth down Antonio's neck, sucking gently to pull a series of breathy moans out of him.

Between the soft sounds escaping him, Antonio said, "I was trying to take this slow."

"Do you want me to stop?" Lee murmured against his neck.

"Oh, don't you dare! I was just trying to do this...sensibly." Antonio's hands slid under Lee's sweater. His nails dragged lightly across Lee's chest and dipped down to his stomach. "You know, court you or whatever before fucking you."

Lee did stop at that. *Like, not just a hookup?*

Antonio took advantage of his stillness and pulled Lee's sweater and undershirt off, hands and lips caressing Lee's bare skin.

Lee ignored his fluttering heart and the hope coursing through his veins. For the sake of his heart after Venus's warning, he pretended to be unaffected by Antonio's words. "Court me, huh?" his inner flirt teased, nudging his forehead against Antonio's. "I'm pretty sure we've had like four dates today. That's practically virginal."

Antonio laughed, tracing both hands up Lee's torso. He cupped Lee's jaw, his arresting eyes searching his face. "What I'm trying to say is I want to see where this goes. Not just physically, I mean. Like, I feel really connected with you. And frankly, that's unusual for me. The old me would have already had you six ways to Sunday, and I don't want my bad habits to ruin whatever this might become."

Exhilaration coursed through him, silencing the reasonable voice that always brought him back to earth. Lee fought to keep his heart from flying from his mouth. He'd always longed for that emotional connection Antonio talked about. To be adored as much as he adored them. To have someone who cared about him beyond their immediate desires. To prove he was worthy of love.

*Chill. At best, this will be a fling.* This was probably what Venus was talking about. His chest ached as he forced himself to remember that Antonio would get bored with him eventually.

For better or for worse, his traitorous inner flirt had the situation in hand, a bitter reminder of what Lee's purpose was here. "Unless you're a serial killer or give trash head, I wanna see where this goes, too."

"Wow." With a scoff of mock offense, Antonio gently slapped him with one of his hands cupping his face. "My head game is fire."

Lee grinned and tightened his grip on Antonio's ass. "I'll believe it when I see it."

"You won't see it. You won't be able to keep your eyes open when I get my throat around your dick!" Antonio's hands drifted down to his belt, unbuckling it.

Lee stopped him, fingers tangling with Antonio's. He'd lived with Blanche long enough to insist that the awkward conversations come first, even if it killed the mood. "Hold on. We should talk about the basics, things I usually ask on Grindr first. I got tested a few weeks ago. I'm vers, and I assume you are too. You would have told me by now if you weren't."

Antonio chuckled. "You caught me. I'm pan. I'm more into someone's energy than if they're a bottom or their gender or whatever. That said, thanks to taking thousands of pills on an empty stomach, I should top. Other than that, I have a surprisingly good bill of health, all things considered. Does all that go on a dating app? I've never had one."

Lee's mouth opened in shock. "Never? Damn! How old are you?!"

Antonio made a face. "Okay, rude. I'm only twenty-eight. I just prefer to meet people in person. I can't have an emotional connection with a picture or a message, you know? Some people on Insta try, but I ignore those DMs."

"I wish that worked for me." All of the guys he'd met in person—even the ones from work—hit him up on apps later instead of flirting with him in person.

"Well, *we* met in person, so I'd say it's working pretty well."

Lee lost control of his inner flirt. Instead of another meaningless quip, he murmured, "Considering you keep surprising me in the best possible ways, I'd say so."

"Sweet talker." Antonio smiled, unzipping Lee's jeans without breaking eye contact. "Now, this might be the only time you'll hear me say this, but I'm tired of talking. Anything else you wanna ask, or can I suck your soul out of your dick?"

Lee swallowed hard as Antonio traced the outline of his erection through his boxers. He managed to squeak, "By all means." *Really? "By all means?" Why would you say that? Stick to flirting.*

Despite the amusement in his eyes, Antonio refrained from laughing at him, instead climbing off Lee's thighs. While Lee pulled off his jeans and boxers, Antonio tossed a throw pillow on the floor and settled between Lee's open legs.

He touched Lee tentatively at first, admiring his length in his hands. Taking in a shuddering breath as Antonio stroked him, Lee struggled to keep Antonio's excited smile from boosting his ego.

"I still can't believe you're real," Antonio murmured, running his tongue along the underside of his erection. "You're charming and funny."

Another lick.

"You've got the sexiest voice."

His fist pumped once, twice, making Lee fight to keep still.

"You're hot as fuck, and you kiss so good I had to untuck and rub one out before I went home the other night." Antonio shook his head with a laugh. "*And* you're hung? You're a literal dream come true."

Lee's hands gripped the couch cushions. He fought to keep his composure against Antonio's onslaught of praise and pleasure. When Antonio sealed his lips around the head of his dick, Lee's eyes rolled back with a loud moan.

Antonio took him deeper, wrapping his hand around the base, gently pumping in time with his mouth. Hazel eyes smiled up at him where Antonio knelt between his thighs. The image of this incredible man with his mouth wrapped around him was shorting out Lee's brain. Antonio's hot tongue swirled around his head and back down, sending sparks down his spine.

A moan tore from Lee's throat. "Damn, you feel amazing."

Antonio grabbed Lee's hand, helplessly gripping the couch cushion, and dragged it to his hair. Lee tangled his fingers in the soft brown curls as Antonio moaned encouragingly. The vibrations from his mouth shot up Lee's spine. Antonio sucked him hard, cheeks hollowing as his hands left Lee to unzip his own jeans, moaning as he touched himself.

Lee's hips jerked. Antonio gagged but kept taking Lee deeper down into his throat. Tears sprang up in those hazel eyes looking up at him with adoration.

With spit dripping down his tightening balls, Lee couldn't hold back anymore, moaning out a string of curses. His grip on Antonio's hair tightened. Antonio's eyes never left him, exhaling hot air in between thrusts. His vision blurry from delirious pleasure, he let go of Antonio's hair and rasped out a warning that he was about to come.

His spine arched as he came with a muffled groan. The wet heat never left him as Antonio choked around his orgasm, sputtering around his pulsing dick. Lee was half-tempted to pull him off, but the determined glint in Antonio's eyes and overwhelming pleasure from the throat gagging around him brought his hands back down to the cushions.

"You were not kidding about your head game." Lee grinned lazily at Antonio as he pushed off Lee's knees to stand up.

Antonio wiped away the tears and drool and cum dripping down his face with his t-shirt before tossing it aside. "If you're still able to talk, I need to do better," he teased in a raspy voice, "but apparently sobriety brought back my gag reflex. Rude. Want to help me get rid of that again?" He pushed his jeans down his thighs, shooting Lee a wink.

"I'm yours." Too blissed out to care about how that could be interpreted, Lee couldn't take his eyes away from Antonio's body. He was surprisingly built for someone so slender. He knew Antonio was fit—the backflips and the splits and his ass in those leggings had told him that. But Antonio naked took his breath away. Wiry muscles rippled in his chest and shoulders. Hints of abs lined his toned stomach, highlighted by a light trail of hair leading down to the breathtaking erection Lee would be dreaming about for the rest of his life.

Antonio fiddled with his pearl necklace as he waited patiently for Lee's judgment.

"Fuck, you're gorgeous." Lee held out his hands. "Come here."

Beaming, Antonio climbed into Lee's lap as Lee pulled him in for a kiss, the salt from his own cum flooding his taste buds as his tongue pressed against Antonio's. Without breaking their kiss, Lee looked around for lube, but not even lotion was in sight. He spat into his hand instead, wrapping it around Antonio's dick.

"I'm not going to last long," Antonio admitted, panting into Lee's ear. "Watching you come was the hottest shit I've ever seen."

"Hottest shit *you've* seen? Should have seen it from my perspective." Lee sucked behind Antonio's jaw, setting a slow pace. Antonio panted and thrust up into Lee's hand.

The precum leaking from Antonio's tip was slick under his thumb. Lee nibbled on his earlobe around the pearl stud, muttering, "I want to replay that every time I close my eyes. You on your knees, taking my whole dick down your throat. You were so good."

Antonio moaned at the praise, his hips stuttering, losing their rhythm. Lee smiled against the pulse fluttering under his lips. His inner flirt was decent at dirty talk, and Lee often used it as a cover. Any romantic and needy sentiments that escaped along with the filthy praise could be chalked up to getting caught up in the mood, instead of his true feelings.

Lee sucked Antonio's neck behind his ear. The moans grew louder, higher pitched. Slowly sliding his hand around Antonio's ass, Lee pushed hard against his perineum. "I can't wait to find out if your ass feels as good as your mouth. I wanna hear you scream my name when I'm fucking you."

Lee hoped there would be a next time. That shit that Antonio had said about courting him—whatever that meant—had settled in his heart despite his best efforts.

With a loud whine, Antonio shuddered in Lee's lap. Cum spilled over Lee's hand as he murmured filthy praise until Antonio stopped twitching.

The lithe body in his arms sagged against him, panting against his collarbone. "That was intense."

"Good intense, I hope." Lee kissed a trail down Antonio's neck.

"Very good intense," Antonio confirmed, sitting up to kiss Lee. He shifted in Lee's lap to cuddle against him. "That voice of yours is sinful."

With a bashful smile, Lee found the unused napkins to clean them up. Even in a dreamy haze, Antonio lying against him put him at ease. Like they fit together.

He sometimes felt insecure about his naked body, especially when guys would stare not out of attraction but in comparison. But under Antonio's gaze, Lee simply felt wanted. Like they could exist naked and it wasn't a performance. Normally, Lee would already be dressed and heading out the door, but today he was reluctant to find his boxers.

As if reading his thoughts, Antonio pulled a blanket off the back of the couch to cover them, seemingly reluctant to end the afterglow, too. Lee settled back to lie on the couch and pulled him close, watching as Tai called Cher a virgin who can't drive. He could stay to finish the movie. Or at least for another round, if that's what Antonio wanted.

Antonio looked at him with those hazel eyes smiling at him again.

Lee bent down to kiss him.

---

# Antonio

"You gonna answer that?" Lee murmured, curled around Antonio in bed.

Antonio blinked sleep from his eyes. His phone rattled on the nightstand, but he'd been planning to sleep through it. He'd rarely slept as soundly as he had last night. *Not that we got much sleep.* His alarm had woken them before the sun rose, but they'd never made it out of bed.

"Nope." Antonio burrowed deeper into Lee's arms, ignoring the bright light of the morning sun streaming in through the windows. The sheet he'd pinned up the night before had fallen at some point during the night. "It's my sister calling to chew me out for missing our yoga class this morning. I'll call her later."

"You skipped yoga for me?" Lee teased. "I'm flattered."

Antonio laughed. "Let's see, yoga at the ass crack of dawn with a dozen middle-aged moms, or another round with the hottie I can't get enough of? Tough call."

Lee's phone buzzed once from the coffee table. He sighed. "I should check that. Tara's probably freaking out that I didn't come home yesterday."

"You told her you were staying over, right?" Antonio asked, disappointed Lee didn't want to ignore the real world with him. *He's a real person with a real life. Like I'm supposed to be.*

"I did, but we've never spent a whole twenty-four hours apart since we met. I should get home before she hunts me down."

"Sorry!" *Ten years and they've never spent a day apart?* Yet another reminder that Lee was a whole person with a whole life outside of his bed, albeit one far different from Antonio's. He grinned over his shoulder, heart burning when Lee's sleep-filled eyes gazed into his. He rubbed his chest to ease the ache. "I mean, not *that* sorry, but you can tell her I'm sorry."

Lee smiled instead of answering. In the morning light, and with Lee's glasses on the nightstand, his warm brown eyes were pools of honey. A faint scar that had been covered by the rim of his glasses lined one cheek.

Antonio's ribs cramped, making it hard to breathe. "Has it actually been that long?" Turning away, he grabbed his phone, ignoring the missed calls from Cassie. "Oh my god, it *is* after ten! Babe, our first date lasted a literal day!"

Lee smiled softly. "Best first date I've ever had."

"Our second date will be even better. When can I see you again?" Cringing at how bad he was at taking this slow, Antonio turned back into the comfort of Lee's arms, blood humming in his veins. Safe to say the weird emotional spark was real because even with Lee wrapped around him, Antonio was still craving more. Somehow that was more terrifying, especially considering how intense this achy yearning was. He pressed a kiss to his clavicle. "Sorry, have I mentioned I can't get enough of you? I have no chill, and I don't care."

"You're bad for my ego." Lee grinned. "But no, yeah—if you wanna see me, I wanna see you. I'm flexible."

"Is tonight too soon?" Antonio laughed. "I should make an appearance at home so my sister doesn't worry, but after? I'll have leftovers if you want to come over for a late dinner. My stepdad's a great cook."

"I'm down." Lee kissed his shoulder. "Can I shower before I go? I'm a little sticky."

"You weren't complaining last night." Antonio winked. For as sweet as Lee was on their date, he was delightfully filthy during sex. That deliciously sweet baritone, begging Antonio to take the condom off and come on his ass during round three, would be playing on repeat in Antonio's head until the day he died. As would the moans he'd pulled from Lee when he'd cleaned his own cum off with his tongue.

But he was obsessed with every aspect of Lee so far: The way he'd been so nervous on their date; how he'd listened and just…understood when Antonio opened up about his sobriety with him; the heavy want darkening his eyes whenever he looked at Antonio.

"Not complaining now, but getting dressed while covered in lube and cum doesn't sound great." Lee kissed him deeply once more before climbing out of bed.

"There's washcloths and towels in the cabinet." Antonio drank in Lee's naked body as he crossed the small apartment. *God, he has the best ass.* He let out a howl at the sight of the wolf print tattoo on Lee's lower back.

"Hey, what did I say?" Lee whirled around and pointed a finger at him in warning, using his other hand to cover his tramp stamp.

Antonio blatantly checked out Lee's muscular chest and soft belly, his dick heavy between his thick thighs. "No howling if I want to eat that juicy ass again?"

Lee grinned, shaking his head. "If you want me bent over in any capacity, no talking shit about the poor choices I made when I was nineteen."

"Wouldn't dream of it, Angel." Antonio smiled innocently as his phone rattled the bedside table again. He picked it up as soon as Lee shut the bathroom door. "I told you I was on a date."

"Must have been some date if you overslept this late." His sister's voice was too calm.

"I just slept in, Cassie. Still sober. Don't worry."

"I'm always going to worry. I hope you're not giving up on the plan we made. What did your therapist say about you dating?"

*My therapist doesn't know. Yet.* He had therapy on Monday afternoons—he was supposed to update Joy about how his first weekend at

Confession went during their session today. *She's in for a damn rollercoaster.* "I'll tell you tonight."

"Tonio."

"Cassie." He loved his sisters, but they worried too much, Cassie especially. Though, he'd given them every reason to.

She sighed through the phone, breaking the long silence. "Fine. How was your date?"

"I'll tell you later."

"Don't act like this, Tonio."

"Like what? Entitled to privacy?" Annoyance spiked through him. *I give her ten seconds before she starts talking about her damn plan for me again.*

"Evasive."

Lee emerged from the bathroom, towel wrapped around his hips.

"I'm not being evasive, Cass. I just woke up. I'll talk to you tonight." Antonio pointed to the phone with an apologetic smile.

"Having a healthy morning routine sets the foundation for the whole day, Antonio..."

With a roll of his eyes, Antonio tuned out while Cassie went on her usual rant about the importance of structure, preferring to admire his...*date? Lover? Boyfriend?*

*Don't get ahead of yourself.* He drank in the view of Lee's broad shoulders as he searched for his clothes around the couch.

Too soon, Lee pulled his sweater over his head and mouthed that he'd let himself out.

"Hold on a sec, Cass." Antonio beckoned him over and put his thumb over the microphone. "I'll see you tonight?"

Lee nodded. "No, yeah, text me when you get home."

Antonio grinned, tugging on Lee's sweater until he bent over for one last indulgent kiss. Lee's lips and tongue made him forget everything, until Cassie's voice calling his name reminded him she was still on the phone.

"Sorry, I'm here." *No, I'm not. I must be in Heaven because Lee is an angel.*

Lee pressed a small kiss to his forehead and shut the door behind him.

*Oh, my god, a forehead kiss?* Antonio kicked his feet but kept his squeal inside.

"Have you heard of a mute button?"

Antonio laughed. "Sorry, I thought I covered the mic. How much did you hear?"

"Enough to be uncomfortable," Cassie teased. "Didn't you get coffee *yesterday*?"

"Yeah, and lunch and dinner and so on. He just left. I wasn't being evasive, but I couldn't exactly tell you about him when he was here."

"Sounds like the date was good. Was this the first time you've had sex since moving home?"

Antonio cackled. "Cassie! I am not talking about my sex life with you."

Cassie laughed. "Whatever. You were never discreet when you lived at home before. Not sure what's different now."

He was sober now. That was the difference. Antonio had been an anxious wreck since Saturday, wondering if they would end up in bed or not, and what that would be like. He hadn't had sex sober since…well, he couldn't remember. At least a decade.

But it'd been fine. More than fine. Amazing. Wonderous. Lee's encouragement and that "fuck, you're gorgeous" had washed away any of his doubt and self-consciousness.

"So, what does Joy think of you dating, then?" Cassie's voice jolted him back into reality.

"Oh, I *was* being evasive about that. I'll tell you tonight." Antonio laughed.

"Tonito! You are so frustrating!"

"Sassy! You are so nosy!" He mimicked her pouty tone.

"Seriously, I worry about you. Is this guy good for you or just making you feel good?"

"Damn, Casshole, way to burst my bubble," Antonio scolded, his annoyance getting the better of him. "I know you don't trust me yet, but I need you to back off on this. I wouldn't be risking everything for someone who wasn't good for me." *I hope.*

Cassie sighed. "Fine. Just trust yourself too. Listen to your gut, even if it's saying something you don't want to hear."

"You want me to trust my *gut*? It can't even digest cheese," Antonio joked to hide the pang of insecurity. *I can't figure out if something's coming from my gut instead of my demons. How am I supposed to trust myself?*

# Sunday, May Fifth

# Chapter Nine

## Lee

Lee locked the front door behind him, smiling at the red curls poking through the crocheted blanket on the couch.

After nearly a week of spending every free moment (and every night) with Antonio, he had expected Tara to complain by now. But she'd been "fine" every time he'd checked in with her, which he'd done several times a day because Lee doubted either of them was "fine" with so much time apart. Tara had been his better half for a decade. No guy, not even an affectionate charmer who wanted to spend every second with him, would come between them. Hopefully, Tara believed that as much as he did.

He gently shook Tara's shoulder, crouching in front of her. "Buttercup, go to bed."

Tara jumped and blinked the sleep from her eyes. "What time is it?"

"Almost four in the morning. Why are you on the couch?"

"Waiting up for you." She rubbed her face. "I've barely seen you in days."

Lee winced at the resentment in her voice. He should have guessed she'd feel left behind, even if he was home for at least a couple of hours every day. Tara would always say she was fine, even when she wasn't. "Sorry. Antonio keeps asking me to hang out and—"

"I'm not mad, dude. I just miss you." Tara sat up and patted the seat next to her. "As long as you actually want to hang out with him, and you're not just saying yes because you're a doormat. I'd be mad about that."

Lee shook his head as he sat beside her. "Thanks for the vote of confidence. But no, yeah, I do actually want to hang out with him. I think he likes me?"

"Oh really?" The sarcasm in Tara's voice was thick. "What gave that away?" She sniffled and wiped her nose on her sleeve.

*That's so nasty.* He nudged the box of tissues closer to her. "Are you crying?"

"No! Just a cold." With an offended scoff, Tara elbowed him. As if it were preposterous that she would cry when she, in fact, cried more often than anyone he knew. "Don't change the subject. He wouldn't ask you to hang out constantly if he didn't like you, dumbass."

Lee smacked her thigh before draping his arm around her shoulders. "It's not what I'm used to, you know? I've never stayed the night at anyone's before, and now this is the first time I'm sleeping at home all week. It's a lot. But I'm into it."

"So why didn't you go home with him after the party?"

Anxiety shot through him, but he hugged her closer. "Antonio went home after the show. I invited him, but he said a party wouldn't be great for him. He's sober, but it's a pretty recent change, so I get it."

Tara glanced up at him. "It's cool that he's setting boundaries for himself. From what you've told me, he seems to thrive off people. That's probably been a huge adjustment for him."

"Right. I wouldn't want to make him uncomfortable."

"So then why are you upset?"

"I'm not upset." He pushed his glasses up his nose.

"Lee, you're squeezing me so tight I can barely breathe and your nose is sweaty as hell. You're a big ball of anxiety right now."

He sighed. "I guess... He always asks me to hang out and the one time I ask him, he doesn't want to. What if I'm just...convenient, you know? Not saying he needs to do *everything* with me, but it would have been nice having him there. You know how they are normally, and the shit-talking was even worse this week. Me talking to Antonio gave them more ammunition. I spent most of the night talking to new people. Met this guy who cuts hair though, so that's cool."

"I keep telling you, I can do your hair for you."

"Respectfully, no fucking way."

Tara sniffled again as she grinned. "Lee, this isn't about you. If Antonio wants to hang out with you everywhere but the stupid parties with your bitchy friends, then maybe the stupid party or the bitchy friends are the issue. Both, most likely. Invite him to do something besides a party before you take it personally. And your bitchy friends are just jealous."

Lee snorted. "Sure. Because my life is worth getting jealous over."

"Hey now, I'm right here," Tara teased. "Your life would be so much worse without me."

Lee kissed the top of her head. "I wouldn't be alive without you, Buttercup."

---

"Hey, man, thanks for getting me in." Lee held out his hand to dap up his newest barber, a recent transplant from Indianapolis Lee had met at the party the night before and promptly forgotten his name. The guy had saved his number as his social media handle, so Lee had no hope of ever learning any name besides Hot Barber.

His handle wasn't inaccurate. Hot Barber was hot. His veiny forearms and muscular biceps sharply contrasted with his lanky build. He'd shaved geometric shapes into his fade, and the ends of his loose curls were bleached blond.

"Honey, you don't have to act straight." Hot Barber looked skeptically at Lee's hand hanging midair. "We're doing this in my bathroom, not in public."

"Sorry." Lee let his hand fall. "Since when is giving dap straight behavior?"

"It's not, but that whole greeting was performative. Your voice was so deep!" Hot Barber's laugh cut through the quiet of his apartment. "That wasn't you on Saturday, why do it today?"

"Sorry. Habit." Anxiety simmered in him every time he got his hair cut. He could practically hear his dad reminding him to speak from his chest, hands straightening Lee's shoulders as they walked into the barbershop. Leland Sr was a whole different dad around those other men, laughing and pretending to be an affectionate dad.

"I know, but obviously, my apartment isn't full of judgy straight men. It's just us here, you don't have to do all that." Gesturing at the mostly bare studio that reminded Lee a lot of Antonio's, Hot Barber led him to the bathroom and gestured to a stool in front of the sink. "So, what'll it be?"

Lee ran a hand over his hair as he sat, avoiding his reflection in the mirror. "Just a basic, uniform buzz cut. Nothing fancy."

He had tried to get an appointment at his last newest barber, but the guy never responded to his texts. When Lee went by the shop, the building was surrounded by construction barriers like the ones across the street from Blanche's apartment. He was getting close to a month without a line-up. For someone raised to believe that his Saturday morning visit to the barber was almost as important as church on Sunday mornings, Lee was starting to look like the abomination his dad had decided he was.

Antonio was way too nice to say anything, but the employee appreciation thing was later that afternoon. Tucked away in the control room, he rarely saw any coworkers besides Freddy for longer than a passing hello. He should look his best.

Hot Barber pouted. "I was hoping for something a little more fun. Not even a little fade for the 'gram? I'm trying to build a client base out here. Can't do that by posting something you could do yourself in five minutes."

Lee winced in apology, ignoring his dad's lectures of *"Vanity is a female sin,"* and *"Real men show their worth through action, not their looks."* He knew—*knew*—that was bullshit. Admittedly, Lee could be vain. He'd accepted his desire to look his best. And yet, considering anything other than the military-approved hairstyle still made his chest tight. "No, yeah, whatever's fine."

"Wow, you're easy," Hot Barber teased, running his hands over Lee's scalp and turning his head. "You can have your buzz cut, you know. I was just giving you shit."

"It's fine." Lee shrugged. "Whatever you wanna do."

"Oh my god, you're one of those!" Hot Barber laughed. "This jawline deserves a low fade at the very least. But full disclosure, I'm going to peer pressure you into growing your hair out. It's so thick and shiny! Let it live!" He patted Lee's cheek. "Can I tag you? My followers will ask for your handle. They always do with the hot ones."

Lee shook his head with another apologetic wince. "Sorry, I'm not really on social media." He only used it to keep up with music trends, respond to the endless memes Sunny sent him, and secretly message his little sister. He couldn't risk any pictures of him showing up on Jazz's phone where their parents might see.

"Your loss." Hot Barber draped a towel over Lee's shoulders. "Just keep coming back to see me for your basic ass buzz cut. Trying to find an affordable chair here is impossible."

"Tell me about it. Every time I find a new shop, the next week the building is gone."

Hot Barber laughed. "That explains why no one is getting back to me. Any suggestions on where to look for a real barbershop and not an overpriced salon?"

"Honestly, I stay close to the river, so I'm not sure." Lee's parents lived over on the far end of Eastside; he tended to stay away from his old neighborhood. But the barbershops farther away from downtown were probably faring better than the ones by Blanche's apartment. "Ask the night manager at the Kum & Go on Fifth. He knows everything and everyone."

"The weed guy?" Hot Barber asked skeptically, palm pushing Lee's head to the side.

Lee laughed. "Yup. He's the real 411 in Eastside."

They made small talk about life in Bellamy while Hot Barber buzzed Lee's hair close to the scalp. It was nice, talking and joking with the man doing his hair without having to act straight for the sake of his hairline.

"There, all cleaned up." Hot Barber brushed off Lee's neck. "What do you think?"

Lee put his glasses back on, risking a glance in the mirror to make sure Hot Barber hadn't fucked him up.

He flinched at his father's accusing glare looking back at him.

"Whoa, that bad?"

"Sorry, no!" Lee shook off the memory of the last time he'd seen his dad's face. "It's good. I just don't really like looking at myself."

"That makes one of us," Hot Barber teased. "If I looked like you, I'd be checking myself out every chance I got! Hell, if it wasn't obvious, I *have* been checking you out."

"Oh." Lee froze. "I...uh...am..." Lee hadn't considered that Hot Barber might be into him. He and Antonio hadn't talked about being exclusive, or what they were doing. Regardless, Hot Barber wasn't Antonio—Lee couldn't think about anyone else if he tried.

"You're talking to someone new and don't want to mess that up?" Hot Barber shrugged. "I heard your friends talking shit about your new girl, but I figured I'd shoot my shot if you were hanging out with so many queer men."

"Oh, he's not my—that is..." Lee pushed his glasses up. "No, yeah, other than the 'girl' part, that's pretty on point. They just talk shit 'cause Antonio does drag."

Hot Barber laughed. "That's so fucked up! You'll keep coming to me for your hair, though, right?"

Lee laughed. "No, yeah. I'd hate to have to find someone else to cut my hair already."

Hot Barber grinned. "Good, because I don't have many friends here yet, and you seem cool. Now hold still so I can get a few angles for my Insta."

Fighting a smile, Lee held still. Maybe he was reading too much into whatever was happening between him and Antonio if he was already rejecting attractive guys, but it felt like he'd made the right move. And maybe a friend, too.

# Chapter Ten

## Antonio

Antonio shut the door of the supply closet behind him. "Jackie, I need your help."

"I'm not helping you flake on the party tonight." Jackie didn't look up from her clipboard as she checked off her inventory counts.

"No, it's not that." Antonio paused. He'd forgotten about the damn employee appreciation shit. Dread sank his stomach. "But if you *wanted* to…"

"I don't. Chas loves these things. If you want to disappoint her, that's all you."

"Don't worry. I'll be there," Antonio grumbled. Chas was the best boss—she didn't micromanage what anyone did as long as their job got done well, and no one broke any important laws. She cared about the people who worked for her. *Including me, even if I don't deserve a second chance.* "I just wanted to ask uh…what love feels like?"

Jackie turned away from counting vodka cases with a slow grin.

"Don't look at me like that." Antonio pointed at her in warning. "I don't exactly advertise this, but I fall somewhere on the aromantic spectrum. Greyromantic is the label du jour. I am intimately familiar with sexual attraction, but romantic? Completely foreign. And I figured since you have the opposite experience, you maybe could…explain it?"

Jackie's grin softened. "The fact that you're asking should tell you everything."

Antonio glared. "Ugh! Forget I asked. I have to go get ready." He didn't move.

Jackie laughed. "I'm not going to stop you from dramatically storming off."

"Okay, fine. Help me. I'm so confused." Antonio threw his arms around her. "Please! I googled it, but it sounds like anxiety. I already have that, so it wasn't very helpful."

Jackie patted him awkwardly on the back. "Tonio, any other time you thought you caught feelings because you were dickmatized, you wouldn't let anyone question it. Not even yourself. The fact that you're unsure says a lot."

"I've been gone for five years. Maybe...I'm less confident now." The tremble in his voice was thankfully muffled by her shoulder.

"Doubtful. Your ego is the biggest part of you."

Antonio grinned. "You're just saying that because you haven't seen my dick!"

Jackie's shoulder shook as she muffled her laugh. "Why do you always say the most out-of-pocket shit?"

"My therapist says I use humor as a defense mechanism."

"Was that not obvious without therapy?" Jackie teased. "Okay, I'm not super alloromantic myself, so sometimes it's hard to tell if I like someone romantically or as a friend or if they're just cool. And the only reliable way I've found to tell the difference is by spending quality time with them. Like, with my ex, I was sure it was a squish—like I wanted to be their friend because they were intimidatingly cool. But then they introduced me as 'just a friend' and I was devastated. It felt like a bubble popped, and my heart landed on its neck."

"What'd you do?" Antonio asked into Jackie's neck.

"Cried in the car. But after that, I told them how I felt. Like any adult with a crush would." Jackie laughed. "And we were happy but grew apart eventually. And we talked about that, too. Like any relationship that grows apart."

"So how does this story help me, exactly? I don't need advice on how to end things. I'm great at that. Well, maybe 'great' is the wrong word—I've ended a lot of things, Jackie." When he was younger, Antonio had wondered what he was missing. He'd hurt a lot of people by masking friendship and lust as love, not realizing they'd felt something different than he did. Antonio had put his whole heart into every new person but had been left underwhelmed and apathetic every time. That *je ne sais quoi* of romance that everyone talked about was only found in the heartbreak in other people's eyes, when they felt something for Antonio that he didn't feel back.

In time, he'd made peace with the fact that he would probably never feel the love he wanted. But the detachment and disconnect from the people he'd dated had been painful. Antonio had labeled himself as greyromantic, leaving it vague enough to kindle a spark of hope, but not enough to hurt people when he didn't feel the same way. People believed the "it's not you, it's me" when he told them he couldn't love them romantically. He could love them as a friend—with benefits—but he'd never be *in* love with them. Yet even on the rare occasion they were fine with that, it wasn't what Antonio really wanted.

But he'd never figured out how to communicate that—or anything related to emotions —in a healthy way. Instead, he would distance himself, and they would leave. Or start a fight that would give him the excuse to leave. *But the new me doesn't do that anymore.*

"I'm saying give yourself time to figure it out. You met Lee a week ago. Why do you think you're romantically attracted to him? What's different about him?"

"Honestly, it feels like I'm constantly on the verge of indigestion. But I like it."

"Gross."

"Like, I start worrying about gas and heartburn, but then I realize I'm just happy because I'm with him. Even after he goes home, the bubbly feeling in my gut doesn't go away, but it's a little sharper and painful, like holding in a fart because I also miss him."

"You can't be normal and call it butterflies?"

Antonio ignored her. "We've spent every day together for like a week. Isn't that enough time to know if the feelings are romantic?"

"Oh, hun." Jackie rubbed his back. "You're such a fuckboy."

"That was Old Antonio. I'd rather leave that reputation behind, thank you."

"Tonio, this is new to you. Take it slow. Don't take this the wrong way, but it kind of sounds like you're love bombing him. Give yourselves more space so it doesn't burn out."

Antonio groaned into her shoulder. "I just really like him, and I like being with him, and he makes everything so easy. And everything's been fucking hard lately, okay? I'm in the right place and I'm doing the right things, but this is the first time since rehab where my life actually *feels* right."

"But is that romance? I'm not saying you're *not* romantically attracted to him, but you gotta give yourself time to be sure. You have a lot going on right now. You might be projecting your need for stability onto him."

That sounded like his therapist, Joy, who was not super thrilled that he had thrown himself headfirst into a new potential relationship when he was supposed to be focusing on himself. But she understood why he was reluctant to pass up the chance to see where things went with Lee. And it's not like she could stop him; he couldn't even stop himself. "You're right. I should play it cool. But it's so fucking hard! I suck at playing it cool!"

Antonio more than sucked; he was utterly failing at it. Lee was wonderful. And charming. And his body was a goddamn work of art, with the juiciest bubble butt and the cutest coils of hair on his broad chest. Those warm brown eyes made Antonio's brain melt. Everything with Lee was too easy, too perfect. Their connection had become instantly deeper than anything Antonio had ever dreamt possible.

He didn't trust it. Knowing him, he was self-sabotaging another part of his life. So until he could figure out if he was avoiding something and what that was, he had to "play it cool" with the one person he could see himself falling in love with.

Staying grounded in reality sucked. Especially when his brain kept repeating *my boyfriend* and *mine mine mine* every time Antonio woke up with Lee in his arms or fell asleep with Lee's musky herbal scent in his sheets.

A knock sounded on the door. "Jackie, you seen Carlita?"

"Don't come in! We're indecent!" Antonio called out before Jackie could answer.

Chas laughed and opened the door. "Funny, Tonio. Get yer ass in makeup. You're emceein' the first half and you're already late."

"Yes sir!" Antonio had Carlita's makeup routine down to a science to avoid spending too much time backstage when the mimosa pitchers were out. He could transform in fifteen minutes if he had to, but Chas was right; if he had an hour, he should use the hour. And maybe he could bug Lee and Freddy in the control room if he finished—

Chas caught him by the elbow. "And since you disregarded everything I said about bein' careful with Lee, remember that this is a coercion-free workplace with a zero-tolerance policy for non-consent. And lock the door if you get up to anything at work."

Antonio wiggled free of his grip, irritated by the disappointment in Chas's condescending tone. "I didn't disregard *everything*. I plan on sticking around if that's what Lee wants. And so far, he has no complaints." He added an exaggerated wink to lighten the mood.

"Keep that to yourself, Tonio! He's practically my nephew!" Chas cringed.

Jackie pulled a face, too. "I do not consent to hearing about your sex life."

"Who said I was talking about sex? Both of y'all are nasty."

---

This isn't so bad. This is fine. I'm fine.

Antonio was not fine. His heart raced and his palms itched. Dread had settled like a stone in his stomach the second the show had started. He'd tried to chalk it up to nerves for emceeing again, but Carlita didn't have nerves. She'd killed it as the emcee and had gotten more tips during her finale than she'd earned her first weekend.

Everything was easy when he was Carlita. Carlita Asada didn't have problems. She didn't have anxiety or memory loss. Carlita was a strong, independent, badass.

Carlita was an escape.

But Carlita now hung on a garment rack, smeared onto makeup remover wipes in the trash. Antonio was merely himself when he joined the crowd of his tipsy coworkers, who saw what they wanted to believe about him.

For Venus, who'd tapped her nose with a wink on her way to the Confessionals, Antonio was the one who made her look good. They'd always been compared as the two young Black queens, the most athletic dancers of the cast, the messy and dramatic duo. Neither of them had ever won the competition that everyone had put them in. Carlita had more charisma, but Venus could function with her vices. Even sober, Antonio wasn't wholly functional.

For Chas, who had taken him by the elbow after the show and said he'd understand if Antonio wanted to skip the party, Antonio was the disappointment. Chas had taken Antonio under his wing as the next star to lead the lineup. Instead, Antonio had failed him at every turn. Sure, Carlita drew crowds, but Antonio had shirked any responsibility Chas had ever tried to put on him. And then he'd fled to New York the second Chas mentioned she'd be taking a leave of absence five years ago.

Everyone who'd worked with him back then had told enough stories that even the newbies knew Antonio was unreliable and indulgent. Which was unfortunately true. He was all of the things people said about him, and everyone at Confession knew it.

Everyone except Lee. Lee knew about his past, his disaster of a life, and his issues, yet he still liked him. Antonio could be the best version of himself with Lee, without any preconceptions to overcome. He was the brightest spot of Antonio's new-slash-old life.

Antonio searched the bar for his...Lee. He spotted him at a table, nursing a Modelo next to Chas, Freddy, and a leggy blond he recognized as Chas's friend, who used to help out backstage when Confession first opened.

Part of him wanted to join them. But he held back, instead pouring himself a glass of water from behind the bar, humming a reminder to act like the New Antonio he wanted to be. Jackie was right; he shouldn't be too clingy. They'd only been talking for a week.

*That's why I have to prove I've changed.* If Lee could see the best in him, Antonio could make everyone else see it too. He refused to fall back into his old easy-yet-destructive habits.

"Bitch, what the hell? I waited but you never showed." Venus popped up on the other side of the bar. "Hand me a napkin?"

Antonio passed a cocktail napkin to her, trying to soothe the irritation in his chest. "V, what part of 'I'm sober now' was unclear?"

"Yeah, but you're *you*." Venus wiped her nose. "I figured that meant liquor, not coke. You're what, like, California sober, then? You can't be *sober* sober."

Antonio gestured to his water glass, his annoyance rising. "Sober sober."

"Ugh, boring!"

"Do I exist to entertain you? Here, I'll add a lime to my water, spice things up for you." He tried to play it off as a joke to convince himself everything was fine. His razor-thin patience was the only dam against the anxiety that was threatening to drown him.

"Oh! While you're at it, can you make me a tequila soda?"

Antonio slammed his glass down. "I'm not making you a damn drink!"

*And you said you were done fighting,* the demons whispered, reminding him of all the shouting matches he'd started, many at this very bar. *You knew you'd lose your shit here again.*

He swallowed the shame churning in his stomach. Two seconds alone with Venus and he'd already lost his Intentions Song. Turning on his heel, Antonio fled to save himself from the flood as anger erupted in his heart and fear tightened his throat.

Quietly, he sang Joy's questions from when he'd first started therapy. *Where in my body am I feeling my emotions? What does that tell me about my mental state? What lies am I telling myself right now?* With all of his focus fighting to regain control of the inferno in his chest and the ice in his veins, he could only hope he was going somewhere quiet, safe, and secure.

When his anxiety finally let him breathe all the way to the bottom of his lungs, Antonio found himself slumped against the wall in the Confessionals, still humming quietly. *Oh fuck. What did I do?* Heart racing, he made himself take deep breaths, shaky as they were. But there were no signs he'd taken anything. Nothing was numb or buzzing. No part of him floated. He was still shaking with cold, yet burning from the inside out. Every breath was painful, but those were just emotions, not a side effect.

The tune he'd been humming was his Intentions Song; he'd composed it in rehab to help him stay grounded and express his emotions before they exploded. New Antonio wanted to build relationships instead of abandoning or destroying them. But if all else failed and his mood swings got the better of him, the final verse of the Intentions Song was that he should flee instead of fight. Old Antonio could be petty and cruel. That wasn't who he wanted to be anymore.

*I didn't fuck up. Just lost my cool. Went somewhere safe. Good job!*

Feeling this much was dangerous. He'd always felt everything so strongly; addiction had only made the mood swings worse. Everyone else managed to say "I'm upset" and argue it out, or "I'm sad" and cry in the shower, then move on with their lives. Antonio's feelings resonated through his whole body and soul. They lingered for hours, days, sometimes weeks later. The good ones were the highest high, but the bad ones were Hell.

When he was young, he'd coped by getting drunk, high, or laid. At least it had started off that way. But over time, he'd needed more booze, stronger drugs, or new strangers to drown them.

Benzos had erased them completely.

He waved off the blurry memories with both hands. *This is how I got into this mess in the first place. I can't erase myself.*

A gentle knock sounded on the door. A soft baritone asked, "Tonio, you in there?"

Relief washed over him. He pulled himself up and opened the door to let Lee in.

"You okay?" Lee's brow was furrowed in concern.

Antonio stepped into his waiting arms, the anger and fear washing away as Lee surrounded him. "Sorry. I'm not trying to be dramatic. I just hate parties."

"What can I do to help?" Lee tightened his arms around Antonio's shoulders.

"You're doing it." Antonio buried his face into Lee's chest, breathing in Lee's familiar herbal scent. "Can I talk about it? I don't want to unload on you if you're not up for it."

"Of course."

Antonio smiled up at Lee in appreciation. "I actually don't hate parties. I fucking love parties." He dropped his face back on Lee's chest. "I hate being forced to go to parties before I'm ready. I'm doing the right things, but it's so…precarious. I've been sober for six months and two weeks, and this is the longest I've managed so far. I keep telling myself the third time's the charm, but I've attempted sobriety far more than three times.

"At first, I said I was weaning myself off, but then I just went to NA meetings high. And I lied about *everything* in those meetings, like how I could handle booze okay even though I couldn't. Or how tough my life was because no one would sympathize with my bad choices."

"You didn't choose to be addicted," Lee reminded him. "It's a disease."

Antonio smiled against Lee's chest. "True, but I was a middle-class kid with a supportive and loving family. Benzos weren't pushed on me by a doctor. I wasn't peer pressured into taking them. I had options, and I chose the path that led me to addiction."

Lee gave him a comforting squeeze, reminding Antonio that someone was listening. That he wasn't alone. That someone cared about him, even the worst parts of him.

"It felt like everyone else had a better excuse. The real me wasn't good enough. So I made shit up and gave up when I got bored." Guilt and shame still gnawed at him. Admitting he could be a terrible person was always painful, but especially to Lee. "I'm hopeful this time—I went to rehab and made big changes like moving home. And avoiding NA. I can't be around people fighting their own addiction, which seems selfish, but at this point, I have to be selfish. I gave up every dream I had for this. Fame isn't worth dying for.

"It's just hard to stay grounded. When I'm here as Carlita, I can focus on performing. But when I'm here to socialize, I remember everyone is waiting for me to fail. Even my family expects the worst of me, and I'm terrified I'll turn back into the old me. Like Venus said, the new me is boring. How long can I keep this going this time if I can't even hang out with my coworkers?"

Lee kissed his hair before saying, "First of all, Venus is obnoxious."

Antonio laughed weakly.

"And she's wrong. You're not boring. I've had more fun with you than I ever have." Lee cupped Antonio's jaw, thumb running across his cheek. "You even had Freddy laughing when you were emceeing tonight."

Antonio's heart fluttered as Lee drew his gaze up. "Keep talking. I'm funny and..."

Lee grinned. "You're generous and sweet. And so resilient." His grin softened into a sweet smile. "You aren't starting a new you from scratch. You're building from everything you learned when you tried before and making different choices to give yourself the best chance this time. Even though it means giving up the life you thought you wanted. That's strength beyond anything I can imagine."

Tears burned behind Antonio's eyes. "You were supposed to say I give great head."

"See? Hilarious," Lee teased. "Look, I'm here however you need. If you want, we can practice hanging out here before the show, so you can get used to it again."

"Really?"

"Sure, I can even bring Tara, Blanche, and Sunny around too. If you want more people to socialize with. *If* you want to meet them."

Antonio wanted nothing more than to meet everyone in Lee's life. "I'd love that."

Lee kissed his forehead, melting Antonio's brain. "You want to rejoin the party, or should we get out of here?"

The anger and fear overwhelming him were washed away by a deep sense of peace, serenity replacing Antonio's hellish emotions. It was terrifying how fast his nerves had been lulled. Everything was too easy with him. *That forehead kiss worked faster than Triazolam.*

As if it couldn't bear to be forgotten, relentless anxiety shot through Antonio at the thought. *I like Lee for who he is, not what he does for me.*

"Can we go home?" Antonio blurted out. "Back to my place, I mean? Wait, no, *I'm* going home—you don't have to. I've been told I might be unintentionally love bombing you, and I don't want you to feel like you have to spend every second with me if you don't want to. I can go. You stay here and have fun."

"Hey, I'll have more fun with you than I will here. I like spending time with you, and I like that you want to spend time with me." Lee pulled him back into his arms before Antonio realized he was backing away. "Besides, I don't care what Chas says—a party with all of our coworkers is still work. Let me tell Blanche I'm leaving, and we can go. Okay?"

Antonio nodded. "Can you tell Chas I'm fine? And I'm sorry for flaking on the party, but it's too much, too soon. Oh, and no gossiping about this with my mom at Mass. Actually, no, they *can* gossip—just give me a chance to tell my mom first, so she doesn't think I'm hiding things from her."

"Anything else, or should I start taking notes?" Lee teased.

Antonio swatted his chest again. "I don't talk *that* much."

"Mm-hmm. Sure." Lee grinned. "You okay?"

Antonio stood on his tiptoes to plant a kiss on Lee's lips. "More than okay."

# Wednesday, May Eighth

# Chapter Eleven

## Sunny

THE THREADBARE CARPET ON the stairs leading up to Blanche's apartment was gray with grime. Only the sunset shining through the window revealed the emerald in the corners, hinting at its original color. Sunny pulled away from the handrail before she got to the sticky spot between the second and third levels.

For a sugar daddy arrangement, it said a lot about Blanche's patron that he'd put them up in such a run-down building. Still nicer than her mother's apartment, though; their railing had been missing since Sunny was sixteen. Sunny had tried to convince Birdie to move so many times, but her mother was nothing if not obstinate.

Sunny huffed, her stomach clenching. The sound of the jackhammer from the construction outside echoed her pulse around the lump in her throat. She blinked away the burning in her eyes, quickly closing *that* tab. Blanche's apartment was where she went to cool off after an argument; she could forget about everything there.

Well, everything but Blanche. Heat crept up her neck; she'd been too embarrassed to bring up the proposition again. But maybe she should, if her mother was back on her *"you need to find a nice girl"* bullshit again.

The scrap of paper with a phone number that her mother insisted she call was still crumpled in her fist. Sunny shoved it into the pocket of her khakis. She'd barely walked in the door from work when her mother had started in on her. There hadn't been a moment to even change out of her unflattering work clothes before Sunny was running out the door again.

*What does Mae expect? That I'll call some traditional cishet girl up and see if she's into trans women? Especially a socially awkward nerd, who panics at the idea of having sex?*

Looking at the door at the end of the hall, Sunny lingered at the top of the stairs to catch her breath. Maybe the argument was her sign that she *should* hire Blanche. She would have to figure out her hang-ups eventually. Even if the idea of being anyone's son, husband, or father made her insides twist into knots, she did want a family. Preferably where her role was a wife and mother. While she doubted any traditional Buddhist girl her mother approved of would want her, Sunny would honor her duty to the family. Eventually. Hopefully in her own way that didn't make her want to throw up.

She should talk with Lee. He'd get it, even if he didn't understand it. Sure, he'd probably try to talk her out of hiring Blanche, but at least he'd have another idea for her to figure her shit out. Because something had to give. How many more guilt trips from her mother would it take before she gave in?

The taste of blood flooded her mouth. Sunny blinked, touching her lower lip. It was puffy, cracked and raw from gnawing on it. With a shake of her head, she closed the Argument with Mae tab again and knocked on the door.

"One moment!" Blanche called from inside.

"It's only me," Sunny called back.

Blanche let her in. "Oh good. I have a client coming by in an hour, I thought they might be early." The click of the lock blessedly quieted the noise of the construction outside.

As the sanctuary of Blanche's apartment took the edge off her raw nerves, Sunny waved to Tara, who sat cross-legged on the coffee table, topless except for a towel around her shoulders. "Haircut day?"

"That's the goal." Blanche lifted the mop of unruly red hair out of Tara's eyes. "I shaved the rest, but I have no idea what Lee does with the top."

"I told you, he pulls a chunk to the side and buzzes it."

"And I have no idea what the fuck that means, babes." Blanche laughed. "I don't want to mess up your hair."

"Shave it all off for all I care!" Tara shrugged. "I just don't want it touching my neck."

"Here," Sunny ran her fingers through Tara's wiry curls, pulling a fistful to the edge of her undercut. She'd watched Lee cut Tara's hair enough times to know what Tara was trying to say. "Cut anything off past here."

Blanche carefully buzzed where Sunny indicated, covering her fist with their warm hand. Half-listening to the banter between Blanche and Tara as they teased each other, Sunny fought the urge to shiver as they worked in tandem until Tara's hair was relatively normal looking.

The press of Blanche's shoulder against hers, the dry callouses of their palm rough on her skin, were a pleasant distraction from why she'd originally shown up unannounced on a weeknight. Blanche and Tara wouldn't ask; Sunny's arguments with her mother were frequent enough that she didn't need to explain anymore.

"Where is Lee anyway?" Sunny asked as Blanche brushed the hair from Tara's neck.

"Canoodling with his new boyfriend." Blanche bent down with a squint to check they hadn't missed anything.

"He would say that Antonio isn't his boyfriend," Tara corrected. "Even though they're totally boyfriends now."

"Again?" Sunny asked. She hadn't seen Lee since Tara's birthday. Which was weird, because she'd been to Blanche's apartment at least three times in the past week.

Was this her sign that she should go through with it? If Lee wasn't around to talk her out of it...maybe the universe *wanted* her to hire Blanche.

"Yup," Tara huffed. "Again."

At Blanche's confirmation that her hair was as "done as it could be," Tara pulled the towel off her bare torso and headed down the hall without another word. Dropping her shorts—and mooning her friends in the process—she kicked them into her room before disappearing into the bathroom to shower.

Sunny envied Tara's ease with herself. Tara had no shame about her nudity, no discomfort with her body, not even thinking twice about stripping bare in front of her friends. Of course, Tara had nothing to be ashamed of. But neither did Sunny.

Yet the idea of stripping naked and walking around the house made the cut on Sunny's lower lip open up again, flooding her mouth with iron. She'd been avoiding dating the girls her mother had kept setting her up with so she could have fun and explore her sexuality as herself.

But how was she supposed to have fun in a constant state of dysphoric anxiety, merely from the anticipation of being nude around someone else? "When can we have that session we talked about?"

"Oh." Blanche froze as they swept the hair off the coffee table and into their hand. "I didn't think you were serious about that."

Sunny's stomach tightened. "I didn't think I was either, but I am."

Blanche turned away to dump the hair into the garbage can. "Are you sure you want it to be with me? I can refer you to someone else if you'd prefer."

"Why would I want anyone else?" Sunny asked, confused. "You know me better than anyone, and I trust you."

Taking a moment to wash their hands in the sink, Blanche turned and examined her thoughtfully. Sunny had never been great at reading anyone, but Blanche was a one-way mirror. Their green eyes could see right through her, but she could never read what they were feeling behind the half smile they always wore until it became a sneer or a smirk or a snorting laugh. She trusted that they'd be honest with her, like she was with them.

"Remember what I said? I don't want this to mess up our friendship."

"It won't!" Sunny insisted. Her crush on Blanche had never come between their friendship before. This would be no different. "This is strictly professional. Friends supporting friends."

Blanche pursed their lips before their face twisted back into a half smile. "I should have Saturday open. My patron is out of town this weekend."

The shower shut off, signaling for better or worse that the conversation was over. Blanche cared about client confidentiality; they wouldn't want Tara to find out about this.

"I'll text you for more details." Sunny threw her arms around Blanche. "Thank you."

"Of course, Babygirl. Anything for you." Blanche rubbed her back before stepping away. "Now, I hate to sexile you, but I do have a client on the way, so..."

Tara pulled on an oversized hoodie as she reentered the room. "I was going to hang out at Confession, if you don't want to go home yet."

Confession would be quiet on a weekday, and Tara would be quiet because Tara and Sunny didn't talk much when it was just the two of them. Sunny wanted quiet after the argument with her mother, but not *that* quiet. She needed something to distract her.

"I have a better idea!" Sunny grinned.

Tara groaned. "Oh no."

"Let's go thrifting!"

"Oh god, why?" Despite her protests, Tara let Sunny pull her out of the apartment behind her as Blanche wished them good luck.

They walked arm in arm to the bus stop in silence as the street lights flickered to life. The silence continued as the bus brought them to Sunny's favorite thrift store—a quirky salvage shop in a warehouse downtown that had managed to evade the bougie revival for the past decade. The *snick snick snick* of the hangers sliding across the racks; the potpourri scent that clung to the clothes for months; the screaming punk song inexplicably followed by a dreamy new age tune playing on the speakers—thrift stores lulled Sunny into a quiet where she could focus on the textures passing under her fingertips and forget the world.

The nice thing about being friends with Tara was that she gave Sunny as much space as she wanted when she was upset. Blanche asked questions, and Lee gave her advice. As much as Sunny appreciated that when she needed it, the room to escape from her issues instead of having to talk them out was a relief.

It was tempting though, to ask what Tara would think about hiring Blanche. Or if Tara thought she should just bite the bit and text the girl her mother wanted her to meet.

"Why do you keep looking at me?" Tara scowled over the rack.

Sunny blinked, realizing she was, in fact, staring at Tara. "Please, you *wish* I was looking at you."

"Spit it out, Sunny. You want to talk about something." Tara handed her a hanger with a halter top dangling from it. "Here. Your tits would look good in this."

Sunny laughed, tossing it in the cart to try on. "Thanks." She sighed, wondering what Tara would say if she asked. "I got into an argument with my mae."

"Same as usual?"

Sunny nodded, admiring a maroon sweater dress with a heart cutout in the chest. Impractical, because where would she wear it? She'd stick out like a sore thumb at work dressed like that, and she already had too many femme dresses that she never wore anywhere. "Another nice girl to give her grandbabies."

Tara winced sympathetically. "Are you going to ask her out?"

Sunny shook her head. "She's probably feeling the same pressure to settle down and get married. And, well, I'm not exactly the traditional son-in-law that parents are hoping for."

"You could pretend to date? If she's not interested, you could both say you were seeing each other and later say it didn't work out. Get your mae off your back."

With a snort, Sunny shook her head. "Wrong tone, Tara-Bear."

"What'd I say?"

"You told me to get my water off my back." Sunny and Tara laughed at the accidental pun. "Maybe just stick to English."

"You knew what I meant." Tara shrugged, but continued, "So why not pretend to date this girl to get your *mom* off your back?"

"Tempting, but..." Sunny pulled a black sweater off the rack that would be work-appropriate, even if it was boring and shapeless. "It's the principle. I don't want to lie to my mae. I just want her to understand that I'm not ready for all of that yet. That when I do get married, I want someone who likes me as I am, you know?" She paused, gripping the sweater tightly. "It's hard."

"No offense, but that sweater is ugly as hell." Tara raised her eyebrow at the shapeless cable-knit clenched in her fist.

Sunny laughed. Lee would tell her to buy the sweater because work clothes would be practical. But she was shopping with Tara, who would tell her to wear what made her feel good. She put the sweater back and held up the maroon sweater dress instead. "What about this?"

Tara gave her a thumbs up. "Hell yeah! Show off the cleave!"

Sunny smiled and put the dress in the cart. Maybe she didn't need to ask Tara what she thought about the Blanche situation. It didn't matter if Lee would think it was foolish of her, or if Tara would think it weird. Sunny needed help, and Blanche could provide it. That was as much of a sign as she needed.

# Saturday, May Eleventh

# Chapter Twelve

## Antonio

"You actually like this guy, don't you?" Gabe asked in surprise.

"Shocker, right? I actually *do* like this guy. He's so generous and understanding. And he's so fucking hot. And have I mentioned the sex is *amahzing*?" Antonio sighed with a smile, keeping his eyes glued to the TV. He leaned against Gabe, squishing his friend into the throw pillows lining the couch in a last-ditch attempt to keep Yoshi from falling to his doom.

It didn't work. Gabe's Sheik flashed across the winner screen. Sitting back in the corner of Gabe's sectional, Antonio tossed his controller down with a frown. He had never been big into video games. *Mostly because I suck, so why bother?*

"Just one or a few hundred times," Gabe muttered wryly, thankfully turning off the TV instead of suggesting another round. Opening the heavy curtains behind the couch now that they didn't need to see the screen, Gabe sneezed as bright sunshine flooded the living room. "Sorry. Colds are gross." He blew his nose, tossing the crumpled Kleenex into the waste bin piled high with used tissues.

"You don't have to apologize for getting sick, Gabey." Antonio shrugged. "Anyway, I'm gonna gush about Lee a few thousand more times, fair warning." He grinned unabashedly, curling his legs underneath him. "But I can talk about my new job instead for a bit! I start next Monday! Well, I start prep, meetings, that shit. Actual classes start in June. I'm just excited to have money again!"

He tried to put on a confident smile. Inside, anxiety ate at him at the thought of donning his boring teacher drag and walking into a school again. First performing as Carlita sober, and now teaching when Antonio couldn't drink himself to oblivion after work? *What am I thinking? Fuck. I do need money, though.*

His parents had been generous in getting him back on his feet, but he could already taste the resentment from his sisters that he was getting yet another handout. Cassie kept nagging him about "his" plans for structure. Plans he had stuck to for all of two seconds after meeting Lee.

Cassie hadn't been surprised when he'd admitted it. Her resignation hurt worse than he'd expected. *And here I promised myself that I was done disappointing her.* Done taking handouts from his parents. Done being the fuckup of the family.

Gabe stretched out on the couch, using Antonio's lap as a pillow and interrupting his spiral before it could begin. His dark brown curls spilled across Antonio's legs. "You're terrified, aren't you?"

"Extremely." Antonio combed his fingers through Gabe's loose ringlets. His hair had grown so long in their time apart. "There's so much to worry about. Like, can my fucked-up brain handle it? What if I cuss some kid out? And do I tell them about my personal life? Like, 'Hi Timmy, I'm your new teacher, the has-been drag queen who just got out of rehab and oops, I already forgot your fucking name?'"

"Take a breath, Tonio." Gabe huffed a laugh. "It was Timmy, by the way."

Antonio scowled. "That was an example, jackass. You were supposed to say I'm not a has-been."

"Can't be a has-been if you never-was." Gabe's dimples deepened as he smirked.

Antonio gently backhanded his cheek. "Why are we friends?"

"Because we have too much history to give up on each other again." Gabe sat up, tucking Antonio under his arm. Antonio wasn't fond of being reminded of how short he was, but Gabe made *everyone* feel small. "Do you remember why you wanted to be a teacher?"

Antonio shrugged, leaning into his friend's side. The French Vanilla Bean lotion Gabe always used was one of the few scents that still brought up good memories. Like making out on the futon in Gabe's parent's basement. "Because Cassie's pushy and works for the school district.

Besides, what else can a former theater kid with a teaching license do in Bellamy?"

Gabe chuckled. "I meant why you got that teaching license in the first place. You wanted every kid to have someone looking out for them. Unlike us, the only two queer kids of color at Driftwood. All of our teachers were straight, white, and out of touch."

The two of them had been bullied mercilessly at the overwhelmingly WASPy Driftwood Academy of the Arts. No adult had stepped in, leaving them with only each other for support. *You'd think for an art school, people would be more open-minded.* But Driftwood Academy was a private school in an old money suburb. No school where they'd grown up would have treated them any differently.

When he was younger, teaching had been his dream career. The theater program had been his haven, the choir his tiny community of allies. Gabe had been less fortunate in his visual arts program. Antonio had wanted to help keep kids like them safe from the constant harassment for being queer, scrawny, Black, and Latino. Or in Gabe's case, queer, overweight, Native, and Jewish. They had too much "them" and never enough "us" for anyone but each other.

Some people would be nice enough in private, but wouldn't dare stick their necks out for the two weirdos. Antonio had hardened his heart to the slurs; Gabe had left defeated. Before he'd burnt out on teaching, Antonio had resolved to protect the weirdos in his classes, for the sake of the Gabes of the world.

But teaching fourth graders how to play the recorder had turned into a mere temp gig until he'd moved to New York. *And look what good that did me.*

"Yeah, I guess being a role model or whatever sounds like something I'd say. But was I ever a good role model? I used to decompress after work the same way we did when we were in high school."

"Getting high, drunk, and laid?"

"Right. Not exactly Teacher of the Year material. And now weed and booze are off the table. And like, I'm sure Lee wouldn't mind a daily booty call, but that doesn't seem healthy."

"True. You don't want to risk a cross-addiction. Especially a sex addiction with someone your ass actually likes. I mean, you barely avoided that food thing. You ate so many fucking donuts in rehab."

Antonio's stomach rumbled loudly. He patted his gut with a laugh. "Don't you start. You can't handle fried food anymore, traitor!"

"Look, Tonio. You will make it work somehow. You're in a better place now than you've ever been. Give yourself time and space to process so you can make sound decisions." Gabe squeezed him tighter. "And you don't have to tell your students everything. Be open about who you are, but not necessarily what you do. Or used to do."

"Thanks, Gabey," Antonio murmured, before adding with a teasing smile, "I'm a little disappointed I'll have to find a new coping mechanism besides Lee's giant—"

Gabe pushed him into the couch. "Stop! I don't want to hear about your sex life!"

Antonio couldn't help but laugh. He and Gabe had been high school fuck buddies; talking about his sex life shouldn't be a big deal. But Gabe got so flustered anytime Antonio mentioned what he and Lee were getting up to. So of course, Antonio used as many innuendos as possible, even if he never shared the specifics. Embarrassing Gabe was his favorite hobby.

"So you don't want to hear what Lee and I are doing before work?" He waggled his eyebrows.

"Absolutely not. Please stop talking." Gabe shook his head and scrambled off the couch. His chunky pittie mix jumped up to steal Gabe's spot with a heavy flop. Aptly named, Hippo was a massive gray dog who looked too intimidating for his sweetheart personality.

"Gabey! We're just hanging out at Confession before the show, no sexy times involved." Antonio laughed, scratching Hippo's ears. Hippo had taken a while to warm up to him, but several weeks of sneaking him treats had finally paid off. "I had a little baby breakdown at work last weekend. Turns out socializing is more than I can handle, so he's helping me ease back into it with a happy hour date. Which is perfect since you and Richard refuse to socialize with me!"

He considered inviting Gabe along to meet Lee, but Gabe never went anywhere anymore.

"I still think it's weird you're dating your coworker, for the record. Seems messy." Gabe pressed his hands together to stretch his ridiculously built arms. He probably wasn't trying to flex, but Antonio still admired the view of his muscles bulging under his black V-neck. One, anyone with a pulse would ogle Gabe. And two, his brain couldn't reconcile the Gabe in front of him with the Gabe he'd grown up with.

Antonio had been positively shook to discover Gabe had had the glow-up of the century in their three-ish years apart. He'd become a literal bodybuilder and aged into his now objectively handsome features. A far cry from the insecure, chubby boy with a hawkish nose and unkempt hair in high school. On the outside, at least. Gabe was still insecure and emotionally fragile.

"It's a gay bar, not some corporate ladder. The lead king and the lights guy have been together for years. Maybe I'll get to emcee more now that I'm with the sound guy." Antonio laughed. "That's a joke, for the record. I already emceed the brunch show last weekend, but I low-key think that was to keep me from flaking on the employee appreciation party afterward."

*Which Old Antonio absolutely would have. And so would New Antonio.*

Antonio liked performing at Confession, and being around his family when they were drinking was manageable, but his foggy memories of Confession's parties had gotten the better of him. *Thank God Lee was there.* Resisting temptation was easier with Lee around. His calming presence made all of the big feelings that dragged him into dark places more manageable.

*You're using him.*

"And you didn't even have to fuck the boss," Gabe teased, his deep bass voice interrupting his demons.

Antonio rolled his eyes to hide his anxiety. "I wouldn't dare. Chas and Freddy both get incredibly jealous. I don't get it, but *I'm* not a jealous person."

Gabe snorted, dimples returning to his cheeks. "You sure?"

Antonio grinned. "No, I'm not sure of anything. I've heard about the honeymoon stage before, but I always thought everyone was exaggerating. But I literally can't think of anything but Lee. Who knows what I'm like with romantic feelings?"

"True. You've never acted this lovestruck before. Seems like a good relationship."

"Gabey Baby, two weeks of talking is *not* a relationship," Antonio chided as he rearranged himself on Gabe's couch, swinging his legs over the back of the sofa.

Gabe shot him a skeptical look. "Really? Talking?"

Antonio grinned, masking another pang of anxiety, and amended, "Okay, maybe to *your* serial monogamist ass, this is a relationship, but not most people. Yeah, we've spent almost every day together. And yeah, I like him, he likes me, and I hope it eventually becomes a relationship, but it's too soon to label it. Ergo, still solidly in the talking stage."

"You just described a relationship."

Antonio let out a frustrated groan, anger simmering in his chest. "It's not, Gabey! I need to take it slow! This is a terrible time to start a relationship. I just got out of rehab, and you know I have no idea what I'm feeling, let alone what I'm doing. I can't fuck it up before it even starts!" He paused to calm his racing heart with a deep breath, but couldn't resist the urge to clap back. "Or worse, develop a codependent relationship where I change my whole personality for him!"

"Damn, fuck you!" Gabe snapped, but he didn't defend himself. Gabe threw his whole self into his partners, always to his detriment. He was a big, sensitive doormat. Always had been.

*I'm an asshole. Gabe didn't deserve that because I'm in over my head.* Guilt ate at his gut as they fell into silence. That was part of the Old Antonio nastiness he wanted to leave behind.

Gabe spoke first. "Sorry, that reaction was uncalled for."

"No, I deserved it. You were trying to be supportive. This is probably why you hate having people over. I can go." Antonio swung his feet around to get up.

Gabe firmly held his feet against the back of the sofa. "S'ok, Tonio. Don't leave. We promised we'd talk shit out instead of leaving, remember? I just—I need a minute. Um, can I get you a snack? Please?"

"Sure." *I'll let you escape from me.* "And sorry. Feeling defensive isn't an excuse to come at you like that."

"No, I shouldn't have pressed it. All this catching feelings shit is new for you. You're way more sensible about it than I would be." Gabe ran a hand through his hair and left the room.

*Sensible or scared shitless?* Antonio had dated many people and had casual sex with many more, but he'd never experienced anything close to what he felt for Lee. People had professed their love to him many times. A few times he'd said it back because he wanted it to be true. All of his situationships had been fun enough, but he'd never felt an inkling more than sexual attraction or fond friendship.

Eventually, everyone wanted more from him than Antonio could give. Or he lost interest and ghosted them, or they'd dump him after a minor argument because he could never bother to make an effort. No one had ever been worth the work of figuring shit out.

Only Gabe had stayed in his life after they'd broken up. As dramatic emo kids, they both dreamed about meeting their soulmates, someone who would truly see them. Yet they'd gotten together anyway, knowing they weren't each other's Death Cab song. They'd split amicably their senior year, having been friends too long to give each other up. *Besides, high school relationships don't count.*

In repeat after repeat of "Crooked Teeth," Gabe had fallen head over heels for every toxic partner since he'd graduated college. Meanwhile, Antonio had more "Tiny Vessels," meaningless flings that never lasted long. While commiserating over a bottle of wine or three when Antonio had first moved to New York, Gabe had been the first to suggest that Antonio may be aromantic.

Like a cute hat in a vintage shop shaped to someone else's head, "aromantic" never fit him right. The first time he'd heard the definition of "pansexual," it was like putting on a perfectly tailored pair of pants. It fit better than the off-the-rack "bisexual" or "mostly gay" that he'd worn before. Yes, those labels did the job of telling others that he was primarily attracted to men, but open to other genders. But his attraction had never been to a physical body—he was attracted to the person. Queer fit fine, but pansexual was made for him.

Aromantic had never fit perfectly like that. Antonio *wanted* to fall in love. He dreamed of meeting his "Soul Meets Body." Of loving someone for eternity, who understood him on a spiritual level. He just never experienced so much as a flicker of the romantic attraction required.

One person he'd dated when he lived in Brooklyn had told him he was demiromantic. They'd put up with Antonio's avoidant bullshit longer than most, in hopes he might love them back in time. Antonio had worn that label for a few people, and it fit just as awkwardly as aromantic did. Even if it wasn't tailor-made, greyromantic was stretchy enough to fit both his reality and his dreams.

The memory loss from the Benzos hadn't helped; it made Antonio second-guess everything. What if he had fallen in love before and forgotten? What if he'd met his soulmate on a bender? What if the serenity he'd craved had blocked him from the joy he yearned for and he actually wasn't greyromantic, just constantly high? Sure, he'd never felt romantic attraction *before* he discovered Xanax, either, but the imposter syndrome whispering that he wasn't *really* greyromantic made him keep that label close to the chest. Even after months of therapy to better understand his emotions and moods, he still didn't trust his feelings.

That tension between reality and wishful thinking only made his relentless need for Lee even more confusing. Chas's warning about Lee was yet another sobering sign that Antonio had to take this slow. On top of his therapist's concerns that he might not be in the best place for a serious relationship. And Cassie's disappointment that he wasn't forming good habits.

It all added to his mistrust that these feelings weren't real, that he was only using Lee to escape from reality. Being with Lee felt like he was cheating on a test. He was the too-easy answer for all of Antonio's problems.

And yet, he'd never felt quite so whole before. Like Lee was an extension of Antonio that he'd somehow lost. He'd looked up at those brown eyes and felt an innate familiarity, that "there you are" he'd been hoping for all of this life.

Gabe brought a tray out from the kitchen. Hippo opened an eye at the sound of a platter on the coffee table, took one look at the carrot sticks, and went back to sleep. "Okay, so. What you said touched a nerve because I've been working to become codependent with Hippo instead of a significant other. But, given the opportunity, I *would* fall back into bad habits. I'm sorry for taking my insecurities out on you."

"Hold on, being codependent with your dog is a *good* habit?" Antonio raised an eyebrow.

Gabe shot him a look as he sat on the other side of Hippo. "Better than falling for someone who uses me again. Anyway, it's a good segue to tell you that I'm starting a new outpatient treatment! Gotta work on this kinda shit!" Gabe made awkward finger guns, as if joking would make Antonio less concerned about yet another outpatient program.

"What is it this time? Another round of CBT?" Cognitive Behavioral Therapy had proven effective for Gabe's PTSD before, begging the question why he needed another round.

"DBT this time! We're focusing on emotional regulation now."

"Twinning!" Antonio laughed. Dialectical Behavioral Therapy had led to his Intentions Song, which had proven useful many times in the past seven-ish months of sobriety.

Gabe snorted. "Yeah, you know how draining it'll be. So you can't drag me out anywhere or set me up on any more dates. I'm single by choice until I figure my shit out."

Antonio shot him a skeptical look back as he grabbed a carrot stick. "I'm pretty sure it's your mom setting you up with people. I'm just trying to drag you out of your damn house. And now you're going to hide out even more? You're safe here, Gabey."

Gabe's fingers grazed the ends of his long hair. "I need space to figure out who I am and what I want, before I put myself into a situation where I might meet someone. We both know how that goes with me."

"Yeah, you fall for anyone that gets your dick hard."

Gabe shook his head with a wince. "I don't like that you phrased it that way, but you're not wrong. Kinda proves my point."

Hippo rolled on his back so Gabe could rub his belly. Gabe had moved back home from New York himself a year ago. After six months of recovering from his ex, he'd bought a large Craftsman in South Bellamy and adopted Hippo for some much-needed emotional support. Gabe hadn't left his house much since, ready to hide in Bellamy for the long term.

*Thank God he's done with her bitch ass.* His ex was controlling, jealous, and evil. Everyone but Gabe had seen it. Or maybe he had and still chose her. Antonio had merely been the first to get cut out of Gabe's life because he never could keep an opinion to himself.

He'd only learned Gabe had moved home after his mom had mentioned it while visiting him in the hospital after his last overdose; her chisme from Bellamy took his mind off the shakes and nausea. Gabe moving back to Bellamy had been the last straw. Nothing was left for Antonio in New York but demons and temptation.

Antonio waved a hand at the foggy memory of detoxing for the third and hopefully final time. *No, not hopefully. The. Final. Time.* He didn't remember much of detox, or the overdose that brought him there, but he would never forget the broken sob that had escaped his mom when he'd asked if he could come home.

Antonio waved both hands frantically to shoo off *that* memory.

"Gabey Baby, you can figure shit out without swearing off the world. How you gonna figure out what you want out of life if you're not living?" Gabe sat silently, but Antonio hoped some part of him was listening. "You just need...boundaries."

Persuading Gabe's stubborn ass to do anything was pointless. *Probably why he stayed with her for so long. Just to prove us wrong.* Not only Antonio but his exes, too. His past several partners had said the same thing she had—Gabe was too much, too intense. *No wonder Gabe picked her over me. He couldn't take yet another partner leaving him.*

Gabe crossed his arms in defiance. "Right now, my focus is Hippo and myself. There's not many good things in my life that *I* chose. I don't even like my job, for fucks sake! Everyone tells me what to do, and I do it because I don't know what I want in the first place. Like, I resent all of the decisions that I don't make. And then I feel guilty because I could have said no, and I fucking didn't. Working on myself will help me figure that out." Gabe fidgeted with a strand of his long hair, tugging on it absentmindedly.

Hippo snuggled up against him until Gabe pet his giant head instead.

Antonio softened. "Just don't hold yourself back from what you want while you're working on yourself. I'd hate for you to resent *yourself* down the road."

"You sound like my therapist," Gabe chuckled mirthlessly.

Antonio smiled. "That's because we have the same therapist. Does Joy know you're using this DBT thing to hide? I thought she said you needed to get out more."

Their therapist, Joy, was Antonio's savior. A literal miracle worker. Antonio sometimes wondered if having the same therapist as his best friend was a good idea. *But it's not like we planned it.* She'd taken them both on before they'd reconnected, and neither wanted to switch.

Besides, Joy was a professional through and through. She never shared anything about Gabe or Antonio with the other. Yet somehow Antonio and Gabe knew exactly the right ways to support each other. Why Joy kept talking about flashbacks when his issue was memory loss had been confusing, until one day when he'd joined Gabe and Richard's daily workout. While changing in the locker room, Antonio had heard Gabe's deep voice whispering, begging for forgiveness—please don't hurt him, he'd do better next time—while curled up in a ball in the gym shower. Somehow Antonio knew what to say to ground him back in reality and help him through the worst of the episode.

*Really, if anyone's at risk of being codependent, it's Gabe and me.*

Gabe shrugged, eyes downcast. "She thinks it'd be good for me to be single to work through some things, but—like you said—I shouldn't hide away from the world so much."

"Joy's trying to cockblock me, too. She keeps telling me to take it slow with Lee." Antonio sighed dramatically, hoping to bring Gabe's mood back up.

His efforts paid off when Gabe's dimples reappeared. "She's doing a terrible job of cockblocking you. She's just worried about you. We all are. Tell me more about this Lee fellow. Gotta make sure he's good for you."

"Gladly!" Antonio grinned and hummed his Lee Song to remember everything he'd learned about his not-yet-boyfriend. "Well, he likes my music, so obviously he's a keeper." Gabe laughed. "His favorite color is periwinkle. He gets dinner with his little sister once a month. And he dances! He has this wolf print tramp stamp that he's super embarrassed about, so of course I howl every time I see it."

"Of course, why wouldn't you?" Gabe shook his head.

"The point is he likes me at my most irritating." Antonio scowled in mock annoyance. "He is unfairly easygoing. Nothing phases him. Like, during my little breakdown, he just held me and listened. He was so sweet. And we'd only been talking for a week." He paused. "Oh, and I'm no size queen, but he gives *you* a run for your money."

"I don't need to know about his dick." Gabe covered his ears.

"I'm just saying he's tall, Gabey." Antonio grinned at his friend. "Get your mind out of the gutter."

# Chapter Thirteen

## Lee

"Yeah, suck it!" Tara crowed.
Toad went flying from the blue shell Wario launched at him.
Lee groaned. "Come on! Again?"
"Tara, for such a sore loser, you're worse when you win," Blanche teased as they watered the plants lining the sun-filled picture window of their apartment.
Lee didn't care how obnoxious Tara could get. He just liked to spend time with her, even if he lost most of the games they played. Lee had been so occupied with Antonio lately that he hadn't hung out with his family in a minute.
He'd missed his platonic soulmate. And Blanche, though he wasn't as emotionally reliant on them as he was on Tara. He still saw them both every day, but mostly in passing. Today had worked out though: Antonio had plans with a friend before the show, and Tara and Blanche were both home before he had to head to Confession.
"You gonna see that blonde girl again?" Lee asked. Tara had hung out with him in the control room at Confession last weekend and picked someone up while getting a drink. She hadn't returned to the control room, instead going home alone during intermission. Like she usually did.
Lee always encouraged Tara to actually talk to the people who hit on her, maybe even go on a date for once. She never did. He worried

about what that would mean for her future, especially if he kept seeing Antonio. They'd been alone together for so long that he had no idea how she'd handle a new person in their lives. And he *really* wanted to keep seeing Antonio. *Hopefully, she's nicer to him than she was to Sunny when they met.*

Blanche perked up as they draped themself over the chair. "Oh? Tara, you didn't mention a blonde."

"That's because I don't want to see her again. Blondie was hot and all, but she asked for my number. Hard no for me." Tara wrinkled her nose.

Tara's Wario came into first place. Again. Lee set the controller down with a sigh. "You know most people do that when they like someone, right? Exchange numbers, go on dates, or, god forbid, go to their house to fuck instead of in public?"

"I thought we agreed you weren't going to slut shame me anymore." Tara arched an eyebrow at him.

"That's not what I'm doing." He had, in fact, unintentionally slut shamed her in the past because he'd been projecting his own shame. Between the strict purity culture he'd been raised in and the *"Being a whore is all you're good for"* on repeat in his head from the last day he'd seen his dad, Blanche had to help him unlearn a lot of shit. A few months after Blanche had first taken them in, they'd given Lee and Tara a crash course in sex ed, and still dragged them along to their testing appointments at least once a month. "I just think a relationship would be good for you."

Behind Tara's tough independent exterior lay someone who was just as needy and fragile as he was. He wasn't the only reason they'd clung to each other all these years. Tara wanted a relationship, a loving family, all the same things he did. And she wanted them so much that she never allowed herself to admit it. In Tara's head, anything that desirable would only end up hurting her.

Not that he was much better. But at least he could admit it. To Tara and Blanche, anyway.

"Stop projecting your sappy ass heart on me, dude. I have friends—I don't need all that relationship stuff. I want fun, not feelings."

"Buttercup, you have three friends! I'm not saying fall in love, just get to know someone." Hell would freeze over before Tara voluntarily went on a date, but at some point, she needed to get out of her emotional fortress. Being closed off from the world wasn't sustainable, even if it had kept her safe when they were younger. They had beds and a door that locked and regular meals now. They could afford to be more vulnerable.

*Hypocritical much?* Lee hadn't exactly been vulnerable either. Tara, Blanche, Sunny, and his sister Jazz were the only people he let in, and even they never got his whole self. No one did. Not even Lee. *And definitely not Antonio.* His mom had been right about one thing: no one cared about his feelings. Any time he'd expressed what he wanted, the universe went and ruined it. He wasn't going to risk this thing he had going with Antonio too.

"Lee's got a point, babes." Blanche stretched, uncrossing their legs over the arm of the chair. "You may be happier with more people in your life."

Tara got up to turn off the TV, pulling her basketball shorts up when they slipped down her slim figure. "Like you're one to talk."

Blanche made a sour face. "Okay, but Lee is doing it, and he's happier. Right, Lee?"

"No, yeah! I can't even put it into words." He had never laughed as hard or as often as he did around Antonio. No one had ever complimented him so genuinely and wanted Lee around every moment. They talked about nothing and everything and still wanted to keep talking. Everything was easy with Antonio.

Lee fought so hard to keep it together around him. Antonio drew out all of Lee's thoughts and feelings like a magnet. But they were just talking. They weren't serious, no matter how much Lee wanted to blurt out how hard he'd fallen. *No point in ruining a good thing by doing something stupid. Antonio wouldn't want all that, especially not with me.*

Lee hadn't realized he'd been wearing a dopey smile until the ache in his cheeks told him it had faded.

A heavy sigh from Tara echoed his mood as she invited herself into his lap. He put his arms around her and held her close. Her scrawny ass body was home. She'd still be his home when Antonio inevitably got bored with him.

Tara patted his forearms. "How's this? I'll keep an open mind if I meet someone I don't hate as much as everyone else. After all, you found someone to make you all soft and shit. Why can't I?"

Lee was surprised she was willing to try, despite her sarcasm. Maybe his Buttercup wasn't completely hopeless. She'd been strangely supportive of him spending all of his time with Antonio, even though he knew she had to be hiding her hard feelings. Hopefully, she'd talk it out with him before he lost her to resentment. After all, everyone had a breaking point.

*"Lee, the only one who will love you unconditionally is me because I'm your mother. Everyone has a breaking point, and you can't keep driving your father to his."*

Bitterness churned in his stomach. That had turned out to be a lie, too. Not even his mother loved him after the truth had come out. Even if Tara had a breaking point he hoped never to reach, she loved him far more than his parents ever had.

Lee squeezed her tighter, taking a deep breath to ignore the resentment burning his throat. Unsure of how she'd react, he tentatively asked, "Antonio and I are hanging out at work before the show. Do you want to come?"

Tara whirled to face him. "Oh, fuck yeah, dude!"

"Wait, Tara. You'll be nice to him, right?" Anxiety sprang up from yet another unexpected reaction. She never wanted to hang out with his other friends. "Right?"

"Let me go change!" Tara jumped from his lap and ran from the room.

Lee grimaced, already regretting asking her. "Blanche, you want to come, too?"

Blanche shook their head. "I have a client tonight. Next time."

"Tonio wants to meet you. Sunny, too. I must talk about you three a lot."

"I never thought you'd be so smitten. It's cute. Speaking of Sunny..." Blanche's voice took on a significant tone Lee didn't understand. "You haven't spoken to her lately, have you?"

Lee shook his head. "Yeah, no. Just nerdy memes I don't understand. Everything okay?"

Blanche smiled tightly. "Everything is fine."

"Okay, I'm ready," Tara announced before he could ask more. Wearing much the same outfit as before, she was now in her "going out" gym shorts and hoodie.

Blanche and Lee exchanged a smirk. Tara would always be Tara.

> Hey. I invited Tara to join us today. Hope that's still cool? She's weirdly excited to meet you. Maybe be prepared for an interrogation. She's kind of grouchy. And overprotective. You might get hissed at.

Omg I can't wait to meet her! :-) Bestie goals!!!

Lemme ask Gabe if he wants to come.

He says not a chance in hell.

> Oh, damn. Ok…

This is Gabe. I didn't mean that personally. Sorry. I'm just a homebody.

> It's cool. Don't worry about it.

---

# Tara

"Tara! You have no idea how excited I am to meet you! I've heard so much about you!" Antonio grinned at Tara, practically dancing in his seat. The studs in his ears sparkled in the afternoon sun with every shimmy.

Confession's dining area was empty aside from a few straggling day drinkers from brunch. Employees raced between the kitchen and the bar, frantically preparing for the dinner rush.

*Already he's better than Lee's other friends. They don't even look at me.* Tara smiled back. "Good things, I hope."

"Of course—I can tell Lee loves you from how he talks about you." Antonio beamed, eyes flicking to Lee.

Tara's soft feelings flickered to life at his affectionate expression. And the way Lee made moon eyes right back. "Likewise—he never shuts up about you. The past couple weeks have been 'Antonio this, and Antonio said that, and Antonio did this thing with his mouth—'"

"Buttercup, please shut the fuck up," Lee interrupted, face buried in his hands.

Tara and Antonio laughed. While she'd been planning to ice him out, her initial scan showed only good signs. He had enthusiastically greeted Lee with a kiss and seemed genuinely excited to meet her. His leggings and Fall Out Boy t-shirt said he wanted to be comfortable, but not flashy. Except for his sky-high heels.

Still, he seemed confident in himself with no signs of conceit or insecurity. Most importantly, she didn't see any of that catty immaturity Lee overlooked in his other friends, the ones Tara loathed. Antonio seemed genuine, warm, and by every indication, just as taken with Lee as Lee was with him.

"So... How'd you get into drag?" Tara asked. Getting Antonio talking would make sure she didn't have to ask any other stupid small talk questions. Or worse, talk about herself. She had caught the start of Carlita's first number on her birthday but had soon been distracted by Mr. Redwood Tree. To hear Lee talk about it later, she'd missed quite the performance. *He seems biased though.*

Antonio grinned. "Oh, you know, flamboyant theater kid. I signed up for a drag show in college to see how far I could push my parents until they stopped showing up for my shows. Instead, my mom introduced me to her friend from church who was opening a gay bar, which is how I met Chas. Drag just fits. I like entertaining people and my campy alter ego. And I *adore* heels. I'm not short with these beauties." He showed off his stilettos. "I'm at least five-ten today."

Their server came over to take their order. Since it was Saturday, Tara ordered her usual whiskey coke before remembering Antonio didn't drink. "Oh, shit. Is that okay?"

He waved her off. "Go right ahead. You, too, Angel. If I can't handle being around alcohol, I'm in the wrong place! We'll only have problems if you make me drink it."

Lee shook his head. "Just water, please. I'm on the clock soon."

The server nodded and walked away as Antonio made heart eyes at Lee.

*Angel? Lee, you didn't say he calls you Angel!* A rush of affection surged in Tara's heart. *How is he winning me over this quickly?* She hadn't even grilled him yet. But everything Lee had told her was true so far. Antonio was funny and charming. And Lee would never tell her this, but Antonio was completely smitten with him. "I'm sure you know it better than anyone, but you're really strong for getting sober," Tara said before she could overthink the compliment.

"If I was strong, I wouldn't have needed to *get* sober. But thank you. I'm a work in progress." Antonio squeezed her hand.

Tara squeezed back. "Give yourself some credit. Breaking an addiction takes more strength than avoiding one in the first place. My mom tried so many times to get clean but always slipped up. Nothing mattered more than dope." *Not even me.* "I always figured I'd end up like her, so it's reassuring that you pulled yourself out."

Tara made herself shut up before she gave him any other personal details. *I don't know him like that. What the fuck?* She glared and pointed a finger at him menacingly. "And if you ever tell anyone else what I said, you will regret it."

Lee snorted. "Her hiss is worse than her bite."

"Don't lie—you know how hard I bite," Tara said. "I just haven't bit *you*."

Antonio laughed. "You really are a feral little kitten, aren't you? Don't worry, Pussycat, I won't tell anyone your secrets."

Tara swallowed, shoving down the memory of Mr. Brown Eyes calling her Kitten as they locked gazes in the mirror along with the rush of guilt and regret that came with it.

*Maybe I do need to give people a chance.* Lee was happier since meeting Antonio. He hadn't been *unhappy* before, but he had a new lightness about him. *Maybe I could...* A surge of some unknown soft wanting feeling rose in her. "So Lee says you're a teacher?" Tara asked, desperate to change her thoughts.

"Yup! To be honest, my sister works for the school district, so I got this gig purely from nepotism. But money is money, and I have a teaching license, so here we are. I start a summer school program next week and middle school choir full-time in the fall."

"That's cool." Tara struggled to find a better response. "Are you um, excited?"

Luckily, Antonio laughed. "Yes, and fucking terrified. My short-term memory is not the greatest, and I'm supposed to memorize, like, a hundred kids' names? And their parents? And the other teachers? I'm going to fuck this up somehow."

"No, you won't." Lee put his arm around Antonio. "Would a call-and-response attendance song help? No one will question why the choir teacher sings everyone's names."

Antonio made heart eyes at Lee again. "You always have the best ideas!"

Lee gazed adoringly right back at him.

*Oh god, they're really cute. Ugh.* That stupid wanting feeling was back.

"So how did you two meet?" Antonio asked. "Lee told me the basics but trying to get details out of him is impossible."

Tara exchanged an uncomfortable glance with Lee. *Hopefully, he already told Antonio enough so this isn't a surprise.* "Uh... The deacon at the church shelter we were both staying at sent Lee to convince me to join the stupid conversion therapy group. Instead, I convinced him that he didn't need to go and then saved his ass when he got jumped. He's been following me around since."

Lee laughed. "You missed the part where I saved your ass too, but yeah, that's basically what happened. This scar on my cheek would have been worse if it weren't for her. I told my aunt I wouldn't come with her unless Tara could, too."

"You were in conversion therapy?" Antonio asked in surprise.

Lee shrugged. "I was fifteen. It was a weird time."

Antonio turned to Tara with an exasperated look. "See? No details."

Tara shrugged. "Honestly, I'm surprised he told you anything."

"Leland! Just who I wanted to see!"

*This bitch.* Tara shuddered as Lee's friend with the forehead approached. She could never keep Lee's other friends' names straight. Not that it mattered; this one never acknowledged her existence anyway. That was just fine; she wanted nothing to do with his red flags. Vain, insecure, and just nasty.

The open expression on Antonio's face had closed off as well. *Interesting.*

"Hey, man, what's going on?" Lee glued a guarded smile to his face.

"Don't play dumb, Leland. You're not cute enough to be a himbo. You're driving us again tonight, right? We're going over South."

This one was the ringleader of Lee's other friends. She didn't understand why. He wasn't very smart, nice, or attractive. Especially with that big ass forehead. *Aunt Alitrice would tell me that was unkind. She'd tell me to hate him cuz he's a bitch, not for his looks.*

Tara wasn't welcome at their parties. Which, cool, not every space was for her. She'd rather be home anyway. But she had always wondered if Lee would still be invited if he didn't drive them there. Lee always told her to stay out of it though, so she did.

As jealous as she was when Lee constantly ditched her for Antonio over the past couple of weeks, it was easier to handle than Lee's "friendship" with this asshole. It hurt knowing he'd pick him over her, even just once a week. With Antonio, Lee came home glowing and grinning, not with tense shoulders and a defensive attitude. She could handle her jealousy of Antonio; he made Lee happy. This asshole just made him anxious.

Panic simmered in Lee's eyes. He looked at Antonio, searching for a clue.

*Lee, don't put your decisions on him. Say no if you don't want to go.* Tara didn't mind being his excuse to get out of things, but Lee needed to grow a spine.

Antonio shrugged. "Don't worry about me, Angel. I have to get my beauty sleep."

"I was talking to Leland, not you, *Carlita*. If I wanted to hang out with a fish, I'd go to an aquarium," the intruder sneered.

Tara saw red on his behalf, even if the attempt at shade was weak as shit. She was on the verge of cussing him out when Antonio gave her the slightest shake of his head.

She closed her mouth. He'd probably dealt with worse in his time. Like actual insults. *When's the last time I got so protective of someone I just met?*

Lee looked caught. Resigned, he agreed. "No, yeah, I'll find you after the show."

The intruder left victorious. Tara glared daggers into his back.

Antonio grinned at her. "You were about to kick his ass, weren't you?"

Tara laughed, nodding. "Dude, you're so much nicer than that asshole. Sorry, Lee, but I can't stand him!"

Antonio cackled. "I'm glad at least one of Lee's friends likes me. I have no idea what I did to piss him off—I never met him before, as far as I know."

Lee looked abashed. "Sorry, he's like that to everyone."

Tara scowled, but Antonio replied before she could. "Lee, you're not responsible for his behavior. If he has a problem with me, he can bring it up with me. Until then, it's his problem." He stood up. "Anyway, I should get ready. It was lovely to meet you, Pussycat. I can tell we're going to be good friends."

Tara rose too, giving him a tight hug. "Yeah, I guess you're okay. Just know your days are numbered if you do anything to hurt my bestie."

"You gonna make me hang out with the fishes?" Antonio teased.

Tara grinned. "I'll leave you at the aquarium."

They both laughed, still hugging. Lee stood up too, putting his arms around both of them. "This did not go how I expected, but I'm glad you two like each other."

Tara's heart overflowed. Lee had been trying to tell her about this. Not about Antonio per se, but allowing more love in. *I hate when Lee's right.* Antonio had already won her over, and she wasn't even upset about it. A little jealous perhaps, knowing Lee would spend less time with her, but she was happy for him. *Who am I and what have I done with Tara?*

---

# Sunny

SINGING ALONG TO THE Peaches song blaring in her headphones, Sunny booted up her computer while she danced around the bedroom she shared with her little sister. Her red toenails shined like rubies against the Landlord Gray carpet squares.

The apartment was clean and tidy. She was freshly showered, shaved, and with plenty of time to dress in something sexy, then relax and join a game with her online friends before her session with Blanche.

Other than her friends, gaming was her favorite escape. The gaming desktop was the one luxury she'd bought when she'd started working. Her mother had flipped when Sunny had spent two months' rent on her computer, but Sunny would do it all over again. As always, Sunny did what she wanted (within reason), and assumed she'd be forgiven. Sunny had inherited her independent stubbornness from somewhere, after all.

Needless to say, her mother would lay the guilt on thick if she ever found out about Sunny's Vagina Fund, the secret account where she deposited any cash she got. Just thinking about that inevitable conversation made Sunny roll her eyes and groan as she pulled her fishnet stockings up her smooth legs.

Everything Birdie did supported the family; Sunny and her sister Luna were expected to follow her example. Sunny happily complied most of the time; both Sunny and Birdie sent any money left over after bills to their extended family in Thailand. Sunny liked doing her part, contributing to the family however she could, but not at the cost of her life and happiness. She would save the small fortune for her upgrade without her mother finding out.

She'd already saved up enough for the laser hair removal and her boob job, both of which pissed her mother off. Not that she didn't want Sunny to get them, but Sunny hadn't told her mother about her procedures until after they were over, knowing Birdie would have a lot to say about the cost. And she had. But the guilt trip then didn't bother Sunny as much; there was nothing her mother could do about it. What was done was done.

Sunny huffed as she shoved Luna's pastel riot of hoodies over to her side of the closet and pulled a vintage black velvet dress out of the back, where Sunny's more femme outfits were tucked behind her work clothes. She carefully unzipped the low-cut back before working it over her hips.

It was better to ask for forgiveness than be shamed out of something that would bring her one step closer to being her true self. Her mother wasn't transphobic; she just had different priorities, covering the fees for her hormones and the fertility clinic where she'd dragged Sunny before she'd started HRT—

A chime from her computer startled her, disrupting both her off-key singing and her internal monologue. *It's a good thing I'm home alone. Luna and Mae would both be giving me shit if they were here.* Her mother was working as usual, and her little sister was "studying" with her "friend who is a boy but not a boyfriend."

Sunny had chosen an outfit that was admittedly a little risqué. Her mae would say she was dressed like a hooker. Her velvet dress was revealing, and the fishnets wouldn't win her any favors if she got caught by her inconsistently traditional mother. But she wanted to look hot for her session with Blanche.

Her heart pounded at the reminder that she'd be having sex with Blanche in a matter of hours.

Thinking about *that* would do no good. The session was happening, no matter how much she kept overthinking it. Sunny closed the Session with Blanche tab and found a pair of Luna's heels that her sister never wore—she was more of a Crocs girl—to complete her outfit. They pinched her toes, but she wouldn't have to wear them far. Just a few blocks to the bus stop and up three flights of stairs.

*Ugh, the bus.* She'd have to wear a jacket to hide her cleavage from creeps. Such a shame, because she looked amazing.

Sunny checked her reflection in the hall mirror, thrilled as always to see herself dressed femme. The soft curves from her waist, the fullness of her chest, the long line of her legs in the dress...she looked how she felt inside. Aside from a few shadows on her face, but makeup could wait until after her game. Too often, her headset messed up her contouring.

She had fallen in love with gaming in elementary school, after a car accident killed her dad and brother. At the age of six, Sunny had been left as the only AMAB person in the family. On top of the anxiety and grief drowning their home, she had struggled with a confusing understanding of her identity. Sunny, who always pretended to be a mom to her dolls when she played house, suddenly had to be a big brother and responsible son. All of her mother's expectations had landed squarely on her small shoulders; the pressure had never once eased up in the nearly twenty years since.

Gaming had become her escape from her responsibilities, from parenting her younger sister and mother who still grieved for her husband and son that Sunny barely remembered. The mother who never seemed to understand that Sunny's dreams for herself didn't perfectly align with the role her mother needed her to play.

Sunny's mouth filled with blood again. She had to stop chewing on her lip long enough for it to heal. The past few days since their last fight had been tense; Sunny had been avoiding Birdie more than usual by hiding in front of her computer to keep the tension from breaking into another fight. But at least she had that. Online, Sunny had the power to be whoever she wanted.

Sometimes, she wished she could still play house like she had as a kid, drinking pretend tea with her stuffed animals while her brother ran around with his friends. Being someone else for a while sounded fun. Instead of a lonely twenty-four-year-old nerd living with her mother and sharing a room with her sister, she could be a trophy wife with friends who got together for book club but never would read the book. Or the cute girlfriend of someone who wanted to take care of her every wish and whisk her away for romantic weekend getaways.

*I'd be the wine-drunk Stepford Wife, causing drama. On Real Housewives of Bellamy, I'd be the trashy one from Eastside.* "Money can't buy happiness but it bought me these tits."

Sunny laughed at her own joke. Sure, she had other escapes these days—hanging out at Blanche's, for instance—

With a huff, she closed the Blanche tab again, sat at her computer, and opened the server to see what her online friends were up to.

She had no idea who her gamer friends were in real life, but they had been playing together for nearly a decade. They were the first people she'd introduced herself to as "Sunny (she/her)," the first step toward coming out to her mom. She'd practiced for life after transitioning by seeing how it felt to be treated as a woman by people who didn't know her.

And though she never told them anything that might personally identify her—or out her as trans—they were still true friends in the way that only online friends could be. The group was cool, mostly bros who weren't raging misogynists, racists, or homophobes.

A few others in their group were already signed on to the server.

> **Sunnywith0meatballs** Happy Saturday everyone!
> **Black_Hawk_Up88** Hey Sunny!

Sunny squealed in excitement as other greetings rolled in. Black_Hawk_Up88 was her online BFF. They were genuinely good friends, despite knowing nothing about the other's real identity. She wasn't even sure he was a he; he lurked on mute like she did.

He hadn't been on in weeks, which wasn't uncommon. Sometimes he would disappear when he struggled with his mental health. The first time he'd done it, she was sure he had died. But he reappeared eventually, making funny sarcastic comments and bad jokes like he hadn't been missing. She'd learned to trust that Black_Hawk was okay and did her best not to jump to conclusions as the weeks stretched on and her worry grew.

She'd sent him a message the first time he'd reappeared, and they had bonded over their shared experience of parental expectations and anxiety. They'd been tight ever since, with Black_Hawk making puns about her mains in the chat, and Sunny teasing him for always being the first to get taken out when he was supposed to be the healer. Black_Hawk was probably a straight white cis neckbeard, but it was nice that someone in her life understood her.

She sent him a DM as they waited for others to join.

> **Sunnywith0meatballs** Hey! Missed you the last few weeks. Hope everything is good with you?
> **Black_Hawk_Up88** Oh you know, overwhelmed by life. Nothing the gym and therapy can't help with.
> **Sunnywith0meatballs** Want to talk about it? I need a distraction.
> **Black_Hawk_Up88** Not really lol. I just had an intense emotional situation, and then my mom doubled down on how she thinks I should live my life, and work is the fucking worst. The usual.
> **Sunnywith0meatballs** Sorry your mom sucks bro.
> **Black_Hawk_Up88** Lol. She's not as bad as yours. I just can't collect my thoughts when she's on a roll, you know? I wish I could press pause on real life sometimes.
> **Sunnywith0meatballs** Why don't you try it? Boop her on the nose and pause her.
> **Black_Hawk_Up88** lmao I doubt she'd understand. She hasn't played a video game since Duck Hunt, which she thought was too violent. But I'll try it with my next SO (lol like that'll ever happen) and let you know if I survive.
> **Sunnywith0meatballs** Next SO? What happened to E?
> **Black_Hawk_Up88** Ughghghghhfjfsjfioesjo that ended a long time ago. It's for the best. I'd rather not talk about E ever again if that's cool. What's going on with you? Why do you need distracting?

Sunny had been avoiding thinking about how she was hiring her crush to fuck her. And the moral implications of that. And the personal, emotional, and physical implications of that. Sunny was terrified. But excited. Mostly excited. *Because my session is in three hours and I have to be excited. Not scared. Excited.*

But the annoying, irrepressible tabs full of doubt only went away once someone told her she was right. And if she could talk about this with anyone, it'd be Black_Hawk. He was the friend she turned to when she couldn't talk about shit with Lee or Blanche. Lee would have talked her off the ledge by now; he'd probably expect her to struggle with the whole "keeping it professional" aspect. But he'd been too busy with this Antonio character.

Not that Sunny was terribly upset by that. If he'd been around, she probably would have already canceled on Blanche tonight. And frankly, she didn't want to cancel on Blanche.

*If this blows up, I'm blaming Lee.*

---

**Sunnywith0meatballs** You might regret asking lmao. TMI time!

**Sunnywith0meatballs** Have you ever had someone you're not supposed to catch feelings for? But you know you're going to catch feelings? And you're going to have sex with them soon and you have to pretend you don't feel anything after? Even though you know it's going to be mind-blowing, life-changing sex?

**Black_Hawk_Up88** Are you stalking me?

**Sunnywith0meatballs** It's not you, dumbass.

**Black_Hawk_Up88** No, I just had a similar situation recently. I mean, I caught feelings mid-nut instead of before, but same.

**Sunnywith0meatballs** Must have been some pussy. Or dick. Idk what you like.

**Black_Hawk_Up88** It was. Mind-blowing, life-changing, as you said. Now I'm fucked up and stuck figuring out how to move on.

**Sunnywith0meatballs** Would you take it back if you could?

**Black_Hawk_Up88** Fuck no! Best decision I've ever made. Totally worth the emotional whiplash and sore wrist from jerking off to the memory every night since. I'm sure you'll be fine!

**Sunnywith0meatballs** Ha! All I needed to hear.

---

The spark of hope in her heart burned brighter. Emotional whiplash was doable. *And if things go well...* She *shouldn't* hope that Blanche might reciprocate her feelings, but they had so much love between them. Maybe Sunny could show Blanche how that love could grow into something more.

But Blanche had been clear: this was a strictly professional service, one that could change her life for the better. No matter how much Sunny wanted Blanche to return her feelings, Sunny could figure it out afterward. If she didn't go through with it, she'd regret it; the Help From Blanche tab would never close.

# Chapter Fourteen

## Tara

Tara sat at the bar by herself, people-watching after Lee and Antonio had clocked in for work. Blanche had a client, so it'd be a few hours before she could go home. *Might as well stay and watch the show.*

"Hey there." The blonde woman from the weekend before sat next to her.

*Or not watch the show.*

"Oh. Hi..." Tara trailed off, unsure of what to say. Blondie had been nice enough, but Tara didn't leave it on the best terms. *Do I ever? I'm the reason I don't do repeats.*

"Rebecca." Blondie provided, her blue eyes teasing.

Tara nodded. "Right, I remember."

Blondie shook her head with a smile. "No, you didn't. But it's not like you gave me your name either." She rubbed her bare ring finger. "Look, I'm sorry if I did something wrong last weekend. I'm kinda new to this dating women thing."

That was no surprise. Last weekend, Blondie had been anxious, glancing for her friend's approval as she'd nervously introduced herself while Tara waited for her drink. "You didn't do anything wrong that would bother a normal person. I just don't really do the talking and dating stuff. Something I should work on." Tara circled the rim of her drink with her fingertip. *I'm an open fucking book today.*

Blondie touched Tara's hip. "Well, can I make it up to you? I'd love to buy you a drink and see where the night goes."

Tara nodded, surprising herself. "Sure. Fair warning, I'm shit at small talk."

Blondie's lips curved into a shy smile. "Well, I'm happy to practice small talk if you don't mind giving me a lesson in oral. I've never come as hard as I did last weekend. I can't stop thinking about it." A blush crept up her cheeks as she spoke.

"I'm down." Tara grinned, oddly eager at the prospect. After having her mind melted by Mr. Brown Eyes on her birthday, Tara had resolved to make everyone feel the way she had. A new bar had been set for her to reach. And while Blondie had appreciated her skill the weekend before—twice—Tara knew she could do better.

Less than half an hour had passed before Tara remembered why she didn't do small talk. Sexually charged flirting with strangers? Piece of cake. Listening to Blondie ramble on about her job? Hell, even remembering Blondie's name again? Not her lane.

Blondie seemed to sense Tara's interest fading. "Do you want to go back to my place? I live a mile or so away, if you don't mind walking."

Tara swallowed hard as her alarm bells tensed, poised to ring. As a rule, she didn't go to people's houses. But she had promised Lee to try the whole dating thing earlier. *Time to get out of my comfort zone.*

She heard herself agree. Tara followed Blondie out of the bar as she texted Lee.

> Dude you can still see my location right? bcuz im going to Blondies and if i die you have to come get my body so my ghost can haunt you for eternity.

> I thought we were gonna haunt each other anyway? Have fun doing it in a bed for once, Buttercup! Proud of you!

> omg. ur so much. can you or can you not see my location?

> No, yeah, ofc I have your location.

Before she knew it, she found herself stepping into Blondie's apartment. *Her place seems nice. Normal.* Tara tried to take in details, but her mind struggled to focus. Blondie was still talking, now about how this was her first place on her own after she had divorced her husband, who she'd married right out of high school.

Tara hoped she sounded sympathetic as she gave canned responses. As gorgeous as Blondie was, Tara couldn't bring herself to listen. *Why am I like this?* If Blanche were here, they'd make Blondie tea and ask questions to make her feel special. They were better at the whole listening thing than Tara. Hell, even Sunny would be rambling on about the books on the shelf or the art on the walls.

Tara just didn't care. She had read everything she needed to know about Blondie last weekend when she'd scanned her. She had been nervous and insecure. The straight friends with her had looked at everyone like they were in a zoo. The pale band on her finger said she was recently single. The tan lines below her biceps said she didn't normally show much skin.

Even now, Blondie looked more ready to teach kindergarten than drink at a bar in a modest wrap dress. She didn't have any red flags. She just wanted validation that she belonged.

In Tara's experience, baby gays usually wanted a good fuck to break the seal, so to speak. She was normally good at that. *But she just keeps talking!* And Tara was struggling to focus on anything.

"So before me, did you only fuck your husband?" Tara asked, finally coming up with something to say that made it seem like she'd been paying attention. *Sex. I can focus on that.*

Blondie blushed and nodded. "There was one other guy, a friend of my husband's. He convinced me to have a threesome to 'spice up our love life.' They were more into each other, and we stopped making love completely. I was too relieved to care that he was cheating with another man."

*Woof. Bitch, you need therapy. Or a girlfriend. Not a hookup with* me, *of all people.* "I'm sorry. He probably never took care of your pleasure, huh?"

Blondie laughed. "Of course not."

"Oh, shit. That sounds awful. In my opinion, everyone who sleeps with AFAB people should get tips from queer women. Both having a pussy and going down on them is another level of expertise that straight dudes could really learn from. I hooked up with this one guy a few weeks ago, and his head game was so good, he might actually be better than me. He *had* to have learned from a queer woman. I don't know how else he would've..." Tara realized she was rambling mid-sentence. "...been that good."

She kept trying to put Mr. Brown Eyes out of her mind, but he kept appearing, his gaze pleading in the mirror. She didn't want to examine why she kept remembering his pretty eyes when she'd spent most of their time together with her tits pressed against the wall.

Blondie looked surprised. "You sleep with men too?"

Tara shrugged. "If we're into each other, I'm open-minded."

Blondie frowned.

"Is that a problem?" Tara had been burned before by the biphobia of other queer folks. She never understood why they were offended that someone as "butch" as her wasn't a lesbian. She wasn't especially masc, just lazy and comfortable.

"Not at all. Just surprised. I can't personally imagine what it's like to *want* to sleep with a man." Blondie smiled shyly. "Especially when there are gorgeous women like you out there."

Tara relaxed. Relaxed as much as she could while trying not to dissociate, anyway. Already, she was catching glimpses of herself in a strange apartment, her mind floating a few feet over her brain. It was deeply uncomfortable. "Do you want to find out how talented I can be?" she asked suggestively, trying to trick herself into being present. "Last weekend was just a warm-up."

Blondie flushed, nodding eagerly. "Where do you want me?"

Tara enjoyed being bossy, but Blondie needed someone nice. Yet she'd picked Tara. Again. "The couch okay?" *Please don't say you want to go to the bedroom.*

Blondie nodded. "Should I take my clothes off?"

*I don't fucking care.* Tara had gotten Blondie off last weekend fully clothed with minimal effort. "Whatever you're comfortable with."

Turning around while Blondie undressed seemed like a nice thing to do when Blondie was obviously anxious. Tara took the opportunity to take a few grounding breaths, only glancing back when Blondie's dress hit the floor out of the corner of her eye.

Fully nude, Blondie sat on the couch with her arms wrapped firmly around her chest, legs crossed. She was beautiful, all curves and softness and blushing skin, her hips wide and rounded. Tara wanted to run her hands over her soft belly and suck bruises into the peachy thighs that pooled onto the couch cushion.

Tara could tell Blondie was a little out of her element. Hell, *Tara* was a little out of her element. Praise was not her forte, and Blondie needed validation. But if the compliment didn't spill out of her mouth automatically, it always felt fake. Lee was the only one for whom Tara could muster unnecessary validation, and even for him, she meant every word. Blondie was objectively gorgeous and, like an asshole, Tara couldn't form the words Blondie needed to hear.

Instead, she tried to explain what she'd want to hear in Blondie's shoes. "I don't want to do anything that makes you uncomfortable, okay? If there's something you want or don't want, tell me. Like, I don't kiss on the mouth, and I don't like when people grab my wrists. Do you have anything you don't like?"

Blondie shook her head.

"Will you let me know if something makes you uncomfortable?" Blondie nodded.

"Good. I'll do the same. Spread those beautiful thighs apart."

Blondie nodded again, slowly uncrossing her legs. Tara's mouth watered at the sight of her pussy, already wet between her thighs. She might be dissociating in this stranger's apartment, but her face between a pair of thick thighs was familiar territory.

Tara knelt before her, running her hands across Blondie's hips and thighs, admiring her stretch marks and soft skin. "My health status hasn't changed, and I haven't had any other partners in the past week. Is that true for you, too?"

Another nod from Blondie.

*So agreeable. She can't even look at me, let alone answer me.* "I need more than a nod. I need to hear a yes if you want this."

"Yes."

"Good. Eyes on me." Tara gently pulled Blondie's arms away from her chest. Blondie blushed but let Tara capture her dark blue eyes. Tara eagerly sucked a rosy nipple into her mouth, keeping her gaze on Blondie's face to check for signs of discomfort. *Reading body language is so much easier than small talk.* Seeing only pleasure, she slid her hands between Blondie's thighs, massaging the soft skin as she pushed her legs further apart. Gently exploring with her fingers, she slid a finger into her wet heat.

Blondie threw her head back and moaned above her, adjusting her hips to allow Tara more room.

"Look at me—I want to see your face."

As Blondie met her eyes again, Tara rewarded her with another finger, crooking and pressing gently. Blondie gasped but didn't look away. Pleased at the reaction, Tara kissed and sucked marks into her belly, her hips, her thighs, everywhere but where Blondie needed her. Not to tease, but to build anticipation for the stars she wanted Blondie to see.

"Please, please!" Blondie begged, jerking her hips. Tara pressed harder inside Blondie instead, her other hand massaging one of Blondie's breasts. She nipped at her thigh, sucking a mark on the smooth skin there before finally giving Blondie what she wanted.

Tara had barely touched her tongue to Blondie's clit, had barely tasted her, when Blondie fell apart, crying out loudly as she shuddered above Tara. Tara didn't let up, hoping to give her another one. Making people come was her favorite part, even more than her own orgasms.

Blondie had other ideas.

"Thank you thank you thank you," she cried, mascara-stained tears streaking her cheeks. Blondie cupped her face, pulling Tara up toward her.

*It didn't even seem that strong. I can do better. I need to make you see stars!* Before Tara could process what was happening, Blondie planted her lips on hers. A strange tongue pushed its way into her mouth.

Flashes of unpleasant memory rose up in Tara's throat like bile. Stale vodka and blood in her mouth. Shouting and screams and sobbing pleas.

Tara's heart pounded wildly. *I need to get away.*

She shoved Blondie off her before she lost control of herself. "What the fuck!"

Blondie's eyes swam with confusion and hurt. "What? Did I do something wrong?"

"Yeah, I literally just told you no kissing. Half an orgasm in and you already forgot?" Rage and fear coursed through her, burning her from the inside. *I need to run.*

"I thought it was an example or something!" Tears welled in Blondie's blue eyes.

Tara couldn't be bothered to care about Blondie's feelings; she needed to get out. She jammed her feet into her shoes. *I need to leave. I need to run.*

Blondie grabbed her wrist to stop her. "Wait!"

Vice grips around her wrist. The sickening thud of a skull hitting a wall.

Tara wrenched her wrist from her grip, raising her arms over her head in a defensive position, resisting the urge to fight back. *She's not attacking you.* "Don't fucking touch me! You want a lesson? Ask for fucking consent before you start grabbing people!"

Tara slammed the door as she stormed out. She didn't fucking care if that bitch was upset. She needed to get out and find somewhere safe to ground herself.

She'd barely crossed the threshold of Blondie's apartment when she froze. *Fuck. She's sheltered as hell. This will mess her up.* Tara pushed open the door again with a bang.

Blondie looked up in shock, blue eyes watering as she pulled her dress around her.

"Don't take this too personal. I'm a little fucked up. Just...find someone normal."

She slammed the door shut before Blondie could respond. *No more repeats. I knew this was a mistake.* Tara shook her head and counted her breaths. *I have to get in front of it.* She didn't have a safe place to go. Lee wasn't an option—who knew where Confession was from here? And she couldn't go home yet if Blanche had a client over.

*Inhale, 2, 3, 4, 5. I see the streetlights turning on. I see gum on the sidewalk.*

*Exhale, 4, 3, 2, 1. I hear cars going by. Someone's playing piano.*

*Inhale, 2, 3, 4, 5. I feel a breeze. And a little hungry.*

*Exhale, 4, 3, 2, 1. I taste Chapstick. Oh, that's disturbing. I'm not wearing Chapstick.*

*Inhale, 2, 3, 4, 5. I smell tacos. Oh, fuck yeah, tacos!*

Tacos should be comforting *and* cheap. She checked her phone, still breathing deeply to focus on her senses instead of her racing thoughts and pounding heartbeat.

Just another hour or two before Blanche's client left. Then she could go home and meditate and cry and panic. Maybe pretend her vibrator had pleading eyes and called her Kitten. *And listened to my fucking boundaries!*

Tara approached sex with an open mind and low expectations. Usually, she left satisfied. Or she thought she had. Fucking the redwood tree with pretty eyes had been akin to a spiritual experience. She'd seen the universe. And he'd done it without kissing her or doing stupid shit like pinning her hands against the wall. *Did Mr. Stoplight System ruin casual sex for me?*

Rough sex was fun, but feeling forced into it? No. Maybe for some people, but not Tara. *And they never ask first!* Mr. Brown Eyes had checked for consent every fucking step of the way. Sure, maybe he hadn't taken her rejection of him that well, but up until that point, he'd listened and let her know she was in control. *Maybe he's not the exception. There's got to be others like him. Because I'll never see him again.*

That thought made her strangely sad. And *that* was confusing. The feeling wasn't quite sadness, but she wasn't sure what it was. Like something was missing. A needy want akin to jealousy. The strange, vulnerable want that had risen up earlier when she'd hugged Antonio and Lee.

Tara shoved the weird feeling away. No point wasting time on it right now—or ever—if she couldn't figure it out.

She looked around as she approached the taco truck, blinking in confusion to see it was parked in front of the Modern Art Institute. Streetlights flickered on along the riverwalk, reflecting off the water. She was still on the Iowa side. She must have been dissociating harder than she'd thought if she couldn't remember how she got to Blondie's. But somehow, her feet had brought her to a safe place: the art museum.

She loved the MAI, one of those rare public spaces that felt like home. They'd never gotten kicked out when they'd loitered in the atrium on cold winter days in their teens. She and Lee had spent countless hours there without a single complaint. Auntie Alitrice had made them sign up for free programs through the Eastside Community Center when they were getting their GEDs; the MAI always had the best classes. It'd been where Lee had learned how to make music, and where Tara had picked up graphic design, so she'd have something to do after he started spending hours on his laptop.

A happy tune from a harmonica played nearby. When she looked for the source, a familiar top hat caught her eye, poking out above the concrete wall separating the sidewalk from the terraced amphitheater outside the museum.

She smiled at the sight. Yet another source of safety. Standing up on her tiptoes, she spotted only the top hat. No beret with him today. *I should have enough money for a couple of extra tacos. Walter would probably appreciate a meal.*

Tara ordered four chicken tacos and handed her debit card to the woman taking her order, exhaling in relief when it went through. *This is my splurge for the month.*

Tacos in hand, she headed toward the top hat. "Mind if I join you?"

Walter squinted to see who was talking to him. His weathered face broke into a smile. "Hey! It's Anne's girl! How ya doing, Freckles?"

Tara sat down next to him, calmer merely from his presence. "Hungry?"

Walter took the offered tacos with a laugh. "Is water wet? You didn't have to get me anything, but I appreciate it all the same, sweetie."

Tara took in the sight of her old friend. The worn top hat was hanging on, and his black wool pea coat had burn marks singing the sleeves. His rucksack looked new, probably stuffed with clothes, blankets, and whatever baubles Walter had acquired since his camp had burned down. His face was still red and craggy as always. The top hat didn't protect him from the elements, but Wanda liked fancy hats, so Walter refused to wear anything else.

"Tacos are the least I can do." She owed Walter and Wanda everything. They'd helped her whenever she'd needed, finding a spot for her and Lee even after her mom had gotten evicted from the camp. When a resident got violent or brought unwelcome people in, Walter cleared them out. Anne Sanderson had brought around the wrong kind of people. Walter and Wanda had both given Tara a kind hug before she'd followed her mother to go...nowhere.

"How's your mom? And your fella?" He meant Lee. Pretending they were a couple had been safer than being two queer kids. They'd shared a tent and let everyone think whatever they wanted.

"He's good. He's at work right now. We're still staying with Blanche. How's Wanda?" Tara ignored the question about her mom; she hadn't seen Anne in a decade. Walter and Wanda were constants in Tara's life in a way her mother had never been.

Walter's face fell. "She passed last winter."

"Oh, Walter, I'm so sorry." Grief flooded through her for the closest person she'd had to a grandmother. Wanda had painted masterpieces on scrap and hung them around the city. She insisted on her berets but never aprons, so specks of paint covered her from head to toe. When Tara was a kid, she'd leave her mom passed out and hang out with Wanda instead. The kind woman would make her lunch, teaching her about color mixing and visual poetry while Tara ate.

Walter and Wanda had been two hippies in love who'd found themselves outsiders in the '80s, left without the intentional communes they'd stayed in throughout the '70s. So he'd built one for her in Eastside, on a large island under the bridge. They'd driven their bus across the Mississippi ice one winter and stayed. The community they'd created was an ode to Wanda, a display of Walter's love. She'd painted the camp in Walter's favorite colors.

Through floods and cold winters and the Reagan administration, their camp had lasted for decades. Only to be taken down by white women complaining to the city council. By ambitious politicians who had decided riverfront beautification was more important than housing the dozens of people who had lived there for decades. By the activists who'd said they'd protect the camp but turned the eviction into a riot.

It would have happened eventually though. That was the direction Bellamy was headed.

"It was her time." Walter patted Tara's knee. "I just always thought mine would come before hers. I'm surprised I've lasted this long without her. She was my everything."

The love in his voice brought up that weird sad needy feeling in her again. Walter and Wanda had been the one example of true love she'd ever witnessed. She wanted someone to talk about her the way Walter talked about Wanda. She wanted to have that undying devotion like they had. The adoration in his voice, like how Lee talked about Antonio.

*Fuck, I'm going to have to try this dating shit, aren't I?*

# Chapter Fifteen

## Sunny

Sunny sat on Blanche's well-loved floral couch, sucking her lips between her teeth. As her second home, she'd been here hundreds of times, but it felt different as a client. The details she found tonight seemed new, even though she must have seen them all before.

Dozens of rescued plants lined the windows. A hodgepodge of thrifted furniture, mismatched throw pillows, and blankets that someone else's grandma had crocheted decorated the room. The shelves were filled with water-damaged books Blanche had brought home from Free Little Libraries.

Even Tara and Lee had been strays Blanche found on the street. Perhaps Sunny herself was a pet Blanche had felt compelled to nurture, instead of a friend introduced by Lee.

She fiddled with the netting of her fishnets.

Sunny had met Lee in middle school, subconsciously making friends with the only other queer kid in class. He'd instantly become her first friend, even though they'd had nothing in common other than loneliness and secrets. By ninth grade, their afternoons at Lee's house had turned into making out and exploring each other recklessly, the way closeted teens do.

She was grateful for the experience—it had unlocked an awareness that she'd hidden since the accident. It finally had clicked for Sunny that not every boy hated his body the way she did. Fooling around with Lee had been the first crack in her egg.

The budding relationship between her and Lee was cut short when Lee's dad had caught them one day, physically throwing Sunny out of the house. Lee had never come back to school.

Sunny ran into his little sister at Luna's school once and asked about him. Jazz had burst into tears, sobbing that she wasn't allowed to talk about him. Mrs. Jones had glared at Sunny and scolded Jazz for crying in public as she'd dragged her away.

She'd never expected to see him again, or known if Lee was even alive. She'd been too scared to tell Mae what had happened. What if Mae did to her whatever Mr. Jones had done to Lee? Or what if his disappearance was somehow her fault, like how she was sick the day of the accident, leaving Phaw to bring her brother to school while Mae had stayed home with Sunny? After all, she had been the one to ask Lee to...

Sunny shook her head, closing that tab. The accident wasn't her fault. And she shouldn't feel responsible because the Jones' were terrible parents. And yet, like Phaw and her brother, it had been safer to never mention Lee again.

Until one day, when Lee had tagged along with Tara to orientation at Bellamy Community College, where Sunny was getting her certificate. Lee had barely recognized her. Sunny had grown her hair out and been taking estrogen for a year. But Lee looked exactly the same—the spitting image of his dad.

It was like no time had passed. They were instantly fast friends again, despite still having nothing in common and Tara's best efforts to drive Sunny away. Sunny had resolved to win her over—any friend of Lee's would be a friend of hers. And, as always when the two women faced off, Sunny emerged victorious.

Through Lee, Sunny had found Blanche; a mentor, a crush, an idol, and a vision of the future. Blanche answered all of her silly questions and helped her figure out her life. Not even Tara could keep Sunny away from Blanche. In time, Tara had been won over too.

And now here they were, with Blanche about to help Sunny become a better version of herself. A confident, sexual woman. She'd had to dip into her Vagina Fund for this, but she already knew it'd be worth—

"Babygirl, do you want something to drink? I can make you some tea." Blanche's voice cut through her train of thought.

"Got anything stronger to take the edge off?" Sunny joked.

Blanche poked their head into the living room, their usual half smile replaced with a frown. "No. If you need to take the edge off, let's talk about why."

Cursing herself for never thinking before she spoke, Sunny plastered on a grin. The scab on her lip twinged in protest. Blanche might still talk her out of this, and she refused to be dissuaded at this point. "I'm just kidding. Tea would be great."

Mollified, Blanche went back into the kitchen as the teakettle whistled. *Of course, they already knew I'd want tea.* Blanche had the uncanny ability to always know what she needed.

Blanche set two steaming cups on the coffee table and sat in their favorite armchair, their dark green eyes peering directly into Sunny's mind. "So tell me what you hope to get out of this. And be real with me. I am not here to judge, just to listen and help you."

Sunny considered her answer, gazing down at her tea to think. "I want to be more confident in my sexuality and…romanticality? Every time I think about dating, I just freeze up. I didn't date before I came out, you know? I thought it'd get easier as I became more myself, but it's still paralyzing."

Blanche sipped their tea and curled up into the chair. "Safety issues aside, what are you scared will happen if you try? Say someone—not a chaser—asks you out, knowing you're trans?"

*Aside from getting murdered?* Sunny's toes squirmed through the holes of her fishnets. Becoming a headline was enough to keep her from joining a dating app. People would hit on her fairly often, but she'd rarely met anyone who actually liked her once they got to know her. There were even fewer who she was comfortable enough with to let them see or touch or fuck her. The whole idea of willingly putting herself out there made it hard to breathe through the knots tightening in her chest.

"I'm afraid that they'll say or do something to give me the Ick and I'll just accept it. Throw in the fact that I'm Thai and that opens a whole other can of fuckshit!" Sunny scoffed. "As if I don't embody a million stereotypes already being trans and Asian—I'm a fucking software engineer, for crying out loud!—I have to deal with all the chasers with a Ladyboy fetish."

She paused, pursing her lips to keep from chewing them. "I need help figuring out what I like and don't like, so I can be more confident in navigating all of that. With, like, real experience, not just fantasizing about what I might enjoy. I don't want to get stuck in a situation where I don't feel seen for who I am or as beautiful as I deserve."

With a nod, Blanche stretched out, draping their feet over the arm of the chair. "Tell me about the sexual or romantic experiences you have had."

Sunny considered her meager dating history. The few times she'd tried to date—or hook up—had all been incredibly awkward. "I've had a few experiences where I felt, at best, invalidated and at worst, fetishized. I've never been able to...come with another partner since before I started HRT, and I hate being that girl who's like, 'No, this is fine. As long as you're having fun, I'm happy.' Because that's not me! I want to come! I just don't know how to tell someone else how when I can't even get myself off most of the time. I'm hoping once I can afford to install my upgrade, I'll have more luck, but that's going to take me years."

She crossed her arms, irritated. It should be easier to transition. Cheaper. Safer. "This is supposed to be when I get to experience casual sex and get my heart broken. I'm twenty-four. I want normal twenty-something-girl experiences! I should be getting dicked down and ghosted by hot immature fuckboys! I want to join a toxic group of friends where I get passed around the whole sapphic coven. Instead, I'm paralyzed by fear at the idea of someone treating me like I'm just my body. And if I can't do this with strangers, how am I supposed to speak up for myself when I'm married to whatever nice girl my mom sets me up with?" With a huff, Sunny met the green eyes still staring at her, seeing too much of her. "I need help, Blanche."

Blanche's slight nod with the barest twist to their mouth was unreadable. "You've come to the right person."

"Right," Sunny said sarcastically. "I doubt you've ever felt the way I have."

"Remember that I'm a decade older than you and had to confront my gender identity a lot younger than you," Blanche snapped, their placid half smile veering into a sneer. "You try being the adopted brown kid in a cult full of tall-ass Swedes and suddenly they're laying hands on you because you started growing tits in middle school. Or surviving by working the streets as a homeless teenager who doesn't understand who they are or what's wrong with them..." They trailed off, putting their Mona Lisa mask back on. "Sunny, trust me—I get it. You have a lot in your favor that I didn't have. You're confident in who you are. You have a family who supports you. You're educated and earning good money to support yourself. And you have me to help you figure this out."

Sunny flushed. She had trouble imagining Blanche as anything but the ethereal deity who sat before her, but Blanche's life had never been easy. "Sorry."

Blanche shrugged and set down their teacup. "So, what makes you feel good?"

"I'm not sure? I guess I don't like penetrating anything? Like, sure it feels good but it feels wrong for my...appendage to go into things." She blushed. Saying what she liked was harder than saying what she didn't. "I can still get hard but not for very long. And frankly, the dysphoria sucks harder than anyone's mouth can, so that doesn't help at all!"

"Bitch, did you really just call it your 'appendage'?" Blanche laughed kindly.

"I haven't found a better word for it! I hate talking about it!" Sunny covered her face.

Blanche leaned closer. "I know it feels wrong, but it's part of your body. You won't be stuck with it forever, but it's the pleasure organ you have, so enjoy it while you have it. Let's find more comfortable ways for you to enjoy it until your upgrade."

Sunny nodded. "I'll try."

Blanche stood up and beckoned Sunny to follow. "I'm going to be vanilla with you. Not anything so sweet as kissing or anything unless you need it as aftercare, but no paddles or gags for you, Babygirl. Go ahead and get naked. Do you have a safeword you like to use?"

Sunny shook her head, unzipping her dress as Blanche led her to the bedroom. She couldn't imagine a universe where she'd use a safeword with *Blanche*.

"We can share mine. You might not need it because this will stay vanilla, but in case you get overwhelmed and need to stop. Lutefisk. Repeat that back to me."

"Lutefisk. That's so unsexy."

The half smile turned into a smirk. "That's the point, Babygirl."

Sunny hesitated, gripping the halves of the zipper to keep them in place. Blanche had seen her in all states of undress before, but this was different. On the other hand, she needed to get naked for what she wanted to happen. *And I'm objectively hot, "appendage" aside. What is there to worry about?* She closed the Insecurity tab as her dress dropped to the floor. Her bra and panties soon followed.

Blanche eyed her appreciatively. Sunny burned under their gaze. "Go ahead and lay down. I'm going to start by touching you. I'll ask questions to check in, and we'll talk about what language you prefer. Do you want me to fuck you like we talked about?"

Sunny nodded eagerly as she crawled onto the bed. Heat flashed through her body just thinking about Blanche fucking her. "Yes, please. It's the one thing I know I like."

Blanche's robe fell into a puddle on the floor.

Sunny forgot how to breathe. Their muscular thighs and curvy hips drew Sunny's eyes up to their small breasts. A small daisy tattoo decorated their left collarbone.

She swallowed, trying to get control of her heart racing. That tattoo was a reminder that this was Blanche, and while she adored Blanche, they were unattainable. There was a reason this had to stay professional, even if the sight of Blanche nude before her was a revelation. She'd seen all of Blanche in bits and pieces, just like Blanche had seen all of Sunny's bits and pieces over the years as they'd shared complaints and experiences.

But this was all of Blanche, bared to her the way she'd always dreamed of. And here Sunny was, bared to them in turn as they crawled over her.

Their calloused hands skimming up her thighs, their weight sinking into the bed, was a palpable reminder of what had drawn Sunny to Blanche in the first place. They were what she aspired to be, someone who loved themself and their body unconditionally. Sunny envied Blanche's lack of dysphoria, their comfort in looking in the mirror and feeling perfectly at home in their chassis. She'd get there one day, just as Blanche had eventually. Even if her path was much different from Blanche's.

Blanche was intersex, but Sunny doubted if they knew exactly what that meant for them internally. They had run away before their adopted family could "correct" their body, and they'd never gone to a doctor to get answers. They were much happier living as a non-binary femme than a man, despite the difficulties that came with their identity. They deserved a life without the fear of being pressured into surgery, a life with the same opportunities as everyone else. Instead, they'd struggled to survive, to maintain some semblance of bodily autonomy.

And sure, in theory, Blanche could find a different career than sex work if they wanted, but there weren't many options for someone who had never finished middle school. Blanche was a dominatrix so they could control who they interacted with. There were contracts and NDAs and a different power balance than when they'd worked—

"Babygirl, are you with me?" Blanche snapped their fingers in front of Sunny's face.

"Sorry, Blanche." Sunny smiled apologetically. "You distracted me."

"Bitch, you were having a full-on silent conversation with yourself. Your mouth was moving and everything." Blanche straddled her thighs, their hands running up Sunny's neck and down her torso, cupping her breasts. "Focus."

"I'm here." Sunny sighed as her nipples tightened. She gripped Blanche's thighs, grounding herself in the firm muscle beneath her fingers. She wanted to enjoy this fully, not let her brain distract her.

Blanche asked, "What do you call these?" They bent down to lick her hardening nipple.

Sunny groaned. "Um...tits? Titties? Breasts, but that sounds wrong when you're doing that to them."

The puff of air from Blanche's chuckle prickled her skin. "Your tits are so beautiful."

Sunny arched her back into Blanche's mouth around her nipple, luxuriating in the sensation, the praise. She moaned again, surprising herself. She always tried to be so quiet living with her mom and sister. It was a rare occasion when she wanted to rub one out *and* her family wasn't home. Here, she could make noise to her heart's content.

"Turn over. Ass up. Legs apart."

Sunny complied. Being bossed around stole her breath away. She didn't have to tell Blanche what to do. They were going to take care of her. *New kink unlocked, I guess.*

Blanche palmed her ass gently but firmly. "Do you have any words you prefer for any parts below the waist?"

Sunny shook her head.

Their hand made small circles around her hole, her nerve endings singing at their touch. Sunny wanted more, wanted Blanche to go deeper, to fuck her now. She told herself to be patient as she moved against their hand.

"Can I make suggestions?"

"Yes, please. I don't know what to call any of it without sounding like a textbook." All Sunny knew were the clinical terms from hours of researching how vaginoplasties worked. There was something terribly unsexy about most medical terminology for genitals. It was one thing for other transgirls on the Internet to proudly claim the words they used, but Sunny had no idea what she would want someone else to say, what might feel right.

"I'll give you options. You don't have to call your body anything you don't want to, but if there's a word you like, tell me." Blanche's hand pressed against her perineum, fingers gently nudging into her inguinal canals. *Seriously, who named these?* "Gooch, cooch, muff, perineum. Any of those feel right?"

"Muff, I guess?"

"Muff it is, Babygirl. You can always change your mind later if it doesn't stick." Blanche's hand moved to her testicles, gently massaging.

Sunny froze. Wrongness shot through her. "I don't like that part being touched."

*"That part"* was an essential part of her future vagina, but acknowledging the existence of *"that part"* gave Sunny the Ick. She pretended *"that part"* wasn't there most of the time.

Blanche's hand quickly withdrew, pressing into her muff gently. "Yes, ma'am. Can I give suggestions or would you rather not name that part?"

The only half-decent sex she'd had before this had been with a bi guy she'd met at the BCC Gay Straight Alliance. He had always fondled *"that part"* despite her repeatedly telling him to stop. She'd hooked up with him three times before finally giving up on him ever learning that she didn't like the same things he did.

Sunny pushed back into their hand, more comfortable now that their fingers were somewhere she liked. She grew eager in anticipation, the Icky knot in her stomach loosening. "I'd rather not."

"Understood, Babygirl. I'll avoid the area."

"Thank you." Sunny sighed, grateful that Blanche was working around her dysphoria, instead of trying to push her through it.

Blanche kept a hand working on her. Their other hand wrapped under her legs to where her "appendage" hung. Sunny cringed at Blanche's touch as much as she craved it. The Wrongness conflicted with her pleasure.

"You said no penetration, does that include hands going around it?"

"It, um, feels good, just wrong. So like, it's okay but not great. I usually prefer it through my panties or something. Touching it like that is a little dysphoric."

"I have an idea." Blanche's weight left the bed. They came back with dental dams, lube, and a condom. "Sit back against me."

Shivering with anticipation, Sunny leaned back against Blanche's chest, luxuriating in the heavenly body behind her. Blanche's tits pressed against her shoulders, their erection against her back. Sunny's breath caught; they were hard for *her*.

Blanche kissed her neck while they opened the dental dams, laying one across her pelvis. They used another on the underside of her, pushing it up against her body with a cupped hand.

Sunny moaned at the sensation, head falling back on Blanche's shoulder. The pressure and the slick wetness sent shockwaves of pleasure through her whole body. She'd never felt this good whenever anyone touched her before, herself included.

"I'll take the moan to mean this feels good." Blanche laughed before asking, "Girldick? Clit? Mound? Vagina? Cock? Sex?" Blanche listed suggestions, their free hand massaging a tit.

"Clit?" Sunny managed to say. "Maybe girldick."

"Your clit feels amazing, Babygirl. I can't wait to watch you come."

*I might have a praise kink.* Sunny had never felt this comfortable during sex, never felt this free. Never felt so herself. "Can you please fuck me then?"

Blanche smiled against her neck as she begged, earning a nip of their teeth on her earlobe. "So impatient. Can you come like this without me fucking you?"

A pang of anxiety shot through her. "Maybe, but I'd rather not."

Their responding snort blew hot across her neck. "I am still going to, but I'm just curious. Some women on HRT come easier with prostate orgasms versus external touch. Especially considering how long you've been on estrogen, you might have an easier time with that. Less dysphoric, too."

"But this feels good!" Sunny leaned back against Blanche and thrust into their hand.

"You can do both, Babygirl! Just don't feel pressured to touch yourself there if it feels wrong. You might want to get a toy for prostate stimulation and a vibe for your clit, so you can do both depending on what you're in the mood for."

Sunny could never imagine having sex toys in the room she shared with her little sister. But then again, she'd already have to hide her case of dental dams because she was definitely going to buy these in bulk.

"Keep touching yourself for me while I get you ready."

Delirious with pleasure, she rubbed her clit the way Blanche had been moments before. It was slightly less exhilarating than the feeling of someone else—Blanche in particular—touching her, but it still felt better than any other time she'd touched herself.

Blanche pushed her face down into the bed. A fingertip circled her hole again, this time cold with lube. She inhaled sharply.

"Relax, Babygirl. You ready?"

Sunny nodded as they pushed their way in gently with a finger, stretching her slowly open. Sunny moaned into the pillow; the sensation was too strong to contain inside. She worked her clit as Blanche's finger moved deeper. They added another, scissoring her open. She hissed whenever they brushed against her prostate, her nerves alit. *Keep it together, Sunny. I need them to fuck me.*

"Prostate? P-spot? G-spot?" Blanche asked. "Do you want to name that, too?"

"Uh..." Sunny forgot that Blanche had been making suggestions. "Yeah?"

Blanche laughed and continued slowly fucking her with their fingers, pressing into the spot that left stars behind her eyes. "You might also find you can come multiple times this way. Your body may not be your ideal self yet, but the estrogen is already transforming you from the inside out, so let yourself or a partner explore the possibilities. Don't pressure yourself to orgasm. Focus on the pleasure without a destination and see what happens."

Just when she was on the verge of begging them to hurry up, the crinkle of the condom wrapper hit her ears. "Ready, Babygirl?" At Sunny's nod, Blanche's erection replaced the fingers inside her, pushing in agonizingly slow.

They pulled her back upright against their body. The angle sent shivers and moans through her. Fucking Blanche was glorious.

Blanche took over rubbing Sunny's clit. "You set the pace, Babygirl. Fuck yourself using me."

Sunny's orgasm threatened to erupt from their words alone. She rode Blanche, slow at first and then faster and harder, grinding against them as they kept pressure on her clit.

Their other hand pinched her nipples, their teeth and tongue on her neck. "You feel so good Babygirl. I want to hear those lovely moans when you come for me."

The words put her over the edge; she came with a loud cry, tremors running through her body and up her spine.

"See? Fucking beautiful." Blanche kissed her neck once more and started to pull out.

"Wait." Sunny stopped them. "You need to come too. Please, use me back."

Blanche consented with a hum. They gently pushed her down so her face pressed into the pillow before truly fucking her. Biting the pillow, Sunny almost felt like she might come again from the euphoria, from the pride as Blanche's hips stuttered into hers, their moans falling softly in her ears before they pulled out.

"How do you feel?" Blanche asked. "Sunny, you're crying! Are you hurt?"

*I'm crying?* Sunny shook her head. "I've never felt this good before." She rolled onto her back, looking up at Blanche with a hopeless grin, sobs escaping her.

Blanche curled up next to her, gently wiping away the tears and lube and cum with a damp cloth. "What do you need? Anything you want to talk about?"

"Can you kiss me?" She was soft, vulnerable, in a way she had never been before. This rush, this high made her feel beautiful, sexy, *loved* as a woman. She had never felt this euphoric before, this at peace with her body. Her heart flew.

Blanche nodded, lips kissing her tears away, her forehead, and her eyelids before settling on her lips. The kiss was more chaste than she'd wanted, but it was exactly what Sunny needed. A kiss from this deity who made Sunny feel alive and loved for the first time ever.

# Sunday, June Second

# Chapter Sixteen

## Lee

Wrapped in the comforter in Antonio's bed, Lee watched Antonio transform into Carlita, admiring the muscles rippling under his brown skin before it was buried in layers of shapewear and costume. Watching him dress felt intimate. Saturdays, he changed at Confession, but Antonio preferred to get ready at home on Sundays. Lee hadn't asked why, but he imagined the pitchers of mimosas floating around for his hungover castmates had something to do with it.

"Any plans after the show?" Lee asked, breaking the quiet.

This felt ritual by now. After a month of spending most nights with Antonio, Lee had felt bold enough to bring two days of clothes over after the party the night before, assuming he'd be invited back after the brunch show. A safe assumption—every time Lee got ready to leave, Antonio would invite him back the second their free time aligned, no matter the hour.

And of course, Lee accepted, still in awe that this fling with Antonio, this dream from which he never wanted to wake, hadn't yet ended.

The muscles in Antonio's back tensed as he rolled his nylons up. "Dinner with my family. Then probably go to bed early."

There was no invitation, not even a hint that one would come. Lee's heart sank, but he kept his voice steady. "Oh. Cool."

"Yeah, summer school classes officially start tomorrow. I need to get my beauty sleep!" Antonio singsonged, scrunching his nose as he held up his padding to decipher which side went where. His chipper voice fell into one of the many wordless songs he often hummed.

Maybe Antonio was telling the truth and not an excuse, but resignation still burned in Lee's throat like bile. He'd gotten too complacent and ruined it somehow. Maybe he'd not been helpful enough, or too quiet. He should have checked to see if Antonio wanted to fool around when he'd come over after the party last night, instead of assuming they'd go right to sleep...

Taking a steadying breath, Lee focused on the arpeggios in Antonio's humming to clear the clouds of insecurity. He was reading too much into it; Antonio was just worried about classes. Abandoning the warmth of Antonio's bed, he crawled forward and took the padding from him. "Here, I'll help."

"Thank you, Angel!" Antonio waited until Lee held his foam thighs in place before pulling another layer of tights up. Lee stuffed the butt pads into position, about to plant a kiss on Antonio's neck, when Antonio added, "Speaking of classes, I might not have much free time this week."

"Oh?" Lee asked carefully, pulling from the smooth skin before his lips could brush it to sit back on his heels, sinking into the bed. The fight against his disappointment ached with each deep breath.

"Yeah," Antonio's controlled tone made Lee's stomach clench. The same tone that every other guy he'd caught feelings for used when they'd let him down gently. "I'll probably be tired from teaching. It's been a while since I dealt with teenagers I'm not related to."

"No, yeah, that's cool." Lee's heart sank as he forced himself to take Antonio at his word. After all, Antonio would be tired from teaching.

But he couldn't trick himself into tasting anything other than the bitterness of his disappointment. Antonio had showered him with adoration, made him laugh harder than he could ever remember, and treated Lee like he was more than a warm body. He'd been so different from everyone else.

Until now.

*I was right. This one does hurt like a bitch.*

"I just probably can't hang out until next weekend. Sorry." Antonio glanced back over his shoulder, but his hazel eyes never met Lee's.

Lee forced a smile. "I get it. Don't worry about it."

## Blanche

"Blanche, if you were a beverage, you'd be the cereal milk left over from Fruity Pebbles," Sunny said, unprompted. She didn't look up from scrolling on her phone, curled up on the couch. Her face stayed expressionless as if she hadn't spoken.

"Thank you?" Blanche furrowed their eyebrows in confusion. Sunny was in one of her zones, probably unaware that she'd even spoken. "What prompted that?"

Sunny blinked and held up her phone with a bashful grin. "Oh. Meme."

"I'd rather be an Arnold Palmer." Blanche turned back to the window, sipping their herbal tea as they watched the afternoon sun streaming through the rebar and scaffolding of the condo starting to go up next door. They gave it another few months before their plants lost most of the sunlight. Already they'd had to rearrange the dumpsters to protect the cat colony in the alley from the constant construction equipment rumbling by.

They might have asked her what beverage she'd be, but encouraging Sunny to talk seemed risky when they were alone. Tara had been a reliable buffer since their session, but she was on a *date*. And Lee was presumably going to Antonio's after work. Blanche missed him, but they knew the day would come when their ducklings would leave the nest eventually. And Lee was so at ease, happier than they'd ever seen him.

"Do you believe the universe wants what's best for us?" Sunny asked. "Or has a plan?"

Blanche shot her another confused look. "I don't think the universe cares." A half-truth, but getting into the nuances of free will versus fate with Sunny didn't seem like a good idea.

"But what if..." Sunny paused to look at Blanche. "You ever see a sign that you're on the right track? That you're doing the right thing? Or a hint to the answer for a decision you've been unsure of?"

Dread filled them, disrupting their peace like the growing shadows of the rebar across the street. If Sunny was seeing any signs that Blanche wanted more than friendship, she was deluding herself. "Not since Daisy died," Blanche said pointedly. "She was my North Star. She always guided me toward what would be best for me."

Hopefully, that reminder that Blanche was unavailable—and not just because of their friendship—would be enough for Sunny to pick up on the hint. Sunny's crush had shown no signs of dissipating after their session, just as Blanche had feared. She kept tiptoeing closer to the line, giving Blanche long looks and wistful sighs during normal, meaningless conversations.

And yet, Blanche couldn't find the heart to tell her to get it together. The sweet, earnest attention was a nice change from their clients. And Sunny hadn't crossed any lines yet...

A key in the door surprised both of them, even more so when Lee walked in.

"Lee!" Sunny jumped up to hug him. "Where the hell have you been, Loca?"

"Why do you always quote Twilight at me?" Lee snorted as he hugged her back, dropping his backpack by the door. "And you saw me yesterday."

"Yeah, but that was at Confession for happy hour! It's not the same!"

Blanche's smile as Lee kissed their cheek in greeting was more relief than anything. If Sunny was paying attention to signs from the universe, Lee walking in the door should be a sign against talking about her feelings for them. "Not going to Antonio's tonight?"

Lee shook his head as he perched stiffly on the couch, his shoulders rising around his ears. "Nope. He had plans with his family."

Sunny and Blanche exchanged a look.

"You want to talk about it?" Blanche asked.

He shook his head, his smile a pale imitation of the easygoing Lee they knew. "Nothing to talk about."

Sunny and Blanche exchanged another look.

Before Blanche could press, the front door banged open again as Tara stomped into the room. "God, that was fucking weird!" She collapsed dramatically over Lee's lap, who gathered her in his arms. "I'm so glad you're here."

"Your date not go well, Buttercup?" he asked.

"You had a date?" Sunny asked. "Why didn't you tell me?"

"I did, you just don't listen." Tara flicked her off. "But yeah, met up with the woman I hooked up with at Confession yesterday. We went to the art museum. But, get this, so did her ex. She spent the whole time oversharing about their relationship while pretending not to see her, even though she made us follow her around."

"That sounds...hilarious," Sunny teased.

"It was so awkward." Tara sighed heavily. "Especially when I came back from the bathroom, and they were making out in the middle of the gallery."

"What did you do?" Blanche asked, fighting a smile at Tara's expense. She hadn't had the best luck with her fledgling attempts at dating.

Tara chuckled. "Ducked into one of the side galleries before they saw me. Some star installation surrounded by blackout curtains, so I figured I could hide there until they left."

"Why is that funny?" Lee asked with a knowing sigh.

"Because there was this fucking beauty hiding in there, too." Tara sighed contentedly. "Legs for days, long hair, real pretty dress that left nothing to the imagination. She was crying by herself in there. Weird, but she struck up a casual conversation about how dark and hopeless the world can be. So I offered to distract her, and it ended well for both of us."

Lee rubbed his forehead. "Sounds like you took advantage of a sad woman."

"Nah, dude!" Tara shook her head. "She was willing and ready. Busted a vibrator out of her purse and everything."

"How do you do it?" Sunny asked, staring at Tara in awe.

A valid question. Tara didn't try to attract attention, yet people always approached her. Blanche chalked it up to Tara's complete inability to mask her facial expression and extreme thirst for the human form. Anyone with half a brain could pick up on if she was into them.

"Aren't you supposed to be dating? Did you get her name at least?"

"Lee, my *date* was busy playing tonsil hockey in the next room. The sad lady called me 'Stargirl' and talked me through a guided tantric meditation while she edged me. Take a wild guess which experience I preferred?" Tara elbowed him. "I'll keep trying, but not everyone is so lucky to find someone who can't get enough of us like you are."

Lee grunted noncommittal, his nostrils flaring slightly.

Sunny sighed. "I should go. Mae has been on my ass about missing dinner on the weekends."

They all said their goodbyes as she trudged dramatically to the door. Relief, and guilt for feeling relieved, flooded Blanche; they could relax without worrying about what Sunny might do or say for the rest of the night. That walking on eggshells feeling was new; Blanche hated it.

Tara winced as soon as the door swung shut. "I know she has a weird relationship with her mom, but she really doesn't consider her audience, does she?"

Blanche snorted. "Why, you want to have dinner with your mom? Do any of us?"

Tara shook her head, reaching up to rub the furrow in Lee's forehead with a gentle smile. "No, but at least her mom cares."

"We have us to care, babes," Blanche reminded her. And themself. "Let's have our own family dinner. Lasagna night?"

"Hell yeah!" Tara grinned and jumped off Lee's lap. "I'll preheat the oven."

Lee followed. "I'll help. Last time you forgot to take the plastic off the Stouffers."

# Thursday, June Sixth

# Chapter Seventeen

## Antonio

Lifting weights was incredibly boring. Dancing and gymnastics—hell, even yoga—were far superior to picking heavy things up and putting them down. Antonio's exhale was sharp with annoyance more than effort as he prepared to lift the bar at his feet. Sweat trickled down his lower back from the fetid air in the gym, despite the fans humming in every corner.

"Back straight, Tonio," Gabe reminded him as he spotted Richard on the squat rack nearby. They made an odd pair, Gabe's giant frame towering behind the shorter man. Richard's pale face was shiny with strain, bright red against his white-blond hair. Gabe watched calmly, eyes flicking between Richard and Antonio for a sign that either needed help.

Antonio bit back a snarky retort—because Gabe was right, his back was not straight—but he still made a show of shaking his ass while glaring at Gabe over his shoulder before lifting the bar. It wasn't Gabe's fault he was pissy today. And had been the whole week.

Nor was it his students, his new coworkers, or his family's fault—not even Cassie's. Even though she was far nosier than any helicopter parent he'd encountered at work.

The bar clinked as he set it down, and clinked again when he lifted it a half second later. It wasn't even *his* fault he was so irritated this week, even if it felt like it. That was how life was. Sometimes, he was just annoyed and in his feelings, and he had to deal with it like a boring, responsible, mature adult now.

Being New Antonio was agonizing.

Antonio strained through the rest of his set, exhaling his feelings through physical exertion because that was what Gabe said worked for his depression. Just like his sister used yoga to help her anxiety, so he'd been joining her every morning before work. And cooking dinner every day because his stepdad had said infusing food with love brought joy to everyone who ate it. Antonio had not been able to resist a joke about cum being the secret sauce, earning him a swat to the back of his head from his mom.

He set the bar down with a heavy clank.

All of his attempts to manage his emotions and his cravings, while both teaching and performing at Confession, were fortunately working. He should be happy about his progress. The seven-month milestone of sobriety had passed so uneventfully that he'd barely noted it. Old Antonio would never have made it this long without relapsing.

But four days without seeing Lee ached. He'd expected it to suck, but not this much. Maybe it was his fault for asking for space, or never giving them the chance to develop a rapport outside of hanging out in person because they were always together, but Lee's radio silence since Sunday stung.

Antonio crouched to take the plates off the bar, fighting the burning in his eyes and the ache in his chest. That was why he was at the gym in the first place. To prove he was fine on his own. That he didn't need Lee. Even if breathing was easier when Lee's arm was around him. Even if thinking was safer with that soft baritone to drag him back from the darker corners of his brain. Even if he'd barely laughed this week without Lee to tease him for his corny jokes.

"Hey, hope I'm not too late!"

Antonio froze, his thoughts scratching like a record at the sound of a too-familiar, too-upbeat voice. He turned to see Phineas Watkins jogging up to Gabe and Richard, pulling his locs back into a ponytail with a scrunchie.

All of his two-point-five friends together in one place.

Without warning.

Gabe greeted him with a side hug. "Hey, Phin. Didn't think you'd be here!"

*That makes two of us.* Antonio yanked the last plate off the bar.

Phineas grinned, unzipping his hoodie. His loose tank top revealed a spray of freckles dotting the brown skin of his wiry shoulders. Far too much of his ribcage was showing for it to be an accident. "Better late than never, am I right?"

Richard snorted. "Considering you usually show up never, it's a surprise that you're only late."

Turning his back, Antonio racked the plates to avoid the inevitable awkwardness. Already, the demons whispered blurry memories of Phineas. Their manic laughter in club bathrooms; coming down from a high to find himself and Phineas and a few strangers naked when he had no memory of who anyone else was or where they were; panic adding a sour tang to Phineas's tenor as he called Antonio's name over and over while Antonio sank into darkness—

"Tonio." A voice like honey—thick and sweet and deep—interrupted the whispers. A heavy hand landed on his shoulder. "Need a hand?"

Antonio blinked and forced a smile as Gabe took the wipe from his trembling hands.

"Oh shit. Sorry, Tonio. I didn't know you'd be here," Phineas winced apologetically. "You want me to go?"

Antonio's sternum twinged with guilt. Phineas had *said* he'd understood that Antonio needed space from him, however Phineas was a people pleaser through and through. He was probably taking it personally. But being around him without mentally preparing meant getting sucked into bad memories; Antonio had to put sobriety before Phineas's fragile ego. If Phineas hadn't been Gabe's friend, Antonio would have ghosted him without a second thought.

Life wasn't that simple—he refused to be the reason Gabe lost any good people in his life. And Phineas might be a mess, but he was good people. So they had an agreement. As the resident flaky workaholic, Phineas was *supposed* to give Antonio a heads-up if he would actually show up to something. Antonio couldn't blame him for crossing that boundary if he hadn't known he'd be at the gym.

Swallowing his irritation—a skill he'd been mastering this week since he'd been pissy more often than not—Antonio shook his head. "I was just about to head out."

Gabe set the bar back on the rack and tossed the wipe in the trash. "Yeah, Tonio and I were about to leave, but Richard was planning to stay and work out a bit longer."

Richard shot a look at Gabe, his blue eyes narrowing. "Was I."

"Yup!" Gabe shot him a tense smile back. Antonio avoided looking at Phineas, who was far too smart to not pick up on Gabe's ham-fisted attempts to smooth things over.

With a huff, Richard turned to Phineas. "We're not running."

Phineas beamed and clapped Richard on the shoulder. "But cardio is the best part!"

Richard smacked his hand away. "One mile, that's it."

Gabe steered Antonio to the entrance with a thick hand around his neck. "Come on, I'm inviting myself over for dinner."

Antonio let his friend push him out of the gym and toward his car, comforted by the familiar weight on his nape and the fresh breeze in the parking lot. Gripping his neck like he was a puppy had been Gabe's go-to method of keeping Antonio from retaliating against their bullies in high school. Annoyingly, it still calmed him far more than it should. "You don't need to—"

"You look like a sneeze could send you spiraling. This is for my peace of mind, okay? Let me make sure you're okay." Gabe dug Antonio's keys out of his pocket and unlocked his car. "Are you okay to drive, or do you want me to take you home?"

Antonio grumbled over the lump of gratitude in his throat. "I'm okay to drive."

"You want me to text Lee to come over, too?" Gabe asked.

"No, I don't *need* Lee," he snapped, climbing into the driver's seat. His run-down Civic groaned in protest, but she would get him home. Like she always did—for him and all of his siblings, handed down from one Flores to the next until the car was family too. In a softer voice, he added, "I can't rely on one person."

He'd missed Lee too much the past few days. Even if it hurt that Lee hadn't reached out, Antonio was determined not to be clingy. He hadn't checked his phone obsessively like he wanted to, not wanting to be reminded that he had no new texts from the man who brought him so much joy. The one who also acted like it was no big deal when Antonio had said he wouldn't see him for a week. Who had not sent a single text since Sunday, when they'd spent every day together for over a month.

"You're so gone for him," Gabe teased. "Just text him so you can stop pouting."

"Oh my god!" Antonio groaned with a laugh. "I'm fully aware, but I can't rely on him as much as I have been."

"You're doing the right thing, Tonio. Even if it sucks. But maybe find a balance between love bombing and ghosting this time." Gabe patted the roof of the car as he pushed the door closed. "Okay, I'll be right behind you."

With another sigh to cool the constant irritation burning in his chest, Antonio forced the sticky clutch down and turned the key. The car groaned and sputtered to life.

Even if Antonio's confusing riot of feelings was overwhelming him, Lee clearly wasn't there yet. And as uncomfortable as it was to be on the opposite side of the coin for the first time in his life, Antonio could live with that. They hadn't talked about labels or feelings or what this was between them yet. Antonio just had to stop reading into it and deal with the ache in his chest like a responsible, mature adult.

That's what this week was about, proving that he didn't need Lee to function. He had his family, friends, and therapist—all of the support he needed.

Hopefully, Lee would want to stay a part of that, too.

---

## Lee

"He's done with me, isn't he?" Lee checked his phone for the millionth time, dismayed to find no new messages since the "Good Morning" text he'd sent on Monday.

A chorus of "*No!*"s rang out, along with a cloud of smoke from Tara's mouth. She sat opposite him on the couch, where she'd been pouting since Lee had beaten her at Mario Kart for once (they'd then both lost to Sunny). Tara had been hogging the bong since. Which was fine with him—Blanche always smoked shit that made him think too much and then pass out.

Tara chucked a popcorn kernel at him; it bounced off his glasses and onto the floor. "He told you he started teaching this week. He's probably just tired and on the verge of murdering teenagers. Don't be illogical about this."

Lee huffed and wiped the smear of butter from the lens. "Yeah, but he hasn't texted me this week. I've almost considered double-texting him."

"What's wrong with double-texting?" Sunny asked from her spot on the floor by Blanche, sipping the cider Lee had picked up so Sunny would have something to drink besides straight whiskey. "I double-text all the time."

Lee bent down to retrieve the popcorn from under the coffee table and set it on a napkin. "It can make you look desperate."

"It does?" Sunny looked to Blanche and Tara for confirmation.

Both of them shrugged.

Lee shook his head. "It's different with us—we're friends. Double-text away. But you may want to consider that next time you're talking to someone new."

"Oh, it'll be a while before I talk to someone new," Sunny muttered.

"What do you mean?" Lee asked. As far as he knew, she wasn't seeing anyone. She wouldn't have been able to keep something like that to herself.

"Nothing." She smiled innocently.

Lee narrowed his eyes—Sunny's fake ass smile always meant she was hiding something—but Blanche changed the subject before he could press it. "Do you have plans to see him again, Lee?"

"No." Lee huffed in annoyance as he nursed his cider. Sunny was his excuse, but he'd bought the cider for himself, too. He didn't understand how Tara and Blanche could drink brown liquor straight. "I haven't needed to make them. He always asks me to come over before I leave. At least he did until Sunday."

"So make some plans," Tara suggested.

"But he hasn't texted me back." Lee shouldn't feel as disappointed as he did. He knew this was coming eventually.

Tara passed him the bong. "Here. You're overthinking. Why are you following this stupid double-text rule? If you want to hang out with him, ask him to hang out."

Lee took it with a laugh. "Buttercup, *you* really wanna talk about stupid rules?"

Tara rolled her eyes. "My rules are *not* stupid, they're sensible."

He fiddled with the bong as an excuse not to reply, hoping the conversation would move on by the time he gave it to someone else. Getting too high would make him impulsive, and he wasn't sure he wanted to go there when he was already in his feelings.

Blanche swirled their whiskey. "She's not wrong. You've been seeing him for over a month now. You can look a little desperate. And knowing you, you haven't told him you're upset about anything."

*"Never let anyone know they have power over you. Shows them where you're vulnerable."* With a wordless puff of smoke to blow away his father's voice, Lee handed Blanche the bong.

"Oh, have I said too much?" Blanche raised an eyebrow. A smile played on their lips. "He probably thinks you're not interested if you won't even send him two texts in a row or tell him you want to see him. Give him a chance to do better."

That sounded entirely too logical to be reasonable after days of feeling worthless. "I miss the days when we didn't talk about my dating life."

"Seriously, Lee, you're so silly sometimes." Sunny huffed. "When we met him, he was super into you. He won't care if you text him more. He'll be happy you're thinking about him."

"I hate to agree with Sunny, but she's right," Tara joined in. "Text him. Ask him to hang out tomorrow after you're done with work."

Lee grumbled as he took out his phone. Still no reply from Antonio. But maybe they had a point. Maybe Antonio wouldn't think anything of it. After all, Lee didn't think Antonio looked desperate, and Antonio had sent four texts where most people would send one.

There was no way he was high, not from that little puff. But here he was, typing and sending a message before he could second-guess it.

> Hope your first week of teaching is going good. Is it cool if I come over tomorrow after the show? I want to hear all about it.

A constant chain of vibrations buzzed in Lee's hand before he even had a chance to put the phone down. The hum from each new notification soothed the sour twist of his stomach that had grown with each passing day. Lee sank into the couch as his screen lit up over and over again.

> OMG yes plz!!! I miss youuuuu! :-D

> I have so much I want to tell you but the overarching theme is: kids are annoying, but I am even more annoying!

> Oh my goddddd I am so sorry! I never saw your text! >.<

> Good morning, Angel!

> Pretend I sent that on Monday

> And Tuesday and yesterday and this morning

> And let's be honest, tomorrow too

> Because I'll probably forget

> Anyway, come over when you're off! I'll wait up for you!!

Sheer relief sat uncomfortably with the realization that he'd wasted all of these days worrying about looking desperate. But Antonio could have texted him, too, and he hadn't. Lee had imagined that Antonio hadn't thought about him once, but with this response? Maybe he'd been pining like Lee had been. Maybe Sunday hadn't been the end, after all.

Tara nudged his thigh with her foot, grinning at him. "Told you so."

Lee realized he was smiling too. "Shut up, Buttercup."

> Looking forward to it.

# Saturday, June Eighth

# Chapter Eighteen

## Lee

Lee rapped softly on the door to Antonio's apartment, hoping he was still up. He had come straight from the burlesque show at Confession, but it was after two in the morning. Antonio didn't perform on Fridays, but Lee needed to see him after five days of overthinking what he'd done wrong.

Antonio opened the door, blinking up at him with a smile. "Hey, Angel."

"Sorry, did I wake you?"

Antonio nodded and pulled Lee down for a kiss. "Yes, but I fell asleep on the couch so I'm glad you did. My back would be a mess if I stayed there."

Lee grinned, wrapping his arms around Antonio. "You're so old, babe."

Antonio looked up at him with a confused smile, his cheeks darkening.

"What?"

"I don't know whether to be annoyed because you just called me 'old' or kiss you because you just called me 'babe'."

"Oh. Is that okay?" he asked cautiously. *Now is not the time to be getting clingy if he's getting sick of you.*

"That you called me 'old' when I'm only four years older than you? No, not okay at all." Antonio laughed. "But 'babe'? Angel, you can call me that anytime!"

Lee grinned. He'd been debating all evening if he should ask outright if this was ending to cut his losses. But with Antonio blushing up at him, those hands sliding around his shoulders to pull him down for a quick kiss, Lee decided against it. He wanted to enjoy this while he could.

Antonio pulled Lee further into the apartment. "How were the titties tonight?"

"Jiggly as always." Lee wasn't exactly the audience for their burlesque shows. The dancers were artistic and athletic, he supposed, especially the routines with silks and poles. "Chas sits in the booth with us on Fridays, which...you know how they are."

Chas spent most of the show teasing Freddy. Flirting aggressively with Freddy, more accurately. She often sat in Freddy's lap and put her hat over his eyes as the dancers got increasingly naked. All while Lee third-wheeled next to them.

Antonio laughed. "She's the one who wanted burlesque. Dunno why she's jealous."

"Honestly, Freddy isn't much better. He covers her eyes the whole time and they miss half the lighting cues." Lee leaned on the kitchen counter as Antonio washed dishes, grabbing a towel to help dry. He found it endearing that Antonio always started tidying up as soon as Lee walked in. "How was your first week of summer school?"

Antonio grinned as he handed Lee a fork. "Oh, you know. Summer school kids. They were resistant to everything until they learned I live over Eastside. I guess that has more clout than being a short twink who went to Driftwood Academy."

"You told them you're gay?" Lee asked, surprised.

"Babe, I didn't need to tell them," Antonio laughed. "I can't exactly hide it. But yeah, I want to be open about who I am, you know?"

"Have I told you how amazing you are?" Lee asked.

Antonio shook his head with a grin, squeezing out the dishrag. "Nope, definitely the first time I've heard you say that. Tell me again?"

Lee smiled back, happy to pretend they hadn't had the same conversation many times before. "Seriously. That's braver than I could be. Proud gay man and all that, but it's not anyone's business but mine for a reason."

Antonio shrugged. "I majored in education because it would have been nice to have an adult I could relate to. Not that Bellamy Public Schools are as overwhelmingly Caucasian as Driftwood Academy, but there may be one kid who needs someone like me in their life."

Lee might have paid attention in class if he'd had a teacher like Antonio. He'd never had any connection with the adults at school; all of his teachers in Eastside were burnt-out idealists with overwhelming class sizes, and Lee had always kept his head down to avoid attention. "How'd you end up going to school in Driftwood anyway?"

"I grew up there."

"What?" Lee had never met a single Black person living in Driftwood at all, let alone a whole family. "Why?"

Luckily, Antonio laughed at his confused expression instead of taking offense. "My parents thought Driftwood would have more opportunities for us. Same reason they moved to Bellamy from LA in the first place. I dunno if it panned out. I still got bullied and into fights and shit. I just had fewer friends and better drugs." Antonio blinked, falling silent, his eyes focusing on nothing in particular the way he did when the conversation turned too close to certain topics.

"So you had a shit time at school but still went into teaching," Lee murmured, hoping to bring him back. "Those summer school kids don't know how lucky they are."

"Sweet talker." Antonio waved a hand and smiled up at him, fully present once again. He wrapped his arms around Lee. "Still, it might be easier to connect with them if the curriculum wasn't so out of date. If it's not referencing classical music, it's about Frank Sinatra and Elvis. I just want to throw something newer in there, but none of it is 'appropriate'."

"Want me to make you a track with the samples you want?" Lee suggested, hoping his desperation to be useful wasn't obvious. "I can bleep out the bad words and whatever else you need."

"Can you do that?" Antonio asked. "Like, legally?"

Lee shrugged. "I mean, probably not *legally*, so don't sell it. Just send me a list of what songs and concepts you're teaching, and I'll throw it together."

Antonio's smile sent his heart fluttering. "Have I told you how amazing *you* are?"

"Have I told you how bad you are for my ego?" Lee basked in the dreamy haze of that smile before pushing the glow down. *Don't read too much into it. You don't know how long this will last.*

"No, I'm great for your ego! Seriously, you're so talented. I appreciate you helping me out on this, when you could be making real music."

"That's enough of that." Lee laughed. Antonio's words always got to his head. "It's just a hobby to make some extra cash."

Antonio smiled. "No, I loved the bounce track you posted the other day!"

"Oh, God, you listened to *that*?!" Lee covered his face in embarrassment. The bounce track had just been for fun. No one was supposed to listen to it, let alone Antonio. "Tara just discovered Big Freedia, and she gets a little obsessive, so after hearing *3rd Ward Bounce* nonstop while she just sat there working, I made a track to try and get her to dance."

"Did it work?"

"No! You ever seen someone listen to bounce and just sit still? It's so weird! Anyway, no one was supposed to hear it but her."

Antonio laughed, looking earnestly into his eyes. "I listen to everything you post, Angel. I promise, from one musician to another, you're so talented!"

Lee's heart skipped a beat as those hazel eyes looked at him with adoration. "'Musician' is a strong word. I just push some buttons on my computer."

Antonio shook his head and pulled out his phone to play the song Lee had made. Lee tapped his fingers automatically in time to the Triggerman sample that filled the room. "You made music. Good music. Ergo, you're a musician. An artiste!" He set his phone on the counter and tugged on Lee's hand as the heavy beat took over. Lee pressed his forehead against Antonio's as they danced together, bodies moving in time to the beat.

Unable to fight his smile, Lee closed his eyes, enjoying Antonio's body pressed against his, cupping his ass to pull him closer. Strong hands gripped Lee's hips. Their breath mingled as they clung tightly to each other, syncing their movements.

The quiet validation of the moment—dancing to a song Lee had made simply because Antonio liked it, liked *him*—finally overshadowed the angsty-ass funk he'd been in the past week. He never expected to find this, let alone with who wanted him, who believed in him. And he'd found it with Antonio.

He was so screwed and he loved every moment of it.

A banging sound interrupted their trance. "Shut the fuck up!" came a shout from one of Antonio's neighbors.

"Sorry!" Antonio called, pausing the music with a sheepish grin. "I forgot it's late."

Lee pulled him close again, steering him to the couch, needing to be near him. He sat and pulled Antonio into his lap, pressing kisses into his neck.

"I missed you this week." Antonio exhaled softly. "It was weird not seeing you."

Smiling against Antonio's collarbone, Lee murmured, "I missed you too."

That was an understatement. Tara was probably right; Antonio was just busy. But it didn't make the five days without him any easier. Thanks to his near-constant presence since they'd met, Lee's hope that Antonio might return his feelings had grown roots in his heart. But over the past week of silence, that hope had wilted along with his ego. Hearing that Antonio missed him back was enough to unfurl the smallest blossom again.

*"Never let your guard down. People will always tell you what you want to hear until they get what they want from you. You can only trust God and me to steer you straight."*

Lee kissed Antonio's neck, breathing in the warm, clean smell of his skin to remind himself to stay present. Now was not the time for one of Dad's toxic life lessons. His dad would say it was a red flag that Antonio was saying everything Lee wanted to hear, but his dad's unbending paranoia was unimaginable in a moment like this. Antonio could take whatever he wanted from Lee, and he'd gladly give it to him.

Antonio gasped as Lee hard sucked on a sensitive spot behind his jaw. "I was trying different ways to decompress after work, but I have to say this is way more effective than a movie."

"Happy to help," Lee teased, gripping the muscular ass in his lap. "Any requests? To help you decompress, of course."

"Just want you to fuck me, Angel." Antonio kissed him.

"You sure?" Lee asked against his lips.

"When I said I missed you, I meant it. I've been digestively preparing for this since you texted me yesterday." Antonio smiled into their kiss before it turned passionate, tongues and hands roaming. Antonio's whine as Lee thumbed his nipple blended with Lee's moans when Antonio ground against him, ringing through the small apartment.

"You really need to start keeping condoms and lube by the couch," Lee teased as Antonio pulled his shirt off. Lee's tongue was running up his chest before the shirt hit the floor.

"This apartment is tiny. It's like a whole five feet away," Antonio replied, hands fumbling with the buttons on Lee's shirt.

Lee pulled it over his head instead, ignoring the sounds of thread snapping as a button flew off. "Five feet too far, babe." He wrapped his arms around Antonio's waist and stood up.

Antonio's lips found his neck and sucked hard, just as Lee stumbled into the bed over him with a groan, kicking off the rest of his clothes. He pulled Antonio's shorts off and pushed his knees up to his chest.

Pressing kisses down his leg, he glanced up, breath catching in his chest at the desperation in the hazel eyes looking back at him. Lee held his gaze as he sucked a mark on the sensitive skin of Antonio's inner thigh. "Hand me the lube and keep your knees up like this."

Antonio grabbed the bottle from the nightstand and passed it to him, along with a condom. He wrapped his arms around his legs, keeping his ass exposed for Lee. "You're making me do so much work."

Lee laughed as he licked a stripe up Antonio's erection. "Okay, pillow princess."

"I am *not* a—" Antonio's retort was cut short by a moan as Lee swirled his tongue around the head of his dick and worked a lubed finger past the tight ring of muscle. "Fuck!"

Lee pleasured Antonio with his mouth as he worked him open, opening his throat to take him deeper. He had to make this good. He wedged another finger in as Antonio relaxed around him, sighing a contented babble of praise when Lee brushed his prostate.

If he gave this everything he had, maybe sex would be enough to keep Antonio around; it was the only part of Lee that anyone had been interested in before. Antonio made him feel like he was worth so much more than that, like the past month was a dream from which Lee never wanted to wake. His eyes burned as Antonio's hips bucked impatiently, his dick bumping the back of Lee's throat.

"Lee, get up here," Antonio whined. "I don't want to come before you fuck me."

With a grin, Lee slowly kissed his way up Antonio's body, until Antonio got impatient and pulled him up by the ears.

Antonio gently wiped the tears dotting Lee's eyes and the spit from his chin. "You're so fucking beautiful." He pulled Lee into a kiss, his tongue slipping between Lee's lips to devour his mouth.

His heart melted at the earnest honesty in Antonio's compliment. Fumbling with the condom, Lee managed to roll it on without breaking their kiss. Their moans harmonized, buzzing against Lee's lips as he pushed into Antonio, the tight heat sucking him in. His fingernails digging into Lee's ears and neck made him shudder.

He gripped Antonio's calves resting on his shoulders, fighting to stay in control after so many days apart. His mouth didn't cooperate, a "Fuck, you feel so good" spilling out. Lee bit his lip. Now was not the time to blurt everything out. Not while Lee didn't know where they stood.

"I missed this," Antonio panted.

Fighting the desire to read too much into all of the sweet things Antonio said, Lee smiled down at him and rolled his hips slowly. "Missed fucking me?"

Antonio propped himself up on his elbows, bringing his hazel eyes intoxicatingly close. "I missed everything about you."

Heart fluttering, Lee kissed him. The romantic shit Antonio said made it so hard to keep his heart from flying from his mouth. Reading too much into this was dangerous. Saying it out loud and being left in the cold again would ruin him. Instead, Lee kissed his longing into Antonio's lips, fucked that aching need that had plagued him all week deep into Antonio's body, where it was safe.

Wrapping his hands under Antonio's hips, Lee lifted him roughly against the headboard, fingertips digging into his skin to keep him close. Antonio cried out, eyes rolling back as Lee fucked him harder, desperate to show Antonio how much he'd missed him, how he belonged with him. Even if he couldn't bring himself to say it, Lee wanted him to feel it.

The bed banged loudly against the wall with each thrust. Antonio's long fingers grasped the headboard behind him for support, calves tightening around Lee's neck like he wanted to keep Lee there forever.

"I've got you, Tonio. Touch yourself." Lee managed to say, swallowing the more romantic words that threatened to spill out.

Wrapping one hand around himself, Antonio bit his lip, cheeks puffing out as he panted. "I won't last much longer."

"Don't hold back." Lee wasn't sure he would last either. He was already fighting his orgasm. The feelings he'd been ignoring all week were rushing to the surface, making him terrified of what he might do or say when he came. "Say my name when you come. Let all your neighbors know who's fucking you like this."

Antonio huffed a laugh and cried out Lee's name loudly as he came a few moments later, back arching against the headboard.

Lee lost what little composure he had. The deep groans from Antonio's throat echoed the devotion that Lee couldn't voice. The pulsing of Antonio around him ached as hard as his bone-deep want. Pleasure contorted Antonio's face into a mask of agony, mirroring the discord in Lee's heart. A string of curses and thankfully nothing else flew from his mouth when his orgasm sent him curling around Antonio, burying his face in his neck.

"Some of us are trying to get some damn sleep!" came a shout from the neighbor.

Antonio banged on the wall. "Buy some fucking earplugs!"

They looked at each other and burst into laughter. Lee fell back, pulling Antonio over him as they shook. Lee couldn't remember if he'd ever laughed so much before, if he'd ever been so comfortable with anyone else. Even Tara, who knew him better than he knew himself, never drew all of him out like this. The surge of vulnerability was almost enough to make him confess how much he wanted—no, not just wanted, loved—Antonio.

*Really? Love?* Lee tried to scold himself. But honestly, yes. Love. Lee had tried to stay rational, but he was in deep. As if catching feelings too fast again wasn't bad enough, now he'd fallen head over heels when they were just talking. His jaw ached as his smile fell. The least he could do was keep it to himself and not ruin the moment.

Antonio kissed his chest. "You're fucking perfect, Angel."

Lee's heart fluttered at the praise. Antonio always said shit like he meant it. It was hard to remind himself not to believe it. He shook his head. "You're just saying that because you're—what'd you call it? Decompressed?"

"Nope. You are literal perfection. Even if I am very decompressed." Antonio smiled shyly at Lee from where he lay on his chest. "You want to come over tomorrow and help me 'decompress' again?"

"No, yeah. Should be fine." Lee nodded, forcing a smile back. Whatshisname could figure out another ride. At least until Antonio got tired of him and he woke up from this dream. For now, Antonio wanted to spend time with him, and that was music to Lee's heart.

# Chapter Nineteen

## Antonio

"How do regular people do this?" Tara pulled out a chair, scraping the concrete floor. She threw herself down at the table in Confession's downstairs restaurant.

Since Antonio had first met Tara a few weeks ago, Blanche and Sunny had been added to the open invitation for their Saturday happy hours. Hanging out with Lee's family was delightful. Especially somewhere beside their apartment. He'd only been there once, but the skunky smell was…a lot. The demons in his head had plenty to say about weed.

"Do what, Buttercup?" Lee asked, rubbing her shoulders between the straps of her tank top. Her skin was ghostly pale beneath the scattering of freckles.

Tara dramatically sighed into her arms. "Get to know people? Date? Active listening? I hate it. Why can't we just order sex like pizza? I'd tip extra if they don't talk to me."

"Did something happen?" Blanche asked.

"I gave someone my number and he's texted me six days in a row. It's so much."

Antonio's laughter rang with everyone else's. As strong as his unspoken feelings were for Lee, he had fallen equally as hard for Lee's family. He liked Sunny's snarky comments and self-righteous rants. Tara's unapologetic authenticity and begrudging affection. The knowing looks he exchanged with Blanche.

*Other than the one where they obviously recognized me.* Thankfully, Blanche had pretended not to. They had woken him up from a drunken stupor to go perform more than once before he'd moved to New York. But if Blanche wanted to give him a chance to be a better person, he wouldn't let them down.

Hopefully, they liked him, too. New Antonio's social life was restricted to his family, Lee, and two-point-five agoraphobic friends otherwise. Being included in Lee's chosen family was exactly what Antonio needed. They didn't care that he was a walking disaster, instead welcoming him as he was. No pressure. No judgment. Just friends hanging out in a relaxed, low-anxiety social situation. He couldn't imagine going back to life without them, especially Lee.

His heart fluttered as he stole a glance at his...*Boyfriend? Lover? Future husband?*

Antonio froze, shocked by his own thoughts. *Future husband? Really?* While it felt like he'd practically fallen in love with Lee at first sight, he'd minimized it as merely lust with an emotional spark. And maybe that had been true at first, but he was increasingly sure his romantic feelings for Lee were real. He wasn't gaslighting himself. Or just gassy. He wanted everything—a future—with Lee.

That was terrifying.

Lee filled all of the empty parts of Antonio's heart, shooing away his demons without realizing it. Considering what it would feel like to lose Lee, if he had to be alone with his demons— *Slow down, Romeo. I cannot rely on one person to stay grounded. I refuse to put all that on Lee.*

He started when Lee met his gaze; he'd been caught staring. With an unabashed wink, Antonio stayed drowning in Lee's eyes. The late afternoon sunlight had brought out the lighter flecks of amber. He imagined how Lee's brown eyes would look with his glasses off. How his rich brown skin would glow in the golden light pouring in through the windows. How those eyes would look up at him through half-closed lashes, while Lee sucked...

*Okay, that's enough.* Antonio turned back to Tara with burning cheeks. He had no shame about staring at his...*boyfriend?* But ignoring Lee's friends to fantasize about him was too far. He risked another glance at Lee, who hid a knowing smirk behind his fist.

"I'm destined to be alone. This is the universe confirming it," Tara complained. "I just find everyone so boring when they talk at me.

They're all too nice, but like in a way where I can tell they aren't listening to me either."

"Maybe you just suck at texting? Or anything less drastic than a pre-ordained lifetime of loneliness," Lee teased.

"Maybe it's a sign to take the stick out of your ass," Sunny said, abrasive as always when it came to Tara. Sunny had been charming when Antonio was introduced to her. Tara got a different side of Sunny than the bashful smiles he'd experienced.

"Yeah, I'll take the stick out of my ass and shove it up yours!" Tara retorted.

Sunny batted her eyelashes in Tara's direction. "Promise, Tara-Bear?"

"Don't call me that!" Tara crumpled a cocktail napkin and threw it at Sunny.

Antonio added a lyric about "Tara-Bear" to his Tara Song. He loved annoying nicknames. She had been briefly taken aback when he'd called her Pussycat, but Tara-Bear got a stronger reaction out of her.

"Not to interrupt...whatever is happening here," a grating voice cut in. Lee's so-called friend sneered as he sidled up to Lee.

Antonio fought the urge to tell this guy to fuck right off. Lee had insisted they were cool, so Antonio kept quiet. Lee still had never introduced them, but this "friend" obviously didn't like Antonio. *Not that I care.* If Forehead had a problem with him, that was on him.

*Maybe it's good Lee keeps that part of his life away from me.* Antonio couldn't imagine leaving one of these parties with his mental health and sobriety intact. Lee had barely mentioned what exactly happened, just that they weren't that fun and he'd rather hang out with Antonio instead. The omission of any detail was all Antonio needed to know that he should stay away.

"Leland, you're driving us tonight, right? There's a party in Drift-wood." Forehead positioned himself between Lee and Tara, leaning his hip on the table. With anyone else, it would have seemed casual, but blatantly blocking Tara felt intentional.

Tara met Antonio's eyes with a deadpan blink.

Antonio glanced up to catch a glare from Lee's friend. He exhaled slowly, stifling his annoyance for Lee's sake. Lee's shoulders, already rising to his ears, grew more tense as he pushed his glasses up. A pensive moment lingered while Lee formulated a response.

Maybe the delay meant Lee was deciding how to tell his friend to find another ride. They'd talked about hanging out tonight after the show, so

Lee had an excuse this time if he didn't want to go. *He didn't exactly say yes, but he'd rather hang out with me, right?*

Regardless, he didn't want to control Lee's choices. Antonio had come between Gabe and his ex. He was resolved to take the high road so that Lee wouldn't have to choose between his friends and his partner like Gabe had. Even if Lee's catty friend reminded him of his former friends back in New York, the ones who had become his only support system after Gabe (and by extension, Richard) had cut him off and Phineas had already moved to Bellamy.

Unlike Gabe, his New York crew had given him no tough love or understanding. Just sex and poppers and coke and molly and weed and Adderall and endless vodka sodas. And when those didn't work, Xanax and Klonopin and Ativan. Whatever feeling he was overwhelmed by, someone had a pill to erase it.

Darkness crept in as he half-remembered those blurry nights.

*Stay present. I'm around good people.* With a wave of his hand and a quiet hum of his Intentions Song, Antonio shook off the brief flashes of bad memories. He'd cut personal ties with everyone from New York for a reason. Antonio hadn't bothered setting boundaries; they wouldn't have respected them. Instead, he'd ghosted everyone and announced his move back to Bellamy on his Insta once he was out of rehab. Now they were mere social media connections.

"Um…" Lee searched Antonio's face as if for clues.

*Please come home with me,* Antonio silently willed. He tried to look patient as his not-yet-boyfriend made up his mind. Lee could be indecisive, but that didn't bother Antonio. He was learning to read Lee's nonverbal answers. But this wasn't a decision Antonio should make.

Lee turned back to Forehead. "No, yeah, I got you."

*Dammit.* Hurt scratched at his ribs. *You should have said something.*

"Great choice, Leland." The friend walked away, throwing one last glare at Antonio.

The negative energy Forehead had brought lingered on Lee's face.

"You okay, Angel?" Antonio asked quietly, swallowing his disappointment. Lee's heavy expression worried him.

"Weren't we gonna hang out tonight?" Lee stared at some imaginary spot on the table.

*Is he upset I didn't say something?* Anxiety flared in his throat. This was one of the moments when he wished he'd made an effort with his past situationships. Navigating this tension was foreign. The demons whispered that Lee would leave if he messed this up.

Antonio ignored them. *Keep a friendly tone. Be reasonable. Play it cool.* "Yeah, but if you want to drive your friends, that's fine. We can hang out whenever."

"So you didn't forget. You just didn't say anything." Lee's normally warm brown eyes were hurt, his gaze accusatory.

"Why should *I* say something if you'd rather hang out with *his* ass instead?" Annoyance shot through any echoes of the Intentions Song, drowning out the verse about not lashing out in anger. "You're the one who didn't give me a straight answer if you wanted to come over. I guess that answers that question!"

"Yeah, that answers a lot of questions." Lee pushed away from the table and stood up. "Freddy needs me for something." He left without looking at Antonio.

Antonio sat frozen, stunned into silence as Lee walked away. *He just...left?* Shame burned away his annoyance and hurt spread from his sternum; Lee had assumed the worst from him and had been driven away simply by Antonio defending his silence. "What the fuck just happened?" Antonio turned to Lee's family. "Is *he* mad at *me*? What the fuck did *I* do?"

"It's not what you did. It's what you didn't do," Blanche answered. "Lee wanted you to tell his friend that he had plans. And yes, we all know how irrational that sounds."

"Why is it on *me* to do that? That guy hates me for no reason." Antonio gestured to Tara for help. "Saying he should go last time almost caused an argument. It would've been worse this time if I told that bitch to get lost because Lee said he'd hang out with me first!"

Tara looked confused. "That wasn't your fault. He opened his damn mouth and I got angry. It doesn't take much to piss me off, especially around that misogynistic, shallow bitch. You kept me from cussing him out." She exhaled sharply. "Look, Lee is loyal to a fault. Even to fake ass bitches. Saying no to a friend is hard for him."

*Like Gabe.*

Sunny nodded, joining in. "He likes when we make decisions for him. It keeps him from being the bad guy so he doesn't have to stand up for himself. He can say 'Oh, Tara needs me for such and such' instead. He *hates* arguing."

*Okay, not exactly like Gabe.*

"And he thinks if he stands up for himself, he'll lose his friends. Again, that motherfucker is a fake ass bitch, so he probably would." Tara aggressively stirred her drink, the paper straw bending in her grip. "Like, he can stand up for himself with *us* because he knows we won't go anywhere. I'm honestly surprised he said anything to you just now."

"Relationships have always been conditional in Lee's experience," Blanche said. "Lee needs to work on this—and he *knows* it—but until he does, he wants reassurance. Specifically, reassurance that you wanted him to come over."

"I always want him around! Why would today be any different?" Antonio buried his fingers in his hair to relieve the itch of frustration trickling down his head.

"Yeah, *we* see that," Tara replied. "But Lee spent the last week overthinking because you barely texted him. Even if you tell him you're not getting bored with him, he might not believe it."

A pang of guilt stabbed Antonio's chest. "No! I was just trying to prove I could handle life on my own. Like, show I can handle the stress of working without needing him."

He'd assumed Lee was fine with the space. Lee had given no indication he wasn't. He'd been his sweet, easygoing self when he'd come over the night before. *Sure, he was kinda touchy. And damn, the sex was intense...* Antonio's heart fell. *Shit. He doesn't talk about his feelings. Ever. He showed you instead.* A wave of shame flooded his lungs.

Blanche looked at him inquisitively. "Why didn't you explain it like that to him? Lee just said you were tired from work."

"Oh, I dunno. Maybe because I'd rather not constantly remind him what a mess I am? I wanted him to have a good impression of me? I didn't think he'd take it to heart?"

"You've never—" Blanche paused, catching themself. "You don't seem the type to shy away from conflict like he does. If you're serious about a relationship with him, you'll have to have uncomfortable conversations like this before they escalate."

"Of course, I'm serious about him!" Antonio desperately needed their insight, especially if he'd somehow given the impression that he wasn't serious about Lee. He liked Lee. A lot. *Like future husband levels of a lot.* "I didn't know we needed the conversation! I didn't think he cared that much if he saw me or not! He is always so easygoing, and he never talks about his feelings." He took a deep breath, the words spilling out in a rush. "Lee's the first person I've ever wanted to be with. Like, we haven't labeled it, but this is basically my first relationship, and I'm in the middle of massive life changes like *sobriety!* I don't know what's real, and I have a lot of feelings that I don't understand. I have no idea what I'm doing with my life or how to be in a relationship. I'm afraid to fuck everything up. It's paralyzing!"

Antonio stopped to catch his breath. "Sorry, I'm freaking out." Fear had his stomach in knots. As the itch of frustration spread down to his shoulders, the hurt in his chest simmered into anger at himself, at Lee, at his past, at Lee's fake friends. He hated feeling this deeply. "The demons in my head are winning."

"Demons?" Blanche asked, their eyebrows raised.

*Ugh, you forgot to filter yourself.* His therapist had reacted the same way. Antonio rubbed his neck and explained, "Metaphorical demons. I promise I don't hear voices. I'm just a dramatic bitch with a Catholic upbringing and an active imagination."

"Oh." Blanche looked down at the table.

"Are you…disappointed?" Antonio asked, confused.

Blanche shrugged. "Demons in your head sounded interesting."

"Sorry? I'm my own demon. I got empty shadows where my memories should be and intrusive thoughts like hanging out there. They get loud sometimes."

If Antonio was his own demon, then Lee was his angel. Lee couldn't make the intrusive thoughts go away, but he made the gaps in his memories a little less dark. Being around anyone helped, but Lee was particularly peaceful. He just had to hold Antonio's hand, murmur something in his sexy baritone, and the demons would become silent shadows in Lee's light.

The past week without him had been hard. Not impossible, Antonio had managed, but it hadn't exactly been fun. Yet he was trying to become stronger and more grounded for his own sake, not Lee's. In Lee's constant presence, it was impossible to tell if he was actually growing or just growing dependent on Lee. *And now you fucked it up by not telling him why you ignored him for a week.*

His chest and back ached. The possibility of losing Lee was painful. That was new; Antonio didn't know if this was progress or just a new way to hurt. In the past, the faintest twinge of annoyance would have been enough for him to end things. He'd never had this many uncomfortable feelings at once without an easy out to shut them off. Watching Lee walk away hurt worse than he'd imagined.

Antonio scratched the back of his neck, trying to reassure himself that the situation was still salvageable. The demons thrived on fear and guilt and hurt. He couldn't focus on it; he'd spiral.

"Would you say being raised Catholic impacted how you process conflict?" Blanche asked, steepling their fingers.

Antonio blinked. "Uh. I guess? I'm not like, Catholic Catholic. More culturally Catholic. I used to go to the same gay-friendly unofficially Catholic church as Chas."

"Blanche, that's so off topic!" Sunny teased. "What I wanna know is how you've never had a relationship when you're hot *and* funny?"

"Speaking of off topic..." Blanche retorted as Tara huffed.

Antonio blinked again, only growing more confused. "Well, I've had situationships, but I'm greyromantic. Lee's the first person I've experienced any romantic attraction for. It's been really confusing. Not to sound like an asshole, but I've never made an effort before. I was just too self-centered to bother until now. That has nothing to do with my lack of romantic attraction, though. My therapist says I have avoidant behaviors because of attachment issues."

"Fascinating." Blanche tilted their head. "How would you—"

"Blanche, stop being nosy!" Tara interrupted. "Does Lee know what you just shared? Before Blanche started psychoanalyzing you, I mean."

"I mean, I've told him a thousand times that I can't get enough of him, and how I've never felt this way about anyone before." Antonio paused. He hadn't *exactly* told Lee what he meant. He'd protected his heart with cliches and humor. Like he always did. He dropped his head in his hands. Lee's reluctance to be vulnerable with him had been irritating, but Antonio hadn't been vulnerable, either. "So, no, he doesn't. What do I do?"

"Talk to him, dumbass!"

"Tara!" Blanche tried to reprimand her.

"No, she's right," Sunny agreed with Tara for once. "Talk to him, dumbass."

Blanche sighed. "I won't call you a dumbass, but I suppose they're right. Tell him how you feel; he deserves the truth. He can handle it. Lee doesn't scare easily."

*I'm done running from hard shit, aren't I?* That was why his Intentions Song included the verse on talking through his feelings, instead of lashing out in anger like Old Antonio was wont to do. If he and Gabe could agree to work through their myriad issues, he could do the same for Lee. Giving up was out of the question.

"You're right! I'm going to talk to him!" Antonio stood up. *I have to fix this.*

"Oh no, hold up." Tara pulled him back down. "After the show. You might not be conflict-avoidant, but Lee is. He needs time and space to turn his feelings into thoughts, or he'll never get them out. Trust me, after a couple of hours of watching you onstage, he'll be begging for forgiveness for getting upset and several other things that never crossed your mind."

Antonio hoped his resolve would last until then. *I may not be conflict-avoidant, but I am resolution-avoidant. And I can't do that to Lee.*

⋅⋅╫⋅⋅

CHAS LEANED AGAINST CARLITA's makeup table and crossed his arms over his cow-print vest. "Everythin' okay?"

"I could use your help zipping up this dress." Carlita gestured to her silver sequin bodycon gown that hung open at the back. She'd been waiting for anyone but Venus to walk by while she touched up her makeup between numbers.

"You know what I mean, Tonio."

Carlita turned her back on him. "You zipping up this dress or not?"

Chas tugged the zipper up, the sequins scratching Carlita's shoulder blades. "You wanna tell me why Lee's poutin' up in the control room? Freddy says he's never seen him so quiet."

"Why doesn't he ask Lee?"

"Tonio, we talked about this. Lee needs people to stick—"

"Tara told me to give him space, so I'm giving him space." Antonio glared at Chas for dragging him out of the safety of his alter ego. "Trust me. I'm sticking around as long as Lee wants me."

Chas held up his hands. "Okay. Okay. That's all I ask. Your track record—"

"Chas! Please stop reminding me of my track record." Antonio huffed. "When's the last time I no-showed? I haven't drank anything but water, let alone brought enough blow for the class. I haven't hooked up with any coworkers—Lee excluded—and I've been staying out of drama! What more do you want from me?"

Chas sighed, rubbing his belly. "You're right. I'm sorry. You've turned over a new leaf. I just get so Mama Bear over him—well, over both of you. Freddy keeps telling me to mind my business."

Antonio narrowed his eyes at Chas's hand on his stomach. "Mama Bear, huh? Again?"

Chas scoffed a laugh, nodding to the stage manager cueing him to emcee. "Shut yer mouth, Carlita. At least until I make an announcement to the crew."

"Stay out of my business, I'll stay out of yours, Chas." Carlita laughed as Chas walked away.

"Trouble in paradise?" a cool voice behind him asked.

"Do I need to repeat myself about staying out of my business, V?" Carlita shifted in her chair to see Venus's back to her in the mirror.

Carlita and Venus used to be besties backstage, but Venus had pointedly ignored her since the employee appreciation party. Five years in New York, and Antonio's newfound sobriety, had erased whatever camaraderie Carlita and Venus used to have.

Antonio hadn't read too much into it. *She's probably salty because I stopped bringing eight balls backstage.* Other than Chas, Venus was the only cast member who'd outlasted Carlita's five-year stint in New York. But the newer performers had warmed up to Antonio over the past couple of months, even if she hadn't.

Besides, there was a reason Chas never let Venus emcee, no matter how hard she begged. *She's all talent, no charm.*

Venus leaned close to her mirror, touching up her lipliner. "I heard you. I'd just feel responsible if Lee gets hurt, even though I warned him about you from the start."

"Warned him about what exactly?" Dread curled in his stomach.

Venus shrugged. "Just how you are with your flings. The hotter it burns, the quicker you burn out. I'm sure he'll find someone to comfort his broken heart tonight."

*Don't lash out in anger.* Antonio's heart churned at the idea of Venus making a pass when Lee was still mad at him. That she'd tried to sabotage his relationship with Lee before it had even begun. That Lee had never shared that with him. Then again, he'd never told Lee that Chas had warned him off, either. It didn't matter; Venus was just trying to stir shit up.

But the stage manager called her, so instead of cussing Venus out, Carlita stalked over to her mark behind the curtain, heels clicking loudly against the wood floor.

*Tara, your ass better be right about this whole "give him space" shit.* Carlita rucked up her dress and switched on the mic pack tucked into her stockings. "Hi Angel, can you hear me?"

"Yup." Lee's curt reply in the earpiece hurt more than Carlita would let Antonio admit. His baritone was cold when it crackled in her ear. "Your mic is live in 3, 2, 1..."

The first chords of her number made Antonio cringe as the curtain rose. Cher was usually a solid choice, but "If I Could Turn Back Time" was far too melodramatic for the situation. But if there was one thing Carlita was good at, it was channeling Antonio's melodrama into tip money. *Hopefully, I can earn Lee's forgiveness, too.*

She took a quiet breath and entered the spotlight with a smile.

# Chapter Twenty

## Blanche

Sunny had followed Blanche and Tara home from Confession, claiming she'd wanted to hang out. Blanche didn't want to be suspicious; Sunny came over often. There was just something...off. A gleam in her eye, a forced air of nonchalance that she had never been good at hiding. Blanche kept their guard up, mask firmly in place. Sunny would be hurt if Blanche treated her any differently and her behavior was normal. So far.

Sunny and Tara played their video game, arguing when Tara lost again. Same as always.

While Tara and Sunny cussed each other out in good fun, Blanche busied themself by making a batch of margaritas for Sunny's sake. Blanche and Tara both took their whiskey neat, but Sunny preferred fruitier drinks.

Blanche didn't understand the appeal of video games. They never bothered to keep up with the latest gadgets unless it was useful, like texting. Lee (the music producer), Tara (the graphic designer), and Sunny (the software engineer) never understood why Blanche shunned technology so hard, especially at the ripe old age of thirty-three. Blanche just didn't see the benefit.

Ignoring Sunny's gaze as they deposited the margarita in front of her, Blanche reminded themself to stop being suspicious. Sunny's motivation for coming over was probably to avoid her mom. That was why she always came over to begin with. But the new light in Sunny's eyes had shone brighter every day since their session a few weeks ago. Adding sex to a crush—no matter how educational Blanche had tried to keep it—had made Sunny's lingering feelings grow.

*Hopefully, she'll get over it.* Blanche refused to fuck up their friendship; Sunny was one of five people still alive who loved Blanche. That was far too important to let go of.

In many ways, Sunny reminded Blanche of their younger self. But Sunny also reminded Blanche of *her*. With long black hair and pretty dark eyes, she and Daisy shared some physical similarities. But moreseo, Sunny's propensity to blurt out her thoughts and rant about the world reminded Blanche of Daisy. All of it got played off with an innocent smile and a dorky laugh.

Daisy had always let out a small sigh after she laughed. *She was so charming.*

Blanche shook the rising memory from their brain like an Etch A Sketch. They squeezed their eyes shut until the disembodied screams and the empty eyes flashing through their mind faded. *I'm too sober to think about that.*

They'd hate themself if their indulgence ruined their friendship. *I should have found another way, someone else, to help her.* They just couldn't say no to someone in need, especially someone as dear to them as Sunny. Someone who looked up at them with pretty eyes begging for help and a sweet voice saying "I trust you." No one afforded Blanche that softness that cut straight to their heart. Not anymore.

With a yawn, Tara polished off her margarita after Sunny beat her yet again and said her goodnights, flicking Sunny off one last time before disappearing into her room.

*This would be a great time for Lee to come home.* Unease picked at Blanche's heart like a vulture on roadkill; he wouldn't come home tonight. And why would he? He and Antonio were such fools for each other. Of course they would work through their disagreement earlier.

Sunny made no move to leave.

Lee didn't miraculously walk in the door.

"Want some coffee, Babygirl?" Grandma Rose had always offered coffee as a hint for guests to start their Minnesota goodbyes. As much as they loved Sunny, Blanche dreaded the conversation they were sensing on the horizon. Sunny had to leave before it did, or Blanche wasn't sure they could say no like they should.

Already they could feel themself folding under the sweet onslaught of her begging, rationalizing all the ways that this terrible idea would be fine: This would be a good learning experience for her. Sunny would still be their friend after it all went to shit. She would stay safe because Blanche knew better now, knew to keep their private life private and hidden from clients who would hurt their loved ones.

Just like they had rationalized it when Sunny had hired them in the first place.

Work Blanche would shut the whole conversation down before it even started. They would take control and tell Sunny what was best for her. But Work Blanche had no arrangement with Sunny, not once their session ended. Sunny would be pleading with Real Blanche.

And Real Blanche would do anything for the people they loved.

"No, thanks," Sunny replied, oblivious to social cues as usual. "I wanted to talk to you about something you said earlier."

*Well, fuck me. Here we go.* "What did I say earlier?" Blanche was fully aware of what they'd said to Antonio. *"Tell him how you feel; he deserves the truth. He can handle it."* Sunny had perked up as if Blanche was giving *her* a hint instead of encouraging Antonio. *Of all the times for her to actually listen to a conversation.*

*Could* they handle what Sunny was about to say? *Lee might not scare easy, but I do.*

"You told Antonio to tell Lee how he feels. Well, I should tell you how *I* feel. About you." Sunny took a deep breath. "Blanche, I've never felt this way about anyone before!"

*You've never felt "this way" about anyone, or no one has ever made you feel "this way" about yourself? Do you even know what "this way" is?* Blanche tried to let her down easily, their placating smile in place. "Look, Babygirl, you're lovely and everything someone might want—"

"Then let's try it!" Sunny interrupted. "We could be good together."

Blanche sighed, closing their eyes, but Sunny's sweet smile and the bat of her eyelashes were already imprinted in their mind's eye. *You're asking too much of me.* They shook their head. "Sunny, we wouldn't be good for each other. I'm a professional dominatrix. A sex worker. I don't want to bring that side of me into our friendship or any romantic relationship, and I have multiple long-term clients who take priority. There's too much of myself I can't give you, and that's not fair for either of us."

Sunny would be a delightful sub with that pushy attitude, but that was for Work Blanche, not Real Blanche. Those two halves needed to stay separate. Real Blanche wanted sweetness. Wanted someone to take care of them for a change.

Blanche's heart lurched in longing; it'd been so long since anyone had truly seen them. *Not since Daisy...* They wanted to be selfish. To have the cute, easy relationship growing pains like Lee and Antonio. To have someone to call theirs again. Someone who encouraged them with soft words and put Blanche first.

Clients did nice things for them. Blanche's patron had been housing them for years now. Their laptop had been a gift from another client for his work trips. One of their regulars even insisted on throwing them a "birthday gala" next month. But they did those things for themselves, not Blanche. Blanche was but a muse for their whims.

*Who would want a "birthday gala" anyway?* Blanche just wanted a guaranteed night where no one could reach Work Blanche. Painful memories always erupted uncontrollably on the birthday that Daisy had picked for them. And now Work Blanche had to go to a fucking party, when Real Blanche just wanted quality time with Freddy and Chas to reminisce about their past, like they did every year.

Blanche reached for the remaining sip of tequila in their glass to stop the memories that threatened to drown them.

"I'm okay with all of that!" Sunny protested, taking Blanche's hand halfway to their glass. She laced their fingers together, rubbing featherlight brushes on Blanche's knuckles with her thumb. "It doesn't bother me. I can learn to sub. I liked it when you were bossing me around during our session."

*Please, that was not "bossing you around."* Sunny needed more experience if she couldn't tell the difference between direction and domination. *She's so naive. I envy that about her.* Sunny had never experienced real heartbreak. Never faced the risks that being with Blanche could bring. She could never truly understand the stalking, the obsessed client who— *Don't go there.* Blanche looked at Sunny, silently begging for her to take it back.

"Please, Blanche, I want to try." Her onyx eyes pleaded. "No one has to know but us."

*Why can't I say no to her?* Blanche knew why. Because they were selfish and seeing Lee fall head over heels for Antonio—even watching Tara's misadventures—reminded Blanche just how alone they were.

How they'd been happiest with someone sweet and earnest and vivacious looking out for them. And how Sunny needed this—ill-fated as it was. She couldn't go into her first real relationship as naive and unsure of herself as she was now.

*If I can't turn her down, I need boundaries.* Already regretting their selfishness, Blanche ticked off a list on their fingers. "No jealousy. No say in decisions about my life. No telling anyone, not even Tara or Lee or your sister. And we need to keep it vanilla."

"I can do all of that. I promise." Sunny beamed, her pretty eyes sparkling.

Blanche's heart softened at the joy on her face. Their friendship needed to survive this indulgence, so Blanche had to make sure it would. "And when this blows up, promise me you'll still be my friend."

"But what if we—"

"Promise me, Sunny." A warning edge seeped into their tone.

Sunny nodded. "I promise."

"Good girl." Blanche reprimanded themself at the slip. *Keep it vanilla.* "Cross any of those boundaries and we go back to being friends and move on."

Sunny squealed in delight and kissed Blanche eagerly. "Yes! You won't regret this. We're going to be great together."

*I already regret this.* And yet, Blanche kissed her back.

---

# Antonio

After the show, Antonio didn't waste time removing Carlita's face. He needed to find Lee. Shame ate at his gut, nerves itched his palms. He wondered if Lee could tell what a mess he was from the control room. If Lee could see his regret when he'd read the straight bachelorettes for trash, heard the apology in his voice as he sang his heart out.

He found Lee in the wings where they'd first kissed, hefting a monitor onto a cart. Antonio's heart fluttered. *Boyfriend. Lover. Future husband.*

Whispers from his demons had been licking at his heart all night. Maybe if he had tried harder with others in his past, he would know how to explain himself now. He was anxious to mess up again, but he had to try. "Leland!" he called out in a singsong voice, hoping to trick himself into optimism.

"Give me a damn minute!" Lee snapped without turning around, picking up a mic stand.

Anxiety smashed against his chest like a tidal wave, the demons roaring as his pulse echoed in his ears. His heart ached like it'd been dropped on the floor and stepped on by his own stiletto. *You did fuck this up.* "I... Can we talk?"

Lee whirled around. "Oh shit! Tonio!" He dropped the mic stand with a clatter and strode over to him. "You never call me by the full name. I got confused."

Antonio's panic melted. "Sorry. I'll stick to Lee."

"No! Call me whatever you want. I just only get the full name when I'm in trouble." Lee grabbed his hand, drawing it to his chest. "I'm not, am I? Are we? Please tell me we're okay."

"Why would you be in trouble? I'm here to apologize to *you*!" The worry in Lee's eyes swept away any lingering irritation. "For acting like I didn't care if we hung out."

"What? No! I'm sorry for flaking on you!" Lee kissed Antonio's wrist. "And for getting upset for no damn reason. You have to know I'd rather spend time with you any day. I just thought you'd speak up for me, tell them we had plans, you know? I'm so used to everyone telling me what they want me to do, it's kind of weird you don't. In a nice way!"

"I was annoyed that you'd rather drive a bunch of drunk bitches around than hang out with me," Antonio admitted primly, brushing his thumb over the scar on Lee's cheek. Lee leaned into his hand. "But that's on me for making you choose between your friends and me."

Antonio took a shaky breath before continuing. "It's just, I have no idea what I'm doing. I've told you before how I've never felt this way about anyone, but I am serious when I say that. I know my past reputation isn't great, but you should know that I literally have *never* had these feelings for anyone before you. Or come close to a connection like we have. Ever. Real talk because I know I come across as joking half the time and melodramatic the other half, but I'm pretty much aromantic."

"Oh. Okay." Lee's face fell briefly before a controlled, understanding expression took over. "What does that mean for you? For us?"

"Oh! Fuck! No! This is coming out all wrong. The feelings I have for you are *definitely* romantic! It's just been very confusing for me because

I've never caught feelings for anyone before. I've always wanted to fall..." Antonio paused, brow furrowing. *Let's not go there.* "I never experienced romantic attraction until I met you. I wasn't sure how to tell you that without giving myself a chance to figure out what I was feeling, and frankly, I'm still processing it. And learning how all this works as I go."

*You should have taken off your face for this conversation.* Lee deserved an honest view of Antonio's expressions, not Carlita's makeup. "But I want to make us work. You're so wonderful, and I love being with you. I've been trying to protect you or myself, or maybe both of us, instead of just telling you how I feel. I mean, I *have* been telling you, but I always make it sound like a joke so I don't overwhelm you or end up hurting you in case the romantic feelings weren't real."

"Honestly, I have been overwhelmed. In a good way!" Lee quickly clarified, tightening his grip on Antonio's hand and drawing him closer with a strong arm around the waist as Antonio pulled away to apologize. "I like what we're doing. I like...us."

Antonio pressed his lips together to hide his smile. *This is Lee talking about his feelings? Adorable.* Lee still remained guarded, as if sharing anything would bite him in the ass.

Lee sighed as Antonio waited for him to continue. "I just...felt some type of way when you barely texted this week and then it was like you didn't care if you saw me tonight. Like you...didn't want me around anymore."

"That's impossible. I always want you around." Antonio gently brushed his lips across Lee's knuckles. "And for the record, I'm sorry for being distant this week. I was just trying to prove that I'm not *reliant* on you, but I should have explained myself better. Not that it's an excuse, but I'm new to the whole 'responsible adult' thing in addition to the 'romantic feelings' thing, so please be patient with me."

"You think you are? Reliant on me, I mean." Lee's voice was nonchalant, but the torso pressing against Antonio's tensed.

Antonio rubbed Lee's shoulders away from his ears. "I've been surprisingly well-grounded this week. I've been going to yoga with my sister and eating right and shit. And I'll keep doing those things, but that doesn't mean we can't spend time together. I may have taken it too far. I like being with you and I want you in my life, fragile as it is. I don't want us to burn out on each other, but I should have realized I was giving you too much distance after weeks of love bombing you. There's balance somewhere and I promise to find it."

"Good. Although, for the record, I like that you want me around." Lee wrapped his arms around Antonio's waist with a flirty smile. "And I volunteer to help you decompress anytime."

"I'll take you up on that, Angel." Antonio grinned, relief washing away the anxiety that had been strangling him for hours. It was strange, explaining himself after a lifetime of spiteful silence and explosions of resentment. But all the hours of therapy, fraught moments with Gabe, and bickering with Cassie had made this more manageable than he'd expected. The words were awkward, but they came. And that was far more than Old Antonio had ever been able to manage. "Just, will you tell me if you're feeling some type of way next time? I've gathered you're a little conflict-avoidant, but I'm trying to be a better me. I'd rather know if I'm doing something wrong so I can fix it."

"You've been talking to Blanche." Lee grinned. "I'll try my best."

"Thank you." Antonio smiled up at him shyly. "And I'll try not to get in between you and your friends again. I can't go to the kiki, but I'll be nice if you ever want to introduce us."

Lee shook his head. "Don't ask me to do that." He peeked around dramatically, making sure they were alone, before whispering, "I don't remember any of their names. And it's been years now so I can't ask anymore."

Antonio laughed in surprise. "And here I thought I had the shitty memory!"

"I'm *so* bad with names." Lee cupped his face. "Are we okay?"

"Angel, we're more than okay."

With a relieved grin, Lee kissed him.

Antonio eagerly kissed his...*Boyfriend. Lover. Future husband* without protest. He sighed with pleasure as Lee held him tightly against his body. Let the bitchy nameless friends see the makeup all over Lee's face, the glitter on his clothes. *He's mine.* He'd rather mark his Angel with a hickey on his neck, with a key to his apartment, and someday with a wedding band. Glitter would do for now.

"Leland!"

They both tensed. Antonio was mildly offended Lee had mistaken his cheerful singsong for this bitch's irritated tone. Lee rolled his eyes and kept kissing him.

Antonio pulled away with a grin, wiping the worst of the makeup off. Considering how much powder covered Lee's face, he must be a mess himself. "You look...well, like you've been making out with a drag queen! Wash your face well before you go to bed."

"Yes, dear." Lee bent back in for another kiss. Antonio let him, even though he'd just cleaned the makeup off of him.

"Leland, seriously! You're taking forever!"

Antonio huffed in annoyance when Lee tensed again. "For the record, Leland Whateveryourmiddlenameis Jones, I will never use your full name because you're in trouble."

Lee kissed him again. "I appreciate that. But I'll never tell you my middle name."

Antonio laughed. "Challenge accepted."

"Leland, I swear to God if you take any longer, I'm going to die of boredom!"

"Can I just flake on Whatshisname?" Lee murmured.

Antonio shook his head. "I'd love that, but you already told him you'd go. And I shouldn't take over your life completely. Get out of here. Go have fun without me." With one last kiss, he gently pushed Lee toward his nameless bitchy friend, waving over his shoulder as he headed back to the greenroom to change.

Behind him, he heard, "What the fuck. You're covered in glitter!"

"It's a good look on me, right?" came in reply as Antonio walked away with a smile.

Hanging up his dress, Antonio wiggled out of his padding and washed what remained of Carlita down the shower drain. Curled up on his couch, he stared at the TV's blank screen.

Nights were the hardest.

Lee had been a light for him lately, staying at his apartment more often than not. On past Saturday nights when he was Lee-less until nearly dawn, he'd performed extra hard so he could sleep right after his shower. Just like he'd been doing at the gym all week.

But on a night like this, when he had been on an emotional rollercoaster, when the demons had been nibbling at his reserves, sleep eluded him. The demons were fucking loud.

*Xanax would shut them up.*

Antonio waved his hand to silence the one reminding him what even half a milligram would make him feel. Or not feel. *I need to talk to someone. Not feeling sounds way too appealing.*

Lee was off having fun with his friends; Antonio didn't want to get in between them again. Guilt and shame danced in his gut. *I can't rely on Lee every time I need someone to talk to.* Instead, he called his favorite moody insomniac. Gabe would probably be playing some nerdy game. *How are we even friends? We have nothing in common.*

Gabe picked up on the first ring. "Tonio? You okay?"

Antonio smiled into the phone. Gabe worried too damn much. "Yeah. I just could use some support right now. Is it okay that I called you? I can call someone else."

"Who else would be awake at three in the fucking morning?"

"Dunno. Maybe I'd call a sex hotline." Antonio already felt lighter hearing his best friend's voice. Gabe was good at shooing his dark thoughts away. His bass voice tasted different from Lee's baritone, more intensely sweet and viscous, like molasses or honey. Lee's voice was rich and thick, like sweet potato pie with a heavy dash of nutmeg. Both were always comforting.

Gabe's laugh echoed in his ear. "Do those still exist?"

Antonio shrugged, forgetting Gabe couldn't see him. "No idea. Remember when we called one our freshman year? Your mom was so pissed when she got her credit card bill."

"Getting grounded was worth every minute with Sasha."

"How do you remember her name?" Antonio laughed. "I still don't know how my mom didn't punish me for that one." Gabe's mom had cussed him out way more than his own parents had. She'd always been the strict parent in his life, even if he technically wasn't her kid.

"Paula lets you get away with everything. She'd never punish her baby boy. Even when you called a fucking sex hotline, and that was the tamest shit you made us do."

"*You* were a bad influence on *me.*"

"Oh really? Do I need to remind you of my mom's necklace that you dropped in the lake?" Gabe teased, "Or the beer bottle that got stuck in your ass? The whipped cream incident? The BB gun? I can keep going."

Antonio couldn't stop his giggles. "What can I say? Youngest child privilege. I'm everyone's favorite person, especially my mom's. Although I think my parents were just too surprised by how hetero the sex hotline was that they forgot to punish me. They were so confused when I told them I was bi, not gay."

"Do you want me to come over?" Gabe asked when their laughter quieted.

"No, but it's sweet that you'd offer at this time of night. I just needed someone to talk to. You know, validation that someone is out there, that I'm not alone."

"What is Lee up to tonight? I thought you guys were glued at the hip these days."

Antonio sighed. "He's out with friends. I'm getting better at existing around parties and drunk people, but nothing good ever happens this time of night. Don't want to chance getting caught up."

"Does Lee uh, partake at all?"

Antonio heard right through Gabe's controlled tone. *Gabey, you worry too much!* "No. I mean, he smokes weed and drinks sometimes, but he's the DD. I just don't know these friends that well. The one I have met reminds me of my old crew from New York. I can't be around catty bitches and temptation." He paused. "We kind of got in a fight today."

"You wanna talk about it?"

*He hasn't met Lee yet. I don't want to ruin his first impression.* He backtracked. "I don't know if it was a fight. Like Capital F Fight? Lee's kind of like you, where he just takes all of my bullshit. But unlike you, he doesn't call me out on said bullshit. I didn't realize he was taking it to heart until it came to a head. But we talked it out before we left work. Kissed and made up. I just don't know how to navigate that stuff."

Gabe chuckled. "That doesn't sound like a fight. At least not one of your normal fights. Sounds more like a healthy relationship, not that I would know what one looks like."

Antonio laughed sardonically. "You would know it more than I would. It hasn't even been six weeks, and this is already one of my longest relationships. And we haven't talked about if it's a relationship yet! Besides, you and Hippo have a super healthy relationship."

"Yeah, me and Hippo have a great relationship, don't we buddy?" Hippo whined in the background. "He tells me what he needs, and I give it to him."

Antonio rolled his eyes. "Sounds like all of your relationships, Gabey."

"Wow, damn! At least Hippo doesn't tell me what to do. And I'm getting better about saying no. I told my mom I wouldn't go to an MAI fundraising event with her. I set a boundary and told her I wasn't ready yet and she listened. Eventually." Gabe sounded really proud of himself.

Antonio saw through it. "How much did you donate instead?"

"Seriously, did you call to attack me?" Gabe asked before he muttered, "Just a thousand dollars. And two Saturdays a month volunteering at an art class."

"A stack and two weekends a month to not spend an evening with your mom? Your boundaries are not cheap." Antonio adored Miriam, but Gabe could never stand up to her. He cared too damn much about what people thought of him. Miriam was a great mom but way too supportive. She was Gabe's biggest cheerleader when Gabe preferred the sidelines.

"Why am I talking to you again?"

"Because you love me," Antonio reminded him saucily.

Gabe chuckled in his ear. "I do love you, Tonio. And I'm proud of you for having your first Not-a-Fight with Lee and resolving it with strangely healthy communication skills. I'm glad you love someone worth sticking around for."

Antonio's heart thumped in his chest. "Who said anything about love? It's barely been a month."

"Tonio, you've never been like this with anyone. Ever. Do you love him?"

He hadn't been sure until there was a real risk of losing Lee. But it was undeniable now. He was in love with Leland Jones. But admitting it out loud to Gabe would make it hard to hold in with Lee. He already struggled to keep himself from calling Lee his boyfriend when they hadn't talked about that yet either. Dumping an "I love you" on him so soon could be a disaster. Antonio didn't want to push Lee for more than he was ready for.

"That's what I thought." Gabe read him through the silence.

Antonio pouted. "Gabey, what do I do? I don't think he's ready for feelings and shit yet. He can barely say he likes me. And I don't know if *I'm* ready for feelings and shit yet. I got out of rehab like four months ago! I have no idea what it means for me to love someone. I don't want to scare him off if I start dropping the L word and he's not there."

"You're feeling the feelings, Tonio. Doesn't matter if you're ready or when you got out of rehab. As someone with a chronic problem of falling in love with people who don't love me back, take my expert advice: be honest, but reassure him that you're not pressuring him into anything.

Tell him intentionally, not in an emotional moment. It's hard to keep that shit in when his face is covered in cum."

"Gabe!" Antonio barked out a laugh just as a gentle knock sounded. "Oh, I have to go. Someone's at the door."

"At this time of night? Don't get murdered."

"Don't put that on me, asshat! It's probably Lee." He paused. "And thank you."

"I'm always here for you, Tonio."

A pang of guilt mixed with resentment in his chest. Gabe hadn't always been there for him. And he hadn't always been there for Gabe. Antonio had taken the easy route, and Gabe had paid the price. He had to make it up to him.

They said their goodbyes. Antonio stood on his tiptoes to look out the peephole—*just in case Gabe jinxed me*—before he opened the door with a big grin.

"I hope I didn't wake you." Lee smiled, fighting the weariness on his face.

"No, I was up. I figured you were gonna go home tonight." Antonio let him in.

"I wanted to see you." Lee rubbed the back of his neck. Glitter still covered his clothes. "I hated leaving you earlier. I don't know why I'm friends with Whatshisname half the time. But you were right earlier, we do need more balance. I should spend time with more people, not just you. And Whatshisname...includes me, I guess. Lets me feel like I'm part of something, even if he is a dick. I doubt any of the other guys would think twice about me if it weren't for him. Not many people other than Tara, Sunny, and Blanche want me around."

"I can't understand why not." Antonio leaned on the door as he locked it behind him. "Though we've established I can't get enough of you."

"Which is one of the many reasons I...like you." Lee smiled as he pushed his glasses up. "I hated how I acted today. That was some shit my mom would pull. The whole 'expressing my feelings' thing is hard for me, but I'll try to be better."

"Oh, Angel. What did I do to deserve you?" Antonio wrapped his arms tight around Lee's perfectly thick waist, wrinkling his nose at the cigarette smell on Lee's clothes. "You know, we had a conflict, we discussed it, and we kissed and made up. I've been told that's healthy communication."

"Did you call your therapist or something when you got home?" Lee teased.

"Nah, just Gabe. He's an expert in unhealthy communication."

"Get any other good insights?" Lee asked, kissing Antonio's forehead.

*That I should tell you I love you.* Considering it made anxiety tighten around his throat. Already regretful at his cowardice, Antonio played it cool yet again with a wink. "He told me to come on your face."

Lee's belly laugh filled Antonio with warmth. "I mean, I was planning on going right to sleep, but if you want…"

Antonio smiled. "No, let's go to bed."

As Lee lay snoring softly in his arms, his emotions at long last overwhelmed him. His appreciation for Gabe's constant support leaked out of his eyes. His gratitude for the insight from Blanche, Tara, and Sunny tugged at his lips. Every overwhelming feeling for Lee was silently exhaled in an "I love you" between Lee's broad shoulders.

His demons would stay at bay forever as long as he had this much love in his life.

# Saturday, July Thirteenth

# Chapter Twenty-One

## Tara

"Buttercup!" Tara's earbuds were yanked from her ears, dragging her attention away from her laptop. Janelle Monae's voice blared from Lee's hands instead of through her entire awareness. "Earth to Tara!"

"What?"

"You haven't heard a damn word I've said, have you?" Lee shook his head, smiling.

She shrugged. She'd been drafting a logo and forgotten the rest of the world existed. Confession's top floor workspace was quiet this afternoon. Tara and Lee sat alone in the main workspace, but someone was using the conference room. The kids' laughter from the playroom was the only clue Tara needed to deduce Chas was having a meeting. Normally full during the week, the desks around them sat vacant. Tara preferred to *not* work on Saturdays too, but Blanche had sexiled them; their sugar daddy had scheduled a last-minute session. *Even though it's their birthday. I hate him.*

"Why is your music so loud? You're going to rupture your eardrums."

Tara shrugged again, pausing the song. Loud music drowned out the world around her and inside her head, allowing her to focus on work. "What'd I miss?"

"How much did you hear?" Lee asked.

Tara shook her head, smiling guiltily. "I literally had no idea you were talking to me."

Lee laughed. "Really? I've been over here fanboying about how Tonio recorded a song over a track I made and you missed it? I sent you the link to his Soundcloud."

Tara tapped her phone. Lee's text appeared on her lock screen. "I was in the zone."

"Obviously," Lee teased. "Did you hear anything about the other track I'm making?"

Tara shook her head as he handed her his headphones. "Not a lick."

Lee sighed. "Why do I bother?" He grinned at her. "So, Tonio is teaching a music class at summer school, right? His students liked the other sample mix I made, so I'm putting together a second one that shows how chord progressions and cadences impact the song's mood. I've been putting way too much effort into it, but it's good practice for me. I started making some tracks with specific moods." He paused. "If I ever do any marketing, that'd be a good angle."

The corners of her mouth tugged into a smile. Lee had rarely been so chatty, especially about a boy. He was normally quiet, with the occasional funny quip or shady observation. For him to ramble on without a response? Very out of character.

Seeing him excited about Antonio was cute. Her soulmate was outgrowing her, but she was strangely happy for him. Mostly. His happiness outweighed her sadness and jealousy. She committed his eager chatter to memory for the next time she cried herself to sleep from loneliness, which was most nights Lee stayed at Antonio's.

Settling his headphones over her ears, she listened to Antonio's recording over a familiar house track she'd heard through Lee's headphones dozens of times when he'd asked her opinion on it. *Tonio's a good singer. Funny, too.* His campy persona shone through his voice.

A familiar notification sounded in the headphones. Tara elbowed Lee. "Lee, I know you're afraid of commitment, but isn't it time to delete Grindr?"

Lee's face fell.

*Shit.* "Sorry. Not my business. I was just talking shit." Tara removed the headphones, wishing she hadn't said anything when the furrow in his brow deepened.

Lee worried his lower lip. "You're right, I think? I just don't know. Like, do I delete it? What does it mean if I don't? We haven't talked about what we are yet. Or if we're exclusive. So, like, do I wait until then? Or do it now? I haven't even opened any dating apps since we met. Parties are hella awkward now since I'm not trying to hook up with anyone."

Tara laughed, relieved. Lee was always indecisive, but Antonio had brought him to a whole new level of internal conflict. "Is that what you do at those house parties? Troll Grindr for dick?"

Lee shrugged. "Not *just* that. But it was, uh, convenient. And now..."

"You'd rather be with Toniooo?" Tara smirked.

Lee smiled bashfully. "Honestly, yeah. But you know how *they* are."

"Bitchy."

"Exactly," Lee sighed. "I need a social life, but can't I stay home sometimes?"

Tara dragged her wheely chair closer to him. "Lee, you're too fucking nice. What do *you* want to do? Do that."

"Easy for you to say." Lee pushed his glasses up his nose. "You're a hard-ass."

"And if you were a little more assertive, you could be a hard-ass too," Tara teased. "Look, you want to hang out with Tonio, hang out with Tonio. You want to delete Grindr, delete Grindr."

Lee shifted in his chair, avoiding her eyes.

"Do you *want* to delete Grindr?" Tara pressed. "Yes or no."

He nodded.

"Then fucking delete it. It's simple."

Lee groaned and threw his head back. "I wish it was that simple."

"It is. If you want to do something, do it!" Tara argued. "Do it. Delete it. Right now."

Lee stared at his phone. "I could always download it again if that isn't what this is."

"Exactly. It's not a big deal." She didn't understand Lee's hesitation. If she wanted something, she made it happen. The world really was that simple.

"And if I *don't*, then it could become a big deal if I should have deleted it already."

"You lost me, but as long as you're rationalizing it to yourself." Antonio didn't seem to have a strong opinion over what apps Lee had. But then, she didn't know Antonio like Lee did. Nor did she understand the appeal of relationships to begin with, let alone exclusive ones. Tara barely understood the point of talking to someone before she had sex with them, even after her attempts at dating.

But being with Antonio was good for Lee. A small confusing part of her wondered if it'd be good for her, too. Even if dating was already emotionally draining enough.

Lee stared at his phone so long that Tara was on the verge of doing it for him, until at last he took a breath and deleted the app. He threw his phone down. "There. It's gone."

Tara hugged him. "I'm proud of you. Scruff next."

"You're so right, Buttercup." Lee laughed and picked the phone up again. "You're never allowed to leave me, okay? I need someone to make all of my decisions."

Tara laughed, nuzzling into his shoulder. "As if I'd ever leave you, Lee. We're family. But have you considered *talking* to him about what you two are doing?"

"Uh... Hi, I'm Lee Jones, apparently we've never met."

Tara gently smacked the back of his head. "I'm serious, dude. If you're unsure about where you stand with *him*, he's probably unsure about where he stands with *you*. He's obviously crazy about you, and you're ready to be exclusive with him. That has to mean something, right?"

"Yeah, that I'm about to get my heart torn out." Lee pushed his glasses up. "Why am I taking relationship advice from you?"

"Hey, I give great advice. I just don't take it." Tara paused. "Speaking of...have you talked to Sunny lately?"

Lee shook his head. "No, just memes. Why?"

Tara sighed. "She's been coming over more lately, but not to hang out with me." She raised an eyebrow, hoping that would be enough for him to get what she was saying. It was awkward enough without saying it out loud.

"So, she's hanging out with Blanche?" Lee shrugged. "Why is that weird?"

"Because they're hanging out in Blanche's room. *After* I go to bed," Tara whispered, glancing at the door to the playroom. Best to keep her voice down if she was talking about Blanche's personal life. "And then Sunny leaves like an hour later."

"Oh." Lee grimaced. "*Oh...*"

"Yeah. I was hoping Sunny would have mentioned it, since she usually tells you everything, because neither of them has told me anything." Blanche wouldn't bring Sunny over in *that* capacity with Tara home if she were a client. Something more had to be going on.

Lee shook his head. "Honestly, I've barely seen her other than when I drag you guys to hang out with Antonio on Saturdays."

"Yeah, I'm aware. She's been making me go thrifting with her since you've been too busy," Tara grumbled, still quiet. She didn't like shopping, but it was...*nice* that Sunny wanted to hang out without Lee or Blanche.

Lee snorted. "Are you sure something's happening with Blanche?"

Tara groaned. "Noise-canceling headphones aren't enough. Yes, I'm sure."

He winced in sympathy. "Do you want me to ask her?"

Blanche likely wouldn't talk if either of them asked, but Sunny would spill any and all information they wanted and then some. She didn't talk much, but once she got on a roll, it was hard to stop her.

"Not unless you want to. I was just curious if she'd said anything. Maybe they're just hooking up, and I'm overthinking it."

The conference room door opened, cutting off their hushed conversation. Chas walked out, dressed spectacularly feminine. Still in her signature cowboy boots and hat, she wore a pink sundress, barely concealing any of her voluptuous apple-shaped body. Chas was off-limits, but keeping her eyes to herself had never been Tara's strong suit.

Two men followed, both dressed in suits. Tara recognized them as Confession's other owners but didn't remember their names; Chas was the real boss. The suits were just the bank. Chas shook their hands goodbye as they headed to the exit.

Grinning at Lee and Tara, Chas walked over, the sundress barely covering her slender thighs. *Dammit, stop staring!* "Y'all comin' to Blanchy's party tonight?" Chas asked, her Texas accent thick even out of drag. Blanche always said that Chas may have left Texas, but the accent followed her.

"Wouldn't miss it!" Lee grinned at his boss.

Chas leaned her arm on the back of Lee's chair, leaving Tara's eyes level with her tits in the thin fabric of the neckline. "I've been lookin' forward to it all week! A gala is a fancy step up from our usual birthday party for Blanchy. Tonio's comin', Lee?"

Lee nodded. "Yeah, he's driving us there."

Chas laughed. "Good luck ridin' in that death trap of a car. Not that yours is any better."

Tara couldn't look away as everything bounced with Chas's laughter.

Chas was a friend. Even if she wasn't married with three kids, Tara didn't mix her sex life with her personal life. *This dating shit is fucking up my rules. I can't start ogling people I know just because I'm trying to give strangers a chance.*

A cough sounded from the playroom door. Freddy glared at her with an eyebrow raised.

Tara gave him a guilty smile. *Busted.* Freddy crossed his arms and leaned against the doorframe until Tara scooted back to her desk and turned her gaze to her laptop.

---

# Sunny

Sunny sipped her pinot, the bitter tannins dry on her tongue. She should be happy. It was her partner's birthday after all. While they hadn't spent a *ton* of time together in the thirty-five days they'd been seeing each other, she enjoyed the time they did have. *Like tonight. I should be enjoying this.* Even if she was on the sidelines watching Blanche from afar, pretending they were just friends.

The setting sun shone pink through the art gallery where Blanche's client was hosting a swanky party in their honor. The drinks and appetizers in front of her were free. Sunny looked elegant in a slinky red dress she had thrifted the other day with Tara. A lively blues band played for the couples on the dance floor. She'd never get the opportunity to meet this many people in Blanche's life again. *So why do I feel sick?*

Blanche worked the room, musical laughter ringing. Stunning as always, their blond hair fell to their waist. A tease of bronze skin peeked out from the low back of their midnight blue evening gown. From the leather-clad pups wearing their best collars to the older men in designer suits, Blanche was effortlessly at home with everyone.

Maybe that explained why Sunny was on edge. She was an ugly duckling, trying to pass as a swan. *Imposter syndrome. That must be it.* As diverse as the cast of Blanche's life was, Sunny didn't belong in it. She was an outsider among them. It was draining. She wondered if she'd ever be the woman, the partner she wanted to—

"You gonna eat that?" Tara pointed at the taquito on Sunny's plate.

Sunny snatched it up and stuffed it in her mouth.

"Bitch, you could just say yes!" Tara laughed. "I just didn't want it to go to waste."

Sunny shrugged, still staring at Blanche from across the room, who hugged Freddy tightly. Bitter anger surged in her stomach.

*No jealousy, Sunny. That's a rule.* The suggestion was irrational, anyway. Nothing would ever happen between Blanche and *Freddy*. Still, it hurt knowing she would never hug her partner around all of these people, not like Freddy got to. She tried to close the Jealousy tab, but could only minimize it.

"What's up with you tonight? You've barely spoken a word. You're irritated. You're hoarding food. You're turning into me," Tara teased. "Stay in your lane."

Sunny smiled despite herself. For all of Tara's bluster and sass, she was a softie inside. *Deep, deep down. Buried underneath a thorn thicket, like a dead body.* She avoided Tara's question the same way she always did, by praising her. "You look lovely tonight, Tara-Bear. You should show off your collarbones more often. They're scrumptious."

Tara had made an effort for the party, a far cry from her usual athleisure. The black satin corset top and crepe palazzo pants Sunny had forced her to buy at the thrift store were stunning on her slim figure. Still Tara, but elevated.

Tara made a face, swirling her wine. "Thank you."

"What? I got a 'thank you'? Forget me, are *you* okay?"

Tara laughed sardonically. "I've been trying to be nicer to strangers. You know, the whole small talk, dating, being a functioning human thing. Might as well practice with you."

"Wow, stay in *your* lane. I'm the nice one."

"Since when are *you* nice?" Tara grinned. "Y'know, I went to someone's house last weekend purely because I liked talking to them. And to meet their dog. And yeah, we had sex, but I went there with zero *intention* of fucking them—I just wanted to keep the conversation going. The sex *was* hot, though! Maybe I should stick to fucking people I like talking to."

"What a concept," Sunny said dryly, turning her eyes to the dance floor to keep from staring at Blanche, who was hugging yet another person who wasn't her.

Antonio was teaching Lee a blues dance. Lee loved dancing, but following a partner looked comically difficult for him. Antonio winced patiently as Lee stepped on his toes.

Tara's gaze followed hers. "He's terrible at that, isn't he? For someone who can do the entire chair routine for "Stronger" when he's blackout drunk, he is struggling."

"Oh, and you can do better?" Sunny nudged her.

"Oh, hell no! But it's sweet he's trying. They're fucking adorable."

Sunny nodded in agreement. "They are. He always had to be so responsible, so serious, even when we were kids. It's nice he's found someone who brings out his fun side."

"I expected I'd be more upset. I've been dreading the time he doesn't need me anymore, but this doesn't hurt as much as I imagined." Tara set her empty wine glass on the white linen-covered table with an exasperated groan. "Like, I'm jealous and lonely, don't get me wrong. It's like I'm falling behind. But do I want a relationship like that of my own?" She made a face of mock disgust. "I think I do, and it's fucking weird."

Sunny smiled despite herself. "Tara? Talking about a relationship? And your feelings? How much wine have you had?"

"Shh. Don't question it." Tara rested her head on Sunny's shoulder. "I thought I wanted us to be alone together forever, but honestly? He's happy and loved on. Why wouldn't I want that for him? Why shouldn't I want that for me?"

Sunny chewed her lip, too taken aback to respond. Not so much because Tara was processing her feelings like a normal person for once. But because Tara was handling her feelings better than Sunny. Here was Tara, queen of panic attacks and abandonment issues, happy that her emotional rock was growing apart from her. Meanwhile Sunny, arguably the most well-adjusted of the four of them, was moping because her partner was popular.

Smoothing the wrinkle in her dress from twisting the hemline, Sunny stuck her tongue between her teeth before her lip started bleeding again. She *should* be happier for Blanche. They were surrounded by love. And yet Sunny sat on the sidelines, hurt that Blanche wasn't introducing her to anyone, even as a friend. If Tara could be happy seeing Lee thrive, why couldn't she be happy for Blanche?

A server refilled their wine glasses for a toast. Blanche walked up to the stage with the host. Sunny barely listened as the host recited kind words about Blanche, raising her glass when everyone else did. She robotically joined in the singing and the applause, never taking her eyes off Blanche as she sipped the too-dry wine.

She lived for the rare occasions when it was just the two of them. But here, around so many people hogging Blanche's affections, she'd become invisible. Sunny felt like a disappointment, somehow not meeting Blanche's needs, even though she was doing everything Blanche had told her to do. Blanche would never, *could* never, acknowledge her in public as more than a friend. She knew that, understood that. Losing Daisy had broken them in half; Blanche was protecting both of them by keeping Sunny a secret.

But Sunny's heart told her if she was somehow better, more, *enough*, then Blanche wouldn't need all of these other people. She could have them to herself—

"Bitch, snap out of it." Tara waved her hand in front of her face, her green eyes searching Sunny's. "Don't tell me what's going on between you two. I know how Blanche is with privacy. But I'm not blind. Or rather, I'm not deaf. Shoulda guessed you'd be a screamer."

Sunny's cheeks burned.

"I want you both to be happy. Right now, you're not happy. And while I'm glad Blanche is finally doing something for themself, I'm not sure they're happy either. Blanche will give you as much as they can, but everyone else takes so much from them, like all of this fuckery." Tara gestured to the party around them. "You need someone who can give you all of themself. That'll never be Blanche."

Sunny blinked to keep her eyes from burning as Tara said exactly what Sunny didn't want to hear. But this—being the wallflower in Blanche's life—was what it meant to be with Blanche, and that was worth everything. Even if everyone else cared for Work Blanche, only Sunny got the real person. When everyone else went home, it'd be Sunny that Blanche invited over. Reminding herself of that eased the bitter taste in her mouth, even if Sunny still wanted more. She forced a smile, reminding herself that this was what she'd signed up for. "Don't worry about me, Tara-Bear. I'm fine."

Tara raised a skeptical eyebrow but put her hand on Sunny's. "We're family. I want what's best for both of you and if that's each other, then you have my support. Even if my sort-of-brother's sort-of-ex is sleeping with my sort-of-parent."

"Oh bitch, don't put it like that. That's weird as hell!" Sunny laughed, smacking Tara's hand. *When did Tara turn into a therapist?*

# Chapter Twenty-Two

## Antonio

"I didn't break your toes, did I? Do you need an ice pack?" Lee rubbed his neck as he locked Antonio's front door behind him. The light over the stove cast just enough of a glow to navigate the shoes strewn on the floor by the door.

Antonio pulled off his kitten heels, pretending not to notice the scuffs Lee had left on his favorite dancing shoes. He winked up at Lee. "You can step on me anytime, Daddy!"

Lee's warm belly laugh boomed, breaking the quiet of the apartment. "Tonio, I'm serious. Need me to carry you to the couch?"

Antonio lifted his arms. "My toes are fine, but I'll let you sweep me off my feet."

"You're *so* corny." Lee bent over and picked Antonio up with ease.

"Onc of these days you'll realize I'm not kidding." Antonio wrapped his arms around his neck, and let himself be carried to the couch by his...whatever they were. *Boyfriend. My charming, caring boyfriend.* Butterflies—not heartburn—quivered in his chest.

At least until Lee dropped him on the couch.

"Hey!" Antonio protested, flailing to sit upright.

Lee grinned innocently at him. "Chamomile?"

Antonio sighed dramatically, but the butterflies fluttered on. *I love you.* "Yes, please."

Lee busied himself making tea in the kitchenette. "Did you have a good time?"

"Way swankier than any birthday party I've had." Antonio stretched out across the cushions. The lights of passing cars danced on the ceiling.

"Right? I'll have to up my party planning game. The disco ball was a nice touch. Yours is next month, right? What do you usually do for your birthday?"

"My mom throws a party in the backyard. The whole family comes for everyone's birthdays, so there's a party somewhere almost every weekend. Big family, you know?"

Lee set two cups of tea on the coffee table. "That sounds amazing. We just went out to eat at Olive Garden or something so I could get the free dessert."

"You and Tara?" Antonio breathed deeply to catch Lee's comforting musky aroma as Lee reached over him to turn on the floor lamp. Warm yellow light filled the room. Lee looked down at him with a soft smile.

After an evening of dancing and teasing touches, Antonio was ready to forget the tea. He ran his hands up Lee's chest and shoulders.

Lee pressed a kiss to his forehead, melting his dirty thoughts like sugar. Lifting Antonio's legs, Lee settled underneath them. "Yeah, no! Tara and I could never afford to eat out. I'm sure Auntie Alitrice would have taken us out, but she was too sick to eat solid food by the time I turned sixteen, so I just never mentioned it. No, I meant my parents and sister.

"We only went out to eat on birthdays, and Jazz and I weren't allowed to have dessert, so cake was a big deal. I always told the server it was my birthday right away because then Dad couldn't say shit." Lee shrugged, a half grin playing at his lips. "At least until we got home, and by then the cake was already eaten. I'd do it for Jazz's birthday too. She didn't want to make Dad mad, not even for cake, but it made her happy. It was the least I could do as her brother, you know?"

Antonio waited for Lee to share more while Lee stared into his tea. He rarely spoke about his family. Nothing else came, and Lee fell into silence. Antonio added a lyric about Lee only getting dessert on his birthday to Lee's Song in his head. The verses about his past were usually sad. Antonio wished Lee's Song was a little happier. *Hopefully, his future verses will be.*

"Do you want to come?" he blurted out. *Oh shit. Is he ready for that? Am I ready for that?* The words had left his mouth without warning.

"Was that a come-on or an invite to your birthday?" Lee asked with a confused smile.

"Well, both!" Antonio winked. "But an invite to my birthday. I want you to meet my family! If you want, of course."

"I want to, just..." Lee trailed off, his face unreadable. "What would I be meeting them as? Your friend or...what?"

*Oh, shit! This is happening!* He'd wanted to have this conversation for weeks. The words lurked in his throat, but he kept swallowing them for fear of overwhelming Lee. He steeled himself before calmly suggesting, "As my boyfriend...?"

Lee froze, lips pursed to blow on his tea.

Antonio's heart raced in impatient circles around his ribcage.

"Boyfriend, huh?" Lee took a long sip from his mug, apparently *still* thinking.

Antonio refused to breathe, in case it'd somehow impact Lee's response. Anxiety clawed at his throat. Hope pounded with every heartbeat.

A smile peeked past the rim of Lee's mug. "I've never had a boyfriend. I'm into it."

Antonio grinned, letting out the sigh of relief he'd been holding. The hope that kept his heart beating turned to joy, taking flight in his chest. "I can't imagine introducing you to my family as a friend. And, to be frank, I haven't been able to shut up about you. There's no way they'd believe me if I said we were just friends."

*I love you.* His throat tightened, trapping the words.

"Honestly, I don't know how I'd handle it if you did say we were just friends," Lee admitted, setting his cup down. He ran his hands up Antonio's bare legs stretched across his lap. "You might have seen me express my emotions. Like, one small tear. Maybe two."

Antonio laughed, charmed by Lee's always awkward vulnerability. Lee wanted him. This. To be his boyfriend. "Wow, I almost got a tear? My boyfriend is so vulnerable."

Lee smiled. "What was that? I didn't quite catch it." He cupped a hand behind his ear.

"My boyfriend!" Antonio couldn't have wiped the grin off his face if he tried. The ache in his cheeks might have been permanent.

Lee was in the same predicament; his charming smile stretched across his face. He took the mug from Antonio's hands and set it on the coffee table next to his own. "I like hearing you call me that," he murmured, leaning over Antonio's body.

"I like saying it." Antonio found a good reason to stop smiling. His mouth had better things to do. Like kissing his boyfriend.

Their kiss deepened, tongues tangling. Hands roamed over their now familiar bodies. Antonio never imagined how in tune he and Lee would be after two months. They were constantly learning new places to touch, new sounds of pleasure to pull from each other. Instead of growing stale like it usually did, the familiarity was comforting.

Lee moaned in frustration, pulling away. "You really gotta start keeping lube over here."

Antonio laughed. "Just lube, huh? Not condoms?"

"Does 'boyfriend' mean exclusive?" Lee asked carefully, kissing the patch of bare chest exposed by Antonio's unbuttoned blouse.

Antonio arched into him. "It does for me. I haven't been with anyone else since long before we met anyway. Is...that what you want?" *This man better say yes.*

Lee's smile tickled Antonio's sternum. "It does for me, too. I deleted all the apps and everything. Not like I've even opened them since we met."

A smile cracked across Antonio's face. "Wow, Mr. Grand Gesture over here."

"Seriously, I can't imagine wanting anyone else when I have you." Lee's brown eyes staring into his made Antonio's brain melt into goo. "So yeah, no condoms. Is that okay?"

At Antonio's eager nod, Lee pulled Antonio off the couch and led him to the bed tucked behind the partition wall. "Come on. I want my boyfriend to rawdog me."

Antonio squealed, dancing after him. "Babe, you're such a romantic!"

He unbuttoned his blouse as Lee yanked his clothes off without care and threw himself onto the bed, bouncing against the pillows. Lee watched him undress, touching himself with slow strokes, his dazed smile matching Antonio's.

Antonio grabbed the lube off the nightstand as Lee pulled him in for a kiss, nibbling gently on his lower lip. Hands roamed over broad shoulders and firm planes of chests and abdomens. Mouths sucked marks and exhaled moans into each other.

For all Lee's impatience, he made no complaints as Antonio showered him with affection, with gentleness, with need. Antonio kissed all of the feelings he'd kept locked up into Lee's skin, licked *move in with me* as he took Lee in his mouth, scissored *I love you* inside him, moaned *future husband* wordlessly into his ear when Lee wrapped a hand around both of them, building their unhurried pleasure with slow strokes. He could die happy as long as he got to do this with his lover, his boyfriend, every day—to come apart along with him.

Lee's brown eyes squeezed shut as Antonio finally worked inside him. Without latex between them, the pressure and heat blazed. Sex with Lee always sent desire burning through his body, but this? An inferno whirled in his soul. Antonio clung to him, fingers digging into the meat of Lee's ass. He fought for self-control as he sank deeper into pleasure.

Lee wound around Antonio as they moved together, rolling them over to ride him. Lee's fingers tangled in his hair and pulled them together into a kiss. Antonio wanted time to stop, for this intimacy, this joy radiating from every cell to last forever. Their tongues and lips collided messily as they breathed each other in.

Antonio edged closer to his breaking point as Lee tugged his hair. He bit down on Lee's lower lip, straining to keep Lee's wonderful, talented mouth tangled with his. He thrust his hips deeper and faster, pumping Lee's erection the way he liked.

Lee gasped and shuddered above him, cum shooting into Antonio's palm. The tight heat as Lee came dragged Antonio over the edge after him.

They caught their breath, reluctant to pull away from each other.

Lee found his voice first, collapsing next to him. "Shit."

"Yeah. Shit."

"Can we never use a condom again?"

Antonio laughed, nodding his head against Lee's neck. "Barebacking only from now on."

He reluctantly pulled away to clean himself off and get a damp cloth for Lee. Antonio wiped away lube and spit and cum, peppering Lee with kisses as he went. *My boyfriend.* He sucked marks along his body, reminders for Lee that they belonged to each other.

"Hey, Tonio?" Lee asked sleepily as Antonio climbed into the bed with him.

"Yeah, Lee?" *Anything for you. Want to move in together?* Antonio cuddled under Lee's arm, snuggling into his boyfriend's side.

"You have, like, a really big family, don't you?" Lee rolled over to face him, eyes half closed with sleep. He pressed a kiss to Antonio's forehead.

There went his brain, puddling into affectionate goo again. "I do." *Want to join it? We can get married.* Antonio kissed the hollow between Lee's collarbones.

"Are they all...you know, cool? With shit? With you?"

His hesitation told Antonio what Lee was really asking. "Of course. I'm not the first queer person in the family. That honor goes to my stepdad. My parents have been outspoken allies since he transitioned before I was born."

"Oh, for real?"

Antonio grinned. "Yeah, my family switched to a queer-friendly church after he came out. He's a real pain in the ass about taking credit for saving me and Cassie from religious trauma."

Eyes fully shut now, Lee mumbled something that sounded like, "Your sister's gay?"

"Yup, as is one of my stepsisters and several cousins." Antonio grinned. "So it was real confusing when I told them I was bi. They didn't believe me because they'd expected I'd be gay since I was old enough to walk." He paused, something about this conversation felt familiar. "Have I told you this before?"

Lee yawned out a "yes."

Guilt crept into his chest, poisoning the once comfortable afterglow. Antonio ran through his Lee Song, but he couldn't recall anything about Lee's own coming out experience, other than it resulted in Lee homeless and going to conversion therapy in a church shelter. "Sorry. Why can't I remember anything about when your parents found out?"

"Because I don't like talking about it. Especially not right now." Lee pulled Antonio tighter against him, melting the guilt with a reassuring kiss to his hair. "Do I need to learn Spanish?"

Antonio barked a surprised laugh. "Babe, I can barely follow a conversation in Spanish, let alone speak it. No, you don't have to learn Spanish, but that's very sweet of you."

"Cool." Lee's breath grew deep and even, but he still fought sleep, murmuring, "Can you make me a cheat sheet or a family tree or something? Don't wanna embarrass myself by forgetting their names."

"Of course, Angel. Don't worry, though. They'll love you." *Almost as much as I do.* Antonio kept that thought to himself, burrowing his face into Lee's collarbone as soft snores filled the room.

# Saturday, August Third

# Chapter Twenty-Three

## Blanche

The rattlesnake plant they'd found on Tara's birthday was barely alive, the new growth already brown from the dry air of their apartment. The sorry state of it was highlighted by the bright lights from the construction site next door, despite the late hour. The steadily climbing concrete and rebar blocked more and more sunlight each day, replaced by constant artificial brightness all night.

There was no point in turning on a lamp; the floodlights were already too bright. As much as they'd miss the view of the river and Bellamy's skyline, the construction couldn't finish soon enough as far as Blanche was concerned.

Whiskey in one hand, watering can in the other, and Mudhoney playing on the CD player, Blanche filled the reservoir of the self-watering pot. "You're not dead yet, sweetie. Keep hanging in there."

They jumped at a buzzing sound from the coffee table, followed by a blue light that cast the room in an even eerier glow.

Ignoring the phone sounded wonderful, but it might be a client. Looking between the whiskey and the watering can with a heavy sigh, they set down the water and looked at yet another text from Sunny. *I don't know what else I expected.*

Being with Sunny wasn't a chore. Far from it. Sunny was dear to them; their time together was not much different from their usual friendship. Even the added intimacy wasn't unenjoyable. Sunny was gorgeous and a joy to bring pleasure to. Doting on her was a pleasant change from their clients, even if Real Blanche still had to keep their walls up.

It was safer that way. Sunny acted so much more entitled—*bratty*—since Blanche had agreed to this indulgence. Instead of the sweet, supportive, charm Blanche had hoped for, Sunny demanded all of Blanche's free time and the little emotional energy they could spare. Sustaining themself until Sunny got what she needed, and they resumed their friendship, was growing to be more of a challenge with every barrage of texts Sunny sent them, demanding more.

The phone in their hand buzzed with another text from Sunny. Blanche fought the urge to toss it back on the table, or turn it off, or just go to bed and hide.

If they let their guard down, Sunny would suck them dry. Not maliciously, of course, but Blanche already struggled to protect their energy. And of course, every time Blanche hinted that Sunny needed to back off, she didn't pick up on it. When they outright asked for more space, Sunny took it personally and pouted.

It'd be easy to chalk it up to immaturity and naivete, considering Sunny had never truly dated anyone before (not since Lee, and that had been short-lived). But Blanche had never truly had a relationship with anyone but Daisy before either. They'd been just as naive as Sunny going into this.

They took a long sip of their whiskey before unlocking their phone.

> Hey <3

> You busy tonight?

> Can I come over if you're free?

> Hello, did you see this?

> Blaaanncchheeeee

> I'll be up gaming so let me know if I can come over. I want to see you. We haven't talked in days. Miss you! <3

Blanche sighed into their glass and forced themself to type a reply.

> Sorry. Can't tonight...I had a client over.

They considered lying and saying the client was still here, but if Sunny couldn't respect Blanche's need for space after a session, this indulgence would need to end.

Sunny's response was instant.

> Oh, they left? So does that mean I can come over?

> No...I need alone time.

> What, you don't want to be alone with me? ;P

> I'm serious, Babygirl. I'm on the verge of a drop...

> Can I help?

> Yes...by giving me space.

> Fine. </3 I'll be up if you change your mind.

Blanche turned off their phone and collapsed into their armchair. *Fuck it. It doesn't matter how much someone would pay. It's not happening tonight.* Their client earlier had been the asshole patron who paid the rent, the one person entitled to a session whenever he wanted, per their agreement. And he wouldn't be back tonight, so Blanche could be truly unavailable.

Which was necessary, since the fragile peace they'd been clinging to had been dashed by Sunny's texts. Blanche was only slightly exaggerating about being on the verge of a drop, but as if they'd spoken it into existence, reality came crashing down hard. Their guilt and irritation physically ached all over, radiating in their jaw and neck.

They pulled out their stash and packed a bowl with Northern Lights. Blanche had hoped the whiskey would be enough, but it was a weed night. *Isn't every night a weed night?* Their session with the asshole hadn't been awful. For their least favorite client, Work Blanche played the priest to whom he confessed his sins. But this one had been cut short by his on-and-off fiancé calling him, so Blanche's drop was unexpected.

Blanche's patron was a pharmaceutical executive in a toxic relationship with the director of a nonprofit for narcotics recovery; the pair had constant arguments about their misaligned goals and his cheating. Watching him struggle in real time to reconcile his controlling relationship with his fiancé with his controlled arrangement with Blanche had been entertaining.

While holding up the phone on speaker, Blanche had kept him kneeling as his fiancé had yelled at him. His hands were physically free, but he'd kept them clasped in prayer as Blanche had instructed. His now ex-fiancé had let him have it, Blanche visibly reacting to every development. The anger in his voice and anxiety flashing across his face from her accusations had been fascinating. Minutes before she'd called, he'd been sobbing from guilt for those very sins during their roleplay.

The less enjoyable part was that he'd cut their session short before Blanche got the chance to punish him. Usually, his penance involved hot wax and a wooden paddle or ruler. The outlet for their resentment made the whole arrangement worth it. *He'll never actually change his behavior. Why would he? He has me as a crutch.*

Tara came home from her date eventually. Their back aching, Blanche forced themself to listen politely while she complained about it. They said all the things Real Blanche should say, brushing off Tara's concern about how they were doing. Tara tucked them in with her blanket and refilled their whiskey when she went to bed.

Despite, or maybe because of, their lack of a full scene, Blanche was unsettled. Unresolved. Lonely. Stuck. *I shouldn't have waited so long to start my aftercare. My usual tricks are taking forever to work.* They continued to smoke, letting the high settle them into a lull. Anger had no place in their real life. That was their fuel for their clients. They had no outlet for it outside of a contract. *Not anymore.*

When they were young, Daisy would drag Blanche to an abandoned warehouse near the mounds, and they'd throw anything breakable they could find. Lightbulbs, window panes, beer bottles. All would be smashed against the concrete wall, while they laughed and drank stolen liquor. That was how Daisy had coped and so Blanche had made it work too.

But the warehouse was sold long ago, destined to become cheap apartments which were later "redeveloped" yet again into luxury condos. Without an outlet for their fury, Blanche had lost their temper when Daisy was cheated by a john. More than their temper—Blanche had lost six weeks of their life in a coma from the injuries he had inflicted. Daisy had found Blanche a mentor before they'd even recovered, so they could have a new outlet through BDSM.

The first step in the long chain of events that had led to Daisy's death.

*Daisy can't be blamed. I knew he was getting too attached and I still took his money.*

The longer this indulgence with Sunny went on, the less she reminded them of Daisy and the more she reminded them of the man who had murdered her. *No, that's unfair. Sunny is nothing like him. She's simply unused to relationships, let alone with someone as avoidant as I am. Sunny is sweet, just a little needy and naive. And stubborn. And bratty.*

Daisy was also all of those things.

But *he'd* been those things, too. He'd pestered Blanche for as many sessions as they'd give him. Demanded kisses and intimacy under the guise of aftercare. Pouted and pushed when Blanche said no.

But Sunny was a saint compared to that monster. The one who had dared wait for Blanche to come home with Daisy bleeding out next to him.

"We can be together all the time now! See? I did this for you!"

Daisy's lifeless eyes had stared into nothing, all of her dreams and love drained into a pool of blood surrounding her.

"Why are you upset? You don't need her! Stop screaming!"

The disembodied screaming that haunted them had been Blanche's. They knew that. But in their memory, it was Daisy. Screaming for help, screaming, *"How could you?"* because it was Blanche's fault. Their client had done this to her.

"You're supposed to be mine!"

*He's dead, too. He can't hurt anyone anymore. Think of the happy times.*

Blanche stared at the wall, losing themself in the memories of Daisy's laughter and misadventures, guiding their brain away from that horrific night. They puffed on the bowl occasionally to keep the memories manageable. Indica was the only way they could remember the love of their life without hating themself. Without drowning in guilt.

A key turning in the lock made Blanche jump. But it was just Lee, coming home from whatever party he'd been at.

He took in the sight of Blanche curled up in the chair, bowl in one hand and whiskey in the other. A gentle smile softened his tired face. "I'll make some tea. Get your ass on the couch."

Blanche somehow found the energy to move the two feet from their armchair to the corner of the couch just as Lee came back. He handed them the steaming mug of chamomile and settled next to them.

"Thank you."

"I'm the designated teddy bear in this family. No need to thank me."

Blanche curled up against Lee, resting their head on his shoulder. Cigarette smoke and sweat clung to his clothes. "Tara is far too bony for cuddling."

"She's all elbows," Lee laughed, pulling them close. "So what'll it be? Therapy session? Silence? Do you want to talk about what's going on with you for once?"

With Sunny, Blanche needed space to get comfortable solitude. But Lee was always safe to be around when they were in a drop, falling into or filling the silence whenever he saw some sign they needed companionship or quiet. "Therapy session. Tell me what's going on with you. How's life with a boyfriend?"

Lee hummed a laugh. "Honestly, good? I keep waiting for the other shoe to drop, but it keeps being easy. Even when I annoy him, he just talks it out and moves on. It's weird."

"Why does the other shoe need to drop? Why can't it be easy?" Blanche breathed in the chamomile steam of their tea before sipping the honey-sweet nectar.

"Because life is never easy for long. You of all people should understand that."

Blanche let out a sardonic chuckle. "I do. But are you letting yourself enjoy the easy times? Or are you protecting yourself because you expect the worst?"

Lee tucked their head under his chin. "Is both an answer?"

"Tell me more."

"Like, I am trying to enjoy it all while it lasts. I say yes to everything because I *want* to spend time with him. I want to meet his family next weekend. I love being with him."

"I sense a 'but' coming."

Lee sighed. "But... How long will it stay easy? How long will he want me around? So yeah, I probably am protecting myself whenever I remind myself to not get too attached or believe the corny, romantic shit he says."

Part of Blanche wanted to tell him to trust that Antonio meant it. Blanche had been more involved with Confession before Daisy's passing. They remembered the entertaining charmer who'd kept morale high whenever Chas had to be the boss, instead of a cast member. The one who slept with half of his coworkers, then caused fights as an excuse to break things off. Who missed shows because he was too drunk to walk, or because he simply didn't feel like it.

There'd been anxiety in Antonio's eyes—he remembered Blanche, too. For his sake, Blanche had pretended they didn't remember Antonio when Lee had introduced them. They had never been close; it was conceivable that they may not remember one another. But Blanche had been friends with Chas and Freddy since they were teenagers, roaming around Eastside under Daisy's leadership. Chas had always been frustrated by Antonio. She'd believed in him, but he'd never believed in himself. He let himself mess up every good opportunity Chas had tried to give him.

Chas had warned Antonio off to protect Lee from being Antonio's latest temporary indulgence. Not that it had worked. Freddy, in a rare break from supporting his beloved's every whim, thought Lee was grown enough to handle himself. Blanche personally agreed with Freddy. Lee protected himself too much; Antonio could be good for him.

And maybe a clean slate was what Antonio needed. Antonio was terrified and heartbroken when Lee had fled from their little lover's spat. The old Antonio would have laughed it off and moved on to someone else. Instead, Lee was throwing the L word around, even as he worried if Antonio liked him. *If he knew Antonio back then, he'd see how head over heels he is now. But that's between them.*

"I'm no relationship expert, but I would have regretted it if I'd had one foot out the door when I was with Daisy."

"Oh, it's one of *those* nights," Lee murmured, reaching for the bowl Blanche had left on the coffee table.

"Shush," Blanche scolded but took the bowl. "You're happy with your relationship, right? How much more would you enjoy it if you let yourself believe it could work out? Daisy and I used to bicker about this all the time. I thought it best to live life like each day was our last. She wanted us to live like we'd have forever.

"I don't know which of us was right, or if either of us was wrong. She let me indulge in everything I was curious about, and I let her mastermind all of her hairbrained schemes that we only pulled off through sheer luck. She had such big dreams for our future." Blanche sighed. "And here we are. She had her last day and I can't figure out how to live without her."

"Your life isn't over, Blanche. You can dream of your future, too. You have us. Tara and Sunny. Chas and Freddy. Me. I might not be home as much, but I'll always be here."

"And I love you for it, darling." Blanche nestled into his side. "If Daisy was right, living like you could die any moment isn't a life. Loving him like you could break up any day isn't love. She'd say you're missing out on building your future together."

*What am I missing out on by living like I'm already dead? Maybe it's time to come up with one of Daisy's hairbrained schemes of my own.*

"It's hard to imagine the future when I've already lived longer than I expected. I never thought I'd make it to sixteen, let alone twenty-five." Lee chuckled.

"It gets worse. Just wait 'til you turn thirty." Blanche snorted. "But if I made it this long, you can too."

It probably shouldn't be funny, but they'd faced their own mortality enough times to resonate. If they were being honest, they'd had far fewer near-death experiences since Daisy had died. Perhaps following her advice would get them in trouble, but both Blanche and Lee had been stagnant for the sake of safety for far too long.

*Lord only knows what Daisy would tell me to do these days. She'd probably have an empire of fetish sites, selling feet pics and used panties. Always creative like that, my Daisy.*

With a sigh, they smiled up at Lee. "When you meet his family next weekend, try it Daisy's way. Enjoy his family as if they're your future. Jump with both feet."

"Why do you and Tara have the most terrifying advice?"

# Saturday, August Tenth

# Chapter Twenty-Four

## Lee

THE SWELTERING AFTERNOON SUN overwhelmed the rattling air conditioner in Antonio's car as they drove to his mom's house for his birthday party. If the crank windows still worked, Lee would have rolled them down in a second. The occasional puff of cool air on his ankles was the only relief from the oppressive heat. Lee had never imagined any car could be shittier than his Sonata, but Antonio's Civic ran on prayer alone. Antonio insisted it would run forever. Blanche would probably say he was projecting.

Despite his apprehensive grip on the door and utter lack of faith in the frayed seat belt, being the passenger was a relief. Driftwood was the bougiest part of the Bellamy metro, across the literal train tracks and Wisconsin border from Eastside. Antonio claimed he grew up in the "cheap part" of town, but Lee doubted Driftwood had a "cheap part".

According to Sunny, Driftwood had been private property until the '50s. When sold to developers, every deed contained a racial covenant barring non-whites from living there. It'd been Bellamy's destination suburb for white flight in the '60s. Lee trusted Sunny to know the history; she actually cared about shit like that. Of course, he *cared* about systemic racism, but he couldn't think about it as much as Sunny did. He had to live it already.

Other than the occasional party Whatshisname dragged him to, Lee tried to avoid Driftwood altogether. Black families, including his parents, tended to stay in Illinois, where they'd been redlined decades ago. Over time, newer immigrant families like Sunny's had joined them in Eastside. Some folks moved to Bellamy proper, but never Driftwood. Antonio's family, transplants from LA, was the only exception Lee had ever heard of.

As they turned off the main road, Lee was pleasantly surprised to find Antonio's neighborhood wasn't full of McMansions. Split-level homes and one-level ramblers—like the one he'd grown up in—lined the streets. No boarded-up windows or dumped cars, but this part of Driftwood still sprouted the occasional condo like the ones going up in Eastside. Antonio's neighborhood looked shockingly normal.

Antonio, effortlessly attractive as always in a yellow tank top and cut-off shorts, put his hand on Lee's thigh once he'd downshifted into third gear. Despite the August heat making his undershirt cling to his skin, Lee couldn't bring himself to dress *that* casually, as much as he appreciated the sheer amount of muscular thigh Antonio's shorts showed. He had to make a good impression on Antonio's family.

Tara had helped him decide what to wear today: bootcut jeans and an orange short-sleeve button-up patterned with blue flowers. He felt both underdressed to meet his boyfriend's parents and overdressed for a backyard cookout.

He'd tried on a few different outfits that were more dressy, a white button-up or a heather gray polo. But he'd looked into the mirror and couldn't see himself—just his dad, who never wore anything more colorful than navy blue. He couldn't stomach the thought of introducing himself to Antonio's family as the spitting image of his father. So orange it was.

"Are you sure it's okay for me to bring this?" Lee pointed to the paper bag between his feet. Antonio had told him not to bring anything, saying his birthday gift from Lee—a songwriting journal—was more than enough. But Lee had picked up a bottle of tequila after Antonio had mentioned it was his stepdad's favorite. His mom's voice had been harping at him all week, alternating between how he should always bring a hostess gift and the sins of alcohol, making Lee question his choice over and over.

"For the millionth time, yes. There'll be more booze than that today. You'll win brownie points just for bringing anything." Antonio patted Lee's leg before shifting gears. The clutch groaned in protest. "Besides, your presence is the real present."

Lee rolled his eyes with a laugh. "I knew you couldn't go long without saying something cliche as hell."

He had spent the past few weeks memorizing the family tree Antonio had diagrammed on the back of a Confession setlist. His parents had five kids, with Antonio the youngest and only boy. They'd split when Antonio was in middle school and remarried. His dad, Pedro, and stepmom, Giselle, had married Antonio's freshman year and had five more kids. His mom, Paula, had married his stepdad, Oscar, Antonio's junior year, adding three stepsisters to the mix.

His parents were still close friends, so all sides of the blended family would be there today. That meant Lee had four parents, four full sisters, five half brothers, and three stepsisters to meet. Along with a handful of in-laws and nieces, nephews, and niblings. And he hadn't even started to learn about all of the aunts, uncles, cousins, and grandparents that came with a big family.

"Oh, by the way, did I remember to tell you my friends are coming?"

*Great.* Lee blinked. "No. Which friends?"

"I pretty much only got two friends, babe! Gabe and Richard, but call him Dicky. He hates it."

"I'm not calling him Dicky, then." Lee couldn't help but smile at Antonio's laugh. "What else should I know?"

Antonio shrugged. "They'll tell you what they want you to know. They're kind of private, and they say I talk too much. I told you Gabe and I dated in high school, right?"

"Yeah, I remember. What have you told them about me?"

Antonio snorted. "What *haven't* I told them?"

*Great.* Lee ran his hands along his thighs. He should have brought Tara as a security blanket, but he had to do this alone. They might be codependent, but he didn't want Antonio's family to know that. He had to make a good impression, and Tara hated parties.

Despite his nerves, he was excited. Lee wanted to learn all about the man he loved. He wanted to see which parent had given Antonio his hazel eyes. What embarrassing stories his sisters would tell about him. Which auntie would spill all of the drama. Whose cooking everyone avoided, and whose was the best. The little things he hadn't appreciated at his mom's family reunions until he was no longer family.

Not that his parents had ever been the big, loud, loving family he dreamed of. But at least they were a connection to church events or family reunions so that Lee could *pretend* he had a big, loud, loving family.

Tara, Blanche, and Sunny might be his true family, but the three introverts would never be the community he craved. Their idea of a party was smoking Northern Lights and Sunny kicking Tara's ass at Mario Kart. Sure, he needed those nights—and their unconditional love and support—but he also longed for something bigger. Being in Whatshisname's circle was a poor substitute, but a poor substitute was better than nothing.

Antonio parked his car, setting the parking brake with a screech. Cars lined the street and loud music blared from a few houses away. Before he unbuckled, Lee popped the door open, breathing in the slightly cooler air with the mouthwatering aroma of grilled meat.

Antonio patted his thigh. "Last chance to run, Angel. Want to back out now?"

Lee shook his head with a grin. "Not a chance. That food smells delicious." He grabbed the paper bag at his feet, eager to meet the people he'd been hearing about. To enjoy the party and pretend Antonio's family was his for a night.

"Hold up a second." Antonio grabbed his arm before he could get out.

Lee turned back in confusion, only to be met with a passionate kiss. He kissed Antonio back eagerly, but this was too intense for a family gathering.

Antonio broke the kiss before Lee needed a moment. "I wanted to do that before we went in. My family won't care, but you're not big on PDA, so we can keep the tongue to a minimum."

Lee nodded. He hadn't considered that they might even hold hands around Antonio's family, let alone kiss. "So, no groping you in front of your grandma?"

"I won't tell you to stop." Antonio winked.

Lee followed Antonio into the backyard, where they were met with a raucous greeting. Despite the many shouts of "Hey Antonio!" and "Happy birthday, cousin!" and "Tonito, is that your boyfriend?", the guests in the backyard didn't rush over to them.

Relief washed over him. He'd worried upon seeing the dozens of people that he'd meet them all at once. Instead, the men standing around the grill raised their beers in a casual greeting. The aunties under the tent stayed in the shade. The folks playing cards were glued to their hands.

Aside from Julio Iglesias playing on the speakers and different seasonings scenting the air, Lee had traveled back in time to his childhood.

A middle-aged woman greeted them first, her thick brown curls pulled up into a puff, flecked with flattering salt and pepper streaks. "Happy birthday, Tonito," she hugged Antonio, smothering his cheek with loud kisses. She squinted up at Lee. "And you must be Lee! Antonio won't shut up about you."

Antonio's cheeks reddened. "Ma, come on!"

"No, I want to embarrass my baby," Paula teased. Lee already loved Antonio's mom, just from watching them interact. His hazel eyes and sharp chin had come from her.

"It's a pleasure to meet you, ma'am." Lee handed her the paper bag. "This is for you."

"Oh, he's got manners, too? Please, call me Paula." Her hazel eyes crinkled, giving him a wide smile just like Antonio's. Lee doubted his own mom had ever looked at him as warmly. "Tonito, how come you're not this polite to me?"

"Must have been my upbringing." Antonio shot a grin at Lee.

Paula swatted his arm. "Don't you start!" She opened the bag. "Oh, it's Oscar's favorite. Thank you, Lee. So sweet of you!"

She motioned for him to bend down. Antonio must have gotten his height from her, too. Lee towered over her as he crouched to hug her. With her welcome, Lee was dragged over to the grill, where Antonio introduced him to his dad and stepdad.

"So, you're Lee," Pedro eyed him up and down, his green eyes bright against his deep umber skin. Antonio's dad didn't have many features in common with Antonio, aside from their slender build. *And the height. Antonio stood no chance against the short genetics.* "What are your intentions with my son?"

"Dad! Why would you ask that? Jesus Christ!"

Before Lee could begin to consider how to answer *that* question, Pedro laughed. He had the same easy, sonorous laugh as Antonio. "I'm just fucking with you, Lee. Hope you're hungry! Oscar and I have been cooking all day!"

"*I've* been cooking all day. You've been supervising." Oscar winked, clacking the tongs as he closed the grill. "Nice to meet you, Lee. Should have guessed Tonio would pick a tall one. About time we got someone else who isn't fun-sized in this family." Oscar wasn't particularly tall, maybe around Tara's height, but he was still taller than Pedro and Antonio.

"Call me fun-sized one more time, find out what happens." Antonio crossed his arms and glared at his stepdad.

"Tonio says you're a great cook, Oscar," Lee interrupted before an argument began, pushing up his glasses as anxiety burned through him. He'd never seen Antonio so defensive. "The food he brings home is amazing. Nice to finally meet the chef."

Oscar's deep brown eyes lit up and a smile grew across his face. "Tonito, I'm a good cook? You said that? About *me*?"

"Oh God, let's go. He's not supposed to know I don't hate him. He's never going to shut up about it." Antonio dragged Lee away as Oscar and Pedro laughed behind them.

*That wasn't... Oh. They were kidding. Duh, Lee.* As if he needed another reminder that Antonio's family wasn't anything like his.

Forcing himself to relax, Lee met Antonio's stepmom Giselle, his sisters, brothers, and their significant others. He met cousins, aunties, and at least nine women who had introduced themselves as Antonio's grandma or abuela or nona (he couldn't figure out where the Italian grandma came in). People who weren't related to Antonio still loved him and welcomed Lee enthusiastically. Dozens of people all melded into a chaotic, loud, cohesive, loving family.

How on earth so many people fit into a small suburban backyard with room left over for a dance floor and a bonfire, he couldn't figure. Lee would never remember their names, but they didn't expect him to. Every single person he met was so nice. Some were funny, some were sweet, others were quiet. But they were all kind and welcoming. Lee felt instantly accepted in a way he hadn't experienced since childhood. *Or ever, honestly.*

A bitter surge of jealousy rose in his chest. Antonio had all of this, and Lee didn't even have his hard-ass parents— With a breath, he squashed it back down; he should enjoy this. He was following Blanche's terrifying advice, immersing himself in Antonio's family for a day. He could unpack the bitterness later.

"Tonio, come watch!" Antonio's youngest brother, Daniel, ran up as Antonio's eldest sister, Cassie, introduced herself. Even at eight years old, Daniel already came up to Antonio's shoulder. Giselle and her kids were the only blood relatives who came close to Lee's height. Daniel tugged on Antonio's hand. "We wrote a song for you!"

"Sure! Let's go!" Antonio grabbed Lee's arm.

With a panicked glance at Cassie, Daniel froze. "No! Just you! Uh, Gracie is shy."

Antonio shot a suspicious glance at Cassie. "Really? Since when is *your* daughter shy?"

Cassie shrugged innocently. "Kids go through phases. Don't worry, I'll keep Lee company while you're gone." She linked her arm through his. Her fingernails pressed into his forearm as she held him firmly next to her.

"Right." Antonio turned to Lee. "Don't let her scare you off with any horror stories about me. I promise I'll be right back."

Lee nodded, pushing up his glasses as his anxiety burned hot enough to make his nose itch. Nervously, Lee faced Cassie, all hope of being accepted by Antonio's family flooding out of him. *It was going too well.*

"So, you're the one my brother's been obsessing over." Cassie's sharp gaze, uncannily like Antonio's, inspected him. She resembled Pedro more than Paula—thick black twists framed her round face and her hazel eyes were greener—but he'd seen her searching expression in Antonio's face many times. "Look, our parents are way too nice to give you the third degree or admit how worried we are. None of us could stand it if he relapsed again. The last detox was..."

She squeezed her eyes shut before leveling her gaze at Lee. "Tonio acts like a cocky little shit, but we're lucky he's alive. He's been in a good place since he moved home, but he needs to surround himself with people who are good for him. You must have something to do with him being so damn happy the past few months, so I'm giving you the benefit of the doubt."

Lee nodded, unsure of how to respond and sensing a "but" coming. Or an interrogation like his mom always did when he looked guilty, asking questions while carefully watching for any sign of the truth. Just in case, Lee did his best to put on the reassuring expression he'd always put on for his mom: a bland half smile and a furrow in his brow, nodding slightly to tell her that her concerns were heard. His mom would have seen right through it.

"But the way he talks about you? He'd follow you into a damn crack house if you led him there. And even though Antonio will not shut up about you, he won't tell us about your life. So what can you tell me to reassure me that your family and friends will be good for him, too? That his soft spot for you isn't going to lead him into a bad situation?"

Lee tucked away his curiosity about how Antonio had talked about him for later, tapping his fingers against his thigh to the beat of the music to focus on Cassie's question. "Uh, well, he's pretty much met everyone except my sister."

Cassie crossed her arms. "He said he met three friends but won't say anything else. You can imagine why that's concerning to hear you say he's met everyone. So which is it? Has he met everyone or three friends?"

He mulled his response, letting the twang of the bass line steady his racing heart. Admitting to Antonio's family that the only people in his life were Tara, Blanche, and Sunny wasn't exactly the good impression he wanted to make. But being cagey would be worse.

"I mean, there's also our coworkers, but he knows them better than I do. And I have some other friends who could be bad for him, but he made the call to avoid them himself, even before he told me about being in recovery. So if you're worried about him following me into a bad situation or 'crack house' or whatever, don't be. I wouldn't pressure him to go anywhere or do anything he doesn't want to, and he'd tell me if something is too far out of his comfort zone."

Lee wondered if he'd said the right thing. He would never have dared say any of that to his parents (imagine telling his *dad* not to micromanage anyone). But the hunch of Cassie's shoulders when she crossed her arms, the slight movements in her eyebrows, were all too similar to Antonio to overthink it.

He didn't appreciate Cassie putting him on the spot, but he understood her worry. It would have been too easy if Antonio's family *didn't* interrogate him. He just wished he had more reassuring things to say. *"I always knew you were a disappointment."* Lee took a breath to keep the reassuring mask up, doing his best to ignore his dad's voice and focus on Cassie.

Her hazel-green eyes narrowed. "And your family? Got any brothers who might pressure him into a drink? Or an unemployed cousin who mysteriously always has money? Or an aunt still taking pain meds for an accident she had years ago?"

Lee shook his head, jaw tightening as anger and shame burned through him, naming the instruments in the song to regain control of his reaction. *Timpani. Guitar.* Cassie had struck a nerve. He'd done *many* things Auntie Alitrice wouldn't have approved of to get morphine because her doctors didn't believe she was in pain as she was dying. *Trombone. Trumpet. This isn't about you.* "I just have a younger sister,

Jazz. She's a freshman at the U. Super smart and annoyingly perfect. I can introduce them soon. I was planning on it anyway."

The yard went quiet as the song ended.

"And when is he going to meet your parents? Your extended family?"

*"I will not allow you to bring shame to our family."* As the ghost of his dad's voice reminded him of his worst memories, Lee's glasses slipped down his nose. *There goes your chance at a good impression.* He'd hoped for more time with Antonio's family before they'd asked about his own. "Uh, Jazz is the only biological family I'm in contact with. She lives with our parents, but Antonio and I wouldn't be welcome there."

Realization dawned on Cassie's face. "Fuck, Lee! I gave this whole ass speech and you just took it? You should have stopped me!"

Scratching his nose to subtly wipe away the sweat, Lee pushed his glasses up, disappointment sinking in like poison. "Don't worry about it. I'd be asking the same thing in your shoes. Tonio is lucky he's got so many people looking out for him."

"And now you do, too." Cassie groaned in resigned frustration. "God, I hate that Mom is always right about her gut feelings. She decided you were ours the second you walked in."

Lee gave her a rueful smile. She was being nice after coming down hard, but the "dream of your future together" advice that Blanche had given him was out the window. Why would Antonio's family want him when his own didn't?

# Chapter Twenty-Five

## Lee

After more stilted small talk with Cassie, during which she tried way too hard to be nice, Antonio finally returned. With a glare at his sister, Antonio dragged Lee away to the table full of food. "Sorry about that. That song was like ten verses long and *apparently*, they needed to perform it *twice* when you were alone with Cassie."

Lee smiled, his nerves soothed now that Antonio was back. Cassie's repeated apologies hadn't eased the disappointed ache reminding him he didn't belong here. Not like Antonio's hand gripping his wrist did, or the faint hum as Antonio sang along to the music under his breath. His dad's voice was easier to ignore with Antonio around. Being constantly showered with praise over the past few months, corny as it was, reminded Lee that his dad was full of shit.

He followed Antonio's lead and grabbed a plate. "She was cool. Barely interrogated me."

Antonio piled more food onto Lee's plate than his own as he huffed in annoyance. "I should have known she'd do something like this. She's always been overprotective."

"Tonio, everyone in your family is great. Don't worry about it." With a reassuring smile infinitely more genuine than what he'd worn for Cassie, Lee pulled the overflowing plate away from Antonio before he could add anything else.

Antonio's presence anchored him, giving him a place in the crowd. Overthinking his conversation with Cassie would be humiliating enough later when he replayed it every night for the rest of his life. Right now, he wanted to enjoy himself. And eat the mountain of food Antonio had handed him. Lee already doubted he'd finish it, but he couldn't wait to try it all.

According to Antonio, his parents were the first of their families to move out of LA, so they'd built a support system with other transplants to Bellamy. Their families had eventually followed, but the community Paula and Pedro had built around them had stayed. The blended background of Antonio's extended family and friends had made a mark on their buffet. Oxtails, pupusa, lumpia, plantains, all of it a fusion of the people who loved Antonio.

Lee's dad always insisted on a strict diet. His mom's family could cook, but Leland Sr couldn't stand his family enjoying anything, especially food. Lee could have grilled chicken, not fried. He could have greens but not with ham hocks. Forget the mac and cheese—dairy and empty carbs were rarely allowed.

He wondered how his strict upbringing had marked him, what shapes Antonio would find if he ever did meet Lee's family. A rush of relief struck him at the realization that he never would; Antonio wouldn't see the version of him that could be controlled, regulated, abandoned. He had spent a decade locking that Lee in the past.

"You doing okay, Angel?" Antonio put a hand on Lee's thigh as they sat down at a table under the tent. "Is it too much?"

"No, this is amazing." Lee smiled as he speared a bit of ham hock on his fork. Antonio's family was...well, *everything* that Lee had wanted from his own family, back when he'd still had one. "Hopefully I'm making a good impression."

"Trust me, you are. My aunt even asked me if you play for both teams." Antonio grinned up at him. "Not that I'd let that happen. You're mine."

Lee covered his mouth as he laughed. "Wait, which aunt? I should weigh my options."

Antonio pinched his arm. "Flirt all you want, but you're coming home with me."

"Of course, babe." Lee patted Antonio's thigh, glancing around nervously as Antonio kissed his cheek.

Antonio's family seemed unphased by their closeness, but why would they be? They weren't Lee's family, who would have coldly asked them to leave long before this. Lee savored the bitter flavor of the greens that reminded him of his aunt's cooking as the impression of Antonio's kiss lingered on his skin.

Even Auntie Alitrice had been uncomfortable with his sexuality, and she'd been the one family member who'd supported him after he'd been outed. Auntie Alitrice's acceptance of Lee had left her isolated along with him. His dad had cut ties with his only sister after she'd taken Lee in, leaving Lee and Tara alone to care for her in her final days.

She'd never had the chance to come around to this version of him; Lee was sure she would have if she'd had more time. Even if she hadn't been thrilled about him being gay, his aunt always wanted Lee to do what made *him* happy, not what his father approved of. He swallowed the lump in his throat, along with the greens, before tentatively wrapping his arm around Antonio.

"Well, isn't that cute?" A deep voice approached them from behind.

"Gabey! Dicky!" Antonio sprang up to greet his friends with a hug. Lee checked that he was presentable before turning around.

The blond man evaded the hug, but the tall one hugged him back eagerly. A mane of long, dark curls fell like a curtain as the man bent down to squeeze Antonio against his massive chest. His shoulders and biceps strained against the sleeves of his black V-neck. Despite his casual appearance, the gold watch and heart logo on his shirt told Lee that Blanche would love to meet the attractive giant.

Lee stood up to introduce himself, wiping his hands on his napkin. "Hi, Lee Jones. You must be Antonio's friends."

The tall one shook his hand, smiling politely. "I'm Gabe Cooper, nice to meet you."

"Richard Carter." The blond one nodded in greeting. He stood a couple of inches taller than Antonio and had a similar wiry build. The similarities ended there. His bright blue eyes were set in a serious expression. The sleeves of his navy blue button-down were rolled neatly up to his elbows, revealing a watch of his own. His khakis were creased sharply, like he was on the way to the country club. *I didn't know people dressed like that unironically. Especially in August.*

"Pleasure to meet you both," Lee replied, astounded at how different Antonio was from his friends. They were reserved, polite, and their appearance screamed money.

"Gabriel, Richard, so glad you could make it!" Paula walked up, greeting them both with a hug. For someone who had dodged Antonio's hug,

Richard embraced Paula fiercely. He handed her a bottle of wine Lee hadn't noticed.

Gabe kissed her cheek. "Paula, lovely to see you. I set some cookies near the desserts on my way in. Mom's recipe."

"You're both always so sweet! Tonito always shows up empty-handed," Paula teased. "Are your parents coming today? Miriam said no, but I'm hoping she changed her mind."

"No, it's their busy season. They say hello though. And happy birthday to this guy." Gabe ruffled Antonio's hair, who swatted his hand away.

"My parents aren't able to make it either," Richard added with a wry grin.

"As if *they'd* ever be invited," Paula laughed. "Make yourselves at home, boys. Get some food!" Paula rubbed Lee's arm with a smile as she wandered back to her hostess duties.

Lee decided then and there that he would die for Antonio's mom. Based on how Gabe and Richard had opened up around her, he wasn't alone. Antonio must have gotten his magnetism from her, too.

Richard turned to Gabe. "I'll get food, you get drinks."

Gabe nodded. "Lee, you want anything?"

"Get him a Modelo, please," Antonio answered before Lee could check with him. "Don't worry Angel, I'm driving. Enjoy yourself."

"If you're sure." Lee nodded, surprised Antonio knew what beer he'd want. He never drank around him. *But social lubricant would be nice right now.*

"Trust me, we'll be here til long past sundown. You don't want to be the only one sober when the party gets started. I'm used to it, but you're new to the chaos."

Moments later, Gabe returned with three bottles of beer and a sparkling water for Antonio. "Cheers."

Lee clinked his bottle against Gabe's. "So how did you guys become friends? Don't take this the wrong way, but you guys seem to be complete opposites."

Gabe nodded with a grin. "We are opposites. I'm not nearly as annoying as Tonio."

Antonio glared. "You're supposed to be hyping me up, Gabey."

"I love you, Tonio, but you can be real fucking annoying," Gabe teased. "We met in middle school. He helped my nerdy, fat kid self fake some confidence."

Lee couldn't imagine the Adonis in front of him being a nerdy fat kid, but high school for them had been over a decade ago.

"You were not fat. Just a little husky is all," Antonio interjected.

"If only everyone else in school thought so, too." Gabe turned back to Lee. "Tonio probably didn't warn you. His family adopts people. One hug from Paula and you're an honorary Flores for life. Even after Tonio broke up with me, she made it a point to remind me that I'll always be her non-biological son. You're invited to every single fucking party for the rest of your life."

Lee's eyebrows raised skeptically before he could stop himself.

"It's true." Richard set a plate down in front of Gabe and sat next to him. "I came to one party when Gabe and I were dating. Paula still texts me every holiday. There's no escape."

"Are you friends with all of your exes?" Lee teased Gabe in an effort to change the subject. He didn't want to admit that he would likely be the exception after his conversation with Cassie.

Gabe winced. "Oh no, just these two. They're the only relationships that didn't crash and burn into a goddamn dumpster fire at the end." He looked at Lee with alarm, as if suddenly remembering his audience. "Oh, fuck. Sorry, I don't know if Tonio told you. He won't shut up about you, but I don't know if he talks about us. That was back in high school, so it doesn't count. I hope that's not weird."

"No, yeah, he did. It's cool. I'd be a huge hypocrite if I had a problem with it. I'm still good friends with my ex from high school, too. Tonio's family is way cooler than hers, though."

"Ooh! What happened? This was Sunny's family?" Antonio asked.

Lee hesitated—Birdie didn't like any of Sunny's friends, not just Lee. "Sunny's mom can be...standoffish, I guess. Sunny says it's because none of us have a 'real job' and we 'lack ambition', but I think her mom blames us for Sunny transitioning. It was a complete coincidence because she came out before we reconnected, but I guess we encouraged her."

Richard huffed. "Glad to know it's not only me." He pointed a thumb at Gabe. "My mom blames Gabe for 'confusing' me into thinking I'm not her cishet little girl anymore."

"And yet, according to your dad, I'm still the one who got away," Gabe teased.

Richard's mouth twisted in a wry smile. "He never lets me forget it."

Lee's initial opinion of Antonio's friends changed rapidly as they spoke. Maybe there'd be some common ground with his friends after all.

He could imagine Blanche and Sunny getting along with them, at least. Tara would take some time to warm up. "So what do you guys do for work?"

"We work at the same investment firm," Richard answered.

Lee's hopes for an idyllic blended group of friends crashed and burned. *Sunny would eat these guys alive. So would Blanche, but for very different reasons.* Sunny would become bloodthirsty for class warfare. Blanche would just be thirsty. "That's cool."

"What about you? What do you do?" Gabe asked.

Lee wondered how to explain what he did to investment bankers without giving them the same aimless impression Birdie had of him. "I'm an audio tech at Confession, which is where I met Antonio. And I sell house beats on the side. I want to go into music production, just waiting for a break."

By "waiting for a break" Lee meant literally. He had no idea how to find a door into the music production world, let alone get his foot in it, but he needed to make music. The secular CDs he'd stolen from yard sales had saved his life. Lee would listen to Prince, Frankie Knuckles, and Tracy Chapman on his Walkman while he'd avoided his parents in his closet. Music had always been his refuge. Still was. And if a break never happened, well, maybe someone somewhere would hear a song he'd contributed to when they were hiding in their own closet. Making beats was enough.

*Maybe I am aimless.* Lee had never bothered to plan beyond the short-term future; he was more worried about where they'd go if Blanche's sugar daddy evicted them. There was no point in starting to build something long-term if he couldn't count on a roof over his head six months from now.

"Sounds way more fulfilling than fucking investments," Gabe said, shooting a teasing grin at Richard, who shrugged.

"How'd you end up working there if it's not fulfilling?" Relieved he wouldn't have to defend his lack of career against Antonio's more successful friends, Lee took a drink to clear his throat and tapped on the bottle in time with the music to clear his mind. *I'm trying to enjoy this, not have an existential crisis.*

"I like it more than Gabe. Getting rich with other people's money is the traditional career for men in my family," Richard said.

Sunny really would not like him.

"But I'm far more successful than my cis brother, which pisses my dad off. It's incredibly satisfying." Richard smirked. "Gabe is just tagging along with me until he figures out what he wants to be when he grows up."

"I'm not tagging along!"

"Find a new job, then."

"But *what*, though?"

"Exactly. You're tagging along. It isn't a bad thing."

Lee wondered what he'd be doing if he hadn't been kicked out. Probably join the Marines like his dad had. Or gone to college on a football scholarship, then to seminary to become a preacher. That's what his dad would have told him to do, and Leland Sr's word was law.

In high school, he'd wanted to join the marching band. Instead, he'd endured one excruciating semester as a defensive lineman on the JV team before he was outed. By the time Aunt Alitrice had found him, she was so sick that he and Tara had to work to keep the lights on. School wasn't an option, let alone marching band. Auntie Alitrice had signed him and Tara up for a GED program at a community center instead.

It was hard not to feel cheated. He'd had Auntie Alitrice, who he'd loved and appreciated, but who had needed him more than she'd liked him. He'd had his mom, the obedient apologist who always took Dad's side and taught him to hide his heart. He'd had his dad, more of a drill sergeant than a father, who looked at him with resignation and disappointment instead of love.

All the biological family he had left was Jazz, and he only had her for one evening a month. Even their few DMs on Instagram had to be coded so that their parents wouldn't get suspicious.

Lee took in the laughter, music, and love swirling around him, radiating from the Flores family. No one was any less kind or welcoming than when he'd first met them. Even Cassie, who caught his eye and grinned from across the backyard. He smiled back. It wouldn't last forever but... *Maybe I can have this. At least for a while.*

Arms wrapped around his middle as a soft sigh escaped Antonio.

He met Antonio's stunning eyes smiling up at him. "Everything okay, Tonio?"

"Yeah, I'm just happy you're here."

"Me too." *He just said no tongues, right?* Reminding himself that the Flores family wouldn't tell him to leave for a little PDA, Lee put his arm around Antonio's shoulders and pressed a kiss to his forehead.

"Ugh, this is nauseatingly sweet," Richard grumbled.
Gabe elbowed him. "Dicky, don't be an ass."
"Don't call me Dicky."

Several hours, beers, and shots of tequila with Pedro and Oscar later, Lee was pleasantly buzzed. Antonio's stepmom was teaching him how to lead; he counted the basic salsa steps to himself as Giselle reminded him to move his hips.

Antonio danced on the other side of the bonfire, Gabe spinning him smoothly without missing a beat. *I need to learn how to do that.* His boyfriend was incredibly talented. And hot. And so easy to love.

Dancing with another person had brought him down to Tara's skillset. He was making a fool of himself, but Lee didn't care. It helped that Giselle had no mean-spiritedness in her teasing laughter. Everyone in Antonio's family had a big heart. This was what parties were supposed to be; not watching Whatshisname start drama and cut him down at any opportunity.

"Can we cut in?" Gabe rescued Giselle from Lee's two left feet.

"Please, he's been staring at Tonio half the time." Giselle teased as she traded Lee's hand for Gabe's.

"Strange, Tonio's been doing the same thing."

Lee should have been embarrassed, but couldn't find it in himself to care. Before he could come up with a decent response, Antonio distracted him with an arm around Lee's waist, leading him into a gentle bachata.

Antonio's hand held firm against his back, brown curls teasing Lee's face. Dancing with Antonio was more familiar, or the bachata was easier, or he had actually learned something from Giselle. His cheeks hurt from the grin on his face as they danced.

"You smile more when you're drunk," Antonio teased.

"I smile more whenever I'm around you," Lee replied, past caring about holding back the romantic thoughts he normally kept muffled. He obediently held up his arm when Antonio lifted it so he could twirl underneath.

Antonio grinned. "Oh, you get sappy when you're drunk? You've been hiding your own corny side from me!" He came back from his spin and pulled Lee into a kiss.

*Guess the no tongues thing is out the window.* He surprisingly didn't worry. Antonio's family lived so openly. Like a family should. His heart soared, fuller than ever.

Someone whistled and Antonio flipped them off without pulling away. Lee smiled into the kiss, grateful for his boyfriend, his welcoming family and friends, and the love Antonio had brought into his world. Antonio was everything Lee never knew he wanted, his family everything Lee never knew he needed. The fiery spark when they'd met had grown exponentially, fanning into a blaze that burned stronger than he'd ever imagined possible.

*So what if this isn't my future?* Every moment of the past few months had been more happiness than Lee—the kid who waited hours, days, weeks, *years* for his parents to come back for him—had ever expected. He had this now, and that was enough.

One day, Antonio might decide the romantic feelings he potentially had for Lee weren't real and move on. Or maybe Antonio would meet someone better, someone who gave him the adoration he deserved and the corny enthusiasm that Lee could never bring himself to express.

Antonio would eventually figure out how easy Lee was to leave.

But until then, Lee would savor every second Antonio gave him.

# Sunday, August Eleventh

# Chapter Twenty-Six

## Antonio

Antonio and Lee walked into Confession for the Sunday brunch show with their hands clasped tight, running late and glowing. Antonio's birthday had left them both exhausted. Leaving the comfort of each other in bed had been an uphill battle, but Lee was impressively unbothered, considering how close they were cutting it to showtime. Most of the brunchers were already deep into their mimosas.

Watching Lee charm his entire family yesterday had sent giddiness bubbling throughout Antonio's whole body. His heart was still floating. He may or may not have stared at Lee the whole night. On a rare moment his gaze had wandered away, he'd been pulled back in by Lee's endearing, toasted marshmallow belly laugh.

Gabe had teased Antonio for his pitiful whine whenever he heard that laugh over the music. *"You got it bad, don't you? Have you told him you love him yet?"* He'd even asked Antonio to bring Lee over after the show to get to know him better. *And Gabe hates company. To be invited to his house is a true honor.*

Antonio longed to tell Lee how he felt, craved the relief he'd feel when he finally gave in. Love was a compulsion constantly on the verge of overpowering his better judgment, bubbling in his sternum every time he looked at Lee. *I love you.* Every time Lee washed dishes with him after dinner. *I love you.* Every time Lee sent him a link to a new song he thought

Antonio would like. *I love you.* Every time he nuzzled Antonio's neck while stuffing Carlita's padding. *I love you.*

He'd tried again and again. The words just kept getting stuck, caught in the snare his demons had looped around his neck. Antonio had managed to hush them, but their doubt and insecurity festered, choking him.

"Leland, where the fuck were you last night?" A bitter voice demanded as Antonio and Lee reached the stairs.

"This bitch," Lee muttered under his breath as they turned around. Antonio snickered.

Whatshisname stood behind them, hands on his hips, a stony expression on his face. The rest of Lee's other friends peered over their shoulders from their table, sipping mimosas as they exchanged heavy looks and raised eyebrows. Antonio wished he could read their expressions, but that would require spending time with them.

"I had another party to go to." Lee exchanged a smile with Antonio.

Antonio hadn't *intentionally* made plans with Lee on a Saturday night. He'd simply invited Lee to *his* party. *And if Lee had a fun time without his "friends," well, that's just a bonus.*

Guilt simmered through him at the thought, considering how recently they'd had their first—and frankly only—conflict on the very topic. *You said you weren't going to make him choose between you and his friends.* Antonio waved that demon away; Lee could have said no if he didn't want to go. He hadn't pressured him. He'd just asked. And Lee had said yes.

"Brandon almost got a DUI because of you!"

A flash of anger crossed Lee's face. Antonio had never witnessed the vein in his temple or the flare of his nostrils before.

*You made him mad.* The demons licked hot shame across his collarbone. He shushed them. This was between Lee and Whatshisname, not him. Not that that alleviated the guilt singeing his lungs.

"A DUI? Damn, you ever heard of Uber?" Lee shot out. "And because of me? What did I do? I didn't make any of you do shit!"

Whatshisname crossed his arms. "You flaked. The Leland I know would never leave us hanging like that."

Lee shook his head, brow furrowed. "You don't even know me! You just use me to drive your ass around."

Antonio sucked in a breath, barely silencing a dramatic gasp. He and Tara had suspected as much, but hearing Lee admit it broke his heart. He hummed his Intentions Song, reminding himself to stay calm.

"I use *you*? You're the boring ass who tags along to everything. You're such a downer. Especially since you started talking to this bitch." Whatshisname gestured to Antonio.

Before Antonio could retort—no, express his emotions calmly—Lee stepped forward, putting himself between them. "Leave Tonio out of it. You got a problem with me, keep it between us. This isn't about him."

Antonio gave his hand an encouraging squeeze. *I love you.* His anxiety and guilt began to ebb under Lee's reassurance.

"I don't know why you fuck with her anyway. You should be fucking real men," Whatshisname sneered, raking his eyes over the padded curves under Antonio's dress, stopping at the heels on his feet.

Fuck his Intentions Song. This bitch needed to be taught exactly what kind of a man Antonio was and what his bitch ass could do about it!

But before he could open his mouth, Lee beat him to it.

"Oh, right! Antonio isn't a real man because he does drag." Lee laughed mirthlessly. "For someone with as big a forehead as you got, you're stupid as hell! Why is the one person who likes *me* the one who doesn't meet your standards? That's bullshit! If I'm a boring ass, why do you care? You obviously don't give a shit about me, so it's gotta be about you! Go deal with how much you hate yourself somewhere else. Stop taking it out on me!"

The temptation to snap his fingers in support was so strong, but the eyes of every diner were glued on them. Lee wouldn't want a scene. From her podium, Jackie gestured to the bouncer in a silent offer, but Antonio shook his head.

"I'm so done with your petty ass. I'm tired of you treating me like your personal chauffeur. I'm tired of you being a bitch to everyone you think is below you, to all my friends, my boyfriend, me! I'm just tired of you, and I don't even know your fucking name! Go find someone else to use."

Whatshisname's mouth gaped. "Whatever. Don't come crying back to me when you realize you lost the only friends worth anything because you had a taste for dried fish." He tossed his hand over his shoulder at them and flounced back to his table. His friends huddled their heads together around him, whispering and staring.

Antonio resisted the urge to glare back, humming the chorus of his Intentions Song because that was the only part he could remember through the adrenaline in his veins. Lee needed his support.

Lee's shoulders, already tight, rose higher around his ears, eyes flickering around the dining room as he realized they had an audience. Even the servers had stopped to watch. Lee's breath shook, sweat beading on his nose.

"Let's go." Antonio tugged on his hand, ignoring the curious looks. At Lee's slight nod, he guided Lee up the stairs and down the hallway to the Confessionals. Bathrooms were always sanctuaries; the doors locked out everything bad in the world.

Lee slid down the tile wall as soon as the door closed behind them, breathing heavily with his head in his hands. "I'm so sorry."

Antonio knelt between his legs. "What for?" He racked his brain. Why would Lee be sorry? "He didn't say anything *that* bad about me. Except he called me dry. Rude. This fish is fresh as hell."

Lee, who normally laughed at all his jokes, didn't react. Didn't even look up. "I try so hard to keep it together, especially around him, and I lost it. My mom would be so pissed at me." His voice was muffled as he spoke into his lap.

Antonio rubbed Lee's thighs soothingly. "No, you were amazing. You said what you needed to say, and you said it with your chest. You kept it together way better than I would've. And can you imagine if *Tara* saw that?"

This time, Lee huffed a small laugh as he covered Antonio's hands where they rested on his legs, his fingers tapping against his wrist. His face was still too serious, his half smile not reaching his eyes. "Are you okay? I got so irritated when he said that shit about you."

"Please, I was raised by my sisters. Being called feminine isn't insulting. I'm more worried about you. You were feeling strong emotions, weren't you?"

"I wear my heart on my sleeve," Lee said sarcastically before softening. "I didn't want to show you, or anyone, that part of me. And now all my coworkers got a show of me at my worst. No one likes someone who loses their temper."

"I hope that's not true—I lose my shit constantly." Antonio squeezed Lee's hands. "I want every part of you, Lee. Temper and all. It'll take a lot more than standing up for yourself to scare me off." He rubbed his thumbs over Lee's knuckles. "I'm proud of you. That couldn't have been easy. I'm sorry if you lost those friends on my account."

"I'm pretty sure your mom adopted me, remember? Your family will take up the slack."

"You sound sarcastic, but you know it's true, right?" Antonio asked, rubbing circles into Lee's hand. "They adored you yesterday. Even

Cassie. Hell, if *Richard* gets invited, then you're in the family for damn sure." *They loved you. I love you.*

Lee's eyes glistened behind his glasses, barely hanging on the end of his nose. "I appreciate you so much. And everything you've brought to my life. Like, I loved you already, but yesterday was one of the best days I've ever had, and I have you to thank for that."

Antonio's heart jumped to his throat. "You...love me?"

Lee looked at him like it should be obvious. "Yeah? I have for months. It's just hard to admit out loud when you don't feel the same. But you just saw the angry side of me, and you're still here. Might as well see the other vulnerable parts while I'm a fucking wreck."

Antonio tried to laugh around the lump pounding against his vocal cords. His voice cracked as he whispered, "We're ridiculous, aren't we?"

"Speak for yourself." Lee took his glasses off to wipe his face, shooting Antonio that guarded half smile even as his eyes swam.

Antonio choked out another laugh, tears springing to his eyes. "Fine, *I'm* ridiculous! I could've been telling you I love you this whole damn time? Why am I keeping that shit in?"

With a gentle stroke of his thumb, Lee brushed away the tears threatening to fall from the corner of Antonio's eyes. "Okay, maybe we are ridiculous." Setting his glasses on the sink, Lee drew Antonio against his chest. "I didn't think you felt that way yet, or if you ever would."

The dam holding back his feelings had finally broken, and they flooded out of him in relief. "I wanted to tell you, but I didn't think *you* were there yet, so I tried so hard to play it cool. Which fucking sucked—I'm so bad at it!"

"God, it's the worst." Lee snorted. "Let's not do that anymore."

"Agreed." Antonio kissed him. "I love you."

Lee kissed him on the forehead. "And I love you."

"Oh god, your sexy voice saying that? And a forehead kiss?" Antonio melted against him. Lee laughed and held him tighter. "You would have stayed even if I didn't love you?"

Most people he'd dated hadn't been content with one-sided feelings. Even the people who'd said they were fine with a one-sided romance had still pushed him for answers he didn't want to give. The fact that Lee hadn't pressured him was everything.

Lee shrugged. "I love you, and I love how I feel when I'm with you. I never expected anyone to love me at all, so why wouldn't that be enough?"

"Angel, you can be more high maintenance, you know," Antonio teased.

Now that the *"I love you"*s could flow freely, a quieter but still persistent thought erupted: *Move in with me. Stay with me every night.* A couple *marry me*s floated past, but even *he* wasn't ready for that conversation yet. Though, signing a new lease and going a whole year with the *move in with me*s floating around in his head sounded awful. He'd barely survived holding in the *I love you*s for two months.

"In the spirit of not playing it cool, my lease is up in October. Do you maybe want to find a place together? No pressure. I know it's soon, but it'd be nice to have you around all the time."

Without looking at him, Lee thought quietly, finding his glasses to fiddle with them.

Antonio waited impatiently as the moment dragged on, humming a reminder to himself to give Lee time and space to respond. *Tara was right—he takes forever to figure out what he wants. But this is a big decision.*

Putting his glasses back on, Lee finally nodded. "I thought you'd be sick of me by now. But if you can put up with my ass every day of the week, I want to. As long as Tara doesn't kill me first, that is."

Glee burst through him. "I could never get sick of you, Angel."

Lee's brown eyes lit up. "You want to meet Jazz? We're getting dinner tonight."

Warmth bubbled in his sternum. "You want me to meet your sister?"

"I just met your whole family. You should meet mine. No more playing shit cool, right?"

"Yes—I want to meet everyone in your life!" He winced. "Except Gabe invited us to his house after the show. I think I forgot to ask you." Antonio was torn; he'd let his friend down before by not being there for him. Flaking on him was Old Antonio behavior.

As if sensing his indecision, Lee gently suggested, "Why not both? I'm not meeting Jazz until seven. Do you want to go by Gabe's place first, and meet her for dinner?"

"Have I mentioned I love you, Leland Middle Name Jones? Even though you won't tell me your middle name?"

"Not nearly enough. I might need a reminder." That easy, genuine smile he loved so much finally returned to Lee's face.

"I love you." Antonio grinned, pulling him down for a kiss. He could remind Lee a million times and never tire of saying it.

A knock rapped on the door. "Boys, there better not be any hanky-panky goin' on in my bathroom stall."

With a groan, Antonio stood, pulling Lee up behind him before opening the door. Chas leaned against the doorframe. "Like you're one to talk, Chas. How many times have you gotten pregnant in these bathrooms? Three? Or was number four conceived here too?"

Chas patted his round stomach. In drag, the growing bump passed as a beer belly. "What happens in the Confessionals stays between me and God." He laughed at his own joke.

Antonio grinned. "Is that what you call Freddy when you're in here?"

"I'd rather not know the answer to that," Lee chimed in.

Chas shot Antonio a smirk. "Tonio, you think I, a devout Catholic, would be that sacrilegious? Besides, they're Confessionals. He's Father Coleman, of course."

"I did not need to hear that," Lee sighed while Antonio laughed.

"What, when else could we roleplay? We got three kids and my mother at home." Chas turned serious. "Jackie told me what happened. You boys okay?"

"We're more than okay, Chas." Lee hugged Antonio from behind, kissing him on the cheek. Antonio leaned into him, a big smile on his face.

"Good, yer late. Show starts in ten. Get yer ass in makeup, Carlita."

---

"Heard you got into it with Xavier earlier." Venus leaned on the counter nearby, making a show of counting her tip money.

"Is that his name?" Antonio inspected the makeup-remover wipe in his hand before glancing in the mirror. "Never bothered to learn it."

"Heard your little boyfriend tore him a new one."

"No one said you were deaf, V. You got something to say, or you just gonna keep repeating what other people said?" Hackles up, Antonio kept Carlita in his head as he removed her from his face. It was safer; Carlita didn't need an Intentions Song.

"I was surprised to hear you just watched. You've never kept your mouth shut before."

Carlita scrubbed her eyebrows free of glue. "It's almost like I'm mature now."

"Don't get ahead of yourself," Venus laughed. "Just observing that you chilled out while Lee grew a pair. About time one of Xavier's pets bit him. You two are cute or whatever."

Carlita blinked. "Are you trying to be nice?"

"Is that so hard to believe?" Venus rolled her eyes. "We've been friends for a decade."

"Some friend! You haven't made eye contact with me in months, and the last time you spoke to me, you threatened to seduce my boyfriend!"

"I didn't say we were *good* friends." Venus shrugged. "Look, Xav is an insecure, manipulative bitch who doesn't reciprocate. And Lee's a sweetheart. I'm just tryna say you've been good for Lee or whatever. And, even though you're all 'responsible' now, he's been good for you. Getting dicked down by all of *that* must have chilled you out."

"Excuse me?!" Antonio whirled around.

Venus smirked. "Calm down. People talk and they always had real nice things to say about Lee. You ruined my chance for that, too."

Antonio felt strangely relieved that Lee and Venus had never— *It shouldn't matter.* He threw the stained wipe in the trash and packed up his bag. "Glad you won't hold it against me."

Venus ignored the sarcasm dripping from Carlita's words as she wrapped her stack of bills in a rubber band. "Don't read into it. Just because I'm being nice doesn't mean you won."

"Won what?" Carlita laughed. "I don't know what competition we're in, but of course I won. Have you met me?"

"I take back what I said. You're still a stuck-up bitch," Venus scoffed. "When you left, I thought I'd get my chance to shine, but Chas just hired more people with half my talent. Then you dragged your ass back here and Chas still fawns over your boring ass!"

"That's because I'm only boring backstage." Carlita teased. This was the Venus she'd been friends with before, who wrapped vulnerability in insults. "Sweetie, your competition is in the mirror. Stop looking at me and focus on yourself."

"I miss when you were the hot mess here."

"V, you know what your problem is? You're cunty until you open your mouth, then you're just a cunt." Carlita closed her makeup bag with a snap, shooting Venus a smile in the mirror so she'd know she was talking shit. "Stick to dancing, darling."

Venus's laughter followed Antonio out. "You better invite me to the wedding!"

# Chapter Twenty-Seven

## Lee

"You worry too much, Angel." Antonio tugged him past a wooden gate, into the backyard of a two-story brick house. "It's totally fine. He's expecting us."

*Expecting us to knock on the front door, not the back.* Lee trusted Antonio to keep them out of trouble. Even if, by all appearances, they were breaking into Gabe's backyard, which went against every fiber of Lee's upbringing. *And over South especially?*

His trust evaporated as Antonio opened the sliding glass door without knocking.

"Seriously?" Lee hurried inside before Gabe's neighbors saw them. South Bellamy wasn't as bad as Driftwood, but there were more than enough "Neighborhood Watch" signs in this predominantly white neighborhood to make him nervous. *Not to mention it's bad manners!*

He shut the door, only to be met with a massive gray dog growling at him. A line of drool dripped from his jowls. Lee blindly reached back for the door handle behind him. *Not today, Satan.* Giant, slobbery, growling dogs were a hard pass.

"Sorry, I forgot you're a monster who hates dogs." Antonio scratched the beast's ears. "It's okay. Hippo is friendly."

The dog wagged his tail but kept his focus on Lee.

"Friendly to *you*, maybe."

"Hippo, chill out." Gabe walked into the eat-in kitchen. Hippo waddled over to Gabe, tail wagging so hard his body wiggled.

Lee took a hesitant step closer, but Hippo whirled to face him, huffing out a deep warning bark.

"Here. Give him one of these." Gabe tossed him a bag of treats. "He's loyal to food."

Hippo sat eagerly, tail thumping on the ground. The blocky gray head cocked back and forth. *Changed his tune quick.* Lee tentatively held a bacon treat out to him.

Taking it gently between his teeth, Hippo scarfed the treat down. Lee took a tentative step into the house, and Hippo let him this time, flopping into a dog bed in the corner.

Back pressed against the stone countertop, he edged into the kitchen, hoping the island would afford some protection in case Hippo changed his mind about Lee. The dog's wide brown eyes tracked every step, but he relaxed into his bed.

"Sorry. I don't have many new people over. He's a big softie, but I guess it's reassuring he'll bark if someone breaks in." Gabe smiled awkwardly in embarrassment.

"As long as they don't bring bacon anyway." Lee wondered if it'd be rude to wash his hands free of dog drool. *Fuck it, I don't care. That's nasty.*

He beelined to the kitchen sink, hyperaware of Hippo's eyes following him. Off-white tile accented the green walls, and light poured in from the giant windows, brightening a wall of pantry cabinets. Pots of fresh herbs lined the windowsill above it. Lee and Tara's bedrooms combined were smaller than the eat-in kitchen they stood in now. The house had looked nice from the outside, but the kitchen was in another tax bracket.

Gabe snorted. "Yeah, he's really food motivated, even if he's a tank now. My dad found him half-starved last November, tied up to a bench by the mounds."

His words knocked the wind out of Lee. He muttered a polite response as he washed his hands, looking over his shoulder at the dog in the corner. He should not be relating this hard with a *dog*. Hippo's tail thumped as he and Lee stared at each other, the rhythmic *tap tap tap* on the tile floor creating a calming beat.

Antonio snooped in a box on the kitchen island. "What's all this, Gabey?"

"My mom found more of my stuff when they were packing up the old house," Gabe explained, adding for Lee's sake, "My parents sold their house in Driftwood and moved closer to work. As if they don't spend enough time there already."

Forcing himself to breathe, Lee dried his hands on a towel. *I should ask about his parents. Right?* He barely remembered most people's names, but Gabe and Richard seemed to be fixtures in his boyfriend's life. He should make an effort.

Before he could come up with a polite question about Gabe's parents, Antonio cried out triumphantly, "Lee, come here!" He held up a picture. "Look at what a cute scene kid I was!"

With a rush of relief at the distraction, Lee peered over his shoulder.

The photo was bent, curved with age. A young Antonio and Gabe had their arms around each other at their high school graduation. Caps in hand, their gowns were draped over their arms as they stood in front of a sign engraved with "Driftwood Academy for the Arts." Antonio looked much the same, just skinnier. He wore spiked leather cuffs on his wrists, tight black pants covered in safety pins, and a fishnet top under a Death Cab for Cutie tee. Most importantly—

"Your hair, babe," Lee breathed out. Antonio's brown curls were dyed black and flat-ironed into a swoop covering one eye, the other heavy with black eyeliner.

"Oh, I know! I looked so hot." Antonio laughed.

"That's so cringe," Lee teased.

"Hey, the emo swoop was the shit back then. You're too young to appreciate it." Antonio elbowed him. "When did you graduate again? In 2012 or something, right?"

Lee looked at Antonio expectantly. Antonio *should* know he'd only gone to high school for a semester. But whether Antonio remembered that at the moment was another story. He'd barely made it past homecoming freshman year, when his dad had thrown open his bedroom door to find him and Sunny—

*Nope.* Lee pushed his glasses up his nose. *I thought I suppressed all that.* Usually, he could recite facts about his past without those memories popping up. *No reason to start that shit up again.* "I was supposed to graduate in 2013."

Antonio smiled apologetically. "Oh, yeah. Sorry."

In the photo, Gabe's appearance was wildly different. *That's an understatement.* Lee might be head over heels for Antonio, but he wasn't blind. Gabe had the body of an Olympian and a face that belonged on a bust in a museum. The kid in the photo, however, was hunched over to shrink himself, buttons puckering around his belly. Acne covered his face, and his short dark brown curls were pressed into an awkward ring from his graduation cap.

"You've had quite the glow-up, Gabe," Lee acknowledged, holding up the picture.

Gabe snatched it away with a scowl. "Tonio, stop looking through my shit!"

Antonio grinned, holding up a couple of Nerf guns he'd dug out of the box. "Oh, come on! You were so cute, Gabey!" He shot a dart at Gabe. It bounced off his chest and onto the floor.

Shame rolled through Lee. *You know better.* Before he could muster an apology, the front door unlocked with a click. Richard entered, nodding in greeting.

Hippo raised his head, wagged his tail, and plopped back down on his bed. Hopefully, Hippo would greet Lee like that from now on. *No barking or licking and shit.*

Antonio fired the Nerf gun just as Richard closed the door. The dart stuck to the window over Richard's shoulder, quivering. Richard slowly turned to Antonio, who tossed the other Nerf gun to him. A mischievous smile erupted on their faces. Richard leveled the Nerf gun and fired back at Antonio, who screamed and ran.

*What the fuck.* Lee watched in amazement as his normally sweet boyfriend fired Nerf darts over his shoulder at the cackling Richard chasing after him.

Gabe wore a bemused smile on his face. "Is he like this with you, too?"

Lee shook his head. "This is a whole new side of him."

"It's annoying as hell," Gabe muttered, but his lips curved into an affectionate smile.

This was probably his best chance to make amends. He did his best to ignore his mom's voice in his head, telling him to stay quiet because he would only make it worse like he always did. If Gabe was Antonio's best friend, then Lee would need to stay on his good side. *And that means apologizing when I piss him off.* Gabe wasn't Tara, who would forgive and forget no matter what.

"Sorry about the glow-up comment. You just look, um, different now."

Gabe's wince didn't help Lee's anxiety, but he'd done it. He'd gotten the apology out relatively quickly. That would have been a ten-minute ordeal if he was apologizing to Tara. It wouldn't have been enough to satisfy his dad's impossible standards, but it was better than nothing.

"Sorry, don't apologize. I'm annoyed at Tonio for digging into my stuff, not you. I just got a lot of shit for my appearance back then, and I'm still insecure about it, is all. Something I need to work on, not for you to worry about."

"Well, kids are assholes."

Gabe huffed out a laugh. "They're not all bad. I've started volunteering at this youth program recently. At least I'm handling the teasing better now than I did then." He picked up the box. "I'm going to hide this before Tonio gets any more ideas. Excuse me."

Lee stood alone in the kitchen, with only the sleeping Hippo and the occasional flash of Antonio and Richard running past. Their footsteps thundered around the house. This was not what he'd expected from the reserved investment bankers he'd met the night before. Antonio and Richard were twenty-nine years old and acting like they were six.

He'd picked up a handful of stray Nerf darts when a knock sounded at the door. Lee looked at Hippo, expecting him to react. Hippo just looked back at him, eyes darting to the door and back to Lee expectantly. He didn't bark. Or even get up.

"Oh, you want me to get it? Not so tough now, are you?"

Hippo thumped his tail and whined softly with pleading eyes.

"Fine. I guess I'll get it." Leaving the Nerf darts in a tidy pile on the coffee table, Lee opened the front door.

DLTopPBW looked at him in surprise, adjusting his glasses. "Am I at the right house?"

"Looking for Gabe?" Lee asked, resigned to an awkward interruption in what *had* been a good day.

"Yes?" DLTopPBW looked around in confusion. His suit made him look significantly more put together than usual. He was the same height as Lee but with a wiry build like Antonio; the tailored suit was a better look for him. He always came across as a manic mess in the oversized, floral-print shirts he wore on Saturday nights.

"Then you're at the right house." Lee stepped aside to let him in. Hippo looked up at the visitor, wagging his tail. *Must be a regular visitor. Which means he knows Antonio. Great. Gotta love how small Bellamy's queer community is.*

DLTopPBW adjusted his glasses again as he stepped inside. "And you are?"

"Lee." *He wasn't asking your name.* "Antonio's boyfriend."

DLTopPBW's eyebrows rose briefly before he schooled his features into an impassive mask. "Phineas Watkins. Gabe's lawyer. Well, and friend. We were roommates. In undergrad. Yale." He paused. "You recognize me, don't you?"

Lee nodded. They'd hooked up once about a year ago and ignored each other at parties since. Lee didn't take it personally; DL guys could be unpredictable, and being ignored was far from the worst-case scenario. He had been memorable, though. Lee wasn't surprised DLTopPBW—*Phineas*—was a lawyer. *The snow job should have been a tip-off he was rich rich.* Already visibly anxious by the time Lee had arrived, DLTopPBW had proceeded to get high on coke and poppers. Lee had stayed sober, concerned that mixing coke and poppers would take a bad turn.

But the sex wasn't bad. *Even if the "top" in his username was misleading.*

Phineas leaned in closer, his long locs falling over his shoulder. "Can you, uh, not tell anyone we've...met?" Phineas asked quietly. "I haven't exactly told everyone I'm bi."

Lee blinked to hide his skepticism. No one would look at Phineas and think he was straight. He had a strong pansexual fuckboy vibe, much like Antonio had when they'd first met. *He's wearing a damn bolo tie, and he thinks he can pass as straight?*

But he knew how it was. His dad's voice still scolded him to "man up" when he acted "too girly" in public. "Look, I get it. But I'm kinda new to this whole committed relationship thing, and this feels like something I should tell Tonio. Other than that, it's your journey."

"Antonio, in a committed relationship?" Phineas smiled, white teeth flashing behind his crooked grin. "There's hope for us all."

A Nerf dart hit Phineas in the glasses, sticking to one lens. Antonio glowered at them from the coffee table as he kept the Nerf gun pointed at Phineas.

Lee snorted. *Message received, babe.* Antonio's jealousy was surprisingly cute. No one had ever gotten jealous over him before. Except Sunny, which had *not* been cute. He returned to his boyfriend, leaving Phineas and his internalized closet behind.

Antonio pushed Lee down onto the couch in the living room and aggressively sat on his lap, sending another glare to Phineas. "Phin. I didn't know *you'd* be coming today."

With a kiss to his shoulder to hide his grin, Lee patted Antonio's thighs reassuringly, tucking away his possessive reaction for later. Antonio normally wasn't this bossy.

Phineas shrugged with a slight roll of his eyes as he wiped his glasses. "I just came to drop something off for Gabe. Didn't know you'd be here."

Richard collapsed in an armchair, straight blond hair flying in all directions. He reloaded his darts, grinning to himself. Richard had come across as serious and composed at Antonio's birthday yesterday. Apparently he also had a fun—if unhinged—side to him.

Gabe walked into the room carrying a tray. "Oh hey—"

A Nerf dart shot bounced off his forehead and landed on the tray, scattering pretzels onto the floor. In an instant, Hippo was underfoot, rooting out every fallen crumb.

Gabe let out a heavy sigh. "Dicky, you're lucky I didn't drop this shit."

"Lighten up, Cooper." Richard smoothed his hair back.

"Man, if *Richard* is telling you to lighten up, you need to lighten up." Phineas laughed. "Here, I've got work shit for both of you."

Phineas avoided Antonio's glare as he pulled two envelopes from his jacket. He held one out to Gabe as he set down the tray on the coffee table. Gabe tossed the envelope on the mantle without bothering to look at it.

Phineas shot a glance at Lee. "That uh...*thing* you wanted me to file is done. The countersuit in New York won't affect anything in the Bellamy metro. Just don't go to the East Coast until it gets figured out."

"Wasn't planning on it," Gabe said. "You're a lifesaver, Phin."

Phineas threw the other envelope to Richard. "And your asset's been moved as requested. But if Dick catches on, oh, maybe within the next year or so, your claim might not stand up in court. After that, it should be in our favor."

"Thanks, Phin." Richard tucked the envelope into his jacket. "Don't worry about dear ol' Dad. He didn't read a thing he signed, but I have it on camera in case he claims he didn't."

Lee sent an inquiring glance to Antonio. *What kind of shit are your friends into?*

"Phineas is their lawyer," Antonio explained in a murmur, leaning against him.

*Obviously. Not what I was asking.* "Ah, cool," is all Lee said.

Phineas gave an awkward thumbs-up. "Okay, back to the office. Nice meeting you, Lee."

A Nerf dart stuck to Phineas's glasses again, this time shot by Richard. "Why are you going to the office on Sunday afternoon? You work too much. Stay a bit."

Pulling the dart off, Phineas sat back down with a nervous glance toward Lee and Antonio. "Like you're one to talk. You're just as much of a workaholic as I am, Dicky."

"No, Richard's right. We haven't seen you at the gym in weeks. And when's the last time you saw your girlfriend?" Gabe asked.

*Girlfriend? Really?* Phineas had Venus's tongue down his throat just last weekend.

Phineas made a face. "What girlfriend? That ended a minute ago. Apparently, I never spent any time with her. And you, Dicky? You can't tell me your dating life is any better."

Richard scowled. "Don't call me Dicky, first of all. And I actually made time for the last person I was seeing, and they still broke it off with me." He smoothed back his hair again. "Called me an emotionally unavailable asshole. I told them that from the jump. Not sure why they were surprised."

Gabe put his head in his hands. "Why are you both like this? You both keep making the same poor choices that your fathers do, and you hate them."

"Sounds like therapy is going well, Gabe," Richard drawled, "but let's not unpack our daddy issues as a group."

"Sorry." Gabe's responding pout was both wounded and sullen.

"At least you have me, Gabey!" Antonio chimed in, his voice slightly higher than normal. "I have a healthy relationship. I don't work too much. I'm in touch with my emotions. Great relationships with all of my father figures. I'm the perfect example of healthy masculinity."

Lee muffled his laugh, but the other three didn't try to contain it.

"Sure, Tonio. We'll ignore all *your* issues," Gabe laughed. "What, a few months of dating and you're the picture of domestic bliss? No offense, Lee. It's just weird to see Tonio like this."

"What, healthy and functioning?" Antonio scowled. "Well, despite your lack of confidence in me, I *am* the picture of domestic bliss! *We're* moving in together!"

Lee had wanted to tell Tara first, but none of these guys had ever met her. He'd tell her when he got home. The prospect of moving somewhere without her made his chest tighten. Trusting someone to still want him when he did something wrong. Hell, *Tara* might not stick around if she felt he was choosing Antonio over her.

Antonio put his hand on Lee's; he was gripping Antonio's thigh so tightly he might leave a mark. With a breath, Lee forced himself to relax and ease up.

This wasn't just anyone; he was moving in with *Antonio*. Tara would be supportive. *Eventually*. Everything was easy with Antonio, and he loved him. Lee *wanted* to live with Antonio, so he'd said yes. *Following Tara's advice is terrifying. Does she just throw herself into everything like this?*

"Oh, you're serious." Richard sounded surprised.

Antonio tensed. "I mean, when my lease is up, yeah."

"Isn't that a little soon?" Gabe asked. "That'll be like what, six months in?"

Antonio cocked his head. "Really? *You're* telling me it's too soon? After encouraging me to have a certain conversation for weeks? Well, we had the conversation, and now you don't like the result? For the first time in my life, I'm making good choices and shit's going well for me, but it's 'too soon' for me to enjoy it?"

Gabe cringed. "Sorry."

Lee intervened before an argument could get started. "We are U-Hauling it, especially by gay standards. But I stay over almost every night already, and your place is a little cramped."

Antonio beamed at him.

"Is this the time for a fish joke?" Phineas grinned.

Antonio and Lee both glared at him. "We've had enough of those today," Lee said.

Antonio rubbed Lee's neck. "It's a sore subject. His friend was not happy that he came to my birthday yesterday."

"Former friend," Lee muttered. After today, he didn't want anything to do with Whatshisname. Or Amen. BJSlut was cool, but he'd stick with Whatshisname. Even Hot Barber had been coming with them lately, so that friendship was unlikely to survive. His standing appointment was tomorrow though, so he'd find out where they stood if Hot Barber fucked up his hair.

He'd always thought he was imagining everything, but Whatshisname blaming him for their bad choices? Even as conflict-avoidant as he was, that was too much. Lee was no longer going to be used for free rides, validation, and Whatshisname's punching bag.

It had hurt, but Lee had already moved on before their argument had even ended. It was no different than being ghosted. And now, he didn't have to pretend to give a shit about Whatshisname's drama. Or suffer the comments about his size, his music, or Antonio. If he couldn't bring Antonio around, then that wasn't the community for him. Lee wanted people like Antonio and his family. People who loved and accepted him for who he was. Who supported him. People like Tara and Sunny and Blanche. *And maybe like Tonio's friends?*

"Oh shit, you're *Leland*!" Recognition dawned in Phineas's voice. "They were pissed at you! I had to call in a favor to keep that Brandon guy from getting a DUI. You know, the one who says 'Amen' every time Xavier says anything?"

*Dude, if you want to pretend to be DL, you gotta stop talking.* Lee shot him another look. *And of course, Amen would risk everything for Whatshisname.* "We're probably not talking about the same people," Lee insisted, avoiding Antonio's curious look.

Phineas nodded. "Right."

"Phin, you got time for a round of Smash?" In a blatant attempt to diffuse the tension, Gabe turned on the TV.

Phineas's eyes flicked back to Antonio again. "Sure, maybe just one. I should get back."

Gabe offered a controller to Lee, but Antonio interrupted, "Shouldn't we go meet your sister?"

Lee grinned, pleased that Antonio was eager to meet Jazz. *Honestly, we might get there early. He must be excited. Or nervous. Or he wants to leave. Fuck. What if he's upset?* Maybe Antonio's jealousy ran deeper than the cute, possessive side.

His smile faded.

"Sister, huh?" Phineas asked. "Is she cute?"

*As if I'd set Jazz up with anyone, let alone DL Top PBW.* Annoyance got the better of him and he snapped, "She's a teenager." *Nineteen is still a teenager. He must be a decade older than her.*

"Oh, my bad, bro." Phineas held up his hands. "I was just playing."

"Sure, Phin." Antonio rolled his eyes as he pulled Lee off the couch. "Come on, Angel."

Lee followed him out, already overthinking how to tell the surprisingly jealous Antonio he'd hooked up with his friend before they'd met. And if Antonio still wanted to live with him after that, then he still had to tell Tara he was moving out. Without her.

# Chapter Twenty-Eight

## Antonio

Antonio glanced at Lee as they drove to the cafe. Lee was looking out the window in silence, rubbing his hands on his thighs.

The cafe was close to the university. Dented cars hogged the street parking. Century-old houses with paint flaking from the porches had plastic cups blowing around the yards, abandoned by students who'd moved in early and had nothing to do but party.

With a wave of his hand, he banished the foggy memories of frat parties from his days at the U. He should have paid closer attention to his demons because what came out of his mouth was, "You and Phineas sure looked friendly."

*Why did you say that?* He'd floated into Gabe's house, high on love. The sight of Phineas standing too close to Lee, with his stupid charming smile, had popped his bubble. Irritation and anxiety brought him crashing back down. *Just seeing Phin unexpectedly was bad enough, but then he smiled like that? At* my *Lee?*

At least Lee hadn't smiled back. *Lee can smile at Phineas all he damn wants.* This bitter irritation, this insecurity weighing on him, wasn't normal.

Phineas's eye roll when Antonio called him out for not giving him enough warning had been irritating, but Lee's presence had been the buffer he'd needed.

Still, the irritation dug its claws in. Antonio braked as the Prius in front of him decided that going twenty miles an hour was plenty fast.

"So, about Phineas," Lee began after the silence had stretched for far too long.

*I already hate this.* Antonio gripped the steering wheel as his palms itched with sweat, knuckles pale. He kept his eyes firmly on the car he was tailgating.

"Sorry if it makes things weird, but *before* I met you, we...hooked up. Not anything serious, and we haven't talked since. He didn't want me to tell anyone because *apparently*, he's DL. Make of *that* what you will. I just wanted to be honest."

Antonio's face contorted in confusion, barely noticing the Prius braking far too early for a stop sign. *Phin? DL? The fuck? Everyone knows he's queer. Except his family.* Antonio wasn't shocked that they'd hooked up. Bellamy's queer community was tiny. *And Lee's hot as fuck.*

He'd suspected something had happened between them; Phineas had been both too familiar and too awkward. He'd been trying to act straight. *He's so bad at it.*

Antonio sucked his teeth as he hugged the center line to pass a biker the Prius had almost hit. At least Lee had told him instead of pretending the weirdness wasn't real. He hated feeling gaslit by his own brain. He'd hate it more if Lee had made him feel that way too. But he was still upset, and now he was confused because he couldn't figure out why. Guilt tightened his throat. He was a fucking hypocrite for being upset about this.

He cleared his throat, keeping his eyes on the tail lights of the slowest driver in the world. "Well, I should tell you I've also slept with Phin. And Gabe, but you already knew that. And technically Richard but just once during a threesome with Gabe. There's also been several group situations with Phin. But all of that's ancient history. So yeah, definitely the first I've heard of him being DL."

Lee made a noise that sounded suspiciously like a laugh. *Why is he laughing? I'd be pissed if I were him.* "His username was even DLTop or something. He blocked me though, so I couldn't check even if I still had Grindr on my phone."

Antonio scoffed, a little mollified to hear Phineas had blocked Lee. *He's mine. Stay away.* "God, he's not even a top! Just a size queen."

"That explains so much. I douched for nothing." Lee paused before adding, "You know, you have *really* hot friends, Tonio."

*Oh, now I definitely do not appreciate his tone.* Anger and irritation flared up again. Spotting a gap in the parked cars, he pulled around the Prius and into a bus stop in front of a pink Victorian. He yanked the parking brake. "Yeah, well maybe you should call *Phineas* to come meet your sister instead if he's so hot!" He whirled at Lee with a glare.

Lee's shoulders shook as he bit his lower lip.

It dawned on him that Lee was laughing. "You're fucking with me, aren't you?"

Lee nodded, the smile he'd been fighting broadening into a grin. "I am. You're cute when you're jealous. Want to talk that out?"

Antonio softened at Lee's loving expression, but annoyance still burned his chest. That bitter, irritated feeling *was* jealousy. He had been envious of people, yes. Protective? Absolutely. But jealous? "I've never had anyone I liked enough to be jealous before," Antonio admitted. "I don't know how to handle it."

Lee touched his cheek softly. "And I've never had anyone who liked me enough to be jealous before. It's flattering."

"So *you're* not jealous that I've slept with literally all of my friends?" Antonio asked, now annoyed for no rational reason. He didn't want Lee to experience the burning insecurity, but he resented how unbothered Lee was. The irritation he'd felt with Phineas reminded him of his irritation with Venus and Whatshisname. *Have I been jealous this whole time?*

Lee calmly shook his head. "Not unless you've been sleeping with them since we met. You're the only person I want. I love you, not anyone else. And I trust you feel the same."

"Ugh, you always say the right fucking thing. Stop being so easy-going." Antonio pressed a quick kiss against his soft lips. "I'll try and figure out this jealousy shit."

"You can be a little jealous. I mean, don't go all Chas and Freddy on me, but it's kinda cute. Just know I'm yours." Lee kissed him again.

Antonio's heart melted as he deepened the kiss, his irritation washing away. He'd never expected to fall in love, let alone with someone as perfect for him as Lee. *Even the hard shit is so easy with him.* The universe had sent his dream man to help New Antonio get his shit together.

He'd never been so hopeful for his future.

Parking near the cafe didn't take long, considering the street traffic. His beloved Civic was small enough to squeeze into unconventional spaces, but they were still late thanks to their impromptu makeout sesh.

Jazz was already waiting for them at a table, herbal tea steaming in front of her. She stood up to hug Lee.

Even if Lee hadn't been there to introduce them, Antonio would have known they were siblings. Jazz had a slightly longer nose and a more oval face, but she otherwise shared Lee's features and larger build. She almost matched his height too, taller than Antonio despite his platforms.

"And you must be Antonio!" Jazz extended her hand.

Antonio pulled her into a hug instead. "I can't believe we're finally meeting!" His anxiety about meeting her hadn't had a chance to take root. His only agenda after the brunch show had been to hang out with Gabe. Instead, he'd been on an emotional rollercoaster and suddenly he was meeting his...*future sister-in-law?*

"Jazz, you want your usual?" Lee asked.

Jazz nodded. "Please and thank you! He won't care about a couple of dollars for tea, but I'll get a lecture on irresponsible spending if I buy a sandwich."

"You really gotta get Dad off your bank account, Jazz." He turned to Antonio. "You want a veggie sandwich?"

Antonio nodded. "Yes, please. I'm not picky."

Lee laughed. "Right. Just no dairy, no meat, low sodium, low sugar, and whole grain everything. Not picky at all."

"Are you vegan?" Jazz asked as Lee walked away. She was dressed modestly for a college freshman in a baggy sweater and jeans. *It's August. How is she wearing a sweater?*

Antonio shook his head. "Not a good one. I try to eat plant-based food for health reasons, but I'll suffer the consequences of the occasional cheeseburger."

Fast food had replaced drugs when he'd first gotten sober. And with how fucked up his digestion had become from taking so many damn pills, his food habit had been particularly unpleasant. *Who knew you could be constipated with diarrhea?* Antonio never wanted to experience *that* again. He always avoided cheese around Lee. *That* would scare him away for sure.

"I've considered going vegan, but Dad wouldn't like it." Jazz rolled her eyes. "Sorry, warning you now I'm going to complain about him a lot. Lee is the only one who gets it."

"Don't let me stop you. Lee rarely talks about him so I haven't heard much. Other than, you know, he got kicked out." It was strange how little he knew of Lee's past. Antonio trusted Lee would tell him when he was ready.

A pained wince crossed Jazz's face. "Yeah. That." Jazz sat quietly for a moment before she broke into a smile. "So Lee tells me you went to the U too?"

*Jazz avoids sore subjects like Lee. Noted.* "I did. But, like, a long ass time ago. Don't ask me how many years."

Jazz laughed the same laugh as Lee. Antonio had liked her already, but that easy booming belly laugh that tasted like toasted marshmallow solidified his opinion. "What did you major in?"

"Music ed and vocal performance. I wanted to teach high school theater." Antonio considered how much to tell her, and decided on a sugarcoated version. "After I visited New York, I decided I wanted to be famous instead. But five years later, I'm back to my childhood ambitions: middle school choir teacher."

Jazz looked at him softly with the same warm brown eyes as Lee. "Was it worth it?"

"Which part?"

"All of it. It sounds like you have a lot of regrets, but were they worth it?"

*Damn. So much for the sugarcoated version.* "I think I'd regret the 'what if' of not moving to New York more than I regret hitting rock bottom. Is that fucked up?" Antonio laughed to mask his discomfort. He hadn't expected Jazz to get so deep while Lee ordered their food.

She shook her head. "Not at all. My 'what-ifs' are heavy as hell. I'm trying to turn them into reality without them becoming regrets later on."

*Girl, you're nineteen. How many "what-ifs" can you have?* Antonio just nodded in sympathy. "Have you picked a major yet?" he asked as Lee returned, handing a glass of iced mint tea to Antonio. Antonio sipped it gratefully.

Jazz perked up again. "I'm thinking ecology. Or maybe botany? I might double major."

"Damn, you sound smart or something," Lee teased.

"'Cause I *am* smart. Not that *you* would know what that's like." Jazz made a face as she pulled off her sweater and hung it over the back of the chair.

"Jazz! What are you wearing?" Lee covered his eyes.

Under her sweater, Jazz had been hiding a neon green mesh shirt with a matching sports bra. Antonio shot a confused look at Lee. *I've worn far more revealing stuff than that in public.*

Jazz rolled her eyes in exasperation. "Clothes, Lee. I'm wearing clothes."

"Does Dad know you're dressed like that?" Lee still covered his face.

"No, obviously. He wouldn't let me leave the house if he knew," Jazz explained for Antonio's sake. "But that's a Dad problem. I'm not going to dress like a kindergarten teacher just to make Dad happy. No offense," she added to Antonio.

"None taken. Teacher drag is boring. Not enough mesh." Antonio winked at her before he pulled Lee's hands from his eyes.

Lee shot him a pleading look.

Antonio shot one back. As mature and understanding as Lee had been on the car ride here, his sister had brought out an annoying overprotective side. "Lee, you're acting like Cassie, and I don't mean that as a compliment. Jazz doesn't need to deal with it."

Lee huffed out a breath. "Fine. You're right. Jazz is grown."

"I'm not the one you should be looking at, Angel."

Lee's huff was closer to a laugh this time. He kept his eyes on Jazz's face. "Sorry. You know. How's school?"

"I know. Life lessons from Dad." Jazz shot a smug grin at Antonio before answering her brother's attempt to change the subject. "School's good. Summer classes are almost over, and I made the dean's list again!"

"That's so impressive!" Antonio clapped. "I barely avoided academic probation."

"Is the dean's list a good thing?" Lee asked.

"Yes. It means I'm smart!" Jazz tapped her temple. "Or...I get good grades, at least."

Antonio was reminded of Lee's unconventional teenage years for the second time today. Guilt twinged in his gut as he remembered Lee's heavy look from earlier. *I wonder if he resents it. Not getting the normal high school experience. I'd resent his parents if I were him.*

Jazz seemed to have a similar thought. "You ever think about going back to school?"

Lee pushed his glasses up. "Yeah, no. I mean, Chas told me I had to when I got hired, but she hasn't made me yet. I don't think it'd be worth the effort or money."

Jazz nodded with a grimace. "It is very expensive."

"Dad is paying, right?" Lee asked.

She sighed heavily. "Is it worth the cost? You don't have to cover your hair at church every Sunday. Or listen to some dusty-ass man with a fragile ego preach that women should submit to their husbands and fathers. And follow all his damn rules! And have him control your every decision! I want to get my degree but he's so damn..." She paused, looking for the right words, "...himself! I can't wait to get out."

The server arrived just in time to break the tension, setting their paninis and kettle chips in front of them. Antonio popped a chip in his mouth, grateful that Lee had ignored his "low sodium" request. *What the fuck kind of church did you go to, Angel?*

"I'm going to shave my head next weekend," Jazz announced.

Antonio choked on the chip. Jazz may avoid sore subjects like Lee, but she was bold.

"Seriously? You're gonna risk the wrath of Dad?" Lee passed his water to Antonio, who guzzled it greedily to wash the chip down. "He's always made you keep your hair long."

Jazz's mouth twisted. "And what's the worst he can do?"

"Beat your ass? Kick you out? Cut you off financially?" Lee suggested.

Jazz huffed in frustration. "Mom would leave him if he tried. She's still upset with him for...you know. Besides, the bald head is supposed to distract him from the septum ring I want."

Lee laughed bitterly. "Jazz, you have completely different parents than I had. Mom didn't even take a shit without Dad's permission."

"He has to learn he can't control me forever. I can't wait to be as free as you are." Her frown twisted into a teasing grin. "Even if you still keep that ugly ass buzz cut Dad always made you get."

"Says the copycat about to shave her head."

Antonio watched them tease each other, smiling along as Lee caught her up on his life and the latest stories about Tara, Blanche, and Sunny. The more he learned about Lee, the more questions he had. How could any parent disown their child, especially someone as easygoing and kind as Lee? Antonio's own childhood—idyllic in comparison, despite his teen angst—had left him with scars that he was only beginning to heal.

Jazz seemed to envy Lee's freedom, but was Lee free? Even when they were alone, Lee often hesitated, cautious about his choices to the point of indecision. Did he feel free from their controlling parents? Or did he just feel abandoned by them?

Taking another sip of his mint tea, Antonio quietly hummed, adding the new things he'd learned to his Lee Song, which was still far too short considering they were about to move in together. But he was excited to discover the many things about Lee he didn't know yet—for better or for worse. *We have all the time in the world.*

# Monday, August Twelfth

# Chapter Twenty-Nine

## Lee

Lee jolted awake, gasping for breath. His muscles were stiff and icy, but his heart pounded hot in fear. *"You know what happens when you're disobedient."*

Streetlights illuminated the ceiling through a thin sheet tacked over the window. *I'm at Antonio's. It was a dream. That wasn't real.*

*"Disappointment."* His dad's voice still rang in his head. *"Abomination." "Sinful."*

He swallowed down the bile rising in his throat, wiping his hands against the sticky cotton of his shirt to convince himself that the leather belt he'd been gripping—wait, hadn't his dad held the belt? No, it'd cut into *his* palms—wasn't real.

He'd been rooted to the spot, forced to watch his dad beat Antonio after he'd caught them together the same way he'd caught Lee and Sunny together all those years ago. Only in real life, Sunny had been safe; Lee had taken the brunt of his father's anger.

But he'd also been Antonio, feeling each crack against his back and thighs.

Worst of all, he'd also been his dad, full of anger and disappointment and resignation.

His mom's hushed sobs were a haunting chorus in the background: *Hide your tears. Say your prayers. It'll be over faster.* Lee hated that he'd caused his mom to break that day, to cry for the first time in his life. He hated even more how she had never once told his dad to stop.

"Lee? You okay?" Antonio murmured next to him. "You were talking in your sleep."

Lee cleared his throat to soothe the lump. "Yeah, just a bad dream." Adrenaline coursed through him. He hadn't dreamt of that day in years. Thankfully, the details of the nightmare were quickly fading. Less fleeting was the guilt and revulsion and fear.

In the silence, he breathed deeply, the way Blanche had taught him long ago. *I'm safe. Antonio is safe. They can't hurt him. I didn't hurt him. We're safe.*

"Wanna talk about it?" Antonio turned over to look at him.

"I'm okay. Go back to sleep."

Antonio's arm draped over his chest. "Come here."

Lee rolled into his arms. The damp sheets peeled off his back as he buried his face into Antonio's neck. Lee's trembling hands ran along his back and thighs, checking Antonio for welts and bruises that couldn't be there, but he had to be sure.

Antonio massaged the tension from Lee's shoulders, softly humming a soothing tune.

"I'm sorry for waking you up," Lee murmured into Antonio's neck. "You don't have to—"

"Angel, you're sweet to me when I can't sleep. This is the least I can do." Antonio kissed his ear.

Antonio's tenderness made Lee's heart ache, made worse with the fresh, visceral nightmare of hurting him. "I love you."

"Love you more, Angel. You okay?"

Lee didn't want to worry him. *I hope moving in together is the right decision. I don't want to hurt him.* "I'm fine."

---

LEE PARKED HIS CAR and double-checked the address, tapping the steering wheel along with the song on the radio to calm himself. Hot Barber had finally found a chair to rent, but his new shop was uncomfortably close to where he'd grown up. *There's no way Dad would be at a barbershop on a Monday afternoon. He would have gone on Saturday morning, and it wouldn't be this one. That nightmare just has me fucked up.*

Opening the door, he stepped into a cloud of Barbasol and sandalwood, a chorus of laughter and buzzing from the clippers. Hot Barber spotted him first, practically jogging up to him in the waiting area.

"Welcome to my new office!" Hot Barber held up his fist in greeting, giving a subtle nod to the group of older men talking in the corner. "Good timing. I just finished a walk-in."

With a wry grin, Lee dapped him up. He teased quietly, "That greeting was so performative. You get a chair, and we gotta act straight now?"

Hot Barber led him to a chair, giving Lee a meaningful look and murmuring, "I didn't want to out you if you didn't want to be out."

Lee glanced back at the trio of older men by the entrance, who looked at him and Hot Barber with more suspicion than curiosity. "That's not stopping you, it looks like." He nodded toward the small pride flag on Hot Barber's mirror as he sat in the chair.

Hot Barber shrugged and fastened a cape around Lee's neck. "Sis, it's August. If they couldn't figure it out from the cutoff shorts and crop tops..." He laughed. "That flag keeps the homophobes out of my chair. Besides, I've heard it all before, and I can dish it back."

"I believe it," Lee laughed. "As long as I'm not about to get bashed out front, no need to act any different with me. I'm gay, no point in hiding it."

"And yet you still want a boring-ass buzz cut. I keep telling you—grow your hair out!" Hot Barber ran his fingers over Lee's hair affectionately before adding quietly, "Xavier was pissed at you on Saturday."

Lee sighed as he took off his glasses. "Do I gotta worry about what you're about to do to my hair?"

He scoffed. "Not at all! Just saying, you missed a shitshow on Saturday!" Hot Barber plugged in the clippers and pushed Lee's head forward. The steady buzz on the back of his head was soothing. "Honey, you need a new best friend. That Xavier is a piece of work."

Lee was pleasantly surprised that Hot Barber was on his side. "He is *not* my best friend."

"Well, you were *his* best friend, then. Mo told me you finally let Xavier have it yesterday. Does this mean we don't have to hang out with him anymore?" Hot Barber laughed. "He's such a controlling ass. Like, Brandon was obviously in no shape to drive no matter what Xavier said, so Mo and I caught a ride with that Phineas guy, who is my hero now.

Normally, he does way too much. But in a crisis? Unreal. He just oozed confidence. Like, we see Brandon get pulled over, right? And Phineas pulls a U-ey on a red, gets someone important on the phone, and walks up to twelve like he's in charge. And they just let them go because some nerd with locs and questionable fashion told them to? Like, if Mo and I haven't been talking lately, I might have considered it! Phineas on a mission could get it."

Lee hoped the awkward tension with Phineas hadn't ruined Antonio's half-friendship with him. He seemed like a good person to keep around. "Which one is Mo?"

"Girl, what? Your friend? Mo?" At Lee's blank look, Hot Barber glanced around and quietly added, "The one with a fleshlight for a throat."

"Oh, yeah. Him." *BJSlut.* He shrugged. "I'm bad with names."

"Are you serious? You don't know his name, but you know *that*?" Hot Barber laughed. "Do you know *my* name?"

Lee sighed. "Look, you saved your number as Hot Barber. I'm *so* bad with names."

"I love that. We're keeping it that way." Hot Barber's grin was mischievous. "So Mo and I have been talking lately. Like actually talking."

Lee grinned, relieved Hot Barber hadn't taken it personally. "Maybe you have. Sounds like his mouth was busy."

"I'm so done with you!" Hot Barber swatted his shoulder with a laugh. "We need to find new people to hang out with. You don't talk much, but we didn't have much fun without you last night. The three of us—and maybe Phin—should find our own scene. Your queen too, of course."

Lee was touched—Whatshisname's words had hurt more than he'd cared to admit. He was never the life of the party, but he didn't think he'd been a drag. "Tonio's not really one for parties," *Or Phin,* "but I'll take you up on that. I figured after yesterday, I wouldn't have many friends left besides Tara and them."

"Well, I'm still your friend, and Mo only put up with Xavier for your sake, so you have at least two friends besides your ladies and your queen. Which is honestly more than I have out here, so lucky you."

Before Lee could respond, one of the men by the entrance called out, "You any relation of Leland Jones?"

Lee froze, his chest tightening. No music played in the barbershop. He did his best to find tranquility in the metallic snips of scissors nearby and the buzz of the clippers in Hot Barber's hand.

"You're right, he does favor Leland. I can't recall the last time I saw his son," another chimed in. "That your old man? Strange, wouldn't have expected *his* son to be hanging around with...folks of *that* persuasion."

Hot Barber rolled his eyes. "Gay, Olly. I'm gay! Saying it won't turn you. But with how much you look at my ass, you probably don't want to take any chances!"

Olly's reply was cut off by the other men's laughter, and the shit-talking carried the conversation away from him. Lee was relieved he didn't have to explain how he was no longer Leland Jones's son to people who still knew him. From what he could see of the men in the corner, Lee didn't remember any of them. But he'd been raised to keep his mouth shut and his eyes down around his elders. He never knew anyone's names; his parents had trained him to address everyone as "yes, sir" or "yes, ma'am." He'd be more likely to recognize their shoes than their faces.

Hot Barber gave him a knowing look in the mirror as he turned the clippers off to take the guard off. "Olly's not so bad. Just old-fashioned."

Lee raised his eyebrows in acknowledgment, catching his own reflection. As always, his dad looked back with angered resignation. Without his glasses, the slight cleft of his chin he'd gotten from his mother and the faint scar on his cheekbone that distinguished his face from his father's were too blurry to see.

For a second, he was fifteen again, glimpsing the weariness in Dad's profile as he drove. Lee trembled in the backseat, staring at his toes in the slides on his bare feet. What was he doing wearing house shoes in the car? With no socks when it was November? Why wasn't he wearing a coat? His back burned against the seat. Why was he so hot when it was so cold?

Lee glanced up, about to apologize for not being properly dressed. Dad's eyes met his in the rearview mirror, resignation simmering with familiar disappointment. Lee closed his mouth, afraid to speak. Why were they in the car? Normally, Dad would have Lee clean as his penance, not go for a drive.

They pulled up to the park by the mounds. Good thing Jazz wasn't with them—Mom would freak out if she found out Jazz was by the mounds, even with Dad. Black girls went missing over here; Lee was supposed to keep her away.

*Oh, Jazz.* She always got so scared when Dad got angry. Maybe he'd sneak some candy from the corner store later. Jazz usually needed a bribe to come out of hiding.

Leland parked by a bench overlooking the river and walked around the car, opening up Lee's door. "I always knew you were a disappointment. But this sin is too great to allow you to poison our home. A life of shame is the punishment for abominations and I will not allow you to bring shame to our family."

"I'm sorry, sir. It won't happen again."

His dad's sigh was heavy. Lee tried not to fidget as his dad considered his words. "No, Lee. It will. You have a sinful nature. I did my best to get you on the right path, but I see now it's impossible. You no longer have a home or a family. You will never return or contact anyone in the family again. You're dead to us, as far as we're concerned. Is that understood?"

Lee nodded, not understanding at all, but asking questions would just make Dad angrier.

"Get out of the car."

Lee panicked. "But I'm not allowed by the mounds. I'm not dressed—"

"Get out!" A heavy hand grabbed him by the shoulder to drag him out of the backseat.

Lee flinched.

"Lee? You're all done." It was Hot Barber's hand on Lee's shoulder. The concern on his face made Lee burn in mortification. "You okay?"

"Yeah, thanks." Lee forced a smile on as he put his glasses back on.

"You don't look so hot." Hot Barber cupped his cheek. "You want me to call Antonio to come get you?"

"No, he's at work. I'm fine. Just tired." He handed over cash for the haircut, anxious to escape the cloud of Barbasol and the memories of his father. The awkward silence of the barbershop pressed on his spine as all eyes followed him. *First the nightmare and now a full-on flashback? What is wrong with me? I thought I had this figured out.* "See you next week?"

Hot Barber's eyes held a mix of understanding and sympathy as he nodded. "Text me. And let me know if you'd rather do bathroom cuts again."

Lee nodded, relief making it easier to breathe. At least until he had this flashback shit under control again, it was best to stay away from the neighborhood he'd grown up in. He hated the trembling in his hands, the queasiness that came with the memories. How weak he still was. The power his dad still had over him.

Olly cleared his throat as Hot Barber walked Lee out. "Hey, we won't tell your old man you're...you know. Lord only knows what his sanctimonious ass would do."

"Gay, Olly." Hot Barber laughed too loudly, practically pushing Lee out the door. "I swear I'll get you to say it one day."

# Chapter Thirty

## Tara

"Buttercup, please don't hate me."

*This again.* With an affectionate chuckle, Tara turned away from the half-finished logo on her laptop to find Lee in her doorframe. He pushed his glasses up before wiping his hands on his joggers, nervous as always about something he didn't need to apologize for.

"What'd you do, Lee?" Tara never understood why he acted so nervous; Lee was stuck with her, no matter what he felt he'd done wrong.

To her surprise, he squeezed into her bedroom. "Can I sit down?"

Tara closed her laptop, anxiety shooting through her. She tucked it into the duffel bag under her bed and scooted over to make room. "Come here."

Lee laid down, wrapping his arms around her waist and tucking his head on her shoulder.

Tara snuggled into her security blanket, waiting for him to speak. Lee would sit there and overthink what he should say. Eventually, Tara would lose patience and make him spit it out. He'd fumble his way through an apology over something she wasn't upset about, but she would make a fuss. Then he'd talk shit and she'd dish it back. They both knew she would forgive him.

This song and dance had happened countless times over their decade together. The ritual was just a formality. They loved each other no matter what.

Today though, Lee seemed legitimately upset, exhaling uncomfortably and tapping his fingers against her ribcage as he overthought whatever he felt called to confess.

Her anxiety climbed higher the longer he took. "That's a lot of heavy sighing, Lee," Tara teased for both of their sakes. "I'm getting nervous."

Lee let out another exhale along with a laugh. "Sorry. Just figuring out what to say."

"I know." Tara kissed his forehead.

He looked at her thoughtfully. "I'm always going to be here for you. No matter what. I love you and we're family forever. Okay?"

A chill stabbed her heart. "If you're trying to reassure me with that, it backfired."

"Just keep that in mind, Buttercup," Lee teased. "It's what I'd want to hear, so hopefully you wanna hear it too."

She froze. *Fuck. He's leaving me.*

"Buttercup, breathe." Lee nuzzled against her.

Tara inhaled deeply, falling into her breathing pattern.

"I'm not leaving you. Yesterday, Antonio asked if I wanted to get a place with him when his lease is up. I told him I want to."

*Inhale, 2, 3, 4, 5. I feel his arms around me.*

"I wanted to tell you now so you have time to process. Even if I move out and get a place with him, you'll always come first in my life."

*Exhale, 4, 3, 2, 1. I smell him, shea butter on his skin and rosemary in his hair, and lavender from our laundry detergent, just like always.*

"Lee, that's fucked up. *You* should come first in your life." Tara sighed. "Maybe Blanche is right. We may be codependent. You come first for me, too."

"I better." Lee laughed softly. "You're right. You're always right. This is why I need you around. You always tell me what I should do."

*Inhale, 2, 3, 4, 5. Keep breathing. I hear his laugh. And mine.*

He lifted his head, glasses slipping down his nose. Fear and confusion swam in those honey-brown eyes she loved so dearly. "It's just...I love him. And he makes me happy. And his family is awesome. And I want all of that but..." he trailed off.

*Exhale, 4, 3, 2, 1. I see my best friend.* "You're scared."

He nodded before resting his head on her shoulder, glasses askew. "What do I do?"

"You'd tell him you changed your mind if I said so?" Tara asked.

Lee nodded against her neck.

"Are you fucking serious?" Irritation exploded through her, blowing her anxiety away like dust. She pushed him onto his back and straddled his chest to make him look at her. Tara pulled his glasses off. "Leland Aloysius Jones! You are so fucking indecisive! You cannot use me as an excuse to hold yourself back. If you want to move in with him, move in with him! It's a simple decision. Don't let our fucking shit keep you from being happy!"

A smile broke through Lee's wide-eyed expression. "Cool. I was probably going to anyway."

Tara groaned in frustration, sitting back on his chest. She put his glasses back on his face. "You knew I'd talk your ass into it! Dammit! I hate you."

"No, you don't. You love me. You wouldn't have brought out the whole government name if you didn't," Lee teased, wrapping his hands around her hips. "And I wasn't lying. I am fucking terrified and indecisive. Like Blanche says, I'm Schrodinger's Gay. I am both going to move in and not move in, and I won't know which one is true until it happens."

Tara snorted and wiggled down his body to lay alongside him. "Oh, Lee. You're a fucked-up mess, aren't you?"

"I know *you're* not talking, Buttercup." He kissed the top of her head.

She rolled her eyes. "We're not talking about me right now. You work so hard to make everyone you love happy. This is your chance to make yourself happy. What is there to be fucking indecisive about?" He'd probably already made a pros and cons list, and one teensy tiny little con would be enough for him to hold back.

Lee let out another heavy sigh. "You know what."

*Maybe not so teensy tiny.* "Antonio is not your dad, Lee."

"I know he's not. But what if I am?"

Tara frowned. "I literally cannot imagine a single way you're like him."

Lee swallowed heavily. "I had a nightmare last night where I was him. And I see him every time I look in the mirror. What if I have more of my dad in me besides my appearance? What if I'm not who Antonio needs? What if I hurt him?"

"Is that why you always ask me how you look? To avoid seeing your dad in the mirror?"

"I don't like to think of it that way, but..." Lee shrugged.

Tara's heart broke for him. "I always assumed you were just insecure."

"What do I have to be insecure about?" Lee asked innocently.

Tara opened her mouth, unsure how to answer. "...nothing?"

Lee snorted. "Damn right."

"Why are you like this?" Tara huffed into his neck. "Look, I've never met your dad, Lee, and he better hope I never do, but you are a million times the man he is. He disowned you because he caught you with someone else's dick in your hand. He abandoned his dying sister because she wouldn't follow his lead. You're nothing like that. You always show up for the people you love, and you're so understanding. Even if you need some space to process, you'd never just leave him when things get tough. Especially if he needed you."

"I just wish I could see the end date," Lee murmured. "Is it worth signing a lease if I get kicked out? If it means hurting Antonio?"

"You can't predict the future, but I'll always be in yours. And so will Blanche and Sunny. We're family. You've got us. Always." Tara touched his cheek. "You're allowed to be happy, you know. We were so relieved when our lives were finally 'good enough' that we got stuck there. This could be good for you, Lee. Antonio is so good for you. And you're good for him."

"I know. But is 'good' worth risking the 'good enough'?"

"Hey now, I'm part of your 'good enough'. You're stuck with me."

At least, she hoped so. Lee might have found something good in his life, but she hadn't. Tara still needed him. She always would. Even if one of these pointless dates ever ended up being worth the effort.

Lee shook his head and held her tight. "You're more than 'good enough,' Buttercup."

Tara clung to him just as tightly. "Do what feels right, Lee. If you want to move in with him, move in. And if things don't work out, I'll kill him if you want."

Lee snorted. "I would never ask that."

"I'm kind of banking on that. I like him," Tara teased. "For the record, I don't think you or Antonio would ever intentionally hurt each other. You guys are perfect together."

"I know. This is the right move, but anxiety doesn't care about logic."

"Maybe talk to Blanche? Or you know...an actual therapist?"

"Sure, I'll talk to Blanche if it gets worse." He rubbed her back. "Are we okay?"

Tara nodded in his chest, though her emotions were going haywire. Her deep breaths cooled her heart, that familiar herbal scent that clung to Lee flooding her with calm. "I'm happy for you."

Lee shook his head vehemently, tightening his arms around her. "Buttercup, the second I leave this room, you're gonna spiral. You've been hiding the hard feelings from me for months. I'll lay here in your tiny ass bed until you tell me everything."

Tara scowled. Yeah, she had been hiding her hard feelings from him. But more importantly, she'd been hiding them from herself. "Fine. Give me a fucking minute."

"Take as much time as you need, Buttercup. I'm not going anywhere."

She fell back into her breathing pattern, keeping her face tucked into his chest. Normally, she only meditated until she could shove her emotions down far enough to keep her panic at bay.

But Lee was right. Figuring out her hard feelings now, where she was safe and had him close by to help her through a panic attack, might be helpful.

The emotions swirled around her head and her heart. She latched onto the loudest one. *Hurt.* Hurt that she was getting left behind, that she couldn't keep up with him. She'd held herself back and Lee had outgrown her. *Except he's just moving out. I'll have to grow with him.*

*Loneliness.* Her whole life, no one had ever been there for her. Not like Lee had. She'd spent the last decade with him at her side. And now he wouldn't be next to her anymore. She hated that chill that reminded her of her mom screaming at her to get lost. *He's just letting Antonio in. Bringing more love into our lives. That's a good thing.*

*Jealousy.* Antonio took up all of Lee's time that used to be spent with her. But maybe she and Lee did spend too much time together. Besides, she'd found other people to spend time with. Shopping with Sunny. The dates she'd had. Maybe she could bring more love into her own life?

That weird, sad, wanting feeling that felt like jealousy but sadder was back. She envied Lee for finding someone as perfect for him as Antonio. Someone who made him happy, when she thought he'd been happy with her. Their happiness was different, though. She hadn't known happiness like that existed; Walter and Wanda's love had been a fluke that normal people couldn't experience. But Lee had found it in Antonio.

And now Tara longed to feel it for herself.

*Longing? Is that what it is? Oh, no, we're not doing that.* She'd be here all night if she had a new soft feeling. Soft feelings took forever to figure out. *This shit is so fucking uncomfortable. Is this how normal people figure this shit out?* Tara felt less scattered and more vulnerable. Why did people sit with their feelings like this? It was so much easier to shove them away.

So she did. They were easier to shove down today, though. Examining them first made it easier to squeeze them into their little box. The hard feelings were smaller. More manageable.

Tara found the words for Lee, honest enough to reflect her hard feelings, but tame enough so he wouldn't worry. "I'm proud of you for doing something you want for once in your fucking life. You never think you're good enough, but you're the best person I know, and you're a million times braver than you give yourself credit for.

"And yeah, I am jealous. And I'm scared of how lonely I'll get after you move out. But I'll deal because I can't expect you to stay in our little bubble forever, you know? I just need to grow with you. I would hate if I held you back from happiness."

"Just remember, I'm not leaving you, Buttercup. I'm always going to be here for you."

Tara nodded. "We're family. You couldn't get rid of me if you tried."

A knock sounded. Antonio, dressed in khakis and a forest green button-down, stood in the open doorframe. *It's weird seeing him dressed so...boring.*

"Blanche let me in. I'm not interrupting anything, am I?" His tight smile looked nervous.

Lee laughed. "You're interrupting a very intimate moment, babe. Jealous?"

"Angel, if it was going to happen, it would have happened by now," Antonio teased.

Tara smiled. "Want to join us? I promise not to hurt you for stealing my soulmate."

"I like your room, Tara. This is cozy." Antonio laughed and crawled over them, sandwiching Tara between him and Lee. The bed groaned in protest. "Intimate, you might say. Y'know, it's been a while since I had a threesome."

Tara groaned as Lee gagged. "Don't make it weird, dude."

"Honestly, she's basically my sister!"

Antonio giggled. "It was just a joke!"

Tara rolled her eyes but laughed along with him. Antonio was a good addition to their family. They needed more fun.

# Saturday, August Seventeenth

# Chapter Thirty-One

## Sunny

Sunny was tired of the routine. She shouldn't be.

Her time with Blanche was absolute bliss, even though they only had a short evening or two together every week. Sunny wanted more, of course, but Blanche always turned her down gently in that sweet, condescending way they always talked to her.

She had what she wanted, didn't she?

"I wish I could get a cat," she announced, unrelated to the conversation the rest of the table had been having over their happy hour drinks, but she hadn't been listening anyway.

"Why can't you?" Antonio asked politely, as if she hadn't interrupted him.

"My mae doesn't want pets."

"I wish our place allowed cats, too," Blanche said, slouching in the chair next to her. "I hate leaving the stray kitties outside."

"Blanche, you literally built them a shelter in the alley, got the whole colony fixed, and you buy hundreds of dollars of cat food every month. They're hardly fending for themselves," Tara pointed out.

Blanche pouted. "Yeah, but I want to take them all home." They sighed. "It's not like we have space for cats anyway."

"Well, funny you should mention that," Antonio said, taking Lee's hand. "We're getting an apartment together when my lease is up in October."

"We're not getting a cat though." Lee smiled down on him.

"Oh, yeah, no." Antonio laughed. "I can barely take care of myself."

"You're moving in together?" Sunny shouldn't be so surprised. They had to grow up eventually. Still, for it to actually happen was weird. She checked for Tara's reaction, worried how she'd take the news.

Tara looked surprisingly calm, not even paying attention. She was avoiding all eye contact, making patterns with the condensation rings from her drink. That could mean either she was about to go on a murderous rampage, or...

"You knew already, didn't you?" she asked Tara, accusatory.

Tara jerked her head up, confusion visible in her green eyes. "What do you— Oh, yeah. Lee told me already. He wanted to give me time to process or some shit." She shrugged, back to avoiding eye contact. "It's cool. It'll be weird without him, but whatever."

"My darling is growing up!" Blanche wore a proud grin on their face. "And the bedroom freed up? Perfect timing for my next venture. I don't suppose anyone knows how to make a SubParty? Chas says it's the next big thing, like YouTube for kink. Apparently, the sub refers to subscribers, not just submissives. And nothing to do at all with sandwiches."

Lee laughed. "Late to the party as always. SubParty has been a thing for years. But I'll help turn my room into a film set if you want."

"I'll help, too! You'd be great at it!" Tara chimed in. "Well, with some technical assistance. We can get a few cameras for different angles. I can take photos!"

"I have a few mics lying around that you could use. Get some ASMR shit going with the floggers and latex?" Lee started a list on his phone.

"To be honest, this is great timing. My patron just got engaged. Again. His fiance is cracking down on his cheating this time, so I need to expand my income streams. Gotta save up for a new place before she finds out about me." Blanche rested their chin on their hands. "Should I specialize my domme content, or..."

The Jealousy tab reopened unprompted. Sunny would never look down on anyone for making money online or digitizing sex work. But the idea of *Blanche* doing it sat ill in her heart. Blanche kept her far away from their domme side, and Sunny did her best to understand that.

But seeing a subscriber count? Blanche sharing themself on the internet?

It was a cruel reminder that she only had a small fraction of Blanche. Sunny wanted all of their life, not just a few hours a week. And now her tiny portion of Real Blanche's free time would shrink even more? Where would Sunny fit into their recording schedule?

Tara's words from Blanche's party echoed in her mind. *"You deserve someone who is going to give you all of themselves. And that's never going to be Blanche."*

THE SETTING SUN ILLUMINATED Blanche's apartment when they returned from Confession, filtering through the gaps of the half-built condo across the street. Blanche headed straight for the kitchen, chattering away happily about their plans for content.

Sunny halfheartedly responded, barely paying attention.

Tara had stayed behind to watch the show. Sunny should be grateful to have this time alone. Any time with Blanche, especially on the weekends, was rare. Sunny cherished the perfect quiet moments when everything felt magical. Moments like...*when? We've had magical moments, haven't we? Besides sex?*

Blanche cleared their throat, waiting expectantly as if they had asked her a question. They were holding out a glass of iced tea.

"Sorry, did you say something?" Knuckles white and her nail beds sore, Sunny's fingers gripped her skirt too tightly to take the glass.

"I asked if you could explain what an algorithm is. Babygirl, you've been off in space all evening." Blanche set the tea down and checked her forehead with the back of their hand. "Are you okay?"

"I'm fine." Sunny sounded childish even to her own ears.

The concern on Blanche's face morphed into a doubtful look, eyebrow raised. "No one says 'I'm fine' in that tone of voice and means it. Talk to me."

Sunny took a deep breath, figuring out what to say. Shifting her weight from one foot to the other, she blurted out, "I don't want you to start a SubParty!"

Blanche's half smile fell into a frown. "And why not?" Their tone had a warning to it. Sunny normally loved when Blanche talked to her like that, but tonight, it rubbed her the wrong way.

Sunny stared at the floor. She wasn't supposed to get jealous, but Blanche had asked. This was how she felt. *That's what relationships should be right? Talking shit out when I feel some type of way.* Not pretending she didn't get jealous because Blanche told her not to. Or that a few hours a week together was enough when she wanted, *needed,* more.

She was so tired of doing what was expected of her. Her mother gave her enough of that constant pressure to be responsible and considerate; being put in a box—put away until it was convenient—was not what Sunny wanted from her partner.

"You're not going to have time for me. For us. You barely have time for me as it is." Sunny fiddled with a fingernail, avoiding Blanche's eye. "And I don't like the idea of a bunch of creeps watching you online."

"But you're fine with creeps touching me in person," Blanche said skeptically.

"That's different." Sunny crossed her arms.

Blanche stepped closer, bending down to stare into her soul with those dark green eyes. "How so? What's so different about people who aren't even in the room?"

"Because!" Sunny stomped her foot in frustration. "Because I don't have to know about it! I can pretend I don't share you with anyone else. You're supposed to be *mine*!"

"There she is." Their tone grew darker as their smirk appeared. Sunny shivered despite the summer heat. "There's the jealous brat I knew was in there."

"What are you talking about?" Sunny backed up as Blanche stalked toward her. Her heart raced, but not from fear. Excitement? Anticipation?

"I'm surprised it took this long. What are the rules, Sunny?"

"Rules? What rules?" Sunny's mind blanked, scattered, scrambling for purchase.

"What are the rules."

Why was their voice so commanding? Sunny wanted to listen, to be good, and make Blanche proud of her. She *needed* to. Words spilled from her mouth, surprising her. "No jealousy. No say in decisions about your life. No telling anyone we're together. Keep it vanilla."

"Good girl."

Sunny shivered again. Arousal coursed through her as Blanche's voice flooded her brain.

"And how many of those rules have you broken?"

Her back hit the wall. "Three."

Blanche stopped, their expression unreadable as the smirk fell. "That's right. Three. Although I can't blame you for the third one. I should have gagged you so Tara wouldn't hear. And here I am breaking the fourth one. You're just so delightfully *bratty*."

Sunny sucked in a breath, her lips parting as Blanche leaned closer.

But they sighed, turning away. "That's why we're done. I'm calling 'lutefisk' on us."

"What? What are you talking about?" Sunny grabbed Blanche's arm. Blanche wrenched out of her grasp, roughly pinning Sunny's arms above her head on the wall, body pressed into hers. Sunny whimpered. Her heart beat violently in her chest.

"We. Are. Done," Blanche hissed. "Babygirl, I need you to listen. Don't argue for once in your goddamn life. I'm not in a good headspace. We haven't negotiated this. We were supposed to stay *sweet*."

Their sharp emphasis on the word flicked saliva on Sunny's cheek. A whimper escaped her as her breath caught in her throat.

"But you can't keep yourself from breaking the rules, and I can't punish you. I *won't* punish you. This isn't supposed to be that." They pulled away but kept Sunny pinned. Their voice softened. "You'll find someone who wants your jealousy, who wants to give you all of them. But that ain't me, Babygirl. Are we clear?"

Sunny nodded.

"Words, Babygirl."

"Yes. Lutefisk. We're over." Her heart broke as she said it, but Blanche was right. She wasn't enough for Blanche. Blanche wasn't enough for her. They were both too much of the wrong things for each other. Sunny wanted more of this exhilaration, and Blanche couldn't give it to her. They couldn't give her all of themself. She needed that. She deserved that.

Sunny fled without a goodbye. And Blanche let her go.

---

# Tara

Tara stumbled into the apartment in the wee hours of Sunday morning. She'd had a couple of drinks past her normal limit to give Blanche and Sunny more time alone for...whatever they were doing together. But her emotions were lighter today. She felt slightly more confident in bending her "Don't get drunk in public" rule. *If Blanche is in a...relationship? And Lee is making decisions for himself, then I can get tipsy in public! And nothing bad happened!*

She cheered internally, laughing as a small "woo!" escaped her. She hadn't even considered hooking up with anyone. The evening had passed without craving external validation or the thrill of danger, and it had been...nice. That weird *longing* still bothered her around happy people, but she'd managed. Tara had had fun tonight, gossiping with Jackie about Antonio and Lee and *finally* watching Carlita perform.

Onstage, Carlita was engaging and energetic. At first, she thought Carlita was lip-syncing until she burst into laughter mid-belt after she slipped on a dollar. And she could sing while doing the splits? Carlita was incredible. *Antonio is so flexible. No wonder Lee likes him.*

The living room rug tripped her.

Blanche sat draped over the armchair, blond hair trailing to the floor. They had a joint in their hand. *That's not a good sign.*

"Oh shit. Rough night?" Tara caught herself as she stumbled again.

Blanche looked up at her where she swayed. "I should ask you the same question."

"Dude, I'm great! I flirted with someone and *didn't* fuck her. I didn't give her my number either, but I did give her my name!" Tara pulled out a bottle of whiskey. She poured them each a generous splash and passed a glass to Blanche, trading them for the joint. She inhaled too deeply, coughing out smoke as she sat on the couch.

"I'm proud of you for sharing basic information," Blanche teased. "What did you learn?"

"I learned I listen better when they talk about shit they're excited about. The lady tonight does photography for weddings, engagements, that sort of thing. Like, I actually listened because she loves what she does, even if Hell will freeze over before I care about weddings and shit!"

Blanche laughed, snorting. Her heart surged with affection. Their genuine laugh was so rare. All of Blanche sat here in front of her tonight.

Tara remembered something else. "Oh, and she does boudoir photos, which are, like, artistic nudes! She gave me some tips for your new SubParty."

The sigh that left Blanche was heavy. "Can you ask Luna to check on Sunny?"

"Hell yeah!" Tara pulled out her phone to text Sunny's sister. "Wait! What happened to Sunny? Shit. Why aren't *you* texting Sunny? Did something happen?!"

Blanche passed the joint back to her. "Chill out. Don't overthink it. Just...get fucked up with me." They leaned back in the chair with a sigh. "I think I broke her. Or she broke me. Either way, it's over. We weren't good for each other."

Tara ran a hand through Blanche's hair, gently massaging their scalp. Black roots peeked out from the blond that Blanche insisted was natural. "I'm sorry. You tried to make her happy."

"No, I was just selfish. I thought I was doing it for her, but I just wanted someone to put me first again. Even if Sunny never actually did. Then again, I didn't put her first either."

"No, you cared. And Sunny cared," Tara murmured. Sunny wouldn't have been so grouchy if she hadn't. She'd been extra bitchy instead of just a ditz. "In her own way."

"We all knew it wouldn't work. I wish I could go back and grow a fucking spine. To tell her no before it started." They shook their head and downed their whiskey.

"Want some of my boundaries?" Tara joked. "I have a few hundred extra."

Blanche laughed. "Girl, what I need is that stick up your ass. Pretend it's a backbone."

"Consider it yours." Tara stuck the joint in Blanche's mouth so she could play with their hair. She wasn't as good at plaiting hair as Mr. Brown Eyes had been, but Blanche needed affection. "Seriously, you give so much of yourself. You gotta protect that big heart of yours."

"And you, my dear, need to give someone a chance to see yours. Not everyone is going to hurt you if you let them in."

"They might though. I've been hurt enough by people leaving." Tara's list of people who had never left her was short. Lee. Blanche. *Sunny, I guess.* Sunny had proven she couldn't be scared off, but the Cookie Incident had set them in a pattern they couldn't escape. *I should be nicer to Sunny. She's a good friend. Even if she is annoying.*

"So have I, but if I let loss stop me, I'd have no love to speak of. Everyone leaves, but they might come back. It hurts forever when they don't, but it's worth the heartache when they do." Blanche tried and failed to blow a smoke ring. "Platonic love, anyway. I doubt I could love anyone romantically again. I just never wanted to lose my friend."

"Sunny's still here," Tara said softly. Blanche must have Daisy on their mind. "You guys tried something that didn't work out, but she'll be back like nothing ever happened."

Blanche sipped their whiskey. "When did you get so wise? Does your sex therapy with strangers actually work?"

"No, but it's fun," Tara laughed. She tried to fix a weird lump she'd made in Blanche's braid. "I'm just trying to keep up with Lee. Can't have him win at this happiness shit."

Blanche laughed. "I didn't know happiness was a competition. We're a fucked up little family, aren't we? One of us gets a boyfriend and we all fall apart."

Tara grinned. Her teeth worried her lower lip as she struggled to end the braid. *How did Mr. Brown Eyes do it? He didn't have a hair tie.* She looped the bottom up messily, pulling it through another strand. The lump came back. Not pretty, but it didn't need to be; she was just babying Blanche. Aftercare.

"I don't think we fell apart. We just grew a little." She kissed Blanche's head. "Speaking of growth, your roots are showing."

"Bitch, this is my natural color. My parents were Swedish, you know."

"You were adopted."

"Not according to Mama. God put her baby into someone else's womb, is all. Lord only knows whose womb, but they for damn sure weren't Swedish." Blanche laughed, then sighed. "Just text Luna, please. If I'm in a drop, I bet Sunny needs some attention, too."

# Sunday, August Eighteenth

# Chapter Thirty-Two

## Lee

"Do they hate me?" Sunny spun around in the desk chair.

In between song changes, Lee was patiently listening to Sunny complain. He didn't have much of a choice. After a "long night of moping," Sunny had dragged herself to where Lee was a captive audience: stuck in the control room for the brunch show. And she hadn't left, continuing to talk while he worked. *I guess I'm her best friend, but damn, this couldn't wait a few hours?*

Sunny was a fucking wreck, looking like a wrung out dishrag. *How are her eyes both puffy and sunken?* She hadn't bothered with makeup, *and* she'd left the house in sweatpants.

"They don't hate you," Lee reassured her. "You're a little annoying sometimes. Right now, for example. But Blanche isn't capable of hating anyone. Least of all you."

Lee hadn't been surprised when Sunny had told him (and subsequently Freddy, also a captive audience) everything that had happened between her and Blanche. Still, he'd pretended he didn't know; Tara wasn't supposed to know either, but that didn't stop her from sending him the latest update this morning.

"You're not just saying that, are you?" Sunny asked. "We promised we'd stay friends if we didn't work out, but I don't know if they still want that."

"If Blanche said it, they meant it." He busied himself with the control panel, confirming Carlita's mic was feeding as she stepped onstage to emcee in a gold halter dress with a high slit. Lee wistfully admired the thigh peeking out.

Part of him was terrified that they were moving in together. But the majority of him—the rational part—was excited to live with Antonio.

Just that one memory of his dad's tail lights, speeding away while Lee sat alone on a park bench, clouded his joy. The burning in his eyes and down his back contrasted against the November air chilling his skin...

It took several steadying breaths for Lee to quash the memory before it overtook him. *Less thinking, more working.* For the first time in years, that day would not stop resurfacing in his psyche. The past week had been exhausting. *I gotta get this shit under control.*

He muted the music feed while Carlita worked the crowd, and queued up Chas' next number to the right timestamp. Even though Sunny knew he had a job to do, she frequently teased that he was a glorified DJ, his whole job simply to hit play on a laptop. And here she was, not paying any attention when he was working.

Instead she spun in her chair, watching the ceiling tiles. "Okay, but staying friends with your teenage fuck buddy is different than paying your friend for sex, pushing them into a relationship, not respecting their boundaries, and then hoping everything will go back to the way it was." Sunny sighed. "I hate it when I have to be self-aware."

Lee met Freddy's deadpan stare with one of his own. *Sunny's not self-aware even when she thinks she is.* "Sun, you may have pushed them for those things, but they still agreed to it. And those aren't good boundaries. Asking you to not feel jealous was never going to happen."

"*Excuse me?!*"

Lee looked at her pointedly. "Remember the homecoming dance?"

His poor date had left in tears after Sunny had accused her of assaulting Lee because she had kissed his cheek when they'd slow danced. Lee still felt bad she'd had to deal with Sunny's irrational anger, when Lee hadn't found the courage to speak up.

Sunny glared at him. "All I did was yell at her."

Lee turned to the stage. "And when you met Tara at BCC and assumed she and I were together?" Sunny had stolen Tara's snickerdoodle, staring her down as she'd shoved the whole cookie in her mouth. It had been the worst possible way for his two best friends to meet.

"What about how Tara treated me? She hissed at me!" Sunny put her hand on her chest, affronted by the suggestion that she'd been the reason for her and Tara's rocky start. Even though she had been. And *still* started all of their arguments.

"Bitch, you stole Tara's cookie! You know how she is about food." Lee rolled his eyes as he hit play at the stage manager's cue. "My point is, Sun, you get jealous. Irrationally. Blanche should have known it was unrealistic to ask that of you. If you had come to me in the first place, I could have told you that before it started."

Sunny scowled. "Maybe if you weren't so busy with your new *boyfriend*, I would have."

Lee whirled to face her. "Don't put this mess on me! You could have texted me. Or cornered me like you're doing now! If you had, I would have told you that if there's anyone who should be exclusive, it's your jealous ass. Express your feelings before you blow up, Sun!"

He shouldn't feel so smug that he and Antonio had handled their jealousy issues better than Sunny and Blanche had. Their relationships were apples and oranges. *And I should also communicate my own shit better.*

Telling Antonio he loved him was one thing. Telling him about the nightmares and flashbacks was another. They'd only started after Lee had decided to move in with Antonio. For years, his brain had blocked that trauma out, but it somehow knew that Lee was putting himself at risk. Like it was trying to stop him by reminding him what could happen.

That wasn't something Antonio needed to know. Antonio loved him and wouldn't take it personally, but his anxiety kept reminding him that his parents had claimed to love him too. Humiliation burned through him just imagining what Antonio would think if he discovered Lee had more in common with Hippo than any of the people in his life.

Lee just had to get his shit under control. Simple as that. He'd done it before; he could do it again. Antonio had enough on his plate without worrying about him, anyway.

He tapped his foot to the intro to Chas's number to focus on Sunny. "But because *you're* stubborn as hell, and *they* can't say no, y'all just thought you could waltz your way through a doomed relationship, like your jealous ass wasn't dating someone with Blanche's...history."

Self-absorbed as Sunny could be, Lee didn't need to remind her about what had happened before Blanche had met them. Besides, Freddy already had to listen to more than he'd ever wanted to without bringing up Daisy's murder.

*Aren't you doing the same thing? Carrying on this doomed relationship with Antonio who has his own history?* A chill ran through Lee at the thought. He didn't like to think of their relationship as doomed, but nothing lasted forever. They had moved so fast in four months; Antonio's love for him had to burn out eventually.

And what would it do to Antonio when it did? Lee would be hurt, but he'd have Tara and Blanche. Antonio had his family and friends for support, but what if living together changed that? What if living together made Antonio too dependent on Lee to maintain his sobriety on his own? And when they inevitably broke up...?

*Is that what the dream is telling me?* In his nightmares, Lee was always in his father's place as he hurt Antonio. Every time, he woke up in a cold sweat, hating himself. What if this step changed things? Turned Lee into a controlling, judgmental partner like his dad? Lee had always been more like his mother in personality, who was controlling and judgmental in her own quiet way. Admittedly, much like Lee. But he never saw Althea in the mirror. Just Leland.

He jumped when Sunny scoffed. "You were nicer before you met Antonio. You never used to bruise my ego like this. This is why I went to Black Hawk in the first place."

Lee pushed his glasses up, but his nose was so sweaty that they immediately slipped down again. "Who?"

"Uh, my online BFF?" Sunny looked at him like he was stupid. "He's been one of my best friends for literal years. We tell each other everything!"

"Oh, so you're getting advice from strangers on the Internet now?" With a cackle and a shake of his head, Lee rubbed the bridge of his nose. Sunny's sense of humor was beyond him, but being her friend was constantly entertaining.

"Online friends are real friends!"

"But he doesn't know the real you, just the you that you want to be. A stranger on the Internet wouldn't know how delusional you can be." A grin cracked across his face.

Sunny tsked. "Maybe if you were nicer, I'd come to *you* for advice!"

"And yet, you're here." Going off on Sunny was easier than Tara. Tara internalized and overthought everything, like he did. Sunny needed someone to tell her shit. She underthought. "Do you remember how when we were young, I thought we were two guys figuring out our sexuality, but you saw us as boyfriend and girlfriend? Like sure, it was a relationship, but we were not a *straight* couple."

"Wait, Lee—are you gay?" Sunny asked sarcastically.

He made a face. "Don't deflect. Isn't there some part of you that liked how Blanche made you feel about yourself? Maybe more than how much you actually liked Blanche? Just like how you felt about me back then?"

*Is that what Antonio and you—*Lee scratched his nose. *I am stressing myself out. I want this. Tonio wants this. Stop overthinking it.*

"Why are you so mean to me, Lee? I thought we were friends." She spun her chair to look at Freddy. "Freddy, what do you think?"

Freddy didn't spare her a glance, keeping his eyes on Chas dancing. He merely gestured his hand toward the stage. He seemed annoyed that Sunny was there at all, let alone oversharing about her secret relationship with his best friend.

Sunny nodded sagely. "You think I was projecting my unresolved mommy issues onto Blanche, seeking the validation my mother won't give me. I get that."

Freddy's loud sigh barely covered his laugh, shaking his head as he tracked the spotlight to follow his spouse's grapevine.

Unable to stand the secondhand embarrassment, Lee grabbed her chair and spun her back to face him. "Look, Sun, however you want to psychoanalyze it, go ahead. Channel your inner Blanche. But you didn't lose a friend. Blanche doesn't have many people in their life, so they're probably worrying themself sick. Just show up for them."

"Yeah yeah, thanks for the pep talk." Sunny got up to leave. "I'm gonna go talk to Blanche. If they let me in, anyway."

The second the control room door shut behind Sunny, Lee and Freddy burst into laughter. Freddy's reedy giggles blended with the big laugh that Lee had picked up from Aunt Alitrice. It was a relief, to just laugh when everything had been so heavy since Antonio's birthday party. Even if he felt bad that Blanche and Sunny had dug themselves into this hole, he trusted they would figure it out. He wasn't confident about many things in his life working out, but his friends? The four of them would get through anything together.

Their laughter devolved into sighs and chuckles. Lee shook his head affectionately as Freddy took out his phone, presumably texting his spouse everything Sunny had shared.

*Blanche is never going to hear the end of this.*

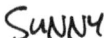

## Sunny

Sunny paced in front of the apartment door. *This conversation is going to suck.* They would not be getting back together, nor did she particularly want to. The past month spent wondering why she wasn't happy was a huge red flag in hindsight. They weren't what the other one needed. Romantically anyway. Lee was right; she couldn't imagine her life without Blanche in it. But she needed her friend who encouraged her and pushed her. Not a lover.

"Are you going to come in? Or just wear a hole in the carpet?" Sunny hadn't realized the door was open. Blanche stood there, waiting for her. Their unreadable half smile was back in place like nothing was out of the ordinary. But their hair was braided messily, frizzy blond strands falling over their face. Their eyes were bloodshot, as if they'd been crying. "Come in. I made us tea."

Sunny followed them in. "How'd you know I would be here?"

"A little birdie told me."

*Lee. That snitch.* She couldn't be mad at him, not after he had just listened to her complain for an hour. Even if he was a little mean.

"It was Freddy, actually." Blanche skewered her with a look. "Did you forget he's family, too? I have a life outside of you three, you know."

"Oh." Sunny hadn't forgotten per se, just...hadn't remembered. "Whoops."

The apartment reeked of weed. She perched on the couch, noting the empty whiskey bottle and full ashtray littering the coffee table. *So they weren't crying. They're just hungover.* Sunny laughed at herself. Blanche hadn't cried in years. She'd been delusional to consider that they would cry over *her*.

"I'm sorry." Blanche handed her a teacup.

That surprised her. "Why are *you* sorry?"

Their words flowed with rehearsed ease. "In my attempts to not be controlled, I became controlling. It was wrong of me to dictate your emotions instead of working through my own. And I'm sorry for projecting. You remind me of me. And her. I knew we wouldn't work out, but a part of me wanted to recreate what she and I had. I was selfish, and that wasn't fair to you."

Sunny waited for some sign of vulnerability, but Blanche merely looked back at her with that opaque half smile. She huffed. "Well, I'm sorry, too. I was scared to lose what I felt with you. I should have realized I was being selfish."

She had craved the bliss Blanche had brought her, but now that she knew euphoria was possible, Sunny could teach another partner to bring her there. She chewed her lip, debating how much she should say. "And, um, sorry for using you to figure out my mommy issues."

Blanche choked on their tea. "Mommy issues?" Their eyebrows furrowed in disbelief as their placid mask fell into a sneer.

Sunny winced apologetically. "Yeah. Freddy helped me realize that I might have been seeking validation from a mother figure since Mae is, well, Mae. And well, I see you as…the mom friend. Total MILF. And when you gave me that validation, it was…nice."

"God, you talked about *that* with Freddy? I'm never going to hear the end of this." Blanche's sneer flipped to a horrified grimace. "I don't do age play, especially mommy play."

Sunny burned hot with embarrassment. "I wasn't trying to! It just…happened."

A smile played on Blanche's lips. "Guess I wasn't the only one who couldn't keep it vanilla. We should have negotiated shit out."

"Probably," Sunny admitted. Their last interaction had awakened something in her. Something to explore with her next partner. *When I'm ready to date again anyway.* "I should figure my shit out with my mom, too. I don't want to put that on someone else."

"I have to say, Sunny, I'm pleasantly surprised. I was wondering how much time and space you'd need before we talked, and I was not expecting it to be this soon. And you've processed so much already? It's surprisingly mature of you."

Sunny wrinkled her nose. "Wow, thanks for the backhanded compliment."

Blanche laughed, letting out a rare snort. "Sorry. It's just, for someone so determined to make this work when it was apparent we wouldn't suit, you accepted it quickly."

Sunny let out a deep sigh. *I hate when Lee's right, but Blanche is too important to not fix us.* She couldn't keep closing the tabs she didn't want to think about. "Well, you were right that it wouldn't work. I've been stubbornly rationalizing my denial."

"You? Stubborn? No."

Sunny shot them a glare.

Blanche smirked. "Babygirl, I knew this wouldn't work, but I also knew it'd be good for you. You needed to learn what you want out of a relationship, not just sex. I'd rather you learn to listen to and advocate for yourself from a fling with me than struggle through a relationship with someone you have more potential with."

Annoyance shot through her. "So I was a charity project for you? You wanted to fix me?"

With their jaw flaring and an eye twitch, Blanche set their teacup down in exasperation. "Seeing potential for growth does not mean you need fixing! You are not and have never been a charity project."

Sunny couldn't help but smile, relief making her giddy after she'd spent all night queasy with anxiety and dread. For as much as Blanche pretended their anger exclusively belonged to Work Blanche, Sunny knew better. The snap in Blanche's voice and the sneer on their face reassured Sunny that their friendship was salvageable. She only got under their skin because they cared about her.

In the sweetest tone she could muster, Sunny couldn't help but egg Blanche on. "So you weren't trying to help me? I thought you cared." She threw on a pout and batted her eyelashes.

"Don't try that shit with me. I know what you're doing." Blanche crossed their arms with a look of disgust. Their condescending serenity vanished as their real thoughts flew from their mouth. "Of course, I care, but I don't do anything out of the goodness of my heart! I might not be good at telling you 'no,' but I damn well would have found a way to curve you if I wanted. But I'm selfish. If I focus on *you*, then I don't have to focus on *me*! I swear, I tried to help you build confidence, but you just turned into a brat!"

Sunny shook her head with a laugh. "God, why is everyone bruising my ego today?"

"You need something else bruised."

"Are you volunteering?"

"Sunny, I swear to god..." Blanche shot her a glare before picking up their teacup. They took a deep breath into the steam rising from the surface. Serenity washed over their face again. "Can't be me, Babygirl, but when you find someone to be all possessive over you, let me know. You both can sit down with me and negotiate it out properly."

"I'll keep that in mind." Sunny held out her hand, craving the touch of Blanche's calloused hand in hers. Needing the validation that everything would be all right. That they'd still be in her life after she'd pushed them so far off course. "We're cool, right? Friends?"

"Friends forever, Babygirl." Blanche took it, twining their fingers together. The small smile on their face matched the warm relief Sunny felt from their touch.

# Sunday, August Twenty-Fifth

# Chapter Thirty-Three

## Antonio

Summer was the best season for family dinners. His stepdad would grill, and there was enough space for everyone to spread out in the backyard and still hear themselves think. The kids could run around without crashing into each other.

"We're looking for a two-bedroom. Between the sheer amount of clothes we have, we need decent storage." Lee chuckled, balancing his paper plate on his thigh as he talked with Antonio's mom. "Just hard to find one in budget."

Antonio's family was taking the news that he and Lee were moving in together suspiciously well. Well, Cassie was ready to interrogate him as soon as she got him alone, but that was expected. She kept pushing off the picnic table to stand up whenever Antonio looked like he was about to go inside. He strolled past the patio door as he got seconds just to fuck with her, sauntering toward the grill with a wink as she rose out of her seat.

Cassie glared and sank back down.

"Two bedrooms? That's more space for you to leave your clothes everywhere," Oscar teased as he handed Antonio another veggie pattie.

"Excuse you, I hang up all of Carlita's clothes." Antonio pressed his hand to his chest in mock offense. Oscar and he had butted heads when he'd first moved in, but enough time had passed where they talked shit out of love, not frustration. "And I have a second laundry basket now, so I don't leave my dirty clothes on the floor before I fold the clean laundry."

That was enough to get all of his sisters to join in the teasing.

"You fold your laundry now?"

"You *wash* your laundry?"

"Ten bucks says that both baskets have dirty laundry." Oscar looked around for takers. His sisters all passed with snarky comments that they'd just lose their money.

"Wow, have some faith in me." Antonio shook the ketchup harder than necessary and it exploded over his hand. He wiped his finger on the bun. "I can clean up after myself."

"Lee, be honest. How messy is his place most of the time?" Cassie pleaded. "He was a hurricane growing up. Left his socks everywhere. Even the stiff ones. It was disgusting."

"Have I witnessed him fold laundry? No." Lee shrugged. "But he doesn't leave clothes on the floor or do a sniff test when he gets dressed, so he's better than my best friend."

"See?" Antonio kissed Lee's cheek as he sat down next to him. "I could be worse."

"True. I'm basically the maid where I live now, and I've never felt the need to pick up after you." Lee looked at him affectionately. "Tara is way worse."

"He's just trying to impress you!" Oscar chimed in from the grill.

"Tonito, promise me you won't make Lee clean up after you," his mom pleaded. "I practically had to be a drill sergeant to get you to pick up after yourself when you were a kid."

Everyone but Paula and Lee laughed. As expected, his sisters burst into another chorus of shit-talking.

"Drill sergeant? What branch of the military is that soft?"

"Pretty sure *we* ended up picking up after him."

"Yeah, he just had to bat his stupidly long eyelashes and say 'Mommy, I don't feel good,' and you'd make us do his chores."

"This is why I'm the favorite," Antonio waved his hands to shush his sisters. "Ma, you don't have to worry. You raised me better than that, and I appreciate you so much."

"Don't be a kiss ass, Tonito." Paula smiled fondly.

Antonio glanced over at Lee, who'd become unusually silent. Lee stared down at his plate, glasses inching down his nose. His shoulders were hunched, curling into himself. A faint murmur came from under his breath. *Another quiet spell?* Over the past couple of weeks, occasionally Lee would almost go blank, staring off into the distance. They didn't usually happen around other people, though.

"Something wrong?" Antonio asked quietly.

Lee didn't respond.

"Lee?" Antonio put his hand on Lee's forearm.

Lee flinched, jerking his wrist away from Antonio's touch. His plate tipped over and his half-eaten burger spilled onto Lee's lap. His brown eyes went wide as he looked blankly at Antonio before Lee finally blinked and forced a smile on his face.

*Oh... Oh! Fuck!* "Oh, shit! Sorry, didn't mean to scare you." Antonio helped him get the worst of the food off of his jeans. *Why didn't you see this before?*

"Everything okay?" Cassie asked.

"Yeah, sorry. I'm fine." Lee's face was ashen. He pushed his glasses up.

"Y'all freaked him out with all your shit talking about my bad habits," Antonio said brightly, hoping to draw his family's attention back to him. Anytime Lee had a nightmare or a quiet spell the past couple of weeks, he'd just say he was fine over and over again until Antonio dropped it. And if he didn't want Antonio asking questions, Lee wouldn't want Antonio's family asking either.

But everyone was looking at Lee with worried interest. Even the kids had stopped running around to see what had caught the adults' attention.

"Your face is really sweaty," Gracie said matter-of-factly. "Are you about to throw up?"

"Gracie, time and place," Cassie sighed. "Lee, you okay?"

Lee smiled tightly, but his skin had a grayish tinge. "Yup, I'm fine."

"Here, let's go to the bathroom. Don't want that ketchup stain to set." Antonio stood up and pulled Lee after him. "Look at me, caring about stains and shit!"

Cassie called after him, "The Tide pen is—"

"I know where the Tide pen is!" Antonio snapped, ushering Lee inside. He led Lee to the downstairs bathroom, digging through the drawers to pull out a washcloth. Soaking it in cold water, he wrung it out and handed it to Lee silently, giving him space. *I hate Tara's advice.*

"Thanks. Not sure what came over me." Lee dabbed the ketchup stain on the front of his jeans, avoiding looking up at Antonio.

"I'm here if you want to talk about it," Antonio murmured.

Lee shook his head. "I'm fine."

"I know." Antonio leaned against the sink, fingers digging into the cool countertop to stay centered for Lee's sake. "And it'd be fine if you weren't fine. Something has been going on with you lately. I'm worried about you."

"I'm fine. I'll get it under control." Lee rubbed harder. "Everything is fine."

Frustration prickled his scalp and the back of his neck, and worry ate at his gut; Lee had never admitted something was wrong before, but why wouldn't he talk about it? "Lee, you don't have to be perfect. You can have problems and we can figure them out together. Tell me what's going on."

"Tonio, I say this with love, but this doesn't have anything to do with you, and I don't need help." Lee looked up at him then, pushing his glasses back up his nose. "Everything is fine. I'm fine."

"You can tell me even if you don't need help." Antonio bit his lip, unsure if he should push it when all of Lee's friends had said Lee needed space to process. Old Antonio would have pushed it. He sighed; that side of him was not who Lee needed. "I want to support you. Like you do with me. You don't have to tell me right now, but I want to know."

*When did this stop being easy?* Lee was so sweet and open when Antonio was having a hard time, but closed off and distant when their roles were reversed. *God, this feels shitty. Is this what it felt like for everyone I was with before? Watching me pull away when things got hard?*

"And I appreciate you for it. But I have to figure this out on my own." Lee drew him into a hug and kissed the top of his head. "I just need time to get myself under control."

"Can we talk about it when you've figured it out? I hate not knowing what you're dealing with." Antonio wrapped his arms around Lee's waist. "When you're ready. Please."

Lee sighed, the frustration apparent in his exhale. "If it means you stop asking if I'm okay, then sure."

Antonio's heart dropped like a stone. It hurt, seeing the parallels between his future husband and Old Antonio. He'd said "sure" in that same tone dozens of times and never meant it once. Not that Lee was the selfish, flaky asshole the Old Antonio had been. But that "sure" was intended to placate, to get Antonio off Lee's back, when all Antonio was trying to do was support him.

Cassie, Gabe, and everyone who loved him had likely been doing the same thing anytime he'd flung the "sure" at them. The hurt he must have caused his family and friends overwhelmed him in moments like this. But nothing had broken through the shield of "sure" until Antonio was ready to accept their support. What would it take for Lee to let him in? How long would Lee suffer on his own, the way Antonio had?

His face must have shown his thoughts because the hard expression on Lee's face softened. "I'm sorry I made you worry—"

"Stop apologizing for shit out of your control," Antonio snapped. "Unless you're choosing to have nightmares and flashbacks, it *is* out of your control."

Lee opened his mouth to speak, but Antonio cut him off once more, still stewing in his frustration and worry, more directed at himself now. "Don't tell me it's not that serious. I recognize a flashback when I see one. My therapist basically trained me on how to handle Gabe's." He paused before adding in a softer tone, "Sorry that I touched you earlier. I didn't realize what was happening."

"No, it's fine." Lee pressed another kiss into his hair. "They're not as bad as they used to be. I just need a little time and—"

"You'll be fine. I know." Antonio squeezed Lee tighter, showing Lee his support, even if he refused to verbally accept it. "You want to get out of here? You did look like you were about to blow chunks earlier so they'll understand if we leave."

Lee snorted. "No, yeah, I wouldn't be mad if we left. Especially if you never say 'blow chunks' again."

Antonio huffed a laugh. "I'll go tell them we're heading out so you can sneak out the front door without having to hug two dozen people goodbye. Meet you in the car?"

Lee nodded. "Thank you."

Antonio kissed him on the cheek before heading upstairs to go out the deck door, so he could distract anyone upstairs from noticing Lee's exit out the front.

As if she'd anticipated Antonio's plan, Cassie waited at the top of the stairwell, her arms crossed. "Well?"

"Well, what?" Antonio sidled around her.

"What was that about?" Thankfully, she followed him to the deck door.

Antonio shrugged. "Couldn't find the Tide pen."

Cassie leveled an expectant look at him and blocked his exit with a hand to the door. "You know what I mean, Tonio. What was with Lee? Was that a panic attack or something?"

Antonio scoffed. "What, are you a therapist now? I thought you were an education strategist, or whatever made-up job you do for the superintendent."

"My career is not made—" Cassie cut herself off, glaring at him. "Don't deflect. You aren't a therapist either, Tonio. You have enough on your plate without having to manage Lee's emotional well-being."

"Can you butt out, Cass?" Antonio snapped. "I know I'm not his therapist, and he's not mine. There are two people—grown adults—in this relationship and neither of them are you."

Cassie sighed. "We're just worried. And you're going to move in with him already? What if whatever is going on with him isn't good for you?"

"What if I'm not good for *him*? I'm not exactly a catch. There's a million 'what-ifs' with us. But we want to move in together anyway because what if we're great for each other? What if we're happy together? That's for us to figure out, not for you to micromanage!" Antonio's anger burned up his neck. He took a deep breath before his temper got the better of him, adding quietly, "Lee tries so hard to be perfect—he's allowed to have problems! In fact, it's a relief that he isn't perfect. He sets the bar so high for himself, it's hard to live up to—"

"That's just it, though. You're on *your* journey, not his. You shouldn't have to live up to the expectations he sets."

"Just yours," he muttered. It was petty to take out his frustration with Lee on Cassie, but he was tired of her constant nagging. She was overstepping, and his patience was running out. *And it's not like you can snap at Lee when he's obviously struggling with something.*

"What's that supposed to mean?" Cassie crossed her arms.

"I'm grown, Cassie! I'm almost thirty, and you still act like you're picking me up from school. I'm not your project! Or your son!" Anger erupted in his chest. "The only one who demands perfection from me is you! I'm tired of it! Lee doesn't expect anything from me that I don't expect from myself. I just want to be as good for him as he is for me."

"I just want to help you, Antonio." Cassie rubbed her forehead, closing her eyes. "I'm sorry for putting pressure on you. I just worry and—"

"I know. I know. I know. I'm sorry for yelling." Antonio held out his arms to offer a hug. Cassie was too sensitive to fight with; they'd endured enough arguments for a lifetime before his parents had accepted that they'd be happier apart. "Come here. I don't want to argue."

Cassie tucked her chin on his shoulder, something he used to do until he'd grown taller than her in eighth grade. His anger melted away as he squeezed his sister tight. She had practically raised Antonio and their other siblings; moving past that dynamic as they grew older wasn't easy.

"Look, Cass, I don't have all the answers to make you stop worrying about me," he murmured. "Just trust me, please. This is my relationship, my partner, my life, okay? I appreciate your concern, but trust me to know what's best for me." Antonio rested his cheek on her hair and spotted his mother hugging Lee by the front door out the corner of his eye.

His heart sank. *How much did he hear?* Both he and Cassie had raised their voices. He'd assumed Lee would stay downstairs longer, but he must have overheard the whole conversation.

Paula smiled kindly at Lee, but the vein in her temple was working overtime. "Feel better, hun. I'll make some soup for you. Just don't let Tonio eat it all, yeah?"

Lee nodded and thanked her before slipping through the front door.

Paula's controlled and passive expression couldn't mask her deep disappointment. Her voice was low and dangerous as she walked past them to the patio door. "Time and place, Cassandra. At least wait until the poor boy is out of earshot."

"Sorry, Ma," Antonio and Cassie muttered together. His mother wouldn't scold him directly—due to some outdated sexist paradigm or out of fear he'd relapse again—but her words were for him as much as his sister.

In the car, Antonio buckled his seatbelt, gripping the strap to hide the trembling of his hands. Shame burned from head to toe. "You heard all of that, didn't you?"

Lee's soft baritone hummed in assent. "You want to talk about it?"

Antonio forced himself to look at Lee, whose brown eyes held far more understanding than he deserved. "Just to explain that it wasn't about you. That was all about me. And a little about Cassie. But please don't take anything she said to heart. Or anything *I* said, for that matter." His heart twinged, hoping Lee hadn't heard Antonio voice his insecurities about meeting Lee's standards.

Lee shrugged. "Sure. Sorry for causing problems with your family."

*There's that "sure" again.* "I've been a pain in Cassie's ass since I was born." Antonio smiled to mask his guilt and frustration. "I love you, and I want you in my life. Remember that."

"Same."

"'Same'? That's it?" Antonio teased, needing some sign that Lee wasn't checked out, like the Old Antonio would be. That even if things weren't easy, they were still okay. "I don't even get a 'Love you, too'?"

A grin broke across Lee's face before he kissed him. "Love you, too."

"Mmm...better." Pulling a smile from Lee—and a kiss—was slightly reassuring. At his core, Lee was nothing like the Old Antonio. Even if he wasn't ready to accept Antonio's support yet, maybe Lee would help himself or lean on his friends, the way Antonio never could until he had no other choice.

Antonio had to trust he knew himself best, just as Lee did for him.

# Monday, September Second

# Chapter Thirty-Four

## Antonio

"How about this one, Angel?" Antonio shoved his phone in Lee's face. "It's charming!"

They were indulging in a lazy morning in bed as rain and wind beat on the windows of Antonio's apartment. Labor Day weekend meant that after today, Antonio would be teaching full time for the first time in...*well, years*. They wouldn't have slow mornings together very often. Antonio wanted to drink in his moments with Lee while he could.

Existing together in their little bubble was sublime. Antonio could breathe deeply and stretch out to his heart's content. Contentment flowed sluggishly through his veins, calmed by the storm outside and Lee's body cradled around him. He couldn't wait to wake up like this every day.

Lee squinted at the phone, his glasses lying on the nightstand. "Eleven hundred a month? Tonio, that's out of budget."

Lightning flashed through the window as Antonio exhaled his frustration, and the bubble popped. They'd had the same disagreement since they'd started apartment hunting. "For the last time, our budget is twelve hundred a month. *This,*" Antonio waved the phone as thunder rumbled in the distance, "is *under* budget. It's got two bedrooms *and* two bathrooms! You know how my Benzo belly gets. You really wanna pass on a second bathroom?"

For some reason, Lee insisted their rent should stay within their individual budgets, not combined. "Just in case" his music sales were slow, or during the summer when Antonio wasn't teaching. Lee's argument was shaky at best. Neither of them would have trouble finding extra work. And, not that he wanted to take another handout, but his family would never let them get evicted. Antonio could not grasp why Lee was so insistent on halving their budget.

*Unless he doesn't want to move in with you.*

*No. Lee said he wanted to live with me. I believe him.* Lee may be indecisive, but he'd been steadfast in that decision. He'd say things like, "When we move in together, you'll see what a neat freak I am" and "We should get a better vacuum for our new place" all the time.

"I just want to make sure we can each afford the apartment. Just in case."

Antonio rubbed his chest in irritation. "The only thing in your half a budget with enough space is literally a garage. I refuse to live in a garage, babe!"

Their requirements stretched far beyond half a budget. They needed a two-bedroom—Lee needed a quiet area to work on his music, Antonio needed a sewing area for Carlita, and they both needed storage—and Lee refused to live somewhere with pests. A garage was out of the question.

"There's got to be something that isn't a garage," Lee countered. "And if there isn't, maybe we just keep looking until rent goes down."

Antonio laughed bitterly. "When does rent ever go down? I have to be out of this place in less than sixty days. I'd rather sign a lease now, instead of scrambling and ending up way over budget because it's the only thing we can find. Or worse, have nowhere to go but my parents!"

Bellamy might not be New York, but rents were rising. Even over Eastside, the smallest studios in the ugly new condos rented for two stacks a month. They were asking for a lot with a twelve hundred dollar budget, let alone six hundred.

A loud clap of thunder rumbled apart, and Antonio realized that Lee had fallen silent. His eyes were unfocused, staring into nothingness, an expression Antonio had seen many times on Gabe's face. One he'd worn himself when fear and anxiety were spreading like poison through his brain. One that broke his heart every time he saw it on Lee's face.

"Lee?" Antonio resisted the urge to touch him. "You with me? You're safe. You're with me—Antonio—in bed."

Though Antonio hadn't touched him, Lee flinched before he put on a reassuring smile. As if it would hide the fear that had flashed across his face. Antonio's heart ached to see his stoic and calm Lee with terror in his eyes. "Sorry, just overthinking. You know how I am."

With a quick hum of his Intentions Song, Antonio snuggled into Lee's side, as if the reassurance could seep in through Lee's skin. "I know how you worry. How responsible you are. How cute and talented you are. How lovable you are."

"Yeah, no, you can stop with all of that." Lee laughed, acting embarrassed. He denied it, but Antonio knew he secretly liked the praise and attention. Lee didn't like when Antonio asked if he was okay, so Antonio had taken to showering him with compliments instead.

"I'm serious, though." Antonio looked solemnly at him. "I love you. I can't wait for us to have a place together, so I can look at your sexy ass every day, forever and ever. Amen!"

"But what if—" Lee stopped himself.

"What if...?" Antonio encouraged him to finish the thought. Fear stabbed him in the heart. *You knew there was a "what if."* "Lee, what if what?"

Lee didn't respond, avoiding Antonio's gaze.

Antonio did his best to keep his composure, to be encouraging despite his own worry. "What if *what* happens? What if the district decides middle schoolers don't need a choir?" Antonio watched Lee's face for any reaction that could reveal Lee's thoughts. "What if I get you pregnant, and we need a third bedroom for our miracle baby?"

A weak laugh escaped Lee.

"What if we break up?"

Lee held his breath. Dread twisted in Antonio's stomach.

"That's it, isn't it?" Antonio brushed his jaw, drawing Lee's gaze to him. "You think we won't last?"

The warm brown eyes he loved so fiercely shimmered with a rare display of emotion, finally looking into his own. Lee tried to push up the glasses he wasn't wearing and scratched his nose instead. He gave a slight nod.

"Did I do something wrong?" Antonio asked softly, his panic leaking into his voice.

"No, of course, you didn't do anything!"

"Then what is it? I'm trying to read your mind and I really suck at it. I can't tell what *I'm* thinking half the time. Help me understand. Is this about what Cassie said? Or something I did?" Antonio's voice broke as he lost his fight for composure. Fear of losing Lee stung his eyes. "We said we'd talk shit out, remember?"

Lee looked away again. "May—maybe we need to slow down."

"Slow down? You don't want to move in with me?" Antonio hated how his voice trembled. *Don't jump to conclusions. Maybe we'll talk through it.* He might be deluding himself, but delusion was the only buoy his heart could find. His Intentions Song was sluggish to come to mind. *Stay grounded. Don't lash out in anger. Build relationships.* He didn't allow himself the temptation of the last verse that told him to run away, instead of causing a fight. It couldn't come to that. They had to figure this out together.

"No! Yes! I do! I just..." Lee's sigh rang deep with frustration. "Maybe we haven't thought this through. I don't want you to get stuck with me. Like, this has been so wonderful and easy, but living together is different. What happens when you're having a tough day, and I'm nagging you about your socks on the floor? What happens when it stops being easy, and I'm not what you need? What happens when you meet someone better for you than me?"

Antonio moved away from Lee, sitting back on his heels to look at the man he planned to spend the rest of his life with. The love of his life, who currently sounded like Old Antonio anytime he'd broken things off with someone. *"It's not you, it's me"* was always true when Antonio had said it, but to hear it from Lee was hell.

The delusion of hope sank. But instead of drowning, his heart burst into an inferno. "Are you seriously breaking up with me right now?"

# Chapter Thirty-Five

## Lee

Lee's body grew cold where Antonio had been pressed against him seconds before. Antonio's hazel eyes burned with fury as he crossed his arms, waiting for Lee to answer the question. Rain lashed against the windows, the batter of the downpour too chaotic for Lee to latch onto any rhythm.

He hadn't expected this to hurt this much. This distance between them felt excruciatingly wrong, but Lee reminded himself this was for Antonio's sake. *You knew this would hurt.* Letting Antonio go now when things were good was for the best. *Less risk for him if this ends here.*

Lee forced himself to answer, overcoming the protest that threatened to fly from his mouth. "If breaking up is what you want."

Antonio's jaw tightened. "Let me recap just to make sure I understand. I'm on the verge of losing my shit, so I'm really hoping this is a misunderstanding. I heard you say that I'll get sick of you, or meet someone 'better,' and regret moving in together."

Lee hated how weak it sounded coming out of Antonio's mouth.

"So we should break up now, so I don't get 'stuck with you' because we live together?"

Lee shrugged as he nodded, fear creeping into his heart at how calm Antonio's voice had gotten. Antonio's face had never been so stony before.

"Is that what *you* want? To break up?"

"No—of course not!"

"Well, now I'm confused, because you just said we *should* break up."

Lee scratched his nose, wishing he had his glasses on to hide behind them. Wishing music was playing so he could escape from his anxiety. Wishing they weren't having this conversation, even if it was for the best. "What I want doesn't matt—"

Antonio held up his hand to stop him. "Shut the fuck up right fucking now! Don't you dare finish that sentence. Or run away from this conversation! Just give me a minute, because I'm already angry with you, and if you're about to say what the fuck I think you're about to say, I cannot be held responsible for what comes out of my mouth."

Lee nodded, scared into silence.

Antonio grabbed a pillow and screamed into it. "Okay, so. We're not doing this! I'm not going to let you do this. I've been trying so hard to be understanding but *this*? This is too much! You are *so* frustrating!"

Lee was scared to ask what he meant by "this." Undefined, "this" made fear freeze his lungs, even as hope kept his heart beating.

"You think I don't recognize self-sabotage when I see it?" Antonio crossed his arms, immediately uncrossing them to gesture between them. "Bitch, I'm the king of self-sabotage! And if I'm not letting *me* fuck up a good thing, I'm sure as hell not letting *you* get away with it! Do you know how hard it is to not be the old me when *you're* acting like the old me?"

Mortification burned every inch of his skin, locking him in place. He hadn't expected Antonio to get angry. He'd expected Antonio to let him down gently in a reasonable conversation, like all of their disagreements. Not this confusing whirl of fear and hope, of guilt and reassurance.

"How *dare* you suggest anyone might be better for me than you? How dare you try to ruin the best fucking part of my life! And yours, which sounds conceited as shit for me to say, but tell me I'm wrong! Look me in the eyes, and tell me I'm not good for you!"

Lee was too terrified to say anything but the honest truth. "You're everything to me."

Antonio screamed into the pillow again, the muffled yell winding down into one of the many songs he often hummed to himself. Anger blazed in his hazel eyes as he looked up. His icy, controlled tone made Lee's back prickle with sweat as Antonio spoke. "Lee, I have been in therapy long enough to recognize that I may be projecting here, but Old Antonio fucked up happiness when I was scared of losing it. You think I gave up on my music career because I couldn't get gigs? No, I'm amazing! But I fucked up every single opportunity I worked for. I took the easy way out every time. I ruin shit before it can ruin me.

"And as frustrated with you as I am right now, I can see you doing the same damn thing. You're skipping the conflict and jumping straight to the resolution. And frankly, this is a bad resolution, and I want a different one! I don't want to fight with you, but you're worth fighting for, and I refuse to let us—let *you* go when that's not what either of us want!"

Lee blinked, struggling to process the rapid tumble of words coming from Antonio. Between one painful breath and the next, it sank in that he and Antonio were not about to break up. Hope won out over paralyzing fear, but guilt and shame surged in its place. He opened his mouth, but couldn't find a response, despite Antonio's silent pleas to say something, *anything*.

With a shake of his head, Antonio scoffed. "We have to talk this shit out together. You said you'd tell me what you're feeling instead of keeping it inside. Your friends said you need space to process and can't handle conflict, so I kept my cool even when I was frustrated. I said my piece and then gave you space to process whatever's been going on with your flashbacks, even when it kills me inside to watch you struggle through them. But if that has something to do with why you're trying—keyword *trying*—to break up with me, then I've given you too much space!

"So talk to me, Lee. Let me in! Let me support you! Or at least help me understand. Give me a chance to be the me I want to be instead of pushing me away! What are you afraid of? What's the worst-case scenario you've cooked up in that beautiful head of yours that you're trying to prevent by breaking up?"

Antonio waited, shoulders and chest heaving.

Lee gaped, scrambling for the right answer—what Antonio would want to hear. But no, Antonio deserved the truth. He swallowed all of the platitudes that would have eased his father's anger. Maybe Antonio was right. He'd been telling himself this was for Antonio, but maybe it was for him. Breaking his own heart was the easiest solution to the anxiety poisoning him since they'd agreed to move in together.

He took a breath and then another, his tongue cotton in his mouth. Every thought he had was drowned by the memory of his father telling him, *"Sorry isn't good enough"* and *"Men own up to their mistakes instead of blaming others"* and *"The world will treat you worse than I do"*.

Lee could barely talk about the nightmares or the flashbacks with *Tara*. Tara understood that part of him, would never judge him for it. Yet he couldn't voice the deepest wounds to her. How could he begin to talk through it with Antonio? His heart fluttered frantically in his chest.

"Please, Lee."

That shaky plea broke him. He had to explain himself, for Antonio's sake. And his own. Antonio deserved to understand. He wouldn't react like Lee's parents had. Even as angry as he was, Antonio would not hurt him like they had. Even Tara would have chucked the pillow by now. Lee counted his heartbeats, forcing them to slow into a calmer tempo before he spoke.

"You'll leave, and then I'll be heartbroken and stuck with a lease I can't afford. Or, more likely, you'll kick me out, and then I'll be heartbroken and homeless again, and *you'll* be paying rent you can't afford. Blanche needs my room, and Tara lives in a damn closet. I'll have nowhere to go, and I won't even have Tara this time." Lee's voice cracked. "And I'm scared I'll hurt you. The nightmares are all from the day I got kicked out. But instead of beating me, my dad makes me beat you. I couldn't live with myself if I hurt you."

Lee slowed his breathing to quell the panic that made his heart race again. He'd already said more than he'd wanted to say, and his eyes wouldn't stop burning.

"God fucking dammit! Why can't I stay mad at you?" Antonio cupped Lee's face gently despite the irritation in his voice. The stony glint vanished; Antonio's hazel eyes grew earnest. "Lee, I don't know how else to say this, but you're it for me. If you were anyone else, I would've been gone months ago."

He crawled over him to straddle Lee's thighs, his voice softening as he spoke. "But with you? With you, I want everything. You make me feel so much, it scares me. But I want more of you, all of you! You are worth more than any frustration because we will be together for as long as you let me love you. Even if one day you break my heart, I'll still love you too much to walk away or kick you out. Okay?"

Shame flooded Lee as a tear rolled down his face. Sheets of rain slapped the window as Antonio waited for him to respond, but Lee didn't trust himself to speak without crying.

"What's it going to take, Lee?" Antonio brushed the tear away gently with his thumb. "What's it going to take for you to believe me? To trust me? To trust us?"

"I believe you. It's just..." Lee took a deep breath, gripping Antonio's thighs to anchor himself. "What if we fight or break up and you relapse? I don't want to put you in a situation where you end up stuck with me because you need me or resent me because I'm not the support you need."

"Lee, this is going to sound harsh, but I don't need you. I want and love you, but I've never *needed* you. I have worked so hard to build a whole life, a whole support system for myself. And you're a part of that, but you're not a crutch." Antonio rested his forehead against Lee's. "I'm learning to trust that I know what's best for me, and I need you to trust me too. If the day ever comes when you're no longer good for me, trust me to advocate for myself. You don't get to make that decision for me."

"How can you love me if you don't need me?" The words flew from his mouth before he could stop them, his voice cracking. "Everyone who doesn't need me leaves. My own parents didn't even want me."

"Your parents—" Antonio stilled in his arms. "Have I done something to remind you of your parents?"

"No, you are *nothing* like them." Shame burned as hot as the tears rolling down Lee's cheeks. "Dad—and Mom—demanded perfection. There were consequences for every mistake or hint of attitude. I thought he treated us like shit because he loved us. That he wanted what was best for us."

Lee pulled Antonio closer, tapping the cadence of his heartbeat against Antonio's spine to work up the courage to explain. He was hurting both of them by keeping this to himself. "The day I got kicked out, Dad came home early and caught me with Sunny. He didn't get physical that often, just when we were deliberately disobedient, like with the birthday cake. Most of the time we could avoid it if we did enough chores and apologized.

"But he didn't give me the choice that day. He beat me harder than he ever had. There was no coming back from breaking that rule." Lee swallowed hard to block out the memory of the screams muffled by his t-shirt, his mom's sobs—the only time he'd ever heard his mom cry—pleading to God to forgive Lee. But not a word to beg her husband to stop, as his dad's shouted slurs got louder with every crack. "When he left me, told me I had no home or family anymore, I just stayed there. I waited for hours on that bench. I thought it was a test to make sure I obeyed him, even though I wasn't allowed to go near the mounds."

Alone on a park bench, Lee sat with *"You're dead to us"* and *"This is where whores belong"* echoing in his ears. The taillights of his dad's car were fading into the distance. And there Lee remained, in just his jeans, t-shirt, and slides as the sun set. The November chill sank in as tears burned hot down his cheeks.

Crying wasn't allowed. He'd have to clean up his face before Dad came back. He was in so much trouble already. He was by the mounds. He wasn't dressed properly. He was gay. He was wearing his house shoes outside. Crying would bring another penance.

It wasn't until the welts on his back and thighs started to throb that the finality sank in. He had done something unforgivable.

Dad had given up on him.

"The mounds? He left you *there*? You were a kid! You could have been trafficked!" Antonio's face contorted in a rare flash of anger as his words snapped Lee out of the memory.

Lee nodded and took a breath. "That was the point. When he left, he told me being a whore was all I was good for now. One of the girls working nearby told me about a church shelter where they wouldn't call CPS. The first week, I went to that bench every day because he might come back. I didn't want to believe he'd given up on me. As if he might come back if I did what he said, so I joined conversion therapy at the shelter so I'd be fixed when he did.

"That place sucked but honestly, it was better than home. Especially after I met Tara. She helped me realize I was free. That I didn't have to go back." He smiled, remembering how Tara had put up with his clinginess and constant fussing about her, when she'd always been perfectly capable of taking care of herself. Her reluctant admission that she didn't mind because no one had ever fussed over her before.

His voice cracked again as he remembered *why* he'd clung to Tara so hard. "I should have gone back for Jazz. Or at least checked on her at school or something. I didn't get to say goodbye to her. Dad told her she wasn't allowed to talk about me anymore. She didn't even know I was alive until she overheard my dad and Aunt Alitrice arguing a few weeks later. She was just a kid."

Antonio hugged him silently, tucking Lee's shoulder under his chin.

"Tara and Blanche have helped me unlearn so much, but it never goes away completely. My brain keeps telling me that everyone will leave me, especially you. That people only stay when they need me. That I'm worthless like he said."

"I thought I had myself under control, but it keeps getting worse since we talked about moving in together. I want to move in with you, but I've been ridiculous about all this." Lee pinched his nose, willing the tears to stop flowing.

Antonio's voice softened. "You're not ridiculous. You've just been dealt a shitty past and shittier parents. And I'm an asshole for not understanding that. I'm sorry for getting upset."

Lee shook his head. "No, I should have told you all of this before. You've been so patient. Tara would have lost her shit so long ago."

Antonio let out a small laugh.

"I just freeze up, and suddenly I'm a kid again, and my mom is trying to figure out why I look guilty. It was easier to stay quiet than tell you the truth if you'd leave me anyway."

"Doing the easy thing is always harder in the long run. Trust me, I've been making shit harder for myself my whole life. But I'm done with that. I want to have these hard conversations with you just as much as the easy ones." Antonio brushed Lee's tears away softly. "Look, we can't predict the future, but I can't imagine my life without you. I want to be with you forever if you let me and I know hearing that probably isn't enough to make you believe me. But I mean it. Like, I don't want to scare you or anything, because we've only been together four months, but I'll go buy an engagement ring if it'll convince you I'm sticking around. I'm serious about us. Hell, I'll go with you to city hall and elope with you right now!"

Lee was stunned into silence, his heart pounding in his ears. He'd never considered Antonio would want anything that serious with him. *Sure, meeting the family and moving in together is serious, but Antonio is marriage serious? About me?* Lee was still processing that Antonio wanted *him* in the first place. "You mean that?"

Antonio nodded. "I mean that. I want to spend the rest of my life with you, and I'll do whatever it takes to prove it. I love you now and I'll love you forever, Leland Aloysius Jones!"

Lee snorted softly. *Of all times to get the full name.* "Who told? Was it Sunny?"

Antonio smirked. "I'm no snitch."

Lee's anxiety about making rent or bunking with Tara seemed manageable in comparison to a divorce. If this wonderful man would *marry* him just to prove he would stick around, Lee could find a way to make rent in case he didn't.

*And what if it doesn't end? What if we make this work?* With a twitch of his lips into the smallest smile, Lee saw a different future for himself that included Antonio. In silk kaftans, complaining about how the newest manifestation of white man-child EDM was ruining the house genre. Old and gray, dancing while they washed the dishes after their friends went home. Sitting in the shade with Antonio's sisters, gossiping about Antonio's nieces and nephews.

Lee wanted all of that. He wanted to be part of Antonio's future. Their future.

"City hall is closed today. It's Labor Day," Lee muttered, fighting the grin that threatened to erupt across his face. *Seriously? That's the best I can come up with?*

Antonio threw back his head and laughed. "That almost sounded like a yes, Angel."

"You didn't ask a question." Lee lost the fight against his smile like he did anytime Antonio laughed. He held up his finger when Antonio opened his mouth to presumably ask The Question. "Let's try living together, so we can make sure living together is good for us. Give me some time to get this shit under control again."

He picked up Antonio's phone and brought up the apartment listing Antonio had shown him. "I'll ask *you* after we've been living here for six months. If we both still want to then. If we're both ready for that."

Antonio's smile lit up. "You take all the time you need to be sure. I'm not going anywhere." He bent down to kiss Lee, lips briefly brushing against his own.

Lee deepened the kiss, needing to show Antonio everything; the vulnerability had drained him, but he still had so much to say. The love, the hope, the exhilaration—he pressed it into the mouth devouring his own. Into Antonio's skin, where Lee's fingertips dragged down Antonio's back. Into the way their bodies moved together. In how he tightened his grip on Antonio's thighs and pulled him closer.

"You know," Lee panted as Antonio's mouth burned hot against his neck. "I hope this place doesn't have mice. It'd suck finding another place after I already decided I'm proposing to you here."

Antonio's hands slid down Lee's chest. "But if you propose to me at home, where will everyone fit for my public grand gesture? You deserve a big, dramatic proposal."

Lee laughed. "What if you propose to me however you want after I ask in private?"

A grin spread across Antonio's face. "What a great compromise. We're so good at this conflict shit."

Lee pulled him close to kiss him again as rain pattered the window. He was *not* good at "conflict shit". But for Antonio? He'd try. He'd practice. He'd learn. Because when he messed up, Antonio would still be there.

# Friday, September Sixth

# Chapter Thirty-Six

## Antonio

"God, this job is the best birth control." The tendons in Antonio's jaw ached from stress. "I'm so glad Lee doesn't want kids."

His chair squeaked as Antonio leaned back with a sigh, grateful for the prep hour between classes. His cramped office in the back of the choir room, originally a practice room, was a refuge with his salt lamp on and the fluorescent overhead lights off. With his nerves stretched tighter than a bungee cord, he desperately needed any peace he could get.

"I thought you liked kids," Cassie replied through the phone pressed to his ear as he fiddled with his stapler. "You're great with everyone in our family."

"Yeah, *they* don't sneak into my office and out me to my entire workplace." His desktop picture, which an asshole seventh grader had forwarded to the whole school the night before, was a shot of him and Lee dancing by the fire. *Thank you, Gabe, for the picture of us with room for Jesus.* The fallout from anything less innocent could have resulted in his termination. Bellamy might be a progressive bubble in the Midwest, but the school district was not.

"The whole district, actually. It's the water cooler talk here at the Super's office, too."

Antonio fired staples across his desk. "Great, really reassuring, Cass."

"Antonio, it'll blow over. It's not like they can fire you for it."

"They can make my life hell, though." The looks and whispers when he'd arrived at school this morning had made his throat tighten. The demons had whispered that of course he'd be fired already, of course they'd found out about Carlita. Of course the five years of his life he barely remembered would come back to haunt him.

"Have they?"

Most of the students didn't care—night and day from his own middle school experience where he'd been The Gay Kid ever since he'd naively declared that Ricky Martin was hot in sixth grade. While he expected most students would speculate about his sexuality, he hadn't planned on becoming The Gay Teacher only a few days in. But many of his coworkers were supportive, taping up Safe Space signs on their classroom doors.

*Still, it's the principle of it.* Antonio huffed. "I got a few nasty emails from one parent, conveniently the mother of the kid who broke into my office. And a few boys were causing trouble, but I just told them their insecurity wasn't doing them any favors."

"You let Carlita out of her closet, huh?"

Antonio laughed. In reality, the retort had come more from Old Antonio than Carlita. Luckily, he'd managed to channel the majority of his pettiness into singing. "I stayed unbothered, and they eventually fell back in line. Still easier than the summer school kids."

"See? You got this! It'll all be fine."

"Cass, you're being weirdly optimistic. You feeling okay?"

A knock on the door made him whirl around. A lanky older man, possibly the assistant principal, stood at the door. "Mr. Flores, got a minute?"

"Cass, I gotta go." Antonio forced a calm smile as he hung up on his sister, running triple time through his Admin Song for his name. "Come on in! How can I help you, Mr. Lindstrom?"

"Please, call me Pat."

With a rush of relief that he'd gotten it right—maybe the personal detail would save him from getting pink-slipped—he dutifully added Pat to Mr. Lindstrom's couplet in the Admin Song. "Call me Antonio in that case."

Pat Lindstrom invited himself to sit on Antonio's desk. "You've caused quite the stir today, Antonio."

"It was certainly a lesson in locking my computer." Antonio forced a smile, craning his neck back to look at the taller man. Was this a power play from Pat, or just an older white man oblivious to the space he occupied in the already small room? *God, I wish I could wear heels to school.*

Pat laughed. "Something I have trouble remembering, myself." He paused. "Listen, we've had some complaints down in the office."

Antonio's heart froze. "Oh?"

"One parent, in particular, does not want her son taught by a homosexual."

"Employment discrimination on the basis of sexual orientation and gender identity has been outlawed in Iowa since 2007," Antonio rushed to recite the laws he'd memorized (and miraculously still remembered) back when he was student teaching. Panic tightened his throat, but he tried to project more confidence than he felt. "And per the department of—"

Pat raised his hand to halt his ramblings. "Yes, we told her as much. Don't worry, you're not in trouble—she complains about everything. Give her a couple of months and you'll look back at this with nostalgia. The reigning champ is when she complained her son did well on a science test. She didn't want him to learn that the Earth revolves around the Sun."

Antonio let out a laugh, relief bubbling out of him. "Sounds like a gem."

Pat hummed with a knowing smile. "Just wanted to tell you we have your back. You've done great work with the kids this week, and we trust you'll maintain professional standards the same as any teacher would. And if her son gives you too much trouble, let me know, too. He's obviously got a lot to deal with at home."

"Thanks, I'll keep that in mind."

"Great. That settles that." Pat Lindstrom's smile looked as relieved as Antonio felt that the awkward conversation was now over. "Any plans for the weekend?"

"Just a quiet weekend at home." His relationship with Lee might be out of the bag, but Carlita was staying in the closet. *Be open about who I am, not what I do.* Flat Earth Karen would have plenty to complain about if anyone discovered his raunchy R-rated alter ego. Not even Iowa's employment discrimination laws would save him.

Antonio sighed in relief once Pat finished his pretense at small talk and left. He pressed a hand over his chest to slow his racing heart. He was on the verge of overthinking himself into a downward spiral. That conversation had been a rollercoaster, and he'd already been stressed. *Journaling! I can journal.*

He pulled out the notebook Lee had gifted him for his birthday and dug around the mess of his drawer for a pen. He scribbled his feelings and thoughts down as quickly as he could, letting them linger just long enough to understand them before finding the next one.

Once again, he'd been terrified by the idea of losing something that he didn't realize was important to him, until losing it was an imminent possibility. He'd assumed he was about to get fired, but was surprised that he'd fought to stay. *Weird, I actually like my nepotism handout job.* Teaching felt like coming home, a natural progression of Antonio's new-slash-old life in Bellamy as much as family dinners, performing at Confession, or dates with Lee.

Teaching was ten thousand times more draining than he'd remembered, but also more rewarding now that he was fully present and not hungover every day. The students had won him over with their enthusiasm for the smallest things, like his corny attendance songs. Antonio couldn't remember the last time he'd been so proud of himself.

His phone buzzed in his pocket with an email to set up a showing at the apartment where he and Lee would hopefully start their future together. Antonio grinned and scribbled out *"PS: I love the life I'm we're building."* in his journal before replying to their future landlady.

---

# Lee

*That one should be higher.* Lee tapped his fingers to the beat of one of his better tracks before doubling the price.

"What are you listening to?" Tara asked, clicking away on her laptop next to him in Confession's coworking space. Again. Blanche had launched their channel already, so Tara and Lee were sexiled even more frequently.

"Just repricing my tracks," Lee said. "I'm trying to be better about marketing and shit. Helping Blanche out made me realize I've been slacking."

Blanche's new SubParty had found moderate overnight success, considering their limited content. They recorded custom messages, usually basic humiliation or praise, assigning punishments or aftercare activities. The full scenes with their exhibitionist clients would happen after Lee moved out. *And if a technology dinosaur like Blanche can make money online, I need to do better.*

Plus with paying rent soon—and saving up for an engagement ring—he had to get his shit together. Antonio was the best motivation for his music career yet.

"Do you use this mass email thing?" Lee asked. "I'm trying to figure out how to send cold emails, but I can't get the fields right."

Tara blinked, visibly confused. "Are you switching your mail merge over from a different program?"

Lee shook his head. "Yeah, no. I just never did much emailing." *Or any.*

She peered at his laptop. "Your merge tag isn't linked correctly. Here." Tara clicked a few keys on his spreadsheet. "Now it should work."

"Thanks, Buttercup!" Lee rubbed her back. "You always know everything."

"I don't understand how you didn't use this before." Tara shook her head. "About time you take charge of your music, though. Blanche hustling, now you? I need to scale up, too."

Lee grinned. "You gotta keep up with me, Buttercup. Maybe you should get a girlfriend."

Tara laughed. "I did have a second date with someone recently. Not worth my time even after a second chance. No point in fucking a straight dude if I didn't like talking to him, even if he does own a taco truck."

"A *straight* guy?" Lee teased. "What's next? Married with kids in Driftwood?"

"Fuck out of here with that hetero shit." Tara gagged. "No kids of mine are going to have a straight guy as a parent! Let alone in *Driftwood*! Ugh!"

Lee laughed. "Wait, kids are fine though?" Tara had never expressed interest in kids before. But she'd also never dated before. "Can't relate."

Tara rolled her eyes. "Lee, don't read into it. It's not that deep. I'll start by meeting someone I can stand to be around. Baby steps."

"Want me to set you up with someone?" Antonio asked from behind them as he emerged from the stairwell. He must have gone home to change out of his work clothes. His leggings and a cropped t-shirt wouldn't pass the dress code in Bellamy Public Schools. But Lee approved, admiring his boyfriend's muscular legs.

"Not Phineas, please," Lee half joked, greeting him with a kiss. He brushed his thumbs along the exposed strip of toned stomach.

Antonio laughed. "Oh, I would never set Phineas up with anyone I like. No, for Tara-Bear, I was thinking more like Gabey or Dicky."

"How about neither?" Tara interjected.

"Are you sure? They're hot," Antonio teased. "And I can personally attest both of them are great in the sack. Dicky is kind of a biter, though. And Gabey might be too emotionally fragile for you."

*That is very on-brand for both of them.* Lee liked Antonio's friends, but he couldn't imagine Tara or Sunny getting along with either of them. Blanche would love them. *Their wallets, anyway.*

"You're really selling it, Tonio. Hard pass." Tara shook her head with a laugh. "As a rule, I don't get involved with people I know in real life, especially a friend of a friend. It'd be awkward when I avoid them like the plague afterward."

Lee pulled Antonio down into his lap. "Not that I'm not glad to see you, but what are you doing here? You're not taking up burlesque, are you?"

Antonio grinned. "I should! But no, I'm here to watch the titties tonight with Tara. Part of my exposure therapy back to socializing without a breakdown."

"Wow. Tara voluntarily socializing? Tonio, I hope you know what a miracle this is." Lee shot Tara a grin, who made a face back to him.

Antonio laughed. "It was far easier to convince Tara than my friends."

"How was your day?" Antonio had made a point to avoid discussing work until they saw each other in person, saying he didn't want to think about work more than he already did with Cassie and his therapist. Antonio had made time for him most nights that week, but Lee had missed their mornings together when they could lay in bed and talk (or not) about anything and everything. *Yet another thing to look forward to when we move in together.*

"I'm *so* glad it's over," Antonio sighed heavily, draping himself over Lee. "It was…so much. Homophobic parents. District-wide drama that ended in a visit from the Assistant Principal. Fragile seventh-grade egos."

"You want to talk about it?" Lee asked, nudging his head against Antonio's.

"Tell 'em to choke on a dick," Tara chimed in.

Antonio snorted. "No on both counts. I honestly thought I could end up unemployed by the end of the day, so I'm not about to tell anyone to choke on anything." He covered Lee's mouth before he could ask. "And I don't really want to talk about it yet. I journaled. I vented to my sister. Can I fill you in when I'm feeling less on edge? I just want to relax, but we can talk about it ad nauseam tomorrow."

Lee nodded. Concern twinged in his gut, but he didn't press it. If Antonio wanted to relax, he could help him relax. "Do you want some help decompressing at least?" Lee kissed Antonio's palm with a wink. "Take the edge off after a long, hard week?"

Biting his lip, Antonio's eyes roved over Lee.

"Lee, weren't you busy with something besides fucking your boyfriend right next to me?" Tara grumbled.

His cheeks burned. "Oh, yeah. Tonio, want to help me with my social media presence?"

Antonio cupped his hands around Lee's jaw, a manic grin on his face. "I'd love to! What platforms are you thinking of?"

"Whichever ones are good?" Lee replied, suddenly nervous. Antonio was too excited about this. "I started a business account on Insta when we were helping Blanche. I don't know what I'm doing."

Lee's phone appeared in Antonio's hand. "Let me see!"

He rested his chin on Antonio's shoulder as Antonio pulled up his business profile. On it was a link to his website, an infographic Tara had made for him on purchasing tracks, and a picture Gabe had taken of them dancing. He normally didn't like pictures of himself, but there was no sign of Leland Sr in the laughter on Lee's face.

"Babe!" Antonio whirled to face him with a grin. "That's my desktop at work!"

Lee smiled back. "I heard you're supposed to post personal stuff, too. I hope that's okay."

"Of course!" Antonio kissed him with a fond look. "By the way, our future landlady got back to me about the apartment. We have a showing tomorrow morning. Is that okay?"

Lee's heart leapt with excitement. And a little fear, but he would manage that. "More than okay."

He pulled Antonio in for a kiss, sucking on his lower lip just hard enough to communicate exactly how okay it was. Enough to pull a gasp from his boyfriend.

Tara balled up a sheet of paper and chucked it at them. "Seriously, get a room."

"Well, I can see we're not wanted here." Antonio laughed. "Come with me?"

Tara grumbled. "Can you phrase that another way?"

Lee and Antonio were already dashing down the stairs, barely containing their scurry to the Confessionals. Lee pressed Antonio against the door the second they were inside, kissing him hard enough to bruise, while Antonio struggled with the lock.

"We gotta make this quick. I'm on the clock in fifteen," Lee managed to say as Antonio sucked behind his jaw.

Antonio smiled against his neck. "Trust me, you'll clock in on time."

Within moments, Lee found himself with his arms braced against the cold ceramic of the sink, jeans and boxers shoved down his thighs. He screwed his eyes shut in pleasure while Antonio's tongue laved his asshole and his fingers delved deep inside him. He forced himself to breathe through the soft moans that escaped him whenever Antonio brushed against his prostate.

"Tonio—" Lee opened his eyes and caught sight of himself in the mirror. Even bent over and his pupils blown wide with pleasure behind his crooked glasses, he still saw his dad first. Always unsettling, it was particularly disturbing when his boyfriend was eating his ass in a public restroom. *I gotta do something about this.* "I should grow my hair out."

Antonio's face popped up in the mirror behind him, one eyebrow raised. "Really? *That's* what you're thinking about?"

"I've worn my hair like this since I was a kid." Lee rubbed a hand over his scalp. "Hot Barber thinks I'd look good with longer hair, and we're moving in together, so maybe this is my time for new hair, new me?"

Antonio pressed a line of kisses up Lee's back, hazel eyes meeting Lee's in the mirror over his shoulder. "Angel, I would love to hear all about this revelation, and we're *definitely* going to talk about 'Hot Barber'. But, later. Okay?"

Lee grinned. "No need to be jealous. That's just my barber's Insta handle. You know I'm worse than you about names."

Antonio pressed hard against his prostate. Lee struggled to stay upright as pleasure shot through him. "*Later.* I better be the *only* one you're thinking about when I'm inside you." Antonio nudged Lee's feet apart. "Spread 'em. You're too tall."

"You're too short."

Antonio smacked his ass. "You want this or not?"

Lee grinned and spread his feet as far as he could. His jeans trapped his legs, but he managed to get his hips low enough for their height difference, still significant even with Antonio's platforms. "You're the perfect height, babe."

"Damn right." Antonio grinned as he drizzled more lube onto Lee's asshole. "Touch yourself for me. Don't want you to be late."

Lee bit his lip as Antonio worked slowly inside him, the breadth of his dick sliding against every nerve ending as it filled him. He could care less about clocking in on time if it meant losing a second of the electric thrill Antonio would bring him. "Go slow. I can be a little late."

# Saturday, October Twenty-Sixth

# Epilogue

## Lee

LEE HUMMED ALONG WITH the radio as he stacked plates in the cabinet. There was something strangely satisfying in deciding how Antonio's stuff—perhaps his now, in a way—would be organized after living with Tara and Blanche's constant chaos. Antonio wasn't exactly orderly, but at least he tried to put silverware back in the right drawer. The plates clinked as Lee lined them up perfectly, making the otherwise empty and sparkling clean cabinets feel a little more lived-in.

They'd paid extra to get the keys early, so Lee could clean to his heart's desire. He'd spent the last week obsessively scrubbing their new place from top to bottom, working all of the weird stains out of the carpet and the crusty bits from underneath the cabinets. Antonio couldn't tell the difference, but Lee felt better moving their belongings into their new home knowing the grime from the previous tenants was gone.

"Where does this box go?" Tara asked from the living room, where his belongings had been stacked earlier that morning. His furniture technically belonged to Blanche's sugar daddy, so he'd only brought his clothing and some music stuff. The handful of boxes he'd brought were sparse compared to the dozens belonging to Antonio that already lined the peach-colored walls, with more on the way.

Gabe was borrowing his dad's pickup to help move the rest of Antonio's stuff and the furniture from his studio. Lee expected them any moment. The pizza he'd ordered for lunch was getting cold, and they might not get any if they took much longer. Even now, Tara was looking at the pizza boxes longingly, while she held up a box that clearly had "Sweaters" written on the top in Sharpie.

"Did you read the label?" Lee couldn't resist teasing her, albeit gently. She'd been asking him questions she already knew the answer to all morning. He'd indulged her for the first few hours out of guilt for moving out, but she'd have to come to terms with it eventually.

Tara looked down at the box. "Yeah, but you have two bedrooms."

"The only clothes going in the guest room are…"

"Carlita's," Tara huffed as she carried the box down the hallway. "All you had to say was 'bedroom,' smartass."

"Love you too, Buttercup!" He collapsed down the box that had held the plates and stacked it with the rest of the moving boxes destined for the recycling bin. His anxiety told him to keep them just in case, but Lee was determined to get rid of every one.

Their apartment was dated, but it was theirs, and he meant to keep it that way. The dark wood cabinets were worn, the peach paint was faded, and the tacky parquet floors snapped loudly underfoot. The dining room light must have been salvaged from a Mexican restaurant because the stained glass had been sticky to the touch (until Lee got his hands on it) and ceramic chilis dangled from the pull chain.

Despite the mess of boxes, their apartment felt like a blank slate. The lack of furniture added to the potential of it. They'd need a dining table, a few rugs, another couch, and maybe some chairs to make the living room more comfortable for company. He and Antonio could truly make this place theirs. Blanche's apartment had been the place he'd stayed at for five years, but he'd never let himself settle in.

But here? This would be their home.

"You're going to love our new place!" As if Lee's thoughts had called him, Antonio's voice echoed from the hallway. "You can actually fit inside this one. Remember that shoebox I rented after I moved out of your place in Manhattan? God, *I* barely fit in there!"

The door thumped and keys jingled. "Which key is it, again?"

"You don't know what key goes to your own door?" Gabe asked, his deep voice strained. "You didn't think to figure that out before I hauled this heavy-ass box up two flights of stairs?"

"Lee color coded the keys for me, but I forgot which colors go to which places."

Lee checked his appearance in the mirror in the entryway, making sure he was presentable before Antonio and Gabe came in. After a month of letting himself get wolfy and obsessively brushing his growing hair into waves, Hot Barber (or Just Barber, as Antonio called him) had lined him up earlier that week, delighted to finally give Lee a more flattering haircut. No one but Antonio had noticed, but still, he hadn't seen Gabe yet. Maybe someone would be more observant than Tara, Blanche, and Sunny and actually appreciate the change.

"Isn't Lee there? Just knock."

"No, he won't let me in." Antonio called, "Because he's a jerk!"

Lee snorted as he brushed his hair into place. After three more keys failed to open the door, it finally unclicked, followed by Antonio with a laundry basket full of clothes and Gabe carrying an unwieldy box.

"Really, you were standing right there?" Antonio grumbled. "Angel, you're killing me!"

"You gotta learn." Lee greeted him with a kiss and took the basket from him. "I'm not like Gabe who leaves the door unlocked. Which key?"

Antonio scowled before singing, "There's no place like home, and nothing rhymes with orange. I need better lyrics. Can't we put a sticker on the door or something?"

"We can do whatever works for you. As long as it's locked."

Gabe set his box down in the living area with a thud, wiping the sweat from his forehead. "We're about to move the mattress in. Can you make sure there's a clear path to the bedroom? Knowing Antonio, there's a box in the hallway. Nice hair, by the way!"

Lee grinned. "Thanks! And I have everything organ—" he paused. Tara should have finished moving that box to the bedroom long before now. Knowing her, she was trying to be helpful. "I'll check."

As they left to go get the mattress, he found Tara in the bedroom, sitting cross-legged in a patch of sunshine, haphazardly pulling the sweaters he'd carefully packed into a heap on the floor.

"You know you don't have to help me unpack," Lee set Antonio's laundry basket of clothes next to the closet.

Tara shrugged. "I want to help. Hopefully, it'll force me to process the reality that your shit will be gone when I get home."

"I support that, but can you help without messing up my system?" Lee teased. "I was going to unpack my clothes *after* we moved in the bedroom furniture. Tonio and his friend are about to move the mattress in here."

With a grin, Tara chucked a sweater across the room.

"Your ass is picking that up!" Lee laughed, putting the sweaters back into the box. "You sure you're okay, Buttercup?"

"Yeah, I'm fine. Your ass has barely been home since you met Tonio anyway. I've had time to adjust." Tara retrieved the sweater with a shrug. "And if not, it's Saturday. Ignore any dramatic drunk texts I send you later."

Lee squeezed her tight. He still felt guilty for abandoning her, even though they both knew that wasn't what he was doing.

"Tonio, can you at least pretend you're helping?" Gabe's deep voice echoed from the front door of the apartment.

"I have the heavy end!"

"It's a mattress! There is no heavy end, just lift it higher. Or lift it at all!"

"How am I supposed to lift it higher when *you're* on the other end of it?"

"Not my fault that I'm a foot taller than you."

"Ten inches! And my dick is bigger than yours!"

"Eleven, and *that's* a lie. Do you want my help moving your shit or not?"

Lee grinned and explained to Tara, "Gabe is Antonio's you—his codependent bestie. They argue more than we do, though."

Gabe backed into the room, dragging the mattress with each step. His long hair was pulled into a bun, showing off his bulging shoulders. Sweat drenched his back, making his t-shirt cling to his rippling muscles. "Lee, you're gonna help me with the couch. Otherwise, you'll end up living here alone because I'm about to strangle him."

"Well, we can't have that." Lee grinned. "By the way, this is Tara. Buttercup, this is Gabe."

Gabe glanced their way and froze. The mattress fell from his hands, buffeting him in the face. "You gotta be fucking kidding me."

Tara stiffened, muttering, "Oh my god!" under her breath.

"You guys okay?" Lee asked, confused by their matching wide-eyed expressions. "You know each other or something?"

"Nope, never seen him before in my life." Tara shook her head vehemently.

Lee glanced between them; she was a terrible liar. But Gabe never left the house, so how would they have met? As much as he wanted to ask, he probably shouldn't press it if Tara was already emotionally fragile.

Antonio attempted to push the mattress from the hallway, barely wiggling it. "Gabe, are you seriously giving up when the mattress is halfway in?"

Gabe's brown eyes blinked rapidly, his mouth opening and closing wordlessly before he shook off his deer-in-the-headlights look. "Sorry, hand cramp." He finished dragging the mattress inside, ducking behind it as he hauled it into the bedroom.

Antonio made a show of pushing the other end into the room, significantly less sweaty than Gabe. "Hey, Tara-Bear! I didn't know you were here! Gabe, this is my new best friend I was telling you about. The one who actually socializes with me, unlike some *other* best friends!"

Gabe didn't reply, propping the mattress against the wall with his back turned.

"I gotta go." Tara bolted out the bedroom door.

Lee met Antonio's confused gaze with a shrug and followed her out, catching up to her by the front door as she put on her shoes. "Hey, Buttercup, you okay?"

"Yup. Fine." Tara let him hug her, burying her face into his chest. "Sorry. Still support you, still want to help. I just need to be home. A little overwhelmed is all." She looked up, worrying her lower lip. "So the redwood tree in there is Antonio's best friend?"

"I know, right? My heart belongs to Antonio, but I got eyes, and *damn*, that's a man!" He grinned as a small smile cracked across Tara's face. "You about to break your 'don't get involved with people you know in real life' rule?"

Tara shook her head with a laugh. "No! It's just sinking in that Antonio has more people than us. Like, I *knew* it, but you're gonna have more people than our misfit family now."

"And so will *you*. Wait until you meet Antonio's family. His parents will send you home with more food than even *your* bottomless pit of a stomach could eat."

Tara squeezed him tight. "Can I come by tomorrow to help you unpack instead? I'm sorry I can't help today. I just... I gotta go."

"Of course, Buttercup. You don't have to apologize. We're family. Me living somewhere else doesn't change that."

Tara gave him one last hug and left.

Lee turned to see Antonio peeking around the corner from the hallway. "She okay?"

"Yeah. Just needs time and space to process. We're fine." Lee was relieved that he believed it. Tara was right; they'd always be there for each other. Even if she was freaked out by the new people in his life—which he totally understood because he was still more than a little freaked out that he had so many people now, too—they'd figure it out.

Lee appreciated that Gabe and Richard—*and Phineas, I guess*—liked him as much as Tara, Blanche, and Sunny did Antonio. They might even learn to like each other if they spent enough time together. But convincing Gabe or Richard to go out in public was like pulling teeth, and Tara and Sunny did not like change.

"Should we have a housewarming party?" Antonio asked, somehow reading his mind as he stepped into Lee's arms.

Lee nodded. "I think we need to."

"New Year's Eve, maybe? It'll give Gabe and Dicky two months to process the inevitable before I start forcing them to hang out with your friends."

"*Our* friends," Lee corrected.

Antonio kissed his chest before smiling up at him. "Our friends."

With time, Tara would adjust to being a part of the new additions to his life. After all, she needed more good people in her life. Just like he did.

Lee's brow furrowed at the realization that *all* of their friends needed more good people. Maybe their housewarming party could be the start of something bigger for all of them.

"Are *you* okay?" Antonio wrapped his arms around Lee, hazel eyes looking at him with adoration and concern.

With a smile, Lee kissed his forehead and held him tight. "More than okay."

# Also by Cozy

**_Confession_ Series**
Book 1: *Loving Lee*
Book 2: *Love on the Sunny Side*
Book 3: *Tempting Tara* – Coming June 12, 2025!
Book 4: To Be Announced

Connect with Cozy on social media or sign up for email updates at cozydubois.com for announcements about upcoming releases.

If you enjoyed this book (or if you didn't!), please kindly show your support by leaving a review and telling your friends about it. Honest reviews and word-of-mouth recommendations make it possible for indie authors to keep writing. Thank you!

# Love on the Sunny Side

**When newfound confidence coincides with an attractive new frenemy, Sunny's heart is torn between happiness and family obligations.**

AFTER RECOVERING FROM AN uncomfortable breakup, Sunny Boonmee sets out to find love. Or at least get laid before her mother pushes her to start a family. Fortunately, the emotionally unavailable Richard Carter—whose red flags are no match for his blue eyes—is willing to help with the latter. He's perfect for a secret fling: a boring snob in the streets, bossy and adventurous in the sheets. No feelings, only orgasms.

The quiet and reclusive Richard is overwhelmed by this argumentative and intelligent woman who understands him better than anyone, including himself. Refusing to ruin another relationship, he endeavors to woo her properly, but Sunny brushes off every romantic gesture he's been taught. His attempts to show that he likes her go unnoticed by everyone except Sunny's ex, Blanche.

When Sunny and Richard discover that Lee and Antonio are conspiring to get them together, they double down on the secrecy by hatching a counterplot: pretending to hate each other. For Richard, their plan is mere amusement until Sunny is ready to go public with their relationship. But for Sunny—oblivious that Richard thinks they're already dating—the act is a desperate ploy for more time before their situationship fizzles out. Even if she accidentally caught feelings, Richard doesn't fit into her mother's plans for her future, and family comes first.

# About the Author

Cozy DuBois (they/them) thought writing fiction was a long-lost hobby. A longtime lover of romance novels, Cozy has renewed their love for writing by telling stories for and about LGBTQ+ people. They hope to bring more books into the world that represent the complex and messy relationships between friends, lovers, and chosen family found in the queer community they love.

Based in Minneapolis, they enjoy life with their partner, two hound dogs, an old ass cat, dozens of houseplants, and a garden that has seen better days. Find them with a beverage in hand on a patio anytime the temp is above freezing or planning their next vacation when it's not.

# Acknowledgements

As someone who still can't quite believe their book is going to be real, the Acknowledgements are very surreal to write. I told myself that was the part I would write last, but I should have written it earlier because now it feels too real!

First and foremost, I want to thank my partner for their sarcastic "If you don't like the way queer people are represented in books, why don't you write one then?" and knowing the best way their Negative Nancy ass could support my writing was to not read it. If you ever read this, I am so proud you finally learned how to read. (A/N: I promise this is a healthy, loving relationship, but we're Earth signs; shit-talking is our love language)

Second, I want to thank my editor, Mikko Lahna at Quick Fox Editors, for seeing the story I was trying to tell, helping me shape it into the best book possible, and encouraging me through my imposter syndrome. Also my cover designer, Marta Susic, for helping me figure out what I wanted and putting up with the many color palettes I went back and forth on.

Third, I want to thank the community of bookish friends I've made since starting this journey. Writing can be a very lonely hobby/career, but the writing community makes me feel like I'm part of something bigger than just my writing desk. Keep being lovely and sometimes dramatic!

Finally, an undying shoutout to my friends, especially Amanda, Christina, Julie, Katie, Kirsten, Rocio, and Nikki, who spent far more time hearing about/reading/giving feedback on/cheering me on about my book than any reasonable person would. Especially in the early months when my writing sucked *so* hard. Seriously, thank you for not discouraging me because I would have discouraged myself if I had an ounce of self-awareness. I appreciate your support, your friendship, and for getting me out of the house sometimes.

And finally (for real this time), to paraphrase Snoop Dogg, I wanna thank me for believing in me, doing the hard work, and never quitting. My own delusion kept me going, and I'm glad I did because writing is such a huge part of my life. I can't imagine what else I could possibly be doing when I'm not spending every spare minute in front of my laptop.

www.ingramcontent.com/pod-product-compliance
Lightning Source LLC
Jackson TN
JSHW021903210425
83012JS00006B/11